W9-BSM-824

Beauty
to
DIE
for

Kim Alexis &
MINDY STARNS CLARK

Beauty
to
DIE
for

a Spa Mystery

WITHDRAWN
LIBRARY OUTREACH
COOPERATIVE LIBRARY SERVICES
111 NE LINCOLN ST MS58A
HILLSBORO OR 97124-3036

B&H
PUBLISHING GROUP

Nashville, Tennessee

Copyright © 2012 by Mindy Starns Clark
and Kim Alexis Pro. Inc.
All rights reserved.
Printed in the United States of America

978-1-4336-7793-9

Published by B&H Publishing Group
Nashville, Tennessee

Dewey Decimal Classification: F
Subject Heading: MYSTERY FICTION
\ HOMICIDE—FICTION \ HEALTH
RESORTS—FICTION

Unless otherwise noted, Scripture version
is New International Version, copyright ©
1973, 1978, 1984, 2011 by International
Bible Society. Also used is King James Version (KJV).

Publisher's Note: The characters and events
in this book are fictional, and any resem-
blance to actual persons or events is coinci-
dental.

1 2 3 4 5 6 7 8 • 15 14 13 12

For the mothers who put their kids first,
the volunteers who serve with glad hearts,
and all who give tirelessly and expect nothing
in return.
Please remember to take care of yourselves
as well,
to be mindful of your health,
and, once in a while,
to indulge in a little pampering.
God bless you for all you do!

Kim and Mindy

Acknowledgments

Kim and Mindy thank . . .

Our amazing editor, Karen Ball: unique visionary, brainstormer extraordinaire, and paragon of patience.

Julie Gwinn and everyone at B&H Publishing Group who have dedicated their time, talents, and incredible enthusiasm to this series.

Chip MacGregor of MacGregor Literary and Frank Breeden at Premiere Authors.

Tracie P. Hall BS, LMT, CMMT, at Restorative Health Therapies in Lansdale, Pennsylvania.

Everyone at Calista Grand Salon & Spa in West Chester, Pennsylvania, especially owners Don Moore and Maria McCool, and stylist Christy Koustourlis.

Susan Page Davis, Leslie Gould, Kay Justus, Joseph Starns, Lori Denton, and Art DiGiacomo at salongalaxy.com; Vanessa Thompson, Helen Styer Hannigan, and Stephanie Ciner.

The helpful management and staff of Two Bunch Palms in Desert Hot Springs, California, on which parts of our fictional Palm Grotto Resort & Spa are based. Special thanks to Mark Eads, Mike Conrad, and Tony Calsolaro for making sure we were more than adequately "Two-Bunched." Any mistakes, changes, or poetic licenses taken are all ours.

Most of all, thanks to our precious families, who help in ways too numerous to count:

John, Emily, and Lauren

and

Ron, Amber, Jamie, Shay, Bobby, and Noah.

We couldn't do it without you!

Chapter One

Kill me now.

Juliette froze at the end of the jetway, staring at the vivid flash of red hair in the crowd up ahead. The woman was just one of many pouring out from a nearby gate, but all it took was a glimpse of those distinctive red waves for Juliette to know exactly who she was.

Not today, not when Juliette was already dealing with so much. Please, not her.

But it *was* her, it had to be. Juliette would know those flaming tresses anywhere. Only one person on earth could carry off that height and color and style with such absolute flair.

The great Raven herself.

Juliette ducked, hiding among the throng spilling out around her, then she worked her way to one side and moved behind a wide pillar. Cheeks burning, she pretended to adjust a strap on her carry-on as the crowd swept past.

What were the odds of ending up in the same gate area of the same airport on the same day as her former cohort? Yet it had happened, even way out here in the middle of the California desert—a near-encounter with a fellow supermodel, one who'd been in the business at the same time as Juliette, back in the '80s. Raven, of all people. The woman was a living nightmare.

The phone in Juliette's pocket gave off the signal for a text, so she pulled it out and checked the message. It was from Didi, her best friend and business partner, who had flown out two days before to prepare for the big event they would be hosting over the weekend at one of the spas that carried their "JT Lady" line of beauty products. The message said: Am in cell lot. Text when you get in.

Thumbs flying, Juliette replied: I'm here, but u'll never guess who else is.

Didi's response was quick: ???

Smiling to herself, Juliette typed, THE RED DRAGON

Didi's reply—!!!!!!!—was followed by a second text: RAVEN? No way!

Juliette nodded to herself as she typed. Yep, am hiding now. Can't come out till coast is clear.

Didi's final response: No prob, take ur time. Oh yeah, check out billboard at carousel 3 before u come out.

Juliette slipped the phone into her pocket and shifted around the pillar to take another look. Scanning the crowd, she spotted the regal redhead at the far end of the hallway. With more of her visible now, Juliette could see the woman was dressed in a flowing mix of purple and teal silk with a couture-like fit. Oh yes, this had to be Raven. Fortunately she was heading straight to the main exit rather than baggage claim. Though the notorious diva had never been known for traveling light, it seemed this trip was an exception. Whew.

Juliette waited until Raven disappeared from sight, then gripped the handle of her carry-on and moved out from behind the pillar. Glad to have dodged that bullet, she made her way to baggage claim and looked around for carousel three. The moment she spotted the sign, her face eased into a smile. Mounted on the back wall, the huge billboard featured an inviting photo of Palm Grotto Spa's world-famous mineral pool, a handsome couple floating side by side in its turquoise waters. Above them was the spa's elegant palm-frond logo. But the best part of the sign was in the lower half. There, in blazing white text against even deeper blue water, were the words:

It's Your Turn . . .
A Juliette Taylor Event
May 11–13

Under that was the contact info for signing up, and across the very bottom was her company's brand new slogan:

Isn't it time someone took care of
you for a change?

The whole billboard really was striking. Standing there and taking it in, Juliette knew she should feel grateful for their gorgeous new "look"—new colors, new logo, new packaging. Instead, all she could feel was fear and frustration and regret.

That's because what had started out as a simple product redesign had ended up bringing to light serious criminal acts that were being perpetrated against Juliette and her beauty supply company, JT Lady. Those crimes had been discovered thanks to the implementation phase of the new design program, which meant it had turned out to be a mixed blessing. They *needed* to know what was going on, of course. But Juliette sure didn't *like* knowing, not at all. How blissful it had been when her head was in the sand! If they hadn't done the redesign, they might never have learned about the crimes at all.

Juliette was startled from her thoughts by a nearby scream.

"You have *got* to be kidding me!"

She spun around to see that she was standing not ten feet from Raven, who then let out a long stream of curses, her voice echoing across baggage claim.

Time for a quick getaway. While the woman's back was to her, Juliette scanned the area for a hiding place, but even as she spotted a restroom she could duck into, she hesitated. Perhaps it was the poor old gray-haired porter, who didn't deserve to be spoken to like that. Or maybe it was the children over by the water fountain, who shouldn't have to hear such blue language. Either way, Juliette let loose a sigh. She couldn't run and hide. In the past she'd seen Raven go on like this for a full five or ten minutes, but she'd also seen the woman's attitude change on a dime, even in the midst of her most vicious rant, if she felt like it. Hoping that would be the case here, Juliette took a deep breath, squared her shoulders, and strode forward.

Time to slay the fire-breathing dragon—or at least keep her from burning someone else.

Marcus Stone stood in the doorway of the old warehouse, looking around at the near-empty space inside. For the past six months this had been command central for JATFAT—the Joint Atlanta Task Force Against Terrorism. Filled with personnel and equipment, it had served as a top-secret beehive of activity, everyone working together toward a singular goal: the seizure of a newly activated terrorist cell based in metro Atlanta. That goal had been achieved last month with the arrest of all the cell's members, and now, after several weeks of processing, investigating, and debriefing, things had finally begun to wind down.

At this point the place held only a few workstations and a handful of people. The rest would be finishing the paperwork at their regular offices and leaving the final wrap-up here to the core members of the team.

Marcus spotted the man he was there to see, Special Agent in Charge Nate Anderson, near the back of the room, trying to close one of the few windows in the place.

He headed that way. "Need some help?"

Nate turned. "Hey, Stone, how you doing?"

The two men shook hands. "Fine. You?"

Nate gestured toward the window. "Not too good at the moment. Somebody thought we needed some fresh air in here today, and now it's stuck open."

"The breeze *is* nice."

"Yeah, but those crickets . . ."

Marcus could hear the cacophony of chirps outside, typical in Georgia for this time of year.

"Still can't tolerate that sound." Anderson's voice was low, guttural. "It's been eleven years, but the minute I hear it, might as well have been yesterday. Three hundred and forty-three of 'em under the rubble, all going off at once, and not a thing we could do about it."

Marcus could feel a tightening in his chest as he, too, remembered. "You're talking about the PASS alarms after 9/11." Short for "Personal Alert Safety Systems," the distress signals were designed to go off whenever the emergency workers wearing them became immobile for more than thirty seconds, to indicate they were in trouble. After the towers fell, more than three hundred firefighters had been trapped, immobile, below the rubble.

Less than a minute later, their alarms began to go off.

Nate nodded. "Sounded just like a bunch of crickets to me. It was bad enough at the beginning, when there were so many and we couldn't get to any of them. But it was even worse when things started quieting down. Batteries dying one by one."

Marcus remembered. It had taken more than a day for the last of those beeps to stop. He'd hated the silence even more than the noise.

With a quick glance his way, Nate added, "You?"

Marcus shrugged, sliding his hands in his pockets. "The sound of crickets, not so much. For me, it's the smell of gasoline or kerosene or diesel. Even lighter fluid. One whiff and I'm back at ground zero, holding my breath from the stench of jet fuel."

"Amen, brother. We're a real pair, huh? Scared of insects and barbecue grills."

Marcus gave a nod and moved to the window. "Let's see if I can help. Maybe together we can get it closed."

Each taking a side, the two men wrestled with the stubborn windowpane and finally managed to break it free from whatever was stopping it from sliding shut. As frame met sill with a thud, the sound of the crickets outside was muffled by more than half.

"Sorry to say, you can still hear 'em a little."

Marcus brushed his hands together to wipe off the dust.

"Yeah, well, I never stop hearing 'em, not completely, anyway." Nate grabbed a rag to wipe his hands. "Then again, who am I to complain? You had it worse there than I did, that's for sure."

Marcus felt his stomach clench at the thought, but he was saved from having to respond when Nate added, "Anyway, what's up? Can I do something for you?"

Marcus took a deep breath and blew it out, not sure how to broach the topic he'd come here to discuss. "I need to talk with you for a minute. It's about that list of names we found among the papers recovered from the terrorist cell."

"Oh?" Nate moved toward his desk and gestured for Marcus to have a seat on the other side.

Marcus glanced around, glad the place was all but deserted, then sat and watched as Nate flipped through the file drawer. He pulled one, opened it onto the desk, and flipped through until he came to a copy of the paper in question, the name list.

Among the evidence that had been collected in the wake of the capture of the terrorist cell had been a typed list of ten names—with no other information at all. Most of the names on it had been immediately recognizable, at least to those on the task force. Three were public figures who spoke out against the counterfeiting of designer goods, such as knock-off purses, counterfeit DVDs, and fake perfumes. Four were members of Congress who were working to toughen federal anticounterfeiting laws. The connection for the remaining three names was less clear, but with some investigation it was determined that the list was comprised of ten people whose actions could be financially detrimental to the cell's counterfeit-based money raising activities in one way or another.

Marcus skimmed the names upside down, remembering the first time he'd seen that list, just a few weeks before.

"Number six," he said gruffly.

Nate ran his finger along the list and stopped there. "Oh yeah, the former supermodel?"

Marcus nodded, swallowing hard. "Yep, that's the one. Juliette Taylor. I'm here because I need to talk to you about her."

"Raven?" Juliette forced a light and happy tone into her voice. "Is that you? I can't believe it. How *are* you?"

Raven turned, and when she saw Juliette,

the expression on her face changed from rage to surprise to what looked like genuine delight.

"Darling! How wonderful to see you! What on *earth* are you doing in this hideous joke of an airport?" Raven threw her arms around Juliette and pulled her in for a hug, seeming to forget her tantrum over the luggage. The porter seized the opportunity and pushed the overloaded cart toward the exit as fast as he could.

Crisis averted. With any luck Juliette would get out of there before Raven started screaming at someone else. Known throughout the industry as a temperamental diva, the woman had never been unkind to Juliette personally—and in fact had once done her a very big favor. But with Raven came drama, which grew tiresome for anyone.

When the hug ended, they stuck to small talk, the two of them trying to remember how long it had been since they'd seen each other last. Five years? Ten? Splitting the difference, they decided it was about seven, when they'd both been in New York for Fashion Week and ended up just one row apart at a Carolina Herrera show.

As they talked, Juliette studied the six-foot-tall beauty, who in her prime had walked the runways for more top-name designers than perhaps any other supermodel in history. It was hard to say whether or not the years had been kind to Raven, but one thing was for certain: The plastic surgeons had not. Between the tightly pulled eyes and the puffed-up lips, Raven looked like a caricature of a human, as though she might melt into a glob of wax at any moment.

How pointless. How sad.

Pity surged through Juliette's heart, and she was glad she'd forced herself to approach her old acquaintance, dramatics or not. Though never best buddies, the two women had moved in the same circles for a number of years. Seeing Raven now made Juliette feel rather nostalgic. Most of all it reminded her of how few people understood the world of the supermodel and the price paid by those who lived it. Despite the decades since either of them had appeared on a runway or a magazine cover, she and Raven shared a bond, one that would be with them for life—just as the title of "Supermodel" was theirs for life, whether they were still in the business of modeling or not.

"So what are you doing out here in the desert?"

She expected Raven to say she was headed for a Palm Springs golf resort, or perhaps a vacation rental in the nearby mountains.

Instead, she ignored the question and began to fidget with the neckline of her blouse. "Let's walk, shall we? Who knows what suitcase of mine that idiot will drop next? Better to be right there, keep him on his toes."

Raven began moving toward the exit, and after a beat Juliette caught up with her. Through the windows she could see that the porter had stopped his cart beside a black stretch limousine and was now loading Raven's bags into the trunk. Juliette sighed. Though she and Raven had both been successful in their youth, they'd handled that success in different ways. Even now, here was Raven with her designer luggage and her limousine, compared to Juliette with her roll-on bag and a lift from a friend. Their careers had been lucrative for them both, but somehow she had a feeling that all the money in the world couldn't buy the one thing Raven needed most: connection to others. Relationship. An end to the loneliness that all but oozed from every pore of her statuesque frame.

If only there was a way to break through that outer, defensive layer that Raven wore like a suit of armor. Juliette slowed, taking her old friend's arm and trying again. "So do you have a house out here or something?"

Raven looked away, her posture stiffening.

"No, I'm . . . I just . . ." Raven cleared her throat. "I came here to relax, pamper myself a little, you know? Take in the desert air and all that. How about you?"

Ah, deflection. In other words, it was none of her business. Juliette sighed, hating to let it go but knowing to back off. Raven had always been a guarded person. There was no reason to think she would've changed by now.

"Why am I here? It's complicated." Juliette hesitated, trying to think of the simplest way to explain that she'd come on JT Lady business, to give training sessions to spa staff this afternoon and then host a signature "Juliette Taylor Event" for a unique group of clients this weekend. "I'm on my way to Palm Grotto Spa, where—"

"*What?*" Raven's head spun toward Juliette, eyes blazing. "How dare you."

Bracing herself for a Raven-sized rant, Juliette took a step back. "How dare I what?" she asked.

Instead of answering the question, Raven snarled, her green eyes flashing. "That part is mine! Steal it from me and I'll kill you!"

With that, she turned on her heel and stomped away, leaving a stunned and confused Juliette in her wake.

She watched as the redhead burst outside and strode toward the limo. Raven's driver jumped to attention, opening the back door and holding it wide as she flung herself into the seat. The windows were tinted, so she disappeared from view as soon as he closed the door. Her driver climbed in front, behind the wheel, and waited as the porter finished loading her bags into the trunk.

What in the world . . . ?

All done, the porter closed the lid with a thud. Immediately the back window of the limo slid down and a claw like hand shot out of the opening, waving a wad of cash in the air until he took it. Just as suddenly, the hand disappeared inside and the tinted window slid closed again.

Well. That wasn't surprising. Almost as notorious as Raven's rants were her generous tips. Those tips were the only reason many people were willing to serve her at all.

Watching the limo pull away, Juliette could only shake her head. How could Raven talk to people that way and still manage to sleep at night? Glancing around, she realized two workers at a nearby car rental desk had overheard their exchange and were gaping at her. Giving them an embarrassed shrug, Juliette squared her shoulders, held her head high, and went through the door, rolling her carry-on bag behind her. She couldn't worry about what other people were thinking—nor about whatever Raven had meant by her bizarre words.

The problems Juliette and her company were currently dealing with were far bigger and much more important than some aging diva's temper tantrum.

Chapter Two

Crystal Walsh spotted the cardboard box between some used strollers and a shelf of old glassware. Scrawled in black marker across the front were the words CDs: $1 each OR 5 for $5. Trying not to roll her eyes at the pointless math, she moved closer, calculating the time in her head. She could take, at most, ten minutes to look them over, and then she would have to run home, eat, and change before heading in for her shift at Palm Grotto Spa.

She pulled out a CD and was reading the back when she realized the vendor was speaking to her.

"You a Julie Andrews fan? I got posters over there. "

Crystal shook her head. "No thanks. This is for my landlady. The movie's kind of special to her, I thought she might like the soundtrack."

The man nodded, gray beard bobbing up and down. *"The Sound of Music*'s a classic. And at just a dollar, a real steal."

"It's not counterfeit, is it?" Crystal's eyes narrowed. She loved a bargain more than most, but she'd been burned by bad knock-offs before. They were everywhere at flea markets, but especially at dumpy ones like this.

"Of course not!" The man pretended to be appalled at the very suggestion.

She rolled her eyes. So far today, she'd walked past a stack of pirated DVDs, a whole table full of fake Fendi purses, and even some bogus JT Lady products. This box of discs *seemed* legit but sometimes it was hard to tell.

"The thing is, I don't even know if she has a way to listen to it."

"Well, then . . ." He stepped over to the next table to retrieve a small, portable CD player with headphones. "Three bucks, take it or leave it."

Crystal hesitated. Mrs. Peterson probably didn't know how to operate a portable CD player, but for just three dollars, it might be worth showing her.

"I'll take it. *If* you'll throw in the CD for free."

He tried to haggle with her but soon she was walking away with the CD, the player—and a fresh pair of batteries at no extra charge. That salesman had been no match for her, which she could've told him going in. She'd been bartering almost since she was old enough to talk. Given that the rare paycheck her mother earned was usually blown before the ink was even dry, Crystal had learned at a young age how to negotiate for better deals.

Those skills were still serving her well now that she was in her twenties and on her own for the first time. She'd only been living in Cahuilla Springs for three weeks, but so far she'd managed to decorate her tiny garage apartment *and* get some nice secondhand clothes for work, all within her meager budget.

Out in the parking lot, Crystal started up her car, but when she put it in gear, it popped forward with a lurch. Soon she was chugging on out of the parking lot anyway, Old Faithful doing its duty to get her where she needed to go.

Others might say she had a transmission problem, but Crystal knew it was more than that. The lurching had started three weeks ago, at the exact moment she'd first put the vehicle in gear to drive away from her mother, her home, and the only life she'd ever known. Faulty transmission or not, Crystal couldn't help but find that leap forward, and every one since, as significant. It was almost as if Old Faithful had been as eager as Crystal was to get out from under the shadows of that dark, dark place, once and for all, and begin life anew—somewhere far away, full of hope and promise.

Marcus waited as the Special Agent in Charge flipped through the dossiers. The team had created one for each person whose name had appeared on the terrorists' list. Marcus first saw Juliette's dossier seventeen days ago.

He'd thought of little else since.

"Here we are." Nate pulled out the report. About ten pages long, it included all of the information the FBI had rounded up on Juliette Taylor, which ranged from general info, such as current and previous home and work details, to more specific reports on her finances, relationships, activities, and more. As expected, no personal ties between Juliette and the terrorist cell had been established.

Nate skimmed the first page, as if to refresh his memory, then handed it over. "Not sure if you've seen the final summary."

"No, I haven't." Pulse surging, Marcus grabbed the page from him and gave it a look.

JULIETTE TAYLOR

Connection-Personal: Subject has no known connection to cell members, radical/militant political groups, Al-Qaeda, or any other recognized terrorist leaders, operatives, or supporters.

Connection-Other: Products created by Subject's co-owned company have been counterfeited, with funds traced to cell.

Probable Reason for Inclusion: 1. Subject has recently become aware of counterfeited products and has initiated an internal investigation. 2. As a public figure, subject has been invited to join forces with anticounterfeiting organizations to increase awareness.

Threat Level: Moderate. At this time, subject is not believed to be a direct target of the larger organization.

Marcus exhaled, handing the paper back to Nate. Though nothing in the summary came as a surprise, it was still a relief to see it all written out this way.

"So what did you want to talk about?"

Marcus cleared his throat, shifting in his chair. "Two things, actually. First, I need to tell you . . . I know this woman personally."

Nate's eyes widened. "And you're just bothering to mention this now?"

Marcus shrugged. "It's complicated. Haven't seen her for twenty-five years. But at one point in my life, she was, uh, important to me."

Nate flipped to the back of the file and removed some pictures. Though most were from Juliette's heyday as a supermodel, one was a more recent publicity photo that Marcus recognized from her company's website. "Beautiful woman, then and now." Nate studied the image for a moment then looked up at Marcus. "So the two of you dated? Is that what you're telling me?"

Again, Marcus squirmed in his seat. This was one reason he hadn't mentioned it before, because it was so hard to explain. "Not exactly. Our time together was short-lived. But she had a big impact on my life, and I'd like to think the reverse was also true."

Nate leaned back and propped his legs up on the desk, crossed at the ankles. "Any contact since?"

"No. Well, yeah, a few years later, sort of. But not exactly."

Nate shook his head. "Man, this is so informative I can't get over your powers of explanation."

Marcus chuckled. "Okay, fine. Short version. Like I said, she and I were together, briefly, twenty-five years ago, but then we went our separate ways. About two years later I was hoping to take our, uh, relationship to the next level, so I went to see her. After I got there, I learned she was engaged. So I left without making contact. And that's it."

"Ouch, Stone, no wonder you don't want to talk about it."

"Yeah, well, lot of water under the bridge since then."

Nate was quiet for a long moment then swung his legs down from the desk and placed his elbows atop it instead. "I don't see where we have a problem. For all intents and purposes, your work on the task force is complete. Twenty-five years is a long time. And we've pretty much been able to identify why her name was found on that list. I assume you concur with our findings? No secret alliances way back when that we should know about?"

"Yes. I mean, yes, I concur. No, no alliances. She's a great person. This is the exact conclusion I expected."

"Good. Okay, well, then, not to worry, but I appreciate you telling me. Better late than never."

Nate began to tuck away the file, so Marcus reached out and placed a hand atop it. "Not done yet. There's still the second thing."

Nate sighed. "Let me guess, your high school sweetheart was number four, the congresswoman? You went to senior prom with number nine, the columnist?"

Marcus grunted. "No, Ms. Taylor is the only one on that list I know personally. But that's just it . . ." His voice trailed off as he tried to come up with the best way to put it. "Look, I know full well that my activities with this task force were and are a hundred percent confidential. I'd never violate that."

"I should hope not."

"But that doesn't mean I can't take steps to protect someone who was once important to me."

Their eyes met, and Marcus could see the shift in Nate's expression. "What're you saying?"

Marcus sucked in another breath and blew it out. "That I made arrangements to attend an event Juliette is hosting, so that we could reconnect. I won't pass along privileged information, but I have to warn her somehow."

"Warn her?" Nate's tone was sharp.

"That she needs to be careful. That she has some dangerous enemies."

Nate studied his face for a moment then stood and began pacing behind his desk.

"Officially, you're pushing the line here, Stone."

"I realize that. But you tell me, Nate, how can I do nothing? Do you expect me to sit here and stay silent? I've been thinking of little else since I first saw her name on that list a few weeks ago. Surely you've been in this position yourself before. Have you never come across privileged information about someone you know being in harm's way?"

Nate did not reply.

"You and I both know it's possible to encourage someone to practice personal safety and defensive living without giving them the full reason why."

Nate did not look happy, but neither did he start yelling or give an out-and-out no.

Marcus drew a deep breath. "Remember, I was brought in as a consultant here, I'm not a federal agent. A lot of guys in my position would've gone to see her and never said a word—especially now that our mission is complete and my contract fulfilled. But I don't work that way. Consultant or not, this has to be above board, at least between you and me. I came here to tell you what I'm going to do because I don't want you to learn of it some other way and think I violated the trust that's been placed in me by you and by the FBI. It won't be. I guarantee it."

Nate gave a weary sigh. "Fine. I'll run this by headquarters tomorrow and let you know what they have to say."

Marcus shook his head. "Sorry, buddy. My flight leaves tonight—and I'm going, whether the FBI wants me to or not."

Still reeling from her encounter, Juliette walked outside, looked around, and spotted Didi behind the wheel of a shiny black SUV not too far away. Looking absurdly small in such a big vehicle, she was inching the rental forward in the traffic.

Juliette gave her a wave, then stood and waited for the car to reach the passenger pick-up area. She felt drained from her encounter with Raven and eager to get out of there. At least the rest of the day should go more according to plan. Within half an hour they'd be at the resort, where Juliette had a 1:30 manicure in the spa, followed by some quiet time in her room to unpack, freshen up, and prepare for this afternoon's staff training sessions. The sessions themselves would be fast-paced and fun—and all finished by 6:00 p.m. or so. Then there would be dinner at the resort's restaurant, final preparations for tomorrow, and, finally, hopefully, a peaceful moonlight soak in the mineral waters of the grotto to end the day. That thought alone had her feeling more relaxed already.

Didi flashed a grin as she pulled to the curb, and Juliette managed a wan smile in return. She tossed her bag into the back seat and climbed in the front, as always feeling about ten feet tall next to her diminutive friend at the wheel.

"Hi there. You okay? You look pale."

"I'm fine." Juliette buckled her seat belt. "Thanks for picking me up." She was quiet as Didi pulled back out into traffic and followed the signs to exit the airport.

"You sure?" Didi glanced her way, brow furrowed. "I can tell something's wrong."

"Let's just say I had a close encounter . . . of the redheaded kind."

Didi laughed. "Oh no. Raven?"

"Raven."

Didi reached the exit and merged onto the road that would take them north to Cahuilla Springs, the town where Palm Grotto Resort was located. "Well, hey, at least that's not serious. We all have Raven-shaped bruises on our psyches, born from years of putting up with the diva of all divas."

Juliette nodded. "She's still the same old Tantrum Queen. You would not *believe* the interaction she and I just had."

"I thought you were going to hide till she left."

"I tried, but I ran into her at baggage claim anyway."

"Ran *into* her? Well there's your problem right there, my dear. For future reference, when it comes to Raven, you're supposed to run *away* from her, not *into* her!"

Juliette groaned. "Trust me, I wish I could have."

"So how'd she look? Is her mouth on her forehead yet?"

Juliette smiled. "No, but—"

"Face so full of Botox she looks like a freeze frame? Lips plumped up bigger than a duck-billed platypus?"

"Didi, stop," Juliette insisted, laughing now. "That's not nice. Yes, she's had some more work done, but that's beside the point." Smoothing out the line of her Derek Lam pants, Juliette grew more serious. "She seemed happy to see me at first, but then I asked what she was doing out here, and it was all downhill from there. She got real weird and vague and then she tried to change the subject."

"If she was being evasive, I'll bet she's here for more plastic surgery. That'd be my guess, anyway."

"Maybe. But then she asked me what I was doing here and I said I was on my way to Palm Grotto Spa. The next thing I knew, she was threatening to kill me."

"What?" Didi veered into the next lane and back again, earning a loud honk.

"Yep. All of a sudden she just flipped out. Got right up in my face, told me the most bizarre thing: 'That part is mine. Steal it and I'll kill you.'"

"'That part is mine? Steal it, and I'll kill you?'"

Juliette nodded.

"Part of what? What part?"

"That's what I said. I have no idea. But whatever she was talking about, she wasn't kidding around. She was furious."

Didi was quiet for a moment, lips pursed. "You know Raven. Do you think it matters what she was talking about?"

Juliette shrugged. "She's always been prone to throwing fits. And we've all heard her go off on other people. But she's never had any issues with me personally, not that I can remember. Now all of a sudden she's hissing in my face, threatening to kill me?"

"That's just a figure of speech."

"I know. But she never used to direct her tantrums at her fellow models. It was you booking agents that she blasted to kingdom come."

"Tell me about it." Didi ran a hand through her limp and lifeless brown hair. It was a move Juliette had seen her do countless times, even way back when Juliette modeled and Didi was her booker. "Raven was difficult from day one of her career, but the more famous she got the worse she grew. She may have been one of the most successful models of all time, but she was also one of the most difficult."

Pushing away an air-conditioning vent, Juliette grew silent as they continued down the road. In her mind she reviewed her conversation with Raven yet again, trying to figure out where it had taken such an odd turn. First, the woman had evaded answering the question about why she was here, then as soon as she heard the words "Palm Grotto," she'd flipped out.

That part is mine.

Juliette gasped, turning to Didi. "I just had a thought. What if she's trying to go into the business? *Our* business?"

"What do you mean?"

"I mean, maybe she's introducing a line of beauty products. Maybe she doesn't realize we've been working with all the major spas out here for years, and that some of them even feature our line exclusively. Maybe she thinks we're crowding in on her territory instead of the other way around."

"So when she said, 'that part is mine,' you think she could've been referring to some sort of region? A territory? Like, 'I'm in this business now too, and I declare that everything within a hundred miles of Palm Springs belongs to me'?"

Juliette nodded. "Exactly."

"How could she think that? We were here first, by far."

"You bet we were, by a good ten years. But maybe she doesn't realize it."

"Okay, let me look into things, make a few calls. If Raven is trying to launch a beauty business in our territory, trust me, hon, I'll find out about it."

"Good. Thanks, Didi."

Settling in her seat, Juliette looked out the window at the rows and rows of spinning windmills in the distance, stark white against the blue California sky. This was her fourth trip to the region, but she was still as fascinated with the contraptions as she'd been on her first visit. The windmills were both hideous and beautiful, functional and artsy, man-made yet almost natural, as if they had sprung up, unbidden, from the ground.

"I hate to mention it," Didi said, interrupting her thoughts, "but what's the latest with the counterfeit products situation? I've been so busy out here getting ready for the event I haven't kept up."

Juliette turned toward her friend. "Well, let's see. The *Harper's Bazaar* people want me to appear at their next anticounterfeiting summit, and the congressional hearings for the new bill are set to begin soon."

"I can't believe this is happening."

Juliette brushed at a smudge on her cuff. "I know. I'm not sure if I'll speak out or not, but I've started jotting down some notes about what happened in our situation, just in case."

"Already making notes? Sounds pretty much like a given to me."

Juliette shrugged. Whether she took a stand against counterfeiting or not, just getting things down on paper had helped to organize her thoughts. Last night she'd written out the whole story, starting with six months ago, when they'd first unveiled the new design for the JT Lady product line. As a part of the transition process, they had requested that all old stock be returned to them for exchange. But when that stock started coming in, they had run across some major discrepancies. It was obvious that not everything they were getting back had been manufactured by JT

Lady. When they looked into it further, they found that counterfeit versions of JT Lady products were being produced and distributed—all over the world—and that some of those counterfeits had made their way into the returns.

Through the process they managed to educate themselves, learning that the counterfeit market was a big, nasty business with direct ties to child labor, organized crime—even terrorism. Juliette found that hard to believe, but when an expert suggested she read up on the 2004 Madrid train attacks, she was shocked to see that those bombings had been funded entirely by the sale of counterfeit goods—with the proceeds being laundered through Al-Qaeda, no less.

After learning that, Juliette finally grasped the scope of the situation.

Didi turned up the air a notch. "I wonder if speaking out on this would put you in any danger? These aren't nice people at the other end of the issue."

Juliette looked at her friend. "I know, but I have to do *something*, Didi, I can't just turn a blind eye. If my words and my image can help create a tougher environment for counterfeiters, then I think I have an obligation here to help."

"You're braver than I, my friend."

Juliette shook her head, her eyes on the road ahead of them. "Not brave, just angry. Angry that someone has been using my name and my products for evil instead of good. Angry enough to do something about it."

Chapter Three

Crystal made it back to her apartment with more than enough time to eat lunch and get dressed. Pulling up the long driveway and coming to a stop at the garage out back, she decided that if she moved quickly, she could even bring Mrs. Peterson her gifts before leaving for work.

Earlier today Crystal had commandeered a perfectly good lawn chair from someone's trash. She pulled that chair from the back seat of her car now, piled the rest of the morning's bounty on top of it, and then hauled the whole lot up the exterior garage stairs. Once inside the apartment, she put some vegetable soup in the microwave then went back out to the landing with her new chair. It fit well along the back rail, so she tested it for sturdiness, then sat to check out the view. After all, that view—or at least one part of it—was what had convinced her to rent this apartment in the first place. Looking down at it now, she inhaled deeply, peace and calm filling her soul.

As a child, Crystal had had a picture book of Peter Rabbit, with pages and pages of glorious, full-color artwork showing a bunny's eye view of Mr. McGregor's garden. Crystal's mother hadn't been much for the details of life, like making sure they had food to eat, so before Crystal was old enough to scavenge at the farmer's market and along restaurant row, she'd often had to go to bed hungry. On those nightsj somehow it always made her feel better to take out that book, turn the pages, and run her fingers across the pictures of fat green watermelons and plump, juicy tomatoes and crispy green spinach. She would imagine that she was eating them, that she, too, had a garden just outside, and that all she had to do to stop the gnawing ache in her gut was to go out and pick from its bounty.

She'd forgotten all about that silly little book until a few weeks ago, when she'd come to Cahuilla Springs for her new job and had gone apartment hunting. Answering an ad in the newspaper for a "small, furnished efficiency garage apartment," she took one look and decided the terms "small" and "furnished" weren't quite correct. The place was downright miniscule, with a sagging bed and rickety table and chairs. Right away she decided to turn it down, despite the affordability of the rent and the sweetness of the older woman who owned it and lived in the main house next door. But then as she was leaving, she'd noticed the garden below.

Though untended, it was easy to tell that once upon a time it had been something, its rows straight and long, its various sections delineated by quaint markers. The whole thing was surrounded by a low, white picket fence, one that looked so familiar. Standing there on the landing, gazing down at it, Crystal hesitated for a long moment, her mind trying to understand the feeling of joy that had surged through her veins at the sight—

She gasped. Of course. Her old picture book. Mr. McGregor's garden. This was it!

Much like the lurching car, Crystal took the similarity between this real garden and the fictional one as a sign. She accepted the apartment and moved in the very next day, feeling sure her decision to live here would prove to be a good one. Though tiny, the apartment had ended up being sufficient for her needs, its location perfect for her job at the spa. Mrs. Peterson was a doll, and even the furniture here was somewhat less rickety once Crystal had taken a screwdriver to it and done a little tightening. With her secondhand decorative touches, a few cans of spray paint, and now a free chair-with-a-view outside, the place was starting to feel like home.

Her thoughts interrupted by the beeping microwave, Crystal took one last look at the neglected garden below, then rose and made her way inside. Someday soon she'd have to suggest to Mrs. Peterson that they bring that little garden back to life, just as Crystal was making a new life for herself in this special place.

They came to a stop at the guardhouse, and Juliette watched as Didi rolled down the window. A man emerged from the tiny building and stepped toward their car, clipboard in hand. He was short and stocky, dressed in a crisp brown uniform, its buttons straining along the slight paunch at his gut.

"Hi, Orlando," Didi called out.

"Uh-oh, here comes trouble," he replied with a broad smile, white teeth flashing beneath a bushy black moustache. After nodding a greeting to Juliette, he returned his attention to Didi. "How was the drive? Was the airport crowded?"

As they chatted, Didi seemed animated, and if Juliette didn't know any better, she'd think her friend was flirting with the man—something the no-nonsense businesswoman never, ever did. Didi was far too self-conscious about her appearance—the extra pounds she carried, her short stature, her dark, limp hair—to put herself out there like this. Yet here she was now, smiling and giggling like a schoolgirl.

Orlando held out a printed paper toward Juliette. "Ms. Taylor, I'm sure I don't have to remind you about the noise policy here."

From previous visits Juliette already knew what the paper would say, but she took it from him and skimmed the words anyway: *To create a calm and peaceful environment, Palm Grotto Spa respectfully requests that guests keep noise to a minimum, avoid cell phone use in public areas, and conduct all conversations at just above a whisper.*

"No problem. Thanks."

The man waved a finger at Didi. "You, on the other hand, better behave yourself. Don't make me have to come in there after you."

Didi giggled.

Juliette's mind raced as she tried to figure this out. Didi had been here for two days, preparing for the weekend and calling on other local accounts. Was it possible that in that short amount of time, she and this Orlando guy had struck up a relationship?

Maybe they'd had coffee—or even shared a moonlight dip in the spa's mineral pool.

Juliette couldn't wait to ask her about it.

Orlando put a finger to his lips. "Just remember, ladies, at Palm Grotto, silence is golden." With that, he stepped back into the gatehouse and raised the barrier. "Have a great stay."

"Will do." Didi gave a little wave then pulled forward, her eyes aglow, her round cheeks flushed a bright pink.

"My goodness, Ms. Finkelton"—Juliette couldn't help teasing her—"that seemed cozy."

"What? Oh please, we're just friends." Blushing furiously, Didi steered around a huge cluster of palm trees and into the resort's main parking lot.

Juliette was about to reply when she spotted it up ahead: a large, black limousine parked front and center.

Raven's limousine.

With a gasp, Juliette pointed left. "Go that way! Quick! Dragonmobile, dead ahead!"

Didi turned, tires squealing, and headed to the far end of the lot. "She's here too? What now?"

"Just park. We need to think."

Didi managed to squeeze their rental car into the last spot in the row.

"I don't get it," Juliette said as they sat

there, engine idling, looking toward the limo in the distance. "Maybe I should go inside, stand our ground, and demand to know why she's trying to infringe on our territory."

Didi shook her head. "You know how Raven is. Soon she'd be screaming and you'd be trying to defend yourself, and the whole scene would be unprofessional. Even though she's the one with the problem, not us, we still don't need the people here at the spa to see us in that light."

"Yeah, I guess you're right. I'm not up to another death threat today anyway."

Before Didi could reply, a smiling, chatty Raven emerged from the main office, walking toward the limo. Another woman followed on Raven's heels, one Juliette recognized as an employee of the resort. In her midforties, she was trim and attractive with shiny black hair and colorful clothing.

Didi sat up straight, trying to get a better view. "That's Iliana. She works the front desk. Do you know her?"

Juliette shrugged. She recognized her, but they'd never interacted much. During events her time was spent with spa staff, not general resort employees. They watched as the two women reached the limo and stood beside it, leaning toward each other as they talked, their body language conspiratorial.

"Well, she's been my primary contact for the group booking, so we've gotten to know each other pretty well in the past few months. She's good, a real pro."

They grew silent as they watched the conversation across the parking lot continue. Studying Raven, Juliette realized that despite the fact that her face was taut and expressionless from plastic surgery and Botox, the redhead still had it, that indefinable quality that drew the eye. With her tremendous height and perfect posture, Raven's bearing was regal and elegant and eye-catching. Who could imagine that this beautiful, seemingly well-adjusted woman could transform into a screaming, ranting she-beast on a dime? The Red Dragon indeed.

"Maybe we're overthinking things," Didi whispered. "Maybe Raven's weird threat was based on a psychotic delusion or something. Maybe all those years of hairspray short-circuited her brain."

"Oh great." Juliette groaned. "That doesn't bode well for me, does it?"

Didi waved off her comment. "I'm just sayin'."

Juliette gave Didi a slap on the arm. "Shush."

"Oh come on. Back in the day, that girl was flatter than Twiggy. Now she could give Dolly

Parton a run for her money. Who does she think she's kidding?"

They grew silent for a long moment, waiting to see what might happen next.

"You know, Raven's no spring chicken." Didi reached out to direct the air vent toward her face. "Maybe it's just early senility kicking in."

"She's not that much older than I am. Thanks a lot."

Didi chuckled. "Hey, I'm the oldest of all."

"Which proves my point. You're not exactly filling your days with shuffleboard." Before Didi could reply, movement caught Juliette's eye. "Looks like they're finishing up."

Both women watched as Raven and Iliana shook hands. Though there was nothing unusual or suspicious about such a gesture, there was still something odd and secretive about their posture. Sliding lower in her seat, Juliette held her breath and continued to observe them.

Raven reached into the pocket of her designer pants, pulled out a wad of money, and held it close to her body as she peeled off a bill. She handed that bill to Iliana, giving the woman's hand one last squeeze before climbing into her limo and closing the door.

"Oh my," Didi whispered. "Did you see that?"

"Sure did. I do believe we just witnessed the greasing of a palm."

Even from where they were sitting, Juliette could see that Iliana's cheeks had turned a vivid red. After glancing around, Iliana shoved the bill deep into her cleavage and strode back to the office.

As the limo began to move, Juliette watched intently, hoping against hope that the sleek black vehicle would veer right to drive out the front gate, pull onto the main road, and disappear into the distance. No such luck. Instead, it veered left onto the road that led downhill to the guest rooms. Obviously Raven wasn't finished here yet. She would be staying at Palm Grotto as an overnight guest.

Kill me now.

Crystal stood on her landlady's porch, holding the gifts behind her back and explaining to Mrs. Peterson that she had a little present for her.

"Didn't you tell me that your husband took you to see *The Sound of Music* on your first date?"

"Why, yes, he did, dear."

"Well then, I thought you might enjoy a CD of the soundtrack." With a flourish, Crystal brought both hands to the front, revealing her gifts.

Mrs. Peterson seemed delighted, if a tad confused. As expected, she did not own a CD player, so Crystal showed her how to use this one. Soon Mrs. Peterson was wearing the headphones, her face aglow as the machine sprang to life and music filled her ears. When the demonstration was finished, the older woman seemed beside herself with joy and gratitude. Face flushing, Crystal waved away the woman's profuse thanks.

"No, really." Mrs. Peterson's eyes filled with sudden tears. "There's something very special about you, you know. I realized that the first time we met. I'm so glad you took the apartment. Already you've been such a blessing to me."

Before Crystal could respond, Mrs. Peterson pulled her in for a warm hug. Crystal's eyes filled with tears as well. It wasn't often that she heard such kind words—especially not from a landlady. As she drove to work, those words kept coming back to her, healing some wounded place deep inside.

Juliette groaned. "The limo turned toward the guestrooms, not the exit."

"I know. I saw."

They were quiet for a long moment until Juliette sucked in a deep breath and blew it out. "We need to talk to Iliana, ask her what Raven is doing here and what that conversation was about."

Didi put the car into drive and moved to a closer slot. "Agreed, though I'm thinking maybe I should do it solo. Iliana might be more willing to spill one on one."

"Guess you're right. We don't want her to feel like we're ganging up on her."

While Didi went to the office to deal with Iliana alone, Juliette decided she would head over to the spa for her manicure. She'd be a little early, but maybe they could go ahead and take her now anyway.

The women climbed from the vehicle and walked together to the bubbling fountain that sat at the resort entrance, flanked by the main office on the right and the restaurant on the left. There they split off, Didi turning to go into the office and Juliette continuing straight and then coming to a stop at the top of the stone steps that led down to the water. Pausing there, she took in the gorgeous sight of Palm Grotto's famous mineral pools below. Supplied by a natural hot spring, the liquid in these pools was like none other in the world, rich with lithium and other elements that somehow managed to calm the body and soothe the soul. Staring down at the shimmering turquoise surface, it was easy to picture herself floating there under the desert sky, relaxing in the water's warm embrace as the minerals worked their wonders on her body.

What an amazing place—and what a beautiful day to be in Cahuilla Springs! The sun was bright, the temperature high, the gentle desert breezes blowing across her skin. Inhaling deeply Juliette continued on to the spa, the door of which was at the far end of the same building that housed the restaurant. The two-story structure was built into a hill, with the spa on the lower floor. She opened the door and stepped inside, pausing for a moment on the landing as her eyes adjusted to the dimmer interior. Engulfed in the scents of sage and lemongrass, she continued down to spa reception at the bottom of the stairs.

The receptionist recognized the supermodel and greeted her with enthusiasm. They chatted as she checked her in for her treatment, and then Juliette continued on to the adjoining waiting room, which was empty at the moment. She chose a seat and perused a stack of magazines, selecting a slick regional publication to get herself into the mind-set of the Southern California desert. As tinkly New Age music played overhead, she flipped through the pages, stopping to read an article about the Cahuilla Indians, from which the town Cahuilla Springs was named. The story featured a photo of what looked at first glance like a big stone pit but was identified as "An Old Cahuilla Indian Well." According to the article, tribe members managed to sustain themselves in a dry desert where surface water was seldom found by hand digging walk-in wells. They would carve crude steps into the sides of the stone walls, and as the water table lowered, they'd just climb down and dig deeper—so much so that some wells ended up more than thirty feet deep. Fascinating.

Juliette was turning the page when she glanced up and happened to notice the new JT Lady display across from her beside the water cooler. Her face broke into a broad smile. Putting the magazine aside, she stood and walked over to it, excited by how wonderful it looked. The unit was well placed and nicely lit, its striking new color scheme and images quite eye-catching.

She was still standing there admiring it when she heard someone clomping down the stairs from the spa entrance above, then calling out to the receptionist. "Hey, you! Young lady? Yes, you there on the phone. Excuse me but I don't appreciate being made to wait."

Raven. The voice belonged to Raven.

And she was right around the corner.

"You must think that call is more important than someone standing here in person, but you're wrong. I demand service! Now! I have an appointment!"

Juliette held in a groan. Goodness gracious, was this woman going to be there every time she turned around? She tried to decide what to do.

If she had any guts, she would go around the corner and talk to Raven, woman to woman, demanding she explain her threat at the airport. If it had been about the beauty product business, Juliette could bring her into the waiting room and show her the display unit and explain how her company had been supplying this spa and others like it with JT Lady products for years. They could make their peace and go on from there.

Yes. That was the thing to do. She just needed to work up enough nerve to—

"This is utterly unacceptable! I *demand* to see a manager! Right now!" Raven's voice was even louder and more shrill than before. Several *thunks* indicated the pounding of fist against countertop.

Oh, great. Never mind, now that Raven was getting herself all worked up. They would have to reconcile some other time. At the moment, Juliette knew, her wiser course of action was simple avoidance.

Hoping to find somewhere nearby that she could hide until Raven was gone, she moved through the door that led to the treatment rooms, then, halfway down the hall, she ducked into an open doorway on the left. She found herself in a large supply closet. The door was propped open by a heavy silver wastebasket, so she moved to the far end to crouch down and hide among the inventory.

As she listened and waited, Juliette remembered what Didi had said earlier about how a public confrontation with Raven would be unprofessional and reflect poorly on the company. With that in mind, she stayed where she was telling herself she was just being a wise businesswoman.

Yeah, right.

She was being a big chicken.

Chapter Four

Even from her hiding place at the back of the closet, Juliette could hear Raven out front as she continued to berate the receptionist. As the moments passed and it didn't stop, she began to feel as guilty and convicted as she had at the airport when Raven screamed at the old luggage porter.

Where was management? Shouldn't they have put a stop to this by now? That poor girl at reception was no match for the redheaded she-beast. Once again Juliette knew she had to intervene.

Rising, she brushed off her pants and stepped forward, pausing at the doorway of the closet to gather her nerve. She was about to turn right and head to reception when she heard a sound on her left and looked to see a familiar spa aide coming in the back door. A handsome young man with the chiseled features and bulging muscles of an Adonis, his name was Ty, if she remembered correctly, and one of his jobs here at Palm Grotto was to escort the clients to their various treatments.

She wasn't sure if he'd come to retrieve her or Raven, but judging by the apprehension on his face, it had to be the latter. He looked like he'd been sent to collect a rattlesnake.

Ty came up the hall but paused when the door of a treatment room swung open in front of him. A woman emerged from inside, and Juliette realized it was her favorite esthetician at Palm Grotto. A short, cute brunette with a blunt haircut and youthful features, Brooke Hutchinson was in her late thirties but always looked like she was about sixteen. She specialized in body treatments—wraps and scrubs—and was renowned as one of the best in the business. She was even leading a lecture on skin care during the retreat, as well as their sunrise hikes on Saturday and Sunday.

When Brooke saw Juliette, her face broke into a smile and she gave her a quick wave. Juliette waved back then put a finger to her lips and gestured toward reception. The aesthetician responded with a nod and a knowing smile, then turned to Ty and asked him if there was a problem. "Shouldn't you be escorting my client to Tamarisk by now?" she whispered.

"Yeah," he hissed, "but I'm not doing it till she calms down."

Brooke rolled her eyes. "Oh good grief, Ty, I'll get her myself."

Turning back around, Brooke gave Juliette a wink as she came up the hall moving past her to the waiting room and the reception area beyond. Right into the line of fire. Brave woman. Juliette gave Ty a sympathetic smile, but he just turned away and exited the building.

Brooke's warm voice rang out from reception. "Raven, welcome back to Palm Grotto!"

Juliette frowned at Brooke's greeting. Welcome *back*? So Raven had been here before? Just how long *had* she been trying to break in on their territory?

"Some welcome," Raven snapped.

"Are you ready?" Brooke's tone remained calm, pleasant.

"I've *been* ready."

"Very well. Follow me and we'll get started. We're out in Tamarisk today."

Quickly Juliette ducked back into the closet and hid, listening as Brooke and Raven moved past the open door. Once they were gone, she waited another thirty seconds or so just to be safe and then stood, startled when she realized she wasn't alone in there. A young woman was standing at the other end of the closet, her eyes on the shelves as she buttoned the signature lab coat of the spa's therapists over her blouse. When the girl heard Juliette's gasp, she turned and gasped as well.

Juliette laughed. "Sorry about that, I didn't see you there."

"Me either. I'm sorry too." After a beat, she added, "Uh, I'm sorry, but clients aren't allowed in here. May I help you with something?"

Before Juliette could respond, the young woman's eyes widened.

"Oh! Wait! I'm so sorry, I didn't realize. You're Juliette Taylor! Of course *you* can be in here. This is where we keep the JT Lady stock, after all."

Juliette glanced at the young woman's name tag as she moved forward and reached out to shake hands. "Thanks, Crystal. I don't believe we've met." The young woman was somewhere in her early twenties with green eyes and delicate features. She wore her pale blonde hair in a casual updo, with loose, wispy strands framing her face and giving her an almost ethereal quality.

"I'm new here, just started a few weeks ago. But I'm familiar with your products." The young woman seemed nervous—starstruck, even—as she continued. "A day spa where I used to work carried the whole JT Lady line. I couldn't afford to buy it myself, not even with my employee discount, but my boss gave me free samples whenever she could." The young woman put a hand to her mouth, her cheeks turning a vivid pink. "Oh sorry, that didn't come out sounding right. The products are totally worth the price, that's not . . . It's just . . . I have to watch every penny—"

"I understand. Quality skin care is expensive. Worth it, but expensive."

Juliette gestured toward the JT Lady products on the shelves and asked Crystal how she liked the new look. The girl responded with enthusiasm, describing the various techniques she used to pitch the products to her clients. Juliette listened, growing more impressed by the minute. This kid was authentic, and she knew her stuff.

Their conversation ended when Ty showed up to retrieve Juliette for her manicure. She bid Crystal farewell for now and followed him down the hall. Soon she was ensconced in a manicure chair, her hands soaking in warm, soapy water as she tried to banish all thoughts of Raven from her mind. The drama was past. It was time to relax and to focus on a little pampering for now—and on the wonderful weekend event that lay ahead—whether she managed to avoid the red-headed she-beast or not.

Marcus drove toward his office, maneuvering through heavy afternoon traffic as he reviewed in his mind the difficult conversation he'd just been through. In the end Nate said that while he would prefer Marcus obtain clearance before seeing Juliette Taylor, he wouldn't try to stop him and he wouldn't mention it to headquarters—at least, not for now.

"You step out of bounds, though, and it'll be a different story."

Marcus appreciated Nate's willingness to work with him on this. Since the day he'd seen Juliette's name on that list, he'd been in agony trying to decide what to do. Eventually an idea formed—to put himself in the same place at the same time so that they could become reacquainted and he could find a way to warn her about the danger she was in without crossing any legal or ethical lines. He'd looked into Juliette's appearance schedule, and when he saw that there were still a few openings for a faith-based retreat she'd be doing at a resort spa in Southern California, he'd decided to go for it.

The retreat was for women only, so to give

him a reason for being there, not to mention to increase their chances for interaction, he needed to bring along a female traveling companion—albeit one that wouldn't confuse the issue and make it look like he was in a relationship. That meant either his daughter or his mother. As it turned out, Zoe's school trip to DC would keep her away till next Tuesday, so his mom had won by default. Once he'd convinced her to go, made the reservations, and bought their tickets, things had started falling into place. Now that he'd broken the news to Nate, all that was left was to wrap up some stuff at work, confirm with his business partner that he'd be out of town for a few days, and then go home and pack his bags.

He could only pray everything would proceed according to plan.

As an expert in disaster prevention and recovery, Marcus was always ready for every contingency. After all, that was the name of his business: BE PREPARED—an acronym for "Bureau of Education, Prevention, Readiness, Evaluation, Preparation, And Resources for Emergencies and Disasters." Better than anyone, he knew how to evaluate a situation and take the necessary preemptive steps for damage control.

So why did he feel so unsettled about this

particular venture? Perhaps it was the emotional aspect, the one part of the equation he'd been able to ignore until now. Once upon a time he'd been crazy about this woman and had hoped to share a future with her. Their lives took different paths after that first meeting, but now here they were, twenty-five years later, but single. Was he ready to open that door again?

Or had he never closed it in the first place?

When he reached the office, Marcus found his business partner, Dean, out back sitting at the picnic table off the break room with their new bookkeeper, Lacey. No surprise there. Dean had been panting after the young woman since the day she'd come for her first job interview the month before.

When Marcus stepped out to join them, Lacey's face broke into a broad smile, though Dean's expression was far less welcoming.

"Am I interrupting anything?" Marcus asked.

Dean grunted. "Just taking a coffee break."

"It's such a gorgeous spring day, we had to come outside." Lacey raised a manicured hand to indicate the beauty surrounding them. "How can we get any work done when the beautiful peach trees are blooming out here?"

Marcus looked around, taking in the vivid pink blossoms that dotted the tree line in the distance. She was right. Even at the back of this old Georgia industrial park, the scenery was something.

"Would you like to join us?" Lacey patted the bench next to her. "There's room right here by me."

"Thanks, but no time. I just wanted to remind you, Dean, that I'll be taking off tomorrow and Monday."

Dean rolled his eyes. "Oh, right, for your fancy trip to the spa—which has to be the lamest use of time off I've ever heard of."

"Dean!" Lacey scolded.

"I'm serious. For the life of me, Marcus, I can't figure out why you would fly all the way to California just to go to a *spa*. Tell me you're going for some water sports at Lake Tahoe, that I would understand. Say you'll be hiking through Yosemite, I could get that. But floating around in a *mineral* pool—and with your *mom*, no less? The two of you sitting there in your fancy bathrobes, getting scalp massages and pedicures? That is so not you, man."

"I think it sounds delicious." Lacey cooed. "I wish *I* were going too."

Dean shook his head. "Man up, buddy. What's happened to you? Your mom's a great lady, but what were you thinking? How could you let her talk you into this?"

Actually, unbeknownst to Dean, it had been the opposite: Marcus was the one who'd had to talk his mother into coming. Beverly Stone was not the "pampered" type, and a weekend at a spa had been a real hard sell. But he hadn't taken no for an answer, and before long she'd acquiesced.

Now, as Lacey babbled on about how wonderful spas were and how sweet it was for a man to go to something like this with his mother, he let their misconceptions stand. Even after six months of serving with a top-secret government task force, he still didn't find it easy to juggle half-truths and omissions, but what choice did he have, really? Once he'd seen that Juliette's name had been typed out on a page by a terrorist, he'd known he would do whatever it took to keep her safe from harm.

"I've been thinking of taking a little get-away myself soon," Lacey drawled. "Hey, I wonder if there are openings left at that 'ol spa for this weekend."

"No," Marcus and Dean replied, in unison.

She jumped, startled by the intensity of their response. Dean tried to smooth things over, but Marcus just looked away. Lacey was nice and all—and as smart as she was pretty—but that didn't change the fact that she was far too aggressive for his tastes, not to mention half his age. While those sorts of thing might appeal to his buddy, who'd been hip-deep in a mid-life crisis for the last several years, for Marcus it was a deal breaker. Idealistic, overeager young eye candy couldn't compare to someone like Juliette, who was refined and classy and had become more beautiful with age. Marcus thought of the recent photo that Nate had showed him, and he had to admit that he was even more captivated by her beauty now than he had been when they were young.

"Anyway, I need to get back to work," he said. "Just wanted to remind you about my trip."

"Got it. Thanks."

"My break time's over too," Lacey said, jumping up and moving toward the building. "Might as well go in with you."

Marcus opened the door, catching a glimpse of his own reflection in the glass as he held it for them. Studying the image, he wondered how Juliette would see him. His hair was silver now instead of black, and his face was a little more lined. But he'd never stopped working out—jogging alternated with strength training, mostly—and in the past six months he'd even gotten in some extra training with the task force. Now he was in top shape, the best he'd been in for years.

But was it enough? After all this time, would Juliette still find him handsome? More importantly, would she be glad to see him?

Or had it been too long?

Once Ms. Taylor left for her manicure, Crystal continued rooting through the supply closet until she found what she was looking for, a net bag to replace one she'd torn the day before. Then she made her way to the treatment room where she would be working for the next hour.

Other than the main building, the spa also featured a series of huts and mud baths and other areas that dotted the sloping lawn outside. To get to the Sweetwater room, Crystal had to go out the back door, down a flight of slate steps, around a small but pretty fountain, and into a long, rectangular structure known as the Arrowscale building. Arrowscale housed four treatment rooms side by side: the Keysia, the Dodder, the Tamarisk, and the Sweetwater.

All of the buildings and treatment rooms at the spa were named after different desert flowers, though some were more poetic than others. With so many beautiful flower names to choose from—Dusty Maidens, Purple Sage,

Evening Snow—they sure had chosen some duds. Like, why call a building Milkvetch instead of Whispering Bells, or Stillingia rather than Shooting Star? She supposed she should take comfort in the fact that at least there was no Bladderpot, no Skunkbush, no Winter Fat.

Then again, given the girth of some of their clients, Winter Fat might not be a bad idea.

Smiling at her own joke, Crystal stepped into Sweetwater, nearly bumping into Ty, who was preparing the room for her upcoming session. Tall and tanned with biceps the size of mangoes, Ty was a total stud and he knew it. Women were always swooning over him, but Crystal was familiar with the type—the overblown ego, the flirty, behavior despite the small gold band on the ring finger of his left hand—and had steered clear since day one, cutting him off the first time he came across as even remotely interested. At least he was a good spa aide, hardworking and unobtrusive.

Stepping around him now, Crystal made her way through the luxurious-but-understated space to the much more utilitarian common area in back, where supplies and equipment were kept for all four of the connected treatment rooms. She opened the sanitizer and began to gather a full set of basalt stones for her first massage of the day, using the net bag to transfer them into the steamer pot in the Sweetwater room. There, the rocks would rise to a uniform 120°, warm enough to be effective but cool enough that they wouldn't burn the skin.

"Okay, linens are changed and out, oil is heated, you should be good to go." Ty headed for the front door. "Be right back."

She thanked him for his help, and once he was gone she took a moment to center and calm herself. Closing her eyes, she breathed in through her nose, enjoying the soothing scents of lavender and jasmine that filled the room. She held that breath for a long moment, then let it ease out through her lips.

Sucking in another breath, she became aware of a noise coming from the room next door. Cocking her head and listening, she could hear what sounded like two women talking—far too loudly, at least by Palm Grotto standards.

Odd.

She tried to ignore them but it wasn't easy, especially when the volume increased even more. Soon, the melodic rise and fall of their speech was punctuated by what sounded like bursts of laughter. Though Crystal had been working here for just three weeks, she knew this was unusual. She decided to take a minute to see who was in there and have a quick word with them about quieting down.

She hated to be snarky, but this was ridiculous.

Chapter Five

Crystal walked to the small bulletin board in the back room, where the day's schedule and room assignments were always posted. She studied the chart, trying to figure out what was going on next door and who was in there. Therapists rotated throughout the facility, but on this day at this time, according to the printout, Tamarisk was being used by Brooke for a chai soy mud wrap. Crystal was surprised. She hadn't known Brooke for very long, but the woman was a professional, highly-respected massage therapist, one who'd been working here for quite a while. If things were louder than usual during one of her treatments, no doubt she had her reasons.

According to the schedule, the wrap was from 1:30 to 2:20. Glancing at the clock on the microwave, Crystal realized the session had just twenty-two minutes to go. She decided not to interrupt after all. As long as her client wasn't bothered by it, she wouldn't take any action, though she intended to ask Brooke about the noise later, if for no other reason than to satisfy her curiosity.

Crystal returned to her treatment room just as there was a light knock at the front door. It swung open to reveal Ty, delivering the man who would be Crystal's client for the next hour, a fellow by the name of Elwood Dowd. Stepping forward, Crystal introduced herself and shook his hand. Barely meeting her eyes, he grunted in return then directed his impatient gaze toward the massage table.

Oh boy, a "Grunter," one of those high-powered executive types who couldn't be bothered with niceties and underlings. Crystal didn't appreciate his abrupt demeanor, but she wouldn't let it upset her. She'd seen all kinds in this business.

Ty gave her the client's intake form and slipped out, pulling the door closed behind him. Turning her attention to the papers, Crystal skimmed through them for any physical complaints, recent injuries or accidents, and any medications the client might be taking. She asked a few additional questions for clarification, taking silent note of one matter he'd failed to mention at all: the visible row of hair plugs clinging for dear life along his pinkish scalp. Though she wouldn't say anything about it, she would be careful not to include a scalp massage in today's treatment.

While the client got situated on the table, Crystal slipped into the back room. She washed her hands at the sink, surprised to realize that the noises in Tamarisk were even louder than before. Unable to imagine what could be going on, she tiptoed up to the door and pressed her ear against it. In between bouts of laughter, she could make out some of the words, in particular when one of the women called out, "A drink! I need another drink!"

Crystal jerked her head away. Was it possible that Brooke and her client were getting drunk? That could explain the noise level, and the raucous laughter. But if that were the case, should she do something about it after all? She considered dialing the extension for Andre, the spa's manager, just to alert him to the situation.

On the other hand, she didn't want to be a tattletale, and she didn't want to get anyone in trouble with the boss. What business did Crystal have coming in here and blowing the whistle? For all she knew, maybe Brooke was using some sort of unorthodox stress-relief therapy or something, and the "drink" in question was water or tea.

Ignoring the noise as best she could, Crystal sucked in one more deep breath, let it out slowly, and tried to focus on her own client.

But it wasn't easy. The sounds from next door continued to waft through the wall, disturbing both her and the tense man on the table in front of her.

Moving to the head of that table, Crystal tried to relax the tension in his jaw by applying gentle, cross-fiber friction to his masseter and mandible. She moved from there into smooth strokes along the neck and upper shoulders, pressing the fleshy part of her fingers against the skin, sensing the many places where muscles and fiber were hard as stale licorice sticks. It didn't seem to be doing much good, so she shifted down to his legs and feet, ready to introduce the stones, hoping the heat they put out would make the difference. Leaning toward the steamer, she retrieved two of the larger ones and coated them with massage oil.

"Let me know if this temperature is too high for you." She kept her voice soft as she placed the warm, oiled rocks in direct contact with the skin.

After a moment, he groaned.

She lifted the stones from his skin. "Too hot?"

"No, it's that noise." He raised himself on

his elbows and twisted around. "What *is* that? It's driving me crazy!"

"I'm not sure. Palm Grotto is such a quiet place, it really is."

Crystal realized that the nature of the sounds next door had changed. No longer did she hear talking or laughter. Instead, it had become more like a high, keening tone, almost as if someone were wailing. Chill bumps rose on her arms, and her stomach began to churn. "Mr. Dowd, can you excuse me for just a minute?"

Without waiting for his reply, she set the stones back in the steamer and grabbed a towel, wiping her hands as she moved toward the back room. She walked straight through, and when she reached the door of Tamarisk, she didn't hesitate this time. Instead, she gave one sharp knock and swung the door open, terrified at the thought of what she might find inside.

Immediately she was assaulted by the sweet, pungent smell of coconut and sandalwood. On the table lay a woman, flat on her back with her eyes closed, her hair wrapped in a towel and her body encased in the white top-blanket of the spa's signature chai soy mud wrap. Much to Crystal's surprise, the client was alone and silent, Brooke nowhere to be seen.

Then Crystal heard that sound again, a high-pitched, keening moan, coming from nearby. Stepping farther into the room, she peered around the open door and spotted Brooke crouched on the floor behind it, knees clutched to her chest, rocking back and forth, her eyes blank, staring ahead as she moaned.

With a gasp, Crystal leaped toward Brooke, but as she did, her feet nearly slid out from under her. Grabbing the doorknob to keep from falling, Crystal looked down to see several open bottles of oil lying nearby, their contents spilled out onto the floor. Moving more cautiously, she skated herself forward then crouched in front of Brooke amidst the oily puddle.

"Brooke." She put her hands on the woman's shoulders and shook her, gently at first and then harder.

Brooke didn't even seem to notice. Instead, she continued to rock back and forth, her eyes blank, her face flushed and sweaty, the eerie sound pouring from her lips.

Crystal's heart pounded. She couldn't imagine what might be wrong. Not only was Brooke unresponsive, but there was something very strange about her eyes. They were dilated—so dilated, in fact, that all that was visible were the big black circles of the pupil, with almost no irises at all.

Crystal pressed two fingers against Brooke's neck. Pulse racing. Skin burning hot. Face flushed. Turning, Crystal called out toward the client on the table. "Ma'am? Can you tell me what happened in here? Do you know what's wrong?"

The client did not reply.

Bile rising in her throat, Crystal stood and made her way on the slippery floor around the door and into the back room. She grabbed the telephone mounted on the wall there, and at the push of three buttons, she was connected with Andre, the spa's manager.

He answered in his usual clipped tone. "Yes?"

"Andre? It's Crystal. You need to come to Tamarisk right away."

"I'm almost there," he snapped. "You're not the first to complain about the noise."

Swallowing hard, she tried to keep from sounding hysterical as she said, "It's not just the noise, Andre. Something's wrong. Something in here has gone terribly, terribly wrong."

Juliette opened her eyes. "What do you think is going on?"

Her treatment almost complete, she was sitting with her hands under the nail dryer as the manicurist added the finishing touch, a light massage of her neck and shoulders. It felt heavenly, but it was hard to relax and enjoy it with so much noise outside.

"I don't know." The woman looked a tad unnerved herself.

They'd been listening to sirens for the past few minutes and had even commented about what had to be a nearby multicar pileup or a raging house fire. But now things had changed. The sirens had gotten louder, so loud that they weren't just down the road somewhere. They had to be on the property of the resort itself.

The two women could hear other noises as well—voices speaking too loudly, footsteps running through the halls, walkie-talkies crackling outside. Finally it struck Juliette that the building might be on fire. Trying to remain calm, she suggested they check things out.

They left the room together, joining in with the flow of people who were moving down the maze of hallways to the spa's back door. Juliette was relieved not to smell or see smoke, though she was disappointed that no one else seemed to know what was going on either. Careful not to nick her freshly-painted nails, she stuck with the crowd until she was on the lawn out back, where there were tons of police cars parked all around, sirens now off but lights still flashing. Continuing on down the slate steps, Juliette saw two ambulances at the ready, parked side by side on the grass in front of the Arrowscale building, their rear doors open and waiting. Paramedics and police officers were milling about the scene, going in and out of one of the rooms, while numerous employees and spa guests hovered along the fringes of the action, craning their necks and jostling for a view.

Juliette searched the crowd for a familiar face. She couldn't find Didi but she did spot Xena, the spa's leather-clad overseer of scheduling. Whip-thin and gorgeous in a fierce, stylish, faux-punk sort of way, Xena was standing about ten feet away, whispering with Andre, the spa's manager.

Relieved, Juliette headed over to them, eager to find out what was going on.

"It's Brooke and a client," Xena told her.

Juliette's eyes widened. "Brooke Hutchinson? What happened?"

Xena yawned. "No one's quite sure exactly. She was giving a chai soy mud wrap in Tamarisk, but something must've gone wrong. Another therapist heard weird noises coming from in there, and when she went to investigate, she found Brooke curled up in a corner in a puddle of oil, babbling and incoherent."

Andre picked up the story from there,

leaning forward and speaking in a whisper. A wiry guy with a shaved head and stylish, square-framed glasses, he'd always been a high energy person, but at the moment he was almost vibrating from the drama of it all. "Crystal called me to come, but I was already on my way. As soon as I opened the door and saw what was going on, I called 9-1-1. Now we're just all waiting to see what happens next."

"You said she was with a client?"

Xena nodded. "Still there on the table, all wrapped up."

With a start, Juliette realized that unless Brooke had already finished up that treatment and moved on to another, the client on that table would've been Raven.

Before she could ask, Andre and Xena were both called away, so as the chaos continued to reign around her, Juliette returned to the slate steps and climbed partway up to get a better view. She couldn't see inside the building because of all the activity, but she did spot Crystal, the new therapist she'd met earlier, sitting on a wrought-iron bench nearby. Spa employees surrounded the distraught young woman. They seemed to be offering comfort, though whether they really cared or were just trying to get in on the drama, she wasn't sure.

Ty must have had some part in things as

well, because he looked traumatized too. He was standing behind Crystal, his face pale, his hands gripping the wooden slats of the bench. His gaze was locked on the Arrowscale building, his eyes narrowed, his focus intent.

Scanning the crowd again, Juliette caught sight of Didi, heading in her direction. Just as she reached the foot of the slate stairs, paramedics emerged from the treatment room, rolling a stretcher toward one of the waiting ambulances. Both women turned to see Brooke lying on that stretcher, twisting her head and body back and forth, struggling against restraints. She was babbling something nonsensical, in a slurred voice.

Once the ambulance was loaded and gone, Didi came up the steps to stand beside Juliette. "Well, I knew it would happen eventually."

"What?"

"Raven has now officially driven someone crazy."

Juliette gasped. "That's not funny, Didi, not at all. This isn't time for jokes."

"You think I'm kidding?"

Ignoring the question, Juliette squinted toward the treatment room, waiting for Raven to appear next. She still couldn't see past the cops blocking the door. Was the woman okay?

Would they be bringing her out on a stretcher too?

Didi stood beside Juliette in silence, the two women watching and waiting together until the second group of paramedics emerged from the treatment room. They, too, were rolling a stretcher, but it was empty. Their faces expressionless, the team put the stretcher in the back, got into the ambulance, and departed without sirens or lights.

"Guess Raven managed to recover on her own." Didi smirked. "Big surprise there. Okay, time to get back to business."

Ignoring her friend's words, Juliette stood on tiptoe, trying to see over the uniformed personnel who once again blocked the treatment room from view.

"Come on, Juliette, we have to go. We can find out more later. Right now we've got to get ready for the staff trainings."

Juliette was reluctant to abandon an old friend in the midst of trouble, regardless of their earlier conflict. What if Raven needed her help? Still, she knew Didi was right. They had their own matters to attend to at the moment. Exhaling loudly, Juliette agreed and they took off toward the conference center. They were just heading past the parking lot when another vehicle pulled into the fray and a man in a suit climbed out and strode toward the building.

Raven's lawyer, no doubt, Juliette thought, but then she spotted the white lettering on the car's door: *Coroner.*

With a cry, Juliette ran back. Police wouldn't let her through, so she scrambled for some position that would at least allow her to see inside the room. When she finally found an angle that gave her a decent view, she saw that the client was still lying on the table, motionless, swathed as if in the midst of a spa treatment, her hair wrapped in a towel and her body encased in a white blanket from neck to toe.

Forcing herself to breathe, Juliette watched as the coroner stood over the woman and peeled down the covers to expose her bare neck and shoulders, which were tinted a sickly color by the thin, greenish residue of the chai soy mud. Juliette sucked in a sharp breath, her knees almost buckling at the sight of the woman's face, lifeless and pale, jaw slack, eyes closed. It *looked* like Raven, though from that angle it was hard to tell for sure.

The coroner leaned in closer. Then, after a long moment, he pulled away the towel that had been wrapped around the woman's head. Immediately her hair sprung free, hanging down from the end of the table in long, wavy locks.

Locks of red—a brilliant, ridiculous, beautiful, vivid red.

Raven was dead.

Chapter Six

Crystal sat on the bench, still seeing everything in her mind, over and over, as vivid as if she were watching it on a movie screen:

Discovering Brooke.

Calling Andre, who burst through the front door just moments later and immediately dialed 9-1-1.

Ty coming in after him and going to Brooke, lifting her off the slippery floor as Crystal threw towels down on the oil so he wouldn't fall.

Ty placing Brooke in a chair then grabbing another towel and wiping the oil from her arms and hands and legs as Crystal continued to try to get her to respond.

Andre focusing on the client, trying to rouse her, to no avail.

Crystal leaving Brooke in Ty's care as she jumped up to help Andre, both of them searching the client for a pulse they never found . . .

Once emergency personnel arrived and the paramedics took over, all three had been brought into the back room, briefly questioned, then sent outside to wait until they would give a more detailed version of events later. Unbelievable.

Dead. The client really was dead. Poor Brooke wasn't doing much better.

What could have happened in there?

Judging by the chatter, everyone seemed to have a different theory, though most people found it far easier to explain the client's death than the employee's breakdown. Surely the one had led to the other, in Crystal's opinion. If the client died on the table of some heretofore-unknown medical condition—a heart attack, a stroke, maybe even an allergy to the soy in the mud—and if Brooke witnessed this woman's death and was helpless to stop it, maybe something inside of her had just snapped and sent her babbling into the corner.

But how did the laughter and noise fit into that picture?

And how could mere shock cause someone's eyes to dilate so completely?

Though Crystal had been relieved to find no signs or smells of alcohol anywhere in the room, she was still puzzling over the words she'd heard earlier, the client's cry for "A drink! I need another drink!" If not booze, what kind of drink had she meant?

Now, the word *dead* began to echo through the crowd. So it was true. The client had died on the table.

Mind reeling, Crystal turned to look at Ty, who had been standing behind her since they'd come out here. He was gripping the back of the bench, his eyes dark and his anguish nearly palpable. She felt so bad for him. Reaching out, she placed a hand over his and gave it a comforting squeeze.

Ty recoiled as if struck, pulling back his arm.

"Take it easy, Ty. I was just trying to be nice."

His face flushed a deep crimson as he looked at her, blinking. "Yeah, well, forget about it. I'm fine. Just fine."

With that, he turned and walked away.

Juliette couldn't stop shaking. Not only was Raven dead, she was dead after having been exposed to a JT Lady product.

"Are you okay?" Didi's question came to her from somewhere far away.

Juliette didn't respond, but soon she could feel her friend leading her over to the fountain. The women sat on the wide stone ledge, side by side, and Didi placed a comforting hand on her back. Juliette's mind reeled.

All she could think about was what they'd learned in recent weeks, that counterfeit cosmetics and perfumes often used illegal substances as fillers or stabilizers or to balance out various properties such as alkalinity. The shocker was that those substances were often things like antifreeze, cleaning products—even *urine*—which could cause caustic rashes, burns, serious allergic reactions, and worse.

"Talk to me, babe. Are you okay?"

Juliette looked at her friend, whose face was finally coming into focus. "Oh, Didi. I just keep remembering what that consultant told us about the dangers of counterfeit beauty products. What if the chai soy mud used on Raven was counterfeit? What if she's dead because of what's been happening with our products? What if she was exposed to some horrible ingredient that killed her?"

Didi also whispered in reply. "Not our fault. We don't deal in fakes."

"You know what I mean. What if she's dead because of a counterfeit JT Lady product?"

"Well, then, that would be Palm Grotto's responsibility, not ours."

Juliette pursed her lips. Didi didn't get what she was saying. This wasn't about legal liability. It was about the tragedy, the senselessness.

The tentacles of evil that kept slithering out from the darkest core of the counterfeiting industry—something she hadn't even been aware of until recently.

Didi continued. "Then again, you have a point. Whether JT Lady is at fault or not, Raven's death could be disastrous for us and the company. There's the inevitable public relations nightmare, the potential of getting pulled in to a criminal investigation. Ugh. I don't even want to think about all that right now."

Juliette stayed quiet, staring off into the distance. Didi was just being practical. They could discuss the less tangible implications later.

"Given the circumstances," Didi added, "I think we should cancel the staff trainings."

Juliette nodded. She felt numb. Lost. No way could she handle something like that right now.

"Let me talk to Reggie, and then I have an idea," Didi said. "While he's busy down here, I think you and I should go pay a visit to Iliana in the main office."

"What for?"

"To talk about Raven's threat at the airport."

Juliette's eyes widened. "What does that matter now that she's dead?"

Didi shrugged, glancing at a nearby officer and lowering her voice. "Maybe it doesn't. But considering that the woman died less than two hours after threatening to kill you, you might want to be somewhat, uh, proactive, in figuring out what was going on with all that."

Juliette studied Didi's face. She was right. Counterfeit products weren't their only concern here. If it turned out that Raven's death wasn't an accident, Juliette herself might be seen as a murder suspect!

Didi disappeared into the crowd in search of Reggie, and by the time she returned, Juliette had managed to calm down and clear her head. She listened as Didi explained that the three afternoon training sessions had been cancelled, but Reggie would lead a single all-staff meeting at 6:00 p.m. instead, where she could give a single, condensed version of the trainings.

Juliette nodded. That should give her enough time to recover from the shock—at least enough time to get through a presentation. The two women headed for the main office. As soon as they were alone and out of hearing range, Didi added yet another concern to Juliette's already overloaded brain.

"I hate to say it, but there's one more thing you ought to keep in mind here."

"What's that?"

"With the whole counterfeiting mess, we already know that there's a chance you have some very dangerous people mad at you."

Juliette grunted. She doubted it. The people at the top of the counterfeiting ring, whoever they were, had bigger fish to fry than the owner of some small beauty-product company.

Didi continued. "A supermodel is now dead at Palm Grotto. You're also a supermodel who's at Palm Grotto . . ."

Juliette shook her head, waiting for a better explanation than that.

"I'm just sayin', we need to bear in mind the possibility that someone was sent here to 'kill the supermodel'—meaning you—and they accidentally killed Raven instead."

"Don't be ridiculous, Didi. Nobody wants me dead."

They walked along until they reached the door of the main office.

"I hope you're right," Didi replied at last. "But if I were you, I wouldn't discount the thought completely. For all we know, there's a big fat target on your back."

Crystal was antsy. She couldn't leave the area until she'd had her second, more thorough questioning by the police, but it didn't look like they'd be ready for her any time soon. She decided to head around behind the Arrowscale building to the employee break room and see if there was anyone hanging around in there to talk to.

Crystal let herself in through the "employees only" gate, and as she neared the break room, she was surprised at the amount of noise she could hear coming from inside. Palm Grotto was such a quiet place; this much chatter happening right at the heart of the property was unheard of. At least the structure was situated in such a way that the sound, even at its loudest, wasn't likely to carry to any public spaces. Not only did the doorway face an enclosed service area and the back of Arrowscale, but on the other side stood a thick stucco wall, beyond which was a barbecue pit, a covered patio, and then the mineral pools of the grotto.

When she stepped in the doorway, she was surprised to see that the place was packed—not just with spa personnel but with those from other divisions as well. Usually resort employees congregated with their own departments in their own separate areas, but right now this was the place to be, regardless of department.

No big surprise there. People always flocked to drama.

Juliette and Didi entered the main office, weaving through the gift shop between display racks of loofahs, lotions, neck pillows, and more as they headed for check-in. The place was empty except for the woman they sought, who was standing behind the desk, keeping up with all that was happening down at Arrowscale via walkie-talkie. In her early forties, Iliana had a pretty face and a warm smile, perfect for a greeter at the posh resort. She was dressed in a fuchsia silk blouse under a multi-colored jacket, pulled together with a bold leather belt and several chunky, color-coordinated necklaces. Her outfit was bright, but she carried it off thanks to her tanned skin and lustrous black hair.

Iliana turned down the crackling walkie-talkie and set it aside. She seemed pleased to see them—until Didi explained why they were there, saying that they had observed something earlier, out in the parking lot, a discussion between her and Raven and wanted to know more about it.

Iliana's lips grew thin and tight. "Why do you ask?"

Didi shifted her weight, crossing her arms at her chest. "Come on, Iliana, you heard what I was in here telling Reggie earlier. Raven threatened Juliette at the airport, and the only reason we can think of for her to have done that was because she was starting her own beauty product line and trying to move in on our territory. We need to know what you know. Why was she here, and what did it have to do with you?"

Iliana's face remained hard for a long moment, then her eyes shifted downward, her face flushed. "It's hard to explain. Raven had just come for her regular visit in January, but—"

"Wait." Didi held up a hand. "Raven's been to Palm Grotto before?"

Iliana blinked. "Of course."

Juliette nodded, telling Didi how Brooke had greeted Raven, not with "Welcome" but with "Welcome *back*."

Iliana nodded vehemently. "Yeah, she's one of our oldest customers. Long before I even started here."

Juliette glanced at Didi, glad they'd never encountered Raven at Palm Grotto before.

If only they hadn't run into her this time either!

Shoulders sagging, Iliana lowered herself into her chair and continued. "Raven had just come for her regular visit in January, so when she called the other day to book a last-minute stay for this weekend, I was surprised. For as long as I've known her, she has come to Palm Grotto twice a year without fail, every January and every July, year after year after year, always scheduled as far in advance as possible. That's why it was just so strange that here it is May, and out of the blue she called and asked me to fit her in. She's never deviated from her regular timetable before, ever."

"Why was she coming now?" Didi pressed.

"She didn't say. But I don't think it had anything to do with you guys, or with a line of beauty products."

"What *do* you think?"

"I'm not sure. But I can tell you this much: It was connected somehow with another one of our guests. A man."

"A man?"

"Yep. Raven was adamant that she needed to come *this weekend*, no later, and that she wanted a guestroom as close to this man's room as possible. She said I was to keep that part of her request a secret—especially from the guy in question himself."

Juliette sighed. "So she was here trying to pursue a relationship?"

Iliana pursed her lips, paused, then looked from one to the other. "I doubt it. For starters, she wasn't even sure of his name."

Chapter Seven

Juliette glanced at Didi, who was scowling at Iliana.

"Let me get this straight," Didi said. "Raven called you and said she wanted to book a stay for this weekend and in a room that was as close as possible to the room of another guest, a man whose name she didn't even know? I don't understand."

Iliana shrugged. "I didn't either, but she's been such a loyal customer here for so many years I tried to accommodate her wishes as best I could. We always try to do whatever it takes to keep our clients happy."

"But how could you do what Raven asked without a name?"

Iliana shook her head. "Oh, I had a name—she provided a whole list of names, as a matter of fact—she just didn't know which one she wanted. Raven dictated that list to me over the phone and asked me to check it against our guest roster, saying that whoever on that list was staying here, that's where she wanted to be. Turns out, there were *three* people on the list who were going to be staying here this weekend—three men who had requested rooms near each other. That made things easier for me. I just had to do a little shifting so that I could assign them to a cluster that had more than three rooms. Then I booked Raven into the fourth and that was that."

Her cheeks colored. "Of course, ethically speaking, I wasn't at liberty to share any guest details with Raven, or even confirm that I'd gotten any hits from her list. The most I could say was that I felt sure she would be pleased with these particular accommodations. That's all she needed to hear. She showed up today and checked in as expected."

"That's it?" Didi demanded. "That's the whole story?"

The woman shrugged. Obviously there was more she wasn't saying.

Juliette gave it a shot. "What were the two of you talking about outside, by the limo? Seemed like quite the conversation."

"I'd rather not say." Iliana's bottom lip began to tremble. "It could cost me my job. Haven't I given you enough info already?"

"Everything's going to come out anyway." Juliette kept her voice gentle.

"Why would it? She's dead now."

"Exactly."

With a deep sigh, the woman placed her elbows on the desk and rested her head in her hands. "Fine. It's not like I did anything illegal. I just violated company policy. If Reggie wasn't such a stickler for doing things by the book, it wouldn't even matter. You know as well as I do, when you're dealing with celebrities, sometimes you have to bend the rules a little."

Juliette nodded. "And how did you bend the rules for Raven?"

"I gave out info I shouldn't have."

"About the three guests?"

"I'm afraid so. Not on the phone, just once she got here. She was so excited, she started throwing all kinds of questions at me at check-in—were the men here yet, how long were they staying, had they scheduled any spa treatments, and on and on. I didn't want Reggie to overhear her and find out what I had already done, so I managed to shut her up until she was all checked in, then I walked her out to her car."

"Where you proceeded to answer every one of her questions."

Iliana looked up at them miserably. "It's not

like I gave her any personal data, like phone numbers or whatever. I just confirmed their room numbers and spa appointments. I know I'm not supposed to do that, but it seemed like the easiest way to wrap things up and get her off my hands."

"And once you told her what she wanted to know, did she say what her interest was in them, or why she was here?"

"No. But she did slip me a hundred bucks as a tip! When she first gave it to me, I about died, like I'd just been paid to violate company policy."

After a beat, Juliette nodded. "Yet you kept it."

At least Iliana had the grace to blush. "Yes. I told myself it wasn't a payoff, it was just a tip. Raven has always been a big tipper, throwing around hundreds like a flower girl tossing rose petals at a wedding." She crossed her arms over her chest. "There's this pair of Louis Vuitton ballet flats down at the mall that I've had my eye on, but I've been about a hundred dollars short—and they're on sale through tonight. When she gave me that money, I decided it was kismet."

"Kismet," Didi echoed.

"I put it out of my mind." Iliana's expression turned grim. "But then you showed up, Didi, asking all of those questions. When you said you suspected Raven was trying to work out some sort of business deal on the sly—one that would undermine our long-standing relationship with your company—I felt terrible. Honestly I have no idea what Raven was doing here or why she wanted a room near those men. But I really, really hope you believe me when I say that if I had known it had anything to do with you or Ms. Taylor and might cause problems of some kind between us, I would never have done what I did. Everyone here at Palm Grotto knows what a valued business relationship we have with you guys. I would never endanger that. You have to believe me. I'm so sorry."

Iliana's face was now slick with tears.

Juliette assured her that they did, indeed, believe her. "You know, there's a chance that whatever Raven was doing here had nothing to do with us or beauty products at all."

Iliana dabbed at her eyes with a tissue. "Really? You think?"

"I guess it all comes down to who those men are. I mean, if we're talking the cosmetics buyers for Macy's or something, then yes, we have a problem. But if she just wanted to stay near a movie star or a famous author or a political figure or whatever, then that's not about us and isn't any of our business."

Iliana nodded. "Well, I didn't recognize a

single one of the names, so they're not movie stars, and probably not authors or political figures either."

"What *were* their names?" Juliette knew that between her and Didi, they would recognize most everyone in the beauty business—especially those who wielded influence over the sales or distribution of product. "May we see the full list?"

Iliana shook her head. "Sorry, I threw the little paper out the other day, as soon as I was finished making all the arrangements."

"Okay, then, just give us the names of the ones who are staying here."

Iliana hesitated for a long moment, then turned to her computer and pushed a few buttons. "In for a penny, in for a pound, I guess. Right?"

They waited in silence.

"Here we go." Iliana lowered her voice and read off the names. "Scott Ferguson, George Bailey, and Elwood Dowd."

Didi repeated the names back to her then looked to Juliette, who shrugged.

"Of the three," Juliette said, "only George Bailey rings a bell, but I can't think why. I'm sure it'll come to me."

Didi turned back to Iliana. "I assume they've already checked in by now?"

"Yeah, they got here around noon. I let

them have an early check-in." Clasping her hands together and holding them in front of her, Iliana looked from Didi to Juliette. "You aren't going to say anything about this to Reggie, are you? That would totally get me fired."

Didi sighed. "I suppose there's no need for that, not yet at least."

Iliana nodded. "Thanks. For what it's worth, I've learned my lesson. Trust me when I say that I won't be giving out confidential guest information to anyone, ever again."

Crystal stood in the doorway of the long, narrow break room, which housed tables and chairs, vending machines, a fridge, and a counter area with sink, microwave, and coffee maker.

At the moment the room was overflowing with people. Glancing around, she decided that most of the faces here were familiar, though she hadn't yet learned all their names. At least it was easy to tell who did which jobs by how they were dressed, from the green-shirt-tan-slacks attire of the administrative folks to the black-and-white outfits of the restaurant's wait staff, to the brown uniforms of the security guards.

The security guards.

Taking a quick, second look, Crystal spotted the handsome face of one security guard in particular: Greg Overstreet, only the best-looking, most interesting guy at the whole spa. Just the sight of him was enough to set her pulse racing, though she tried not to let it show as she continued on to the counter and began making herself a mug of herbal tea.

She had met Greg during her first day on the job and had been attracted to his beautiful brown eyes, chiseled features, and hiker's physique. Unfortunately, other than polite friendliness, he hadn't seemed all that interested in her. Not, that is, until this past Monday night, when they ran into each other at a local health food store. Crystal had wanted to whip up a batch of her homemade hydrating body treatment, so she'd gone there in search of sweet almond oil. Greg was there too, and when he saw her combing the shelves he offered to help find whatever it was she was looking for. They spotted the oil, but at $17 it was too big and too expensive. She was tempted to substitute Patchouli at half the price, but then Greg found a smaller bottle of sweet almond in a different brand, on sale for just $4.99.

She'd almost hugged him on the spot.

After that the two of them stood and talked right there in the store for a good half hour or more. When they parted it was with his suggestion that they "go out for a coffee after work sometime." Her response had been eager and immediate, and they'd made plans for the following night.

Their date went well, though she found it odd that he hadn't tried to kiss her or touch her in any way. Instead, they just talked—for almost two hours straight. He was a wonderful listener, though he seemed kind of shy when it was his turn to speak. She hoped he would soon open up a little more, but at least his shyness made a nice change from the men she usually went for—guys who blathered on and on about themselves for hours on end.

Though Crystal wanted to go sit with him now, she didn't want to seem overeager, so she forced herself to join a group at a different table instead. She took the empty chair at a table with Michelle, a manicurist, Lisa, a spa scheduler, and Beth, an esthetician who specialized in anti-aging facials. They were deep in conversation, and she listened as she dipped the spicy tea bag up and down in her mug of steaming water.

No big surprise, the three women were talking about Raven, the client who had died. Crystal hadn't even met her, but from what they were saying, it sounded like she hadn't been popular with the staff. Sipping at her tea, Crystal picked up conversations at other tables too, all of them about Raven and what an awful person she had been and how much everyone hated her. Wow.

Hoping to change the subject, at least with these three, Crystal asked if there'd been any news on Brooke. They said no, not yet, not that they knew of—then they went right back to the topic at hand.

Good grief. Their talk went on for several more minutes until finally she blurted, "Maybe there was a reason she was so mean. She could've just been going through a difficult time or something."

"Ha!" Lisa cried. "I've been here seven years and she's been an absolute nightmare on every single visit."

"I've been here *fifteen* years," an older man in a cook's apron volunteered from the next table. "Take it from me, she was always that way. Those of us in the kitchen dreaded every visit she paid to this place."

Agreement—and even a bit of applause—sounded from others in the room.

"Was there nothing good about her at all?" Crystal demanded.

Everyone was quiet until a woman from housekeeping volunteered, "She tipped well. I don't know about all of you, but I'll put up with a lot for the kind of money she threw around."

"I wouldn't serve that woman again no matter how much you paid me," the cook replied. After a beat, he added, "Oh, right! Guess now I won't have to!"

As many of the others laughed, he launched into a vivid tale about an altercation he'd had with Raven years ago. No sooner had he finished than another employee piped up with what she called her "own personal Raven horror story." It seemed almost everyone in the room had one—and they were all eager to share.

Eventually Crystal interrupted again, unwilling to hear even one more tale. "You're telling me that in all those years and all those visits, Raven never made a single friend on staff here?"

Everyone grew quiet for a moment, and even when she looked over at Greg and met his eyes, he shrugged and turned away.

"It's not like nobody ever talked to her," said a different security guard, the older one with the mustache and the friendly smile. He was at the vending machine, buying himself a candy bar. "Upper management hung out with the lady almost every time she came."

Crystal watched as that man loaded in his coins. "You mean like Reggie? Andre? They were friends with her?"

"Tell the truth, Orlando," someone called out.

"Okay, maybe they weren't exactly friends, but they'd share drinks with her on the restaurant's balcony or take in the sunrise from reclining chairs by the lake. Stuff like that. They did what they could to make her feel welcome."

"Of course they did," snapped a groundskeeper from a table near the door. "Because they *had* to. Part of management's job is to schmooze the clients, especially the rich ones who throw a lot of cash around while they're here."

Everyone nodded.

"Yeah, but just until that big mess she caused last summer," said the cook as he crossed his arms over his ample chest. "After that, I don't think even upper management wanted anything to do with her. When she came in January, they all steered clear."

Crystal was about to ask what big mess he was talking about when someone hissed, "Speaking of upper management."

Looking up, Crystal spotted Xena Peele, the spa's director of scheduling, coming into the room. Tall and striking, Xena was a force to be reckoned with, the only person here at Palm Grotto that Crystal hadn't yet been able to get a handle on. She was an intimidating woman, but intentionally so, Crystal thought, with her leather pants and chain belts, her black spiky hair, and her blood-red nails.

Mostly, Crystal just tried to stay on Xena's good side—when she wasn't avoiding her entirely, that is.

Xena crossed to the coffee area, the heels of her thigh-high boots clicking a loud rhythm as she went. After pouring herself a cup of the rich, dark brew, she turned to face the group. "'Speaking of upper management,' what?"

Everyone was quiet for a moment until the groundskeeper spoke up. "We were saying nobody liked Raven, not even upper management."

"Ah." Xena sipped her coffee, her eyes moving from one to the other. "Actually, Raven did have one real friend on staff here."

"Define *real*." The cook's skepticism was palpable.

"*Real* as in liked her and confided in her. Cared about her."

Crystal was glad to hear it. Turning toward Xena, she waited for her to elaborate.

Xena's gaze fell on Crystal in return. "Imagine that, knowing the deepest, darkest secrets of a monster like Raven, yet caring about her anyway. Sounds hard to believe, I know, but it's true."

Marcus managed to wrap things up at work, so after one final check of the day's task list to make sure he hadn't missed anything, he neatened his desk, locked up the office, and headed out.

Once home, he launched into packing for the trip but soon found that was easier said than done. Normally he could "load and roll" in under four minutes—a fact he had proven time and again, especially when he was working active response. But this time was different, thanks to the person he was going to see.

The more his small suitcase filled, the more he began to second-guess himself. He had no problems with the initial reason for his visit, the desire to protect an old friend. It was the unofficial, unspoken stuff—the memories, the emotions—behind that reason that gave Marcus an odd lurch in his gut. Was that nerves? Could the man *Newsweek* magazine had once called "the epitome of cool in a crisis" be rattled by the thought of reconnecting with a woman he hadn't spoken to for more than two decades?

Marcus reached for the nearest folded set— blue shirt and silver tie—and tossed them into the open suitcase. There. Decision made. He began to close the lid then hesitated, rethinking the tie, concerned that it might emphasize the silver of his hair. Back then it had been thick and jet black. It was still almost as thick now, thank goodness, but it wasn't black anymore and hadn't been for ten or fifteen years. Not that he'd even given the matter a second thought, before this.

Scowling, Marcus removed the tie from the suitcase, hung it back on the rack in the closet, and chose a different one instead, a mix of blues, greens, and browns that Zoe had insisted he buy during a recent jaunt to the mall. Placing it atop the neatly folded clothes inside the suitcase, he wondered if he should rethink everything else in there as well. Should he have gone shopping for some new things? There was no time left for that now, but maybe tomorrow morning before seeing Juliette he could slip away from the spa and hit a nice men's store out there.

Wait a minute. Shopping? New clothes? Hair color? Marcus groaned—he sounded like a teenage girl.

He couldn't imagine why he was finding it so hard to prepare for this one simple encounter. Lowering himself to the edge of the bed, he had to admit that was because there was nothing simple about it.

Get a grip, Stone.

Looking at his suitcase, he could feel his pulse pounding in his neck. Stifling a groan, he closed the lid, zipped it shut, and lowered the bag to the floor. There. Now he had everything he needed for this trip save one last item.

He retrieved that item from his dresser and then paused and held it in his open palm. He'd just bought it yesterday, for less than a dollar, but to his mind it was the single most valuable possession he owned right now. It was to be his own personal calling card, a secret signal meant to bridge a gap.

A twenty-five-year gap.

With a grunt, Marcus looked down at the silver and blue wrapper in his hand. Who could imagine so much significance being attached to a simple piece of candy, to one small round patty of peppermint crème covered in chocolate?

Tucking it into the front pocket of his suitcase, Marcus couldn't help but grin. A Peppermint Pattie as the must-have item for this adventure?

No one in the whole world would understand.

No one except Juliette Taylor.

Chapter Eight

The room had fallen silent, waiting for Xena's revelation.

"So who was it?" someone prodded. "Who was Raven's friend on staff here?"

Xena stirred her coffee. "Moonflower. Everybody knows that. The two of them were very close—and have been for years."

Crystal frowned. "Moonflower Youngblood? The Watsu tech?"

"No, Moonflower Jones, the dishwasher," Xena snapped. "How many Moonflowers do you think we have around here?"

Crystal didn't appreciate the sarcasm, but it wasn't worth a retort. Not only did Xena outrank her, but as the gatekeeper of the appointments, the woman was in a position to make Crystal's life miserable—or the opposite, for that matter—if she wanted to.

Fortunately Xena soon topped off her coffee mug and left, done with the whole subject.

After that, one of the spa aides turned to Crystal and elaborated. She said that Moonflower had been Raven's favorite therapist for years and that the two of them had grown quite close over time. "Not that they'd hung out after hours or anything, just that they developed a strong therapist-client bond."

Crystal nodded, knowing that was common with masseurs, but especially so with those who specialized in the emotionally intimate art of Watsu. Its name derived from the words *water* and *Shiatsu*, Watsu was a unique form of massage done by well-trained professionals in small, waist-deep heated pools. Most Watsu sessions had the masseuse cradling the client in their arms for many of the stretches, a posture that mimicked the maternal bond and helped bring about physical and psychological healing to the client. It hadn't surprised Crystal at all when she first learned that the naturally-maternal Moonflower was a Watsu specialist, nor did it seem odd to her now to hear that Raven had formed a strong attachment to the woman over the years.

"She was pretty upset when she heard," the aide added. "I think she even went home."

The cook grinned. "Meanwhile, the rest of us munchkins have been running around singing 'Ding Dong the Witch Is Dead' all afternoon."

Heat flooded Crystal's face, but everyone else laughed. This was awful. She had to get out of here. She washed her mug at the sink then made her way to the exit. Outside she took in a deep breath as she headed down the service walkway between the two buildings. Before she got far, she realized someone else had come out and was walking along behind her.

"I'm sorry you had to hear all that."

With a backward glance, Crystal saw that it was Greg, his expression dark.

"The people at Palm Grotto aren't usually so hostile," he added as he caught up with her on the sidewalk. "It's just been a really bad day."

"It's not only Palm Grotto, it's everywhere." Crystal knew the world was a cold and heartless place, but something about the harsh way those people had bandied about the dead woman's name had been especially disturbing.

"Is it just me, or is the world getting crueler all the time?" She could hear the sadness in her own voice as they continued toward the gate, side by side.

Greg's brow furrowed. "Actually, the world has always been this way. Haven't you ever heard the phrase 'man's inhumanity to man'? That was from a poem by Burns, I think, but it was so true people have been using it ever since."

"Man's inhumanity to man," Crystal echoed.

"Even the Bible says, 'They sharpen their tongues like swords and aim cruel words like deadly arrows.' I'm just saying, it's not only here and now. It's everywhere, and for as long as humans have been alive."

"Wow. I guess you're right. And I'm impressed."

Greg gave Crystal a shy glance. "Don't be. My mom was always big on quotes. My sister and I had to recite a new one every week before we could get our allowance."

Crystal nodded but didn't speak. Too bad she hadn't spent more time in college so she could quote something smart back to him. She'd always planned to get a degree, but with money so tight, she had given up after just one semester and switched over to a massage therapy school instead, where her tuition was almost covered by her day spa's work-study program. The school was top-notch and she took the full two-year curriculum, though most of that time was spent learning about things like anatomy and physiology, not poetry or literature.

When they reached the gate, Greg opened

and held it. She stepped through, deeply glad that he had left the others to be with her.

He flashed her a shy smile as he hooked the latch behind them. "Do you want to go somewhere quiet? You know, where we could talk or whatever? This must have been a pretty traumatic day for you. Sometimes it helps to review things a couple of times until the shock isn't quite so raw."

Heart pounding, Crystal resisted the urge to move closer to him. Few people had ever worried or cared about her, at least not to the extent that they offered a shoulder to cry on or an ear to listen. It hadn't mattered, really. She was strong, she had survived. But somehow, this one little show of sympathy pushed past all of her strength, all of her resolve, and left her feeling open and raw and . . . needy.

She didn't want to be needy.

"I'd love to, but the police said I'm not supposed to leave the area." She glanced around then added, "How 'bout we sit on one of those benches around front, near the fountain? We can talk till they come and get me?"

"Sure."

They fell silent as they made their way along the side of the building, the heat of Greg's body making her heart pound. There was something about him that drew her close, made her want to lean against his shoulder or take his hand or reach up and brush the bangs from his forehead. She did none of those for now, but maybe someday she could.

The bench was just ahead, but they no sooner rounded the corner when Crystal heard someone call her name. It was one of the detectives, and he was waving her over to the treatment room.

"Miss Walsh? We're ready for you now."

Swallowing hard, Crystal turned to look at Greg, who gave her a reassuring smile. She tried to smile in return, but she was suddenly so tense, she felt sure it came off more like a grimace.

Juliette and Didi headed away from the main office, foregoing the shortcut that would've brought them directly past the Arrowscale building and using the wide road that led to their guest rooms instead. They were quiet as they walked along the shoulder, the resort coming more fully into view as they rounded the first bend.

Palm Grotto was nestled on about sixty lush, beautiful acres of gently-sloping hillside, with the gatehouse at the top, a small lake at the middle, and a jogging trail rounding out the bottom. In between were the various facilities, such as the conference center, the yoga dome, tennis courts, and of course the world-renowned spa and the mineral waters of the grotto itself. Guest rooms lined the perimeter of the property in clusters of varying sizes, from small single and double units, all the way up to a big block of rooms near the conference center. Most of this weekend's retreat attendees would be staying in that block, with Didi and Juliette in a separate unit next door.

The two women grew silent as they continued to walk. Looking around, Juliette tried to find solace in the beauty on all sides. The sight of this place usually took her breath away, but right now thoughts of Raven's death were casting a shadow over everything. If only she hadn't chosen to hide in a closet rather than risk an encounter with the woman! Now that she'd never have another chance to make things right, Juliette would regret that action forever, no matter how unreasonable the feisty redhead might've been in return.

Didi glanced her way. "You okay?"

"I'm fine." Juliette shrugged. "I'm just thinking about Raven, wishing things hadn't ended this way between us. I feel bad about it."

Didi grunted. "Speak for yourself."

"Yeah, you haven't heard what happened yet." Juliette explained how she'd cowered in the supply closet earlier, until Brooke swept in and saved the day. "I feel terrible. I should have stepped up, not chickened out."

Didi shook her head. "Nah, you were smart to hide. I wouldn't give it another thought."

Juliette grew silent, her heart overflowing with grief and regret and guilt. The woman obviously carried around a tremendous load of pain. If only Juliette had put her personal aversion aside, sought Raven out, spoken to her with kindness. Maybe she could've made a real difference in her life.

Now it was too late.

Juliette's voice was soft. "I should have offered her an olive branch."

Didi barked out a laugh. "Are you kidding? Do you know what she would've done if you had? She would have ripped that branch out of your hand, used it to smack you across the face, then snapped it in half over her knee."

Juliette smiled in spite of herself. "Maybe."

"Forget it, hon. People like Raven don't *do* friendship. They can't be helped, can't be reasoned with or softened or changed. Why would you want to be friends with someone like her anyway?"

Juliette shrugged. "Uh, 'Love your enemies? Pray for those who persecute you?' Book of Matthew? Any of that ring a bell?"

"Don't be sarcastic. You know what I mean. You can love someone and still have boundaries."

"I'm not sure hiding in a closet qualifies as a boundary."

Didi merely grunted in reply.

But maybe she was right. Raven's heart had been so hard it probably would've taken a sledgehammer—if not a jackhammer—to get through to her. Still, that didn't change the fact that Juliette hadn't even *tried*. Shame on her.

"It's just that I owed her one, you know?" she said finally. "Today I had the chance to return a favor and I didn't do it. Now it's too late."

"A favor?"

"From back in the day. That time when she and I were in Italy for the collections, and she taught me self-defense."

"Oh, that," Didi replied. "Please. You were all of, what, eighteen at the time?"

"Yeah."

"That's forever ago. So she showed you a few holds. Some kicks. So what?"

"It was more than just a few. She taught me how to protect myself. Trust me, that knowledge has come in handy more than a few times since."

"But to feel indebted to the woman for

thirty-something years? That's a little extreme, don't you think?"

Juliette thrust her hands in her pockets, not sure she wanted to go down this road. "You have to understand, Didi, guys in Italy were hitting on us right and left. Raven got worried about me, said my naiveté was going to end up getting me in big trouble. And she was right. I was incredibly obtuse and trusting back then."

"She actually said that? That your naiveté would get you in trouble?"

"Actually, I think it was more like, 'Don't be an idiot, men are only after one thing and you're too stupid to see it.'"

Didi chuckled. "That sounds more like the Raven I knew."

"Anyway, you know how it was for my sister and me. We were pretty sheltered growing up. Our parents were wonderful, but they were protective. Then when they died and we went to live with our grandparents, it was the exact opposite, or at least it was for me. I was just fourteen years old, but from then on I had complete freedom to come and go as I pleased, to do whatever I wanted, wherever and whenever. There was no preparation, no transition, no guidance. By the time I was eighteen and trying to break into modeling, I still didn't have a clue how to protect myself.

Raven picked up on that. When we were in Italy, the situation felt dangerous enough that she decided to take me under her wing and teach me stuff. I learned all kinds of things from her, not just holds and kicks."

"Like what else?"

"Like stop making eye contact with every person who walks by. Don't go off alone, especially at night. Always carry cab fare, even if you think you won't need it. Pretty basic, but it was all news to me."

"Still not getting it." Didi shook her head. "That's what friends do for friends. What's the big deal?"

Juliette was silent for a long moment, gazing out at the beautiful scenery that surrounded them. There was such a contrast between the lush greenness of the resort and the dry, brown, desert mountains in the distance. Much like the contrast between Raven's stunning outer beauty and the dark, damaged person within.

"You don't know the whole story."

"No?"

"I guess I can tell you, now that she's passed away." Juliette's voice was soft, their feet crunching rhythmically in the gravel below.

Didi kept silent, waiting for her to continue.

"When Raven first tried to warn me that I

was putting myself in danger, I just blew her off. She knew she'd have to convince me of my own ignorance if I was ever going to listen. So one night she sat me down and told me what the world was really like."

Didi shot her a glance.

Juliette swallowed hard. "You see, there were reasons Raven knew all of that self defense stuff in the first place. Sad, sick, horrible reasons." She inhaled a shaky breath. "When she was younger, she was victimized, repeatedly, usually by the boyfriends her mother brought home. By the time Raven learned to defend herself, she'd already been violated by a dozen different men, starting when she was just a child."

Didi faltered, her eyes filling with sudden tears. "I didn't know that."

"Nobody did. Her bio was pure fiction, and she guarded the real facts of her life with a vengeance. She was an incredibly private person."

Sniffling, Didi dug in her pockets for a tissue. "You can say that again. She wouldn't even tell people her real name."

"I know. But for some reason, that night she decided to trust me with the truth. She *had* to, to open my eyes, and thank goodness she did. I didn't know what the world was really like until then. After that, I was ready to learn whatever she wanted to teach me. And that's why I've been in her debt ever since."

Didi dabbed at her eyes with the tissue.

"Kind of reframes things a bit, now doesn't it?" Juliette added softly.

"To say the least. I wish I had known."

"Yeah, I would've told you if I could."

They rounded the corner on the last leg of their jaunt, their cluster of guestrooms coming into sight.

"Did she tell *you* her real name?" Didi asked suddenly.

Juliette nodded. "Rayleen Eugenia Humphries."

Wiping away a tear of her own, Juliette gazed into the distance, wondering which name would go on Raven's tombstone, the one she was given at birth, or the one she created for herself the day she drew a line in the sand and decided she would never be anyone's victim again.

Crystal stood, one eye on the waiting detective as she wrapped things up with Greg.

She spoke in an urgent whisper. "Listen, I was thinking I might go over to Moonflower's later, just to see if she's okay. Do you want to come with me?"

To her surprise, he declined. "Big mistake.

Moonflower would be furious. She can't stand me."

"What? Why do you think that?"

He shrugged. "It's probably the uniform. I mean, she may be a nice person and all, but at the end of the day she's just an old hippie at heart. To her, anyone in uniform—even a security guard—is 'the Man.' The few times she and I had dealings in the past, she was barely civil. I think she'd spit on me if she could get away with it."

Moonflower? Spitting on someone? Sweet, peaceful, loving little Moonflower? Crystal couldn't imagine such a thing.

"Ma'am?" The detective was growing impatient.

"But, thanks anyway," he said to her.

Then with a quick, reluctant good-bye, she turned and walked toward the scene of the crime.

The two women reached their destination, and Juliette smiled when she remembered that each guest room here had its own private courtyard, delineated by chest-high stucco barriers encircling colorful, blooming vegetation. Didi gave Juliette her room key and the two women parted outside. The plan was for Juliette to unpack and freshen up then join

Didi next door. In the meantime Didi would be on the computer, researching the three names Iliana had given them—Scott Ferguson, George Bailey, and Elwood Dowd—to see if she could figure out who they were.

Opening the door and stepping inside, Juliette was glad to see that her room was spacious, its décor understated, a mix of beiges and browns that created a peaceful, minimalist feel. Hanging in the closet was Palm Grotto's signature white terry bathrobe, the garb of choice for almost every guest who stayed here. The robes were even welcome in the restaurant, and Juliette knew it wasn't unusual to see, among the silk blouses and tailored suits, numerous guests dining comfortably in white robes and flip-flops.

Juliette unpacked and undressed, then brushed her teeth and washed her face. Like most models—even those who'd been out of the business for a long time—she hated makeup and wore it only when she absolutely had to. She preferred to focus on skin care, which was the basis of the entire JT Lady product line.

Her hair was equally low-maintenance, thanks to the expensive-but-worth-every-penny haircut that allowed her natural, short blonde waves to form the perfect, face-flattering shape without much fuss at all. Once she was finished freshening up, she donned the Palm Grotto robe and slippers and padded outside.

"Knock-knock," she said when she reached Didi's door, which was wide open.

Didi was sitting on the bed, a pile of pillows propped behind her, her laptop balanced on her knees. "Come in. My, but don't you look comfortable."

Juliette tugged on her terrycloth belt as she sat on the second bed. "Yeah, love these robes. Find anything?"

Didi returned her attention to the computer screen. "It's strange, actually. I can't make sense of it."

Trying to get comfortable, Juliette leaned over and rested her elbow on the pillows, relishing the soft desert breezes that blew gently through the room and out the window on the other side. "Bad news?"

"Not exactly. I'm not sure." Didi glanced at her, an odd gleam in her eye. "I mean, I got worried at first. When I Googled 'Scott Ferguson,' it came back with a 'Scottie Ferguson Haircutting' in Cincinnati, Ohio."

"I knew it!" Juliette slapped a hand against the bed covers. "Raven was trying to break into the beauty product business!"

Didi cut her off. "Not so fast. I thought that too, at first. But then I Googled the other two names, George Bailey and Elwood Dowd. Neither one came up with any hits that were in any way related to the beauty business."

"Maybe they're up-and-comers who haven't made a name for themselves yet. Maybe they're salon owners who don't have web-sites."

Didi shook her head, giving Juliette a vague, perplexed smile. "Those three names do have something in common, but it's got nothing to do with the beauty industry, or with skin care."

"What, then?"

"Scott Ferguson. George Bailey. Elwood Dowd." Didi turned her laptop toward Juliette. On the screen were three pictures, side-by-side, old black-and-white images of what looked like the actor Jimmy Stewart.

"Spit it out, Didi. Who are they? What do they have in common?"

"Makes no sense to me, but those are the names of the main characters in three differ-ent Jimmy Stewart movies. Remember how you said George Bailey sounded familiar?"

Juliette nodded.

"Duh. Of course it did. George Bailey was the name of the character played by Jimmy Stewart in *It's a Wonderful Life*."

Chapter Nine

Marcus loaded the car then returned to the kitchen for a last-minute check on perishables. He'd be gone for the next four days, which meant that the eggs and cheese would keep but the milk and the leftovers would not. Glancing at the clock, he pulled out everything that would need to be either eaten or ditched and made himself a plate for supper. While that heated in the microwave, he poured himself a big glass of milk and sat down at the table, cell phone in hand, and called his daughter.

He missed having her around, but still he was grateful for the timing of the class trip she was on, which couldn't have been better. It freed him up to go away without having to make childcare arrangements—not to mention that it saved him from any probing questions prior to departure. Zoe was quite perceptive, and if she'd been around for the past few days she would have definitely picked up a whiff that something was going on here beyond a simple vacation to a spa.

The way Marcus had set things up, he'd be back by Monday night, plenty of time before Zoe would return Tuesday afternoon. And though she'd known her dad and grand-mother would be traveling while she was gone, she'd been so excited over her own adventure that she hadn't seemed to give theirs much thought at all, which was fine by him.

At thirteen, Zoe was that age where she flipped back and forth, seemingly at random, between adoring her father and seeing him as the biggest irritant on the planet. He never knew which of her two sides he would get, so as he sat listening to the rings and waiting for her to pick up, he hoped for Jekyll, not Hyde.

"Daddy! Hi!" Her voice was exuberant and loud.

Jekyll, thank goodness.

"Hey, sweetie, how's it going?"

"Hold on, Dad. I told everybody you'd be calling but they're still being really noisy."

He waited, listening as she extracted her-self from a boisterous group of kids and made her way to somewhere quieter. The micro-wave dinged so he grabbed his plate and was just sitting back down to a steaming plate of

Tuesday's chicken casserole when she came back on the line.

"This is better, I'm in the hall now. We're leaving for dinner in about ten minutes and the girls in my room are being all yappy and hogging the mirror. I got ready early so I could talk."

"Good thinking. So how's the trip going?"

"Oh, Dad, it's awesome! Washington is, like, so amazing!"

Grinning, he took another bite and listened to her expound on the joys of DC. He'd just brought her there himself, a few years before, but to hear her talk, it was as if she was seeing it all now for the first time. She recounted the places they'd been so far, including the Capitol Building, two of the Smithsonian museums, and the zoo.

"Oh—and we saw the Spy Museum! It was my favorite!"

Why didn't that surprise him?

"Jamie and Alison have decided that *you're* a spy, Dad."

Marcus nearly choked on his peas. "They *what*? Why?"

"There was a list of how to tell if someone is a spy and a bunch of things on it sounded just like you."

"Oh boy. Guess my secret decoder ring gave me away?"

"No, really, you know how like you're not allowed to talk about your work sometimes? Or how you have phone numbers for all kinds of important people, like high-ranking government officials and stuff?"

"Zoe, that's—"

"You take photos of unusual things, like doorframes or the insides of cabinets."

"Yeah, for structural analy—"

"And you're always being called in to help when there's been a big disaster or something."

"That's because I'm an expert in disasters!"

"I know, but they think that's your cover—for espionage."

Marcus shook his head, not sure whether to laugh or groan. "What did you tell them?"

"I said I could neither confirm nor deny."

They both laughed.

"Great, thanks, Zo. I'm sure after that they were even more convinced than before."

Marcus asked how everyone was getting along. By the time she was done recounting all of the middle school drama, he had polished off his entire dinner, washed the dishes he'd used, and put them away. At least it sounded like she was staying out of trouble herself. She also seemed to be learning a lot, and she was clearly having a wonderful time.

Just before hanging up, as he moved

through the house making sure he'd locked the windows and turned off all lights, they picked the day and time for their next call, Sunday evening at 6:00. He also reminded her that he was about to leave on his trip with Grandma.

"Oh right, to that spa. Jamie wants to know, do you have to get naked for a massage?"

"Zoe!"

"Well, she asked."

He groaned. "No, I think that's optional. Don't worry, I'll keep my shorts on."

"Eww! Dad! She wasn't talking about you; we were wondering about Grandma."

He laughed. "Honey, I assure you that even if your grandmother does choose to disrobe, she'd still have a sheet or a towel over her. Besides, a masseuse is like a doctor. They're professionals about it—not to mention they've seen it all before."

"Well, I hope you guys have a lot of fun either way."

"We'll try."

"Hey, maybe you'll meet some gorgeous manicurist or something and end up marrying her and bringing her home."

The idea of Marcus meeting someone and getting married had become a frequent topic of Zoe's lately. Good thing she didn't know the real reason he was going to California.

Otherwise, she'd already be calling Juliette "Mommy."

"Though I highly doubt I could meet and marry someone in just four days, I'm glad you'd like to see me happy."

"Oh, I don't care about your happiness," she teased. "I just think it would be cool to have someone in the family who could give me free manicures."

He chuckled, checking the thermostat to make sure it was set down. "Zoe, I miss ya like crazy, kid."

"Me too, Dad. Have a good time."

"I will. You too. Be safe." They said their good-byes, and he disconnected the call.

Ready to head out, Marcus gathered his things and paused at the back door, the last bag of trash in one hand and his keys in the other. There in the darkened kitchen, he asked a prayer of protection for his child and travelling mercies for them all. He closed that prayer with a huge thank-you for the best daughter a man could ever ask for.

Crystal had been afraid she might have to go into the room where the death occurred, but instead the detective brought her next door to the Sweetwater, where she'd been giving a hot-stone massage when things first started getting weird. Once inside, the man introduced himself as Detective Lopez, then a second detective joined them, a younger guy with the last name of Bryant. He had a friendly face and a gentler demeanor than his older, more grizzled partner.

The men explained that they wanted to hear what had taken place from her perspective. Ignoring the butterflies careening around inside her stomach, Crystal decided to start at the beginning. She moved closer to the massage table and demonstrated how she'd been standing there, doing some deep breathing in preparation for giving a massage, when she realized she could hear voices coming from next door.

"Actually, we'd like to go a little further back than that." Detective Lopez eyed her intently. "Let's start with your whereabouts since about five p.m. yesterday."

Well . . . that was odd. Why did they need to know that? Trying not to frown, she thought for a moment then listed off her activities after she'd clocked out around 5:20 p.m. First she'd made a stop for free end-of-the-day pretzels near the park, then she'd gone to a pet store in downtown Cahuilla Springs, one where patrons were allowed to play with the puppies. After that, she'd gone home and whipped up a batch of Blueberry and Brown Sugar Body Scrub, which she followed with a bath and then bed.

Lopez grunted, looking down at his notes. "Buying a dog, are you?"

"No sir." Heat crept into her cheeks. How pathetic she must sound to these two men. "I'm new in town and don't really know anybody yet, and I was feeling kind of, uh, lonely. So I went and hugged some puppies. Is there something wrong with that?"

Bryant seemed to understand what she was saying, though Lopez merely grunted. She continued going through the time period in question, ending with this morning's trip to the farmer's market and the flea market, the quick stop at home, and her return to the spa to start her workday.

"From what I'm hearing, Crystal, can I assume you have some financial issues?"

What? Where did Lopez come up with that? She forced her voice to remain calm. "How can that possibly be relevant here?"

"Just sounds like you're having to cut a few corners. I was thinking, if you're pinching pennies at home, it must be hard to work at a place that caters to the rich. Having to serve folks like that all day long must make you kinda resentful."

Crystal did her best to keep the disrespect from her voice. "Why would I resent it if my clients have money? This is my *job*. Thank goodness they do, or I wouldn't get a paycheck!"

She knew she sounded defensive, but the whole subject rubbed her the wrong way. Pinching pennies? Compared to how she and her mother used to live, her new life here was a stay at the Ritz!

Fortunately they seemed satisfied with her answers and told her to continue. She went on to describe parking her car in the employee lot, clocking in at the main building, meeting Juliette Taylor at the supply closet, and finally coming over to the Sweetwater Room, where the aide was getting things ready for her first appointment of the day.

The older detective flipped through his notes. "Right, that was a hot-stone massage at two o'clock with a Mr. VonTassel."

"Who?"

"VonTassel. Your massage was with Quentin VonTassel."

"No it wasn't. My client was named Elwood Dowd."

"I don't think so."

"Yes, he was here earlier. I saw you questioning him. Short guy, runner's body, hair plugs along the forehead?"

Lopez flipped back and forth for several pages, but then Bryant interrupted him, giving him a meaningful look and stretching the name. "*Dowd*, remember? Threatened to call in the big guns?"

The men shared a look and then changed the subject. Crystal wanted to ask what that was about, but soon they were directing her to the back room, where they had some additional questions. Gesturing toward the refrigerator and microwave, Bryant asked if those were used for storing and cooking employee snacks and lunches.

"Gosh, no, there are appliances in the break room for that. We'd never put food in here."

Crystal walked to the fridge and swung open the door, intending to show them the neat rows of various bottles and jars and tubes inside. Instead, it was completely empty.

"I don't understand. Where did everything go?" She started to list the items they should have been seeing, but the young detective stopped her, explaining that the contents had been taken over to the Palm Springs police lab for analysis.

Before she could ask why they'd needed to do that, the older detective looked down at his notes again. "If no one ever puts food in there, how do you explain the large tub of yogurt and the fruits and vegetables that we found? Do you know anything about those?"

"Yes, sir. We use them in some of our

facials. Yogurt is an extremely gentle exfoliant. And the silica in cucumbers is great for nourishing connective tissue in the skin. Lime juice balances pH levels—"

"It's okay, we get it." Lopez scribbled another note on his pad. "What about the various nonfood items that were in there? The tubes and bottles and stuff. Why do they need to be refrigerated?"

"They're more effective when chilled. There's a lot of heating and cooling in our various treatments. It depends on the goal, like if I'm trying to open up the pores or relax the muscles, I'll use warmth. If I want to reduce swelling or soothe the skin, I'll go with cool."

"Okay, got it." Lopez flipped to a new page in his notebook and moved on. "So you already mentioned that you were back here in this area several times today. At any point did you observe anyone else in this room or see anyone going in or out of this building?"

Crystal shook her head then hesitated. "Well, Ty, of course, in the beginning, but all he did was set up the room for me and then leave again to retrieve my client. Once he dropped off Mr., uh, whoever, I didn't see him after that. The spa aides are kept pretty busy, all day long."

Bryant nodded. "And you saw no one else back here other than Ty Kirkland?"

"No sir. No one."

Lopez shifted in his seat. "Let's talk about you. How long would you say you were in this back room before your client arrived?"

"I'm not sure, maybe three or four minutes."

"Then you said you came back here again soon after that, just before the start of his massage?"

"Yes."

"How long were you here that time?"

"A minute or two at the most."

Both detectives were taking notes now. "And what did you do during that time?"

Crystal hesitated. She was picking up on a very strange vibe. Nothing had changed—their voices were still calm and modulated, their expressions neutral—but for some reason she felt uncomfortable. For lack of a better word, she felt almost *accused* somehow.

Trying not to act self-conscious, Crystal walked toward the back door and pointed out the master schedule hanging on the wall. "I washed my hands, then I came over and looked at the printout to learn which therapist was in Tamarisk. To be honest, I just couldn't imagine who was making all that noise, and I was trying to decide whether to knock on the door and ask them to tone it down or call the spa manager so he could deal with it."

"And?"

"And when I saw it was Brooke, I decided to do neither. She's one of the best therapists here. It wasn't my place to correct her. She knows what she's doing." She bit her lip. "At least . . . I thought she did."

She pulled her hand away from the schedule, and as she did she noticed an odd, grayish-black substance on her fingertips. "There's something on here that wasn't there before. Some sort of dark powder."

"Yes ma'am. That's just residue from the fingerprinting."

Crystal turned to look at them. "Fingerprinting? But why?"

The two detectives glanced at each other and then back at her, their gazes narrowing just a bit.

"Standard procedure," the young one said.

"To take fingerprints when somebody dies? That's standard procedure?"

He nodded. "When there are inconsistencies, yes."

"Inconsistencies." Crystal rolled the word around on her tongue and then she gasped, eyes wide.

This hadn't been a death by natural causes, as she'd been assuming all along.

It had been a murder.

Chapter Ten

By the time Crystal finished talking to the police, she was exhausted and in need of a friendly face. Her schedule had been cleared till the meeting at six, so she went in search of Greg.

The main security office was at the other side of the resort, and as she walked there, she inhaled deeply, letting the fresh air clear her head and revive her spirit. At the small tin building, she knocked on the door and swung it open, leaning inside to see an unmanned front desk. She called out a hello, hoping he wouldn't think her pushy or overeager for having come here.

She heard a cough and some shuffling in the back room, and after a moment a man emerged into the hallway, the light revealing him in silhouette. As he came closer, Crystal realized that it was Greg, looking so handsome, as usual, in his khaki security guard uniform.

"Crystal?"

She couldn't quite tell from his tone whether he was happy to see her or not. She stayed where she was, watching as he came toward her.

"Yeah, it's me." She couldn't see his face, which was still in shadow. "Are you busy?"

He paused to twist on a lamp. "Just catching up with some paperwork. How'd it go with the police?" He turned toward her, and as she met his gaze, she realized his eyes and nose were red, as if he'd been crying.

Heart surging with compassion, she stepped inside and pulled the door shut behind her. "Fine. Are you okay?"

"Sure. Why?" His voice was gruff.

Crystal shrugged, resisting the urge to take his hand in hers. "I don't know, you look like maybe you've been crying."

He was quiet for a long moment then he shook his head and gave her a rueful smile.

"What?"

"I was going to say my eyes are red because of allergies or something. But for some reason, the words won't come out. I guess I just can't lie to you, Crystal." He cleared his throat. "You're right, I *was* crying. Don't tell anyone though, okay?"

"Sure. But you don't need to be embarrassed. Everybody cries sometimes, even big strong security guards like you."

Ignoring her attempt at humorous flirtation, he invited her back to his office. As they went, he started right in asking about her interrogation.

Crystal let him change the subject—for now. Maybe if they talked about other things for a while first, he would grow comfortable enough to share what had upset him so.

No matter how many ways they looked at it, Juliette and Didi could make no sense of the Raven-Jimmy Stewart connection. Finally, as it got closer to the time for them to head up to the conference center, Juliette returned to her room to get dressed and review her notes.

Back at her closet she traded the robe for a white blouse and a black-and-white polka-dotted skirt, then she draped a lightweight black sweater across her shoulders and tied it at the neck. Slipping on a comfortable pair of flats, she stepped back, checked her image in the mirror, and then turned her attentions to the materials for the talks she would have given today at the staff meetings, had they not been cancelled. She still had a good ten minutes before it would be time to go, so she gathered up her things and stepped outside.

Out on her own little private patio, she sat on a cushioned wrought iron chair and went through her papers, trying to winnow down an hour's worth of information into a brief, ten-minute version of the most salient points. As she worked, she found herself relishing the warm air and the late afternoon sunshine. A hummingbird darted among a profusion of purple flowers blooming along the privacy barrier. Pausing to watch for a moment, she was struck with the thought that even on the saddest of days, God always seemed to provide glimpses of joy among the tragedy.

Crystal gave Greg what she hoped was a warm and reassuring smile and asked, for the second time, why he'd been crying. "Was it all that stuff with Brooke and the client's death and everything?"

"No." He ran a hand through his hair. "Okay, well, sort of, I guess. But not exactly." He reached for a picture frame sitting on the desk next to his computer. Picking it up, he held it toward himself and looked down at the picture as he spoke. "I'm not exactly buddies with Brooke, and I didn't know the woman who died. So it's not what happened to them specifically, it's just, well, having such a close encounter with death—*any* death—is still kind of tough for me. I'm sure it'll get better with time, but right now I'm pretty raw."

He turned the frame around so that she could see the photo, a portrait of a young woman. She was beautiful, with dark hair and eyes, her lashes long and thick, her lips a deep, natural red. In the picture she was smiling, but her expression seemed tentative, even guarded . . . and sad.

"This was my sister, Valentine."

"She's beautiful." Wait, did he say she *was* his sister? *Oh no . . .*

"She was also one of the most wonderful, amazing people in the whole world." He turned the frame back around, his eyes filling with fresh tears. "She died, just last year. I thought I was doing better, but I guess today's events brought it all back and then some." He grunted and swiped away fresh tears, then he set the picture off to the side of the desk. "They say things get better with time, but right now it feels like it just happened."

"It takes a long time to grieve the loss of a loved one, Greg," What else could she say? There were no words for something so heartbreaking. "Give yourself a break. No wonder today was difficult for you. It was way too soon."

"I guess."

Unable to stop herself, Crystal reached out and took Greg's hand, gently entangling her fingers with his. She met his tortured eyes. "I'm so sorry. I hope I didn't make things worse by marching in here and talking about the police and everything."

He shook his head. "Not at all. If anything, I think it kind of helped distract me for a while."

Greg gave her hand a firm squeeze then disentangled his fingers and moved his hands to his lap. Heat flooded her face. Did she do something wrong? Had she misread his signals?

Looking away, he continued. "You know, some days I don't think about my sister all that much, but then there are other days when she's on my mind a lot. Today, with all the stuff that happened . . ." He looked away. "Guess it just brought it all back, you know?"

"I can imagine."

Returning his gaze to Crystal, he added, "You have to understand, my family wasn't exactly like the ones you see on TV, if you know what I mean."

"I always wanted a family like the one on *Little Bear*."

Much to Crystal's delight, her words brought a smile to Greg's face.

"Yes! Like on *Little Bear*! Exactly! Or *Full House*, maybe." His smile faded. "Trust me, we Overstreets were nothing like that. Things were pretty bad, but at least Valentine and I had each other. The way we survived was by sticking together. That's why we were so close, there was no one else we could depend on."

Crystal's thoughts rearranged themselves in her mind. What Greg had said earlier about his mom loving quotes and making him earn his allowance had sounded so lovely, so normal, that she assumed he'd grown up in one of those perfect homes with a perfect family. Now it turned out that his family wasn't so perfect after all.

Though she hated to admit it, a part of her was actually glad to hear that. Her own childhood had been so crazy, her mom's dysfunction so extreme, she'd never really been able to connect with normal guys, at least not at a deeper level. Now that she knew Greg's childhood had probably been a lot like hers—if not in the specifics, at least in the pain it had caused and the emotional scars it had left behind—that was even more reason they would be good together. Their parents may have messed things up royally, but perhaps the two of them could finally get it right.

Seeming to relax just a bit, Greg leaned back in his chair and ran his hands through his thick, dark hair. "You know what? It's because of Valentine that I work here at the spa—and that I live in this town, for that matter."

"I thought you told me you grew up here in Cahuilla Springs."

"I did, but only till I was seventeen. That's when Val and I moved away, to live with our dad in Utah. I was so glad to get out I swore I'd never return, but Val always wanted to. Finally, a couple years ago, she got a job here and moved back. Things went so well for her, after a while she started trying to talk me into coming back too."

"I guess your mom still lives in this area? She must've been happy about that."

A hardness crossed Greg's features, all traces of relaxation gone. "Put it this way, if my mother were still here, I wouldn't have come at all."

"Ah. Got it."

"I hate to sound harsh, but she was mentally unstable, especially once our dad left. Totally off the deep end."

"Believe it or not, Greg. I think our situations were probably a lot alike."

"Oh yeah? Lucky us."

They shared a sad smile of commiseration.

"Anyway," Greg added, "this town isn't exactly filled with happy memories, but I'm glad I came back, if for no other reason than it gave me a chance to spend more time with my sister before she died."

Crystal wanted to learn more about that but knew she needed to tread lightly. "How did it happen? Was your sister ill? Was she in an accident of some kind?"

At her words, his eyes began to tear up again, but this time he responded by shaking his head and taking a few deep breaths, in and out. "I'm sorry. It's just too hard to talk about right now."

Crystal's eyes filled, too. "I understand. I should get going now anyway."

They parted without any further physical contact, no quick hug nor even a squeezed hand. No last, lingering looks.

Crystal stood to go. *Relax. Stop trying so hard.*

If things between her and Greg were meant to happen, they would. It was that simple.

Chapter Eleven

Juliette and Didi got to the conference center early and saw that the large hall was empty except for two men down at the podium: Andre Leveque, the spa manager, and a man Didi said was Reggie Roberts, the new general manager of the resort.

As the two women walked down the aisle to the front, Juliette couldn't help but notice Reggie's clothing. In his midforties, he had on the resort's administrative uniform of polo shirt, khaki slacks, and brown loafers. But judging by the cut and fit of his neatly-pressed slacks, Juliette knew they were more likely Roberto Cavalli than JC Penney, his shoes Versace, not Sears. Compared to the other employees—most of them long-time locals who sported a far more "relaxed" version of the same look—the guy's upgraded attire, Movado watch, and expensive haircut stuck out like a sore thumb. This was the California desert, after all, not Fifth Avenue.

Down front, Andre greeted them with cheek kisses, then Reggie introduced himself to Juliette and expressed condolences to both her and Didi about the loss of their former colleague.

Once they'd gotten the niceties out of the way, they quickly discussed the meeting's agenda, then Andre propped open the doors and people began trickling in. Didi chose a pair of seats for them near the front while Juliette excused herself and headed to the lobby. She wanted to watch for Ty Kirkland, the spa aide in charge of inventory at Palm Grotto. She was hoping to catch him before the meeting started, pull him aside, and ask a few quick questions about inventory and procedures—information that would help them figure out if counterfeit products could have played into Raven's death in any way.

For the next fifteen minutes Juliette watched as therapists, aestheticians, manicurists, technicians, assistants, schedulers, and more filed into the building and then the auditorium. It seemed everyone from the spa was there—everyone, that is, except for Ty. When it was nearly time for the meeting to begin, she decided to give up and try later. Maybe he was just running late. She returned to her seat in the small auditorium, which was nearly full and buzzing with conversation.

Juliette whispered an explanation to Didi about where she'd been. Then she tried to review her notes, but the various conversations going on around her were too distracting. Most of the talk was about Raven, no surprise there, but what Juliette found disturbing was that these people weren't focusing on what had happened today or why. Instead, almost everyone seemed to be saying how hated Raven had been. Even Andre was talking about "that awful, awful woman," telling a cluster of employees how she'd always mispronounced his last name on purpose, just to get in a little dig.

"She knew it's pronounced Luh-*veck*, but whenever I corrected her, she'd say, 'Sorry, I prefer Lev-a-*cue*, just like the cue ball that is your head.'"

They all laughed, even Andre. He wasn't a bad-looking guy, and thanks to a smooth head and a well-chosen pair of designer glasses, the baldness thing actually worked in his favor. Though Raven could be cruel, Juliette had a feeling that in this case she'd meant it not so much as an insult as a joke.

Juliette tried to return her attention to her notes, but soon a new Raven-centric conversation started up in the row behind her. Unable to tune it out, she could feel her hands slowly tightening into fists as it continued. How dare all these people speak of the dead this way?

But then she heard one of them refer to Raven as a "fire-breathing dragon," and her face flushed. Was she any better? So she wouldn't malign the dead, but she and Didi certainly hadn't held back while Raven was alive. After all, they had plenty of their own nicknames for the supermodel. Red Dragon. Tantrum Queen. She-Beast. How were those any different from this?

Juliette mulled these things over until Reggie took the podium and got the meeting underway. He started with an update on Brooke's condition, saying that her status was currently listed as "stable," though no specific information had yet been released. As for Raven, thus far the cause of death was undetermined. "There's been a lot of gossip flying around, but there's no reason to believe foul play was involved until after the autopsy."

That last comment generated a murmur through the crowd. Though the thought had crossed Juliette's mind, she was surprised to hear it articulated.

Before Juliette could think about that any further, however, Reggie was finished and calling her up to the podium for her turn.

Keeping her voice light, Juliette gave a quick greeting, then launched into the main points she needed to cover, starting with JT Lady's new product design, moving on to their enhanced sales incentive program. She ended with a quick explanation of this weekend's "spa retreat" and how it would differ from the usual Juliette Taylor Event.

Beyond the obvious—that the point of this retreat was spiritual, not financial, and that it was for the general public, not industry professionals—she wanted the staff to understand what kind of people would be coming here to participate. "The theme for the weekend is 'Serving While Preserving: Helping Others without Ignoring Ourselves.' As you can imagine, this one is always especially popular with *doers*. Volunteers, church workers, employees at faith-based charities, people like that."

Juliette looked out at the audience. "You therapists and manicurists and aestheticians, you may find that these women are somewhat resistant to pampering. That's because they are by their very nature givers, not receivers. I'm sure you've encountered this type before." Heads nodded with understanding. "But they do deserve pampering, to be sure. Our goal is to provide them with a time of rest, relaxation, and rejuvenation. With the help of a group of volunteers from Cahuilla Springs Community Church, we're also giving them a time of worship and fellowship and spiritual encouragement. By the end of the weekend, our hope is that each of these women will head home filled with peace and health, reinforced faith, and enthusiasm for what they do. By blessing them with your own expertise, you will be a very big part of making that happen."

Juliette suddenly thought of Brooke, who was one of the best therapists at Palm Grotto. She was also a Christian—the only one on staff here as far as Juliette knew—which made her absence from this particular event even more disheartening. At least Andre would supply someone to fill in for her.

Moving into her conclusion, Juliette took the microphone from its stand and stepped out from behind the podium. "Next year will be the tenth year that JT Lady and Palm Grotto Spa have been doing business together. We value that relationship."

Glancing toward Andre and Reggie, she wondered if they, too, valued it or if they'd been in secret discussions with Raven about a possible change in suppliers. She continued.

"You guys here at Palm Grotto are the very best at what you do. Thank you for a wonderful and rewarding ten years. Thank you, also, in advance, for coming alongside us this weekend and helping to make a difference in the lives of these women. Please feel free to join any of our worship services, sunrise or sunset hikes, or game nights if you'd like. I know you'll find this to be a delightful group of people, and that they would love the opportunity to get to know each of you as well. Thank you for your time."

The audience applauded as Juliette returned the mic to the stand and gave a nod to Andre, who came up to take her place at the podium. As she walked back toward her seat, she searched the crowd for the sight of Ty's face, but he was nowhere to be seen.

Marcus noticed his mother yawning as they waited in the gate area. He felt bad dragging her out on a night flight like this, but when he'd booked their trip, the 9:00 p.m. had been the only one still available. It would take a total of six and a half hours and a change of planes in Phoenix to get from Atlanta to Cahuilla Springs, which meant they wouldn't reach their destination until almost 3:30 in the morning. But because they were moving backwards across the time zones, it would be just 12:30 am out there. That was no problem for him, but his mom might not fare so well.

"Do you think you'll be able to sleep on the plane?" he asked after catching her in another yawn.

"I hope so. I brought an eye mask and a neck pillow so I could give it a try."

Marcus smiled. "Look at you, Miss World Traveler."

"Compliments of the Brood." She used the nickname he'd given her little group of neighborhood friends who were always cackling around each other like a brood of hens. "I do believe they thought of everything."

He nodded, expecting her to return her attentions to the book in her lap. Instead, she shifted in her seat and cleared her throat. "Listen, son, I know I've been pretty resistant about everything, but now that our trip is underway, I have to admit I'm excited. The girls pulled up Palm Grotto's website and showed me some pictures, ones that weren't in the brochure. Such gorgeous flowers and trees! Besides the spa and the mineral pools, there's also a lake and lots of olive trees and even a small grapefruit orchard."

Marcus smiled, sorry he'd never thought to treat her to something like this before.

"I wonder if they'd mind if I took a cutting or two," she added. "We're not in the best zone for it, but I always wanted to try my hand at growing grapefruit."

Marcus resisted the urge to groan. He could just picture it now, little old Beverly Stone making her way into this fancy resort's orchard with a pair of clippers, snipping off a limb from some exotic tree.

"You'll probably be so busy with all of the scheduled activities that you won't have time to glance at the orchard, much less go at it with a pair of scissors, Mom."

She didn't reply.

"Mother?" He recognized that faraway look in her eyes, the one that told him her mind was off and running with a plan, one that could not be contained. "Promise me you won't single-handedly deface any of the trees in Palm Grotto's orchard."

"Of course not, dear. I would never do that."

"Good."

"If I'm as busy with the retreat as you think I'll be, I'll probably need you to get those cuttings for me."

After the meeting, Juliette once again looked for Ty but eventually gave up and headed with Didi to the resort's five-star restaurant for dinner. Soon they were settled at a window table and quietly rehashing the day's events. They tossed around various theories about what might've happened to Raven and Brooke, but until they had more information, there wasn't much to go on.

They agreed to put the topic to rest once the waiter showed up with their entrees— sautéed summer vegetable crepes for Juliette and herb-crusted rack of lamb with roasted potatoes in a garlic mustard sauce for Didi. Inhaling the delicious aroma of both dishes, they said a discreet blessing and dug in, their delicious meal punctuated by the soft clink of glasses and the low murmur of conversation all around them. Lunch for Juliette had been a bag of pretzels on the plane, so she was quite hungry.

Outside the sun slowly set behind the mountains in a magnificent orange and gold display of God's creation. Juliette was admiring the view when she glanced toward a group seated out on the balcony and did a double take. Eyes wide, she leaned in to Didi and whispered, "Don't look now, but there's a big celebrity at five o'clock."

"What kind? Movie star? Rock star? Politician?" Didi set down her fork.

"Director. Outside, to your right, one table back."

Faking a stretch, Didi took a discreet look around then turned toward Juliette. "You're right. That's Quentin VonTassel."

"I know. He's smaller than he looks on the Oscars, isn't he?"

Didi leaned closer. "Forget smaller, how 'bout those hair plugs? With all his money, you'd think he could've gotten better ones than that."

"Shush."

"Hey, I just call 'em like I see 'em. And with plugs that bad, I can see 'em from all the way in here!"

Once Marcus's mom returned her attentions to the book she was reading, he allowed his eyes to roam over the waiting passengers. An edge of apprehension nagged at him, but that was probably thanks to his recent work on the task force. He had terrorism on the brain, and everywhere he looked he saw something that could be construed as suspicious . . .

The man with the sweaty forehead whose eyes had been darting about nervously for the past half hour.

The couple huddled together by the window, whispering, as they looked out at the plane.

The guy hunched protectively over his laptop, typing in a frenzy.

If Marcus had learned anything lately, it was that you never knew. You *never* knew. The family next door could be part of a support cell. The paperboy could be in a sleeper cell. That guy at work could be in an execution cell.

The cell structure favored by terrorists worked on several levels. For starters, it provided a way to limit the damage done when one was exposed and its members captured. Except for the person acting as liaison, cell members rarely knew anything about the other cells in the organization. After all, what they didn't know, they couldn't confess. The cell structure also kept the overall organization strong, since the destruction of a single cell couldn't wipe out the entire effort. Theoretically, even if nine cells out of ten were taken down, that one remaining cell—like a speck of cancer that missed the cut of the surgeon's knife—could regenerate and multiply for the cause, eventually building itself back up into one just as strong as before.

Finally, cells were a unique way to consolidate expertise. Support cells, for example, could focus on what they did best—whether that was logistics, fund-raising, procuring of supplies, or some other task necessary for the larger goal—and leave the actual carrying out of the terrorist act to a different cell entirely. That meant someone could be a terrorist and never once pick up a bomb or plan an attack.

By working toward the cell's goal, they were also working toward the common goal.

When he signed on with the project, Marcus learned that cells could have as few as four members or as many as twelve, but they were usually made up of about eight to ten people. The one JATFAT had brought down was an eight-member fund-raising cell that procured money for the larger organization. That they had been doing so primarily through the sale of counterfeit goods had not come as a surprise. What *had* come as a surprise was how pervasive the problem was, and how little the average person understood it.

Even Marcus had needed convincing in the beginning. He and Nate Anderson had first met during the aftermath of 9/11, when the two men's duties kept them in close proximity. They developed a mutual respect and stayed in touch. When Nate was forming his task force, he brought Marcus in as a consultant to run various disaster scenarios and plot out the necessary steps for prevention and/or response. Those scenarios changed with each new piece of intel they uncovered, and the job had kept Marcus busy for the past six months.

In the beginning, though, he almost didn't take the job, partly because he hadn't understood what was at stake. In the end it took a photograph to get Marcus on board.

Snapped covertly in a third-world sweat shop, the photo showed a group of children assembling counterfeit watches. Those children, valued for their tiny fingers, endured forced labor for as much as twelve hours a day. In the photo Nate pointed out the oddly-disfigured legs of several of the boys.

"These were the rowdier of the kids, so the gang running the shop crippled them." Nate's anger shone in his eyes. "If you can't walk, you stop begging to go out and play."

Marcus still couldn't get that image from his mind.

Now that his work with JATFAT was done and the cell had been eliminated, this one task remained: to help Juliette understand the kind of people she was up against and the precautions she needed to take—all without violating his oath of confidentiality.

He wasn't sure how he was going to pull that off, but he trusted that with God's help, he would find the right words at the right time.

Chapter Twelve

After dinner Juliette and Didi started off toward their rooms on foot but were soon stopped by a friendly security guard, who insisted on giving them a ride in his golf cart. He explained that the resort would be providing security escorts for the rest of the evening, should they care to venture out again later. Though Juliette was a bit unnerved by the thought, a part of her was also relieved.

Better safe than sorry and of all that.

Once they'd been delivered safely, they each went to their own room. While Didi freshened up and got ready to go to the volunteer meeting across town, Juliette changed into a bathing suit, robe, and slippers, then she went back outside. When Didi emerged again, Juliette was there on the walkway waiting for her, room key in hand and a towel over her arm. With a grin, she stuck out her thumb.

Didi smiled, pulling the door closed behind her. "Don't see many hitchhikers dressed like this."

"Yeah, well, it's the grotto or bust. Give me a lift on your way out? I don't want to wait for another escort."

"Of course."

They headed to the car, Didi unlocking it with the remote as they approached. "I'm proud of you, though I'm surprised you made the healthier choice here."

"What do you mean?"

"Going for a soak in the grotto. Good for you. I figured you would spend the evening in your room, obsessing over the whole Raven situation."

Didi hoisted herself into the driver's seat of the SUV as Juliette climbed into the passenger side and buckled her seat belt. "I'll probably do that too, but at least I'll think better if I'm relaxed."

Didi gave Juliette an odd glance as she turned the key and the vehicle rumbled to life. "Think you *can* relax, given all that's going on?"

"I don't know. It's worth a shot."

"Just be careful, okay? Someone did die here today—for reasons that are still unknown.

Even with all the enhanced security, well, just keep your eyes open. And promise me you'll get another escort back when you're done."

"I promise."

"You still remember those self-defense moves Raven taught you?"

Juliette resisted the urge to roll her eyes. "Yes, mother."

Didi pursed her lips as she accelerated up the wide, curving road that led to the grotto and the resort exit beyond. "You know, I wasn't kidding earlier when I said someone could've been sent here to 'kill the super-model' and ended up offing Raven instead of you by mistake. I'm sure the news of her death has hit the airwaves by now. For all we know, somebody's out there just itching for the opportunity to correct their little error."

Juliette gazed out at the lake as they drove past, the moon's reflection sparkling on the smooth, black surface. "I'm not exactly on board with that theory, but I suppose you could be right, that is one more reason to be careful. I will be, I really will."

Didi slowed at the sight of a Palm Grotto golf cart that had pulled over to the side of the road to dispense some passengers. As they moved past, Juliette couldn't help but notice how eagerly Didi scanned the scene.

"Looking for someone in particular?" she

teased, knowing full well her friend had been hoping it might be Orlando, the guard she'd been flirting with earlier.

"No."

Juliette chuckled. "Oh, come on. Why do you keep denying the obvious? It's time to take this attraction to the next level. Ask the man for coffee or something."

"Yeah, right."

"I'm serious. Have you seen the way he looks at you? The way you are around him?"

Juliette was half teasing, but Didi didn't respond with her usual good humor. Instead she remained silent until they reached the top of the hill and turned into the main parking lot. She pulled to a stop near the entrance to the resort and let the engine idle as she turned toward Juliette.

"Let's just say there was something there. What's the use? We live three thousand miles apart."

Juliette laughed. "Gosh, Didi, I didn't say marry the guy. I said go for coffee."

She climbed out but then hesitated, growing more serious. "I'm just saying, don't use the bigger issue of forever as an excuse to miss out on the here and now. Sometimes long-distance relationships work out great, you know."

Didi met her gaze. "No offense, but I have

a little trouble taking advice about long-distance relationships from you of all people."

Juliette's brow furrowed. "Why? What do you mean?"

"Uh . . . TOTGA?"

Juliette gasped and her head jerked back as if struck. "You know how much I hate that word."

"Sorry, but what else could I call him? You wouldn't tell me his name, so I came up with one of my own. TOTGA—'The One That Got Away.'"

"Grammatically speaking," Juliette replied stiffly, "I believe the proper usage would be 'The One *Who* Got Away.'"

"Thanks, Professor. TOTGA, TOWGA, whatever. You call that a successful long-distance relationship? Look what it did to you."

Juliette was quiet for a long moment, wondering how to reply. Yes, he had caused her some heartbreak in the end. But she still wouldn't have traded their time together for anything. "He changed my life."

"That's putting it mildly. You were at the height of your career. You were a supermodel. And yet somehow a man—a perfect stranger no less—convinced you to turn your back on all of it. You were just twenty-four, you still had a few great years left. Instead, thanks to him, you gave up modeling completely, turned your back on millions, and just walked away."

"Best decision I ever made." Juliette's eyes narrowed. "But speaking of millions, are you sure this is about me and not you? As my booker, you lost out on plenty of money too."

"I would never ask someone to stay in a career they hated just so I could collect my twenty percent. I'm not that selfish."

"Well I guess I am, 'cause if I had to do it over again, I would do it exactly the same way." Juliette pinched the bridge of her nose. She could feel a headache starting, deep inside. This was an old argument, one they'd had plenty of times before. "Look, I don't know how else to say it. Yes, I was hurt by the fact that he never came back for me later, but I still treasure what we shared. That man didn't just change my life, he saved it. It's like I was *suffocating*, and he came along and gave me air. He set me free. I'll always be grateful to him for that."

Didi glared back at her, skeptical. "Still, as far as long-distance relationships go, under Pros and Cons, I'd say that's one giant check in the Cons column. He completely disappeared from your life. He said he'd come find you but he didn't."

Juliette swallowed hard, wondering if Didi could fathom how hurtful her words really were right now. "That was twenty-five years ago. I got over it."

Didi rolled her eyes. "Maybe. But you pined after that guy and waited for him for so long that you ended up missing out on other men, other relationships. Sorry, but I don't want that to happen to me. Better never to open that door in the first place."

Juliette resisted the urge to roll her eyes. Didi hadn't dated anyone—near or far—for years. What made her think history would repeat itself here?

"Sorry," Didi added, "I know it's a sore topic."

Juliette took a deep breath and blew it out. "I had other relationships, Didi. Need I remind you, I've even been engaged? *Twice*."

"Yeah, but both times you broke it off."

"That's not—"

"You broke it off because no other man could compare to *that* one, to the only one you ever really wanted. The one that got away. TOTGA."

Ready to end the conversation, Juliette stepped back from the car. "You know what? Do whatever you want with Orlando, I'll stop bringing it up. Just leave me and my past relationships out of it, will you? Thanks for the lift."

With that, she closed the door and walked

off, her heart pounding furiously all the way to the grotto.

The conference center was transforming before Crystal's eyes. To accommodate a variety of group needs, the place featured sliding walls, portable podiums, retracting screens, and more, many of which were being put to use now. Crystal had been tasked with organizing the reception desk in the lobby of the conference center, and soon she was so engrossed in her duties that the time simply flew. She even managed to forget about the day's trauma—until it was time to go and Andre made them wait at the door while he called for their "security escort."

"Oh, please," one of other staffers scoffed. "What for?"

Andre tugged at his collar, avoiding their eyes. "Due to, uh, today's events, security has been ramped up throughout the resort. Until further notice, no employees are allowed outside after dark unless accompanied by a guard."

Crystal's eyes widened. *What* was going on? Had Raven's death really involved some sort of foul play? The detectives hadn't been willing to say either way, but now here was another sign that they were thinking murder.

But how? Who? Why?

She was still puzzling over that a few minutes later when their escort arrived and she saw it was none other than Greg. She pushed those questions from her mind for now. Somehow, just the sight of his handsome face and crisp uniform made her feel safe and secure.

Greg's cart had seating for six, and though Crystal wanted nothing more than to climb up front next to him, she deferred to her boss and slid into the second row. Soon they were off, the cool night air caressing her face, lifting her hair, and raising chill bumps along her arms. Or maybe the chill bumps weren't coming from the air at all but instead from the way Greg kept glancing at her in his rearview mirror.

When they reached the employee parking lot, though he could have dropped everyone at the center and let them disperse from there, he instead ferried each person directly to his or her own vehicle, proclaiming "door-to-door service with a smile."

Much to Crystal's delight, he saved her for last. As the others were driving away, she lingered in her seat, reluctant to part, as he turned so that they could face each other. Their earlier conversation had ended awkwardly, but she was reassured by the way he was acting now—warm and friendly and eager to be together. Once all the cars were gone, however, the parking lot felt dark and empty, and it struck her that this probably wasn't the safest place to linger.

"So what's up with the heightened security tonight?" She glanced around at the encroaching shadows. "Should I worry? Did the cops tell you guys to do this?"

Greg shook his head. "Nah, this was a Palm Grotto decision. People are feeling a little spooked is all, so we've been given extended hours and additional security rounds. It's just for show, mostly, though I think it's also to keep any paparazzi at bay. Nobody needs some nosy reporter or photographer snooping around, you know?"

"Makes sense."

"At least I'll get some overtime out of it. I'm on duty till midnight, and then I've got to be back here tomorrow first thing."

Crystal's shoulders sagged. She had been about to suggest they go for coffee or something, but now that she knew he'd be on duty for a while yet and wasn't free to leave, she held her tongue. It was just as well. This had been a long day, and she was starting to feel tired again.

Sitting there in the cart, she fumbled for her keys, thanking Greg for the ride. As she began to climb out, she felt his warm hand around her wrist. Electricity raced up her arm and through her body, and she turned to meet his eyes. For a heartbeat, she thought he might kiss her, but instead he simply spoke, his tone soft and intimate.

"Crystal, I . . . I just wanted to apologize for earlier."

"Apologize?"

"For blowing you off like that. You were being so sweet, letting me talk about my sister, and I just kind of shut down."

A surge of tenderness rose in her throat. "It's understandable, Greg. I know this can't be easy."

He slid his hand up her arm until it came to rest just above the elbow. "Still, you asked me a question and I didn't answer it. I want to answer it now."

Swallowing hard, Crystal leaned in even closer as she waited for him to go on.

"You asked me if Val had been ill or in an accident. The truth is, she was murdered."

Crystal gasped. "Murdered?"

Greg nodded then looked away. "Oh, not according to the police. They ruled it a suicide. But I know the truth. She didn't . . . it wasn't . . ." His eyes welled up again, as they had that afternoon. "Sorry. It's hard to talk about."

Crystal took him by the hand. "Of course

it is. Just tell me, who did it? Were they caught?"

With his free hand, Greg swiped at his tears. "No. Like I said, police labeled it a suicide and closed the case. I tried to convince them otherwise, but in the end . . ." He shook his head, his grief palpable.

She squeezed his hand even tighter. "Why did the police think it was a suicide?"

"Because there was a note. But it wasn't even a note really, just a quote she'd jotted down. Nietzsche."

Crystal waited, and after a moment he recited it for her.

"It said, 'One ought to hold on to one's heart; for if one lets it go, one soon loses control of the head too.'"

What an odd, sad thought. "What does that mean? Had her heart been broken?"

Greg nodded. "Yeah, she'd had a real run of bad luck. Lost her job, the guy she'd been seeing broke up with her . . . She was depressed. All the more reason for the police to call it suicide. But she didn't kill herself. She was murdered. I have no doubt whatsoever."

Greg's walkie-talkie crackled to life, interrupting them to say that someone else needed a ride. Reluctantly Crystal took a step back. Though she had a million more questions, Greg's work had to come first.

She gave him a reassuring smile as she clutched her keys in her hand, suggesting they continue their conversation tomorrow.

He shrugged, turning away. "I don't like to talk about it. I just thought you deserved to know the truth."

He waited until she was safely in her car and had pulled out of the parking lot before he sped off in the other direction. Once she was out on the main road and driving toward home, Crystal went back over their conversation several times. At least she understood now why he seemed to shut down so abruptly sometimes—he was still grappling with the senselessness of his beloved sister's murder less than a year before.

Poor Greg seemed like the kind of guy who wanted to protect people, to keep them safe. He'd chosen a career as a security guard, after all, and he'd mentioned more than once that his long-term goal was to become a policeman. Given that, no wonder he'd been so devastated by his sister's death! He must've felt that he'd failed her, that in the end he hadn't protected her from the biggest threat of all. Tears formed in Crystal's eyes at the very thought.

Blinking them away, she looked up at the half moon glowing a vivid yellow in the velvety sky. If she believed in prayer, she would say one for Greg now. Instead, she simply sent out good thoughts as strongly as she could and hoped they'd make their way to him across the dry desert night.

Hand on the rail, Juliette walked down the stone steps toward the dark, swirling pool. She was afraid her conflict with Didi would rob this experience of any pleasure, but as soon as she eased first one foot, then the other, into the warm embrace of the mineral-rich waters, she let all that go and focused on the here and now. She'd been anticipating this soak in the grotto so thoroughly that neither Didi's words nor any concerns about her safety could dim the pleasure of the moment. The presence of the roving security guards helped. As they kept watch nearby, she lowered herself the rest of the way and relaxed.

The water was warm but not scalding, its constant 94-degree temperature the perfect compliment to the cool night air of the desert. The ambiance here was peaceful, low key. Inviting. One couple floated near the steps, another sat quietly in their robes in front of the outdoor fireplace. Ignoring them all, Juliette pushed off from the side and allowed herself to relish the warmth, the solitude, and the darkness. Though the grotto was open twenty-four hours a day, no special lights illuminated it at night. Instead, the area was allowed to grow dark and shadowy, which gave the sensation of being alone in a private paradise even when others were nearby. It also made it possible to see the stars, to lie there and look up at the night sky without anything to dim the view.

Taking a deep breath and letting it out slowly, Juliette moved toward the middle of the pool, leaned her head back, and simply floated. As a gentle desert breeze brushed across her cheeks, she closed her eyes and tried to clear her mind—of Raven, of Didi, of the past.

No luck there. Her thoughts were already off and running, and she was helpless to stop them. As she floated in the water, body relaxed, eyes closed, she had no choice but to go with it. Sliding into the memories as easily as she'd slid into this pool, she found herself going back to the day, so many years ago, that changed her life forever.

The day she met Marcus Stone, the one who got away.

Chapter Thirteen

At just twenty-four years old Juliette Taylor was one of the highest-paid and most in-demand models in the world. She walked runways for almost every major designer, appeared on the cover of countless magazines, had an exclusive contract with a top-name cosmetic firm. She was a success.

And she couldn't have been more miserable.

Thinking back, she could still feel the unhappiness of that time, the claustrophobia of her situation. People always thought modeling was such a glamorous profession, but they didn't know what it did to the models on the inside. Like scooping out a pumpkin, the business slowly scraped away almost every shred of a woman's worth, her privacy, and her sense of self. In the seven years Juliette's star rose and her price tag soared, the person she was on the inside had gotten lost some-how, until she no longer knew who she was or what she even wanted in life.

All she knew was that she didn't want this.

Some of her fellow models seemed as unhappy as she. The most successful among them were also as stuck as she, prisoners of their own success, of their own massive pay-checks. She earned more in a week than many people earned in a year. Yet she wanted out. With every fiber of her being, she wanted out. But how could she justify turning her back on that kind of money? The very thought seemed ungrateful at best, insane at worst.

And so she endured. Each day on the job, as she was primped and painted and pow-dered, she would swallow away her growing discontent and press on. By the time she went on that fateful photo shoot on an island off the Georgia coast, the aching, internal claus-trophobia was so strong she feared her heart would burst.

The shoot itself had been grueling, the photographer and the editor constantly butt-ing heads. The photographer had been highly praised by *German Vogue*, but this was his first big shoot for an American magazine and he was clearly insecure. To Juliette's experience, unconfident photographers were the worst, because not only did they not know what they wanted, often they didn't even realize once they had it! They'd just keep shooting, roll after roll after roll, so intent on their creative vision—and so afraid they might fail—that they indulged in complete overkill.

Juliette endured it all in silence, waiting when it was time to wait, lighting up for the camera when it was time to shine, sitting frozen on the sidelines in between lest she smear or smudge or wrinkle someone else's hard work.

She'd been on plenty of tough shoots before, but that day at the coast was particularly unpleasant. If it wasn't the sharp seashells cutting into Juliette's skin, it was the bones of the bodice squeezing her lungs. Worse, a big storm was headed in their direction and the sky grew darker and more ominous by the hour.

At least the rain stayed away. After enduring three hours of hair and makeup and four hours of posing atop a crumbling stone wall at the edge of a churning sea, Juliette had had enough—but every time she thought they were finished, this guy would call for "just one more."

Then a light box blew. That wasn't unusual, but it meant a delay while the technicians scrambled to fix it. Juliette was desperate for a break, but in such situations she never knew whether she could shift or not. No one bothered to tell her, because somewhere along the way they'd forgotten that she was a human being. Instead she'd become a canvas on which they were bringing their own creations to life.

But what about *her* creations, *her* life? Beyond her beautiful face and figure, did she even have any value at all?

While they continued to bustle around and tend to the broken lighting box, Juliette stood at the center of the scene, like a lone bride atop a cake, big fat tears suddenly welling up in her eyes and spilling down her cheeks. On the inside her tears rose up from great, heaving sobs, but on the outside they were simply drips of salty water that seeped out and down, slowly destroying all that was in their path, like floodwaters pouring through a museum.

The makeup girl spotted it first. She'd been standing about ten feet away, chatting with an editorial assistant, when she glanced at Juliette and realized what was happening. Quickly but discreetly, she went to the supermodel's side, powder puff and Q-tips in hand, and tried to repair the damage. She was a nice girl, but the kindness in her voice only made matters worse. Afraid of breaking into audible sobs at any moment, Juliette finally excused herself and stepped away from the scene.

She used a phone in the hotel lobby to call her booker. Didi Finkelton was the best in the business, the one Juliette leaned on when things got tough. The conversation they had that day was one they'd repeated a dozen times before, with the supermodel saying she couldn't do this anymore—not today but any day—and Didi urging her to hang in there "for five more years, just five more years."

She might as well have been asking for five hundred.

"You'll age out around twenty-nine or thirty anyway," Didi cajoled her over the long-distance line. "Nobody will want you then and you can go on with your life. But for now, can't you just milk this? How many women would give their right arm to be in your shoes?"

This time even a call with Didi hadn't made Juliette feel better. When she stepped back outside, almost everyone in the group turned her way, impatience etched in their grim expressions. She knew she was creating a problem, but she couldn't help it. Everything inside of her simply screamed to break free. Lightning had begun to flash in the distance, but the turmoil in the sky couldn't begin to match that in her heart.

Once again the makeup girl rushed to her

side, taking her by the hand and saying under her breath, "I know this has been a tough one for you, but we're almost done. We have to be, or we'll miss our flight out." She led Juliette back into place, again fixed the damage to her makeup, and then gave her an encouraging pat on the arm and a final "Hang in there" before stepping away.

Juliette felt more like she was hanging on than hanging in—by a thread, by her fingernails, by sheer force of will. But she was a pro, and so as the photographer began snapping away, she gave it her all, even as the thunder grew louder and the flashes got closer.

For the final five minutes of the shoot, though there was still no rain, the lightning felt like it was practically on top of them, thunder booming closer and closer. Juliette was terrified, but the photographer was energized, acting as if the dramatic sky was a backdrop created just for him.

Finally the editor called a halt to the shoot, not because the model atop the stone wall was in danger, but because they needed to get going if they wanted to reach the airport in time. As Juliette changed back into her own clothes, the others packed up their tons of gear and loaded it into the charter boat. The crossing was so rough, the waves so high, that by the time they reached the mainland, half of them were pale and sweating and on the verge of losing their lunch.

The first drops didn't hit the rented van until they were almost to the airport, but when it finally came, it came hard. The sky exploded with a flash of lightning, and drops became sheets of driving rain. The wind whipped at trees, bending them low. Once inside they checked their bags and hurried toward their gate but had barely made it through the main lobby when the announcement came from overhead that all flights had been grounded.

Juliette remained silent through it all. It was as though she was seeing things from a distance, like her mind and her body were no longer connected. Despite the others' anxious phone calls to the home office and angry threats made to airport personnel, in the end it all came down to the fact that no matter how important they thought they were or how urgent their business back in New York, the storm was in charge now and there wasn't anything anyone could do about that except sit and wait until it was safe to fly again.

Finally accepting the inevitable, the photographer and his assistants commandeered an entire corner of the airport lobby, taking the equipment that had been too precious to check as baggage and plopping it along the floor like a barricade. Then they spread themselves out inside their little fort and tried to drift off to sleep.

She had no interest in joining them. Nor did she feel like being with the editor and her small entourage who staked claim to a table in an airport coffee shop and leaned their heads in a tight circle to whisper.

Juliette wanted to be alone. After a bit of exploring, she finally found the perfect place, a small alcove that faced a large bank of windows and was hidden behind a divider wall. As she settled into the tight space and drew her knees to her chest, two questions kept rolling around in her mind: *How much longer can I do this, and what do I really want out of life anyway?*

Even now, as she continued to float in the warm grotto under the sparkling desert sky, Juliette could remember that moment from all those years ago as vividly as if it had happened yesterday.

The defeat that had pounded in her heart.

The claustrophobia that pressed in on her lungs.

The ache deep in her gut that told her she couldn't go on like this any longer.

Way back then she had closed her eyes and whispered a frantic, desperate prayer, asking God to show her a way out of her misery.

Little had she known, He was about to answer that prayer.

Marcus loved to fly, and this trip to the spa with his mother was no exception. His apprehension evaporated after takeoff, and he'd been glued to what he could see of the scenery ever since. He would've enjoyed this trip so much more in the daylight, but at least he'd have that opportunity when they returned home on Monday. Day or night, he just loved that feeling of soaring high above the ground toward a new destination.

His mother had read for a while but eventually drifted off. Now, judging by the evenness of her breathing and the tilt of her head in the borrowed neck pillow, she was sound asleep. Good. He exhaled slowly, glad to see her catching some Zs in transit.

Turning, he leaned his forehead against the cold window of the airplane and looked down at the dark earth below. As he did, his mind went to what lay ahead—or, rather, *who* lay ahead: Juliette Taylor, a woman he'd known briefly yet who'd had a tremendous impact on his entire life.

Though he didn't often stroll down memory lane, he let his thoughts wander there now. Soaring westward thirty thousand feet in the sky, the lights of some city twinkling on the distant horizon, he allowed himself to think back—twenty-five years back—to the day they first met.

The day that changed his life forever.

Marcus had been twenty-eight years old at the time, working for an engineering firm in Atlanta. After having spent his first few years after grad school in the employ of Uncle Sam, he'd thought that joining a private firm might be a better way to go. But he'd been wrong. After eighteen months on the job, he had grown cynical and disillusioned. He'd also learned to hate compromise.

As an engineer Marcus knew that every construction project involved concurrent but often competing desires for beauty, functionality, safety, reparability, sustainability, environmental sensitivity, and more, all within the confines of certain cost restrictions. As one of his old professors used to say, "Engineering is always about choice, and the sad truth is that you can't have it all. The key is to find the right balance." Marcus understood that. Though his own personal priority had always been safety, he often made concessions if they didn't endanger life or limb outright.

The problem wasn't that type of compromise. It was the kind of compromise his employer's firm shouldn't have been making, like the use of substandard concrete. Inadequate ventilation. Insufficient wiring. Sometimes Marcus would sit in on a meeting and wonder if he was the only one in the whole firm who really understood the safety implications of the decisions being made. What he saw as unethical, his superiors called "pragmatic." What he said was unconscionable, they considered "realistic." Again and again he'd butted heads all the way up to the big boss, a man whose eyes stayed so glued to the bottom line that he refused to see all but the most dire warnings of catastrophe.

At that time Midtown Atlanta was on the verge of a growth boom—not out but up—and the firm was positioned to become an integral part of the city's burgeoning high-rise construction industry. That was one of the reasons, in fact, that Marcus had sought a position there in the first place, because safety was his specialty, and he knew that the higher the building, the greater the problem of protecting its occupants in case of emergency. Measures that would work for five stories weren't sufficient for twenty-five—from evacuation routes to fire-response tactics to earthquake stability and more. Marcus had come into the job hoping to use his talents, his education, and his experience to meet such challenges. Instead, with every project that involved the wrong kinds of compromises, he felt himself growing more and more frustrated and disturbed.

Then came that fateful trip to the coast, to the site of a new condominium complex that would cover one hundred acres of prime Georgia oceanfront real estate. His firm had been hired to evaluate the design for structural reliability and make any necessary recommendations prior to construction. That part of the job was finished, now all that was needed was a representative to attend the ground-breaking ceremony and perhaps sit in on a meeting afterward to answer questions and see to any final engineering details.

The only reason Marcus had ended up serving as that representative was because the coworker who should've done it had busted up his knee during a basketball pickup game the week before and was still recovering from surgery. Marcus hadn't known much about the project when he was first approached, but his boss said that didn't really matter, that his presence there would be a mere formality. "The structure's only three stories high," the man had added with a smirk. "Are we safe to assume you won't drum up any new safety crusades while you're there?"

Marcus was getting used to the sarcasm. In

the past month he'd endured several rounds of battles over the plans for what would become Atlanta's first fifty-story building. After all that, a mindless trip to the coast to represent the firm at a little groundbreaking ceremony sounded like a welcome escape.

As the whole thing would take place on a Friday, it also sounded like the makings of a nice, long weekend and a good opportunity to get in a few rounds of golf. Marcus agreed to go in his coworker's stead and promptly booked himself a room and a tee time out on Hilton Head for afterward.

As the date drew nearer, the only dark cloud on the horizon was an actual dark cloud, so to speak, a tropical storm headed in the general direction of the Georgia coast. Marcus thought the ceremony might be postponed because of it, but in the days before the trip, the squall began to lessen in intensity.

Plans remained in effect, so that morning Marcus left early for the four-hour drive to the coast. When he reached his destination with plenty of time to spare, he settled down in a comfortable coffee shop to review the project notes and blueprints and other papers and bring himself up to speed as much as possible on the condos, in case he had to field any questions. Reviewing the paperwork, it had been easy to go through the list of recommendations that had been made by his firm and see which ones had been addressed and how.

At first the reports were fairly rudimentary, with small adjustments here and there to the design and the construction materials. Some of their recommendations—like precoating all exposed metal with a tin and zinc alloy to prevent corrosion from the salt air—had been accepted. Some had been modified, and others had been rejected outright, which wasn't unusual. The problem here, Marcus realized once he had finished his review, wasn't the suggestions that had been rejected or the compromises that had been reached; overall, there seemed to have been a pretty fair meeting of the minds when it had come to hammering out the final plan. Instead, at issue was a roofing problem that had never been addressed in the first place.

The award-winning Atlanta-based architect who'd designed the complex had a "signature style" that emphasized distinctive rooflines with wide eaves, deep gables, and varying degrees of pitch throughout. That sort of thing might have been well and good for a more inland location, but Marcus knew that to replicate it there on the coast would be disastrous, an open invitation to the high winds to lift off entire sections of roofing like so many Coke bottle lids being flipped off by a massive, unruly bottle opener. Judging by the blueprints, however, each cluster of these elaborate, oceanfront structures would feature eave after eave, each one wider than the next, some of them even tilted slightly upward at the tips.

By the time Marcus left the coffee shop, he had exactly one goal, to convince the key players why the most prominent element of their new design simply could not stand. The design may have been aesthetically striking, but it was also an engineering nightmare for a coastal region routinely pounded by high winds and subjected to a fierce annual hurricane season.

Not wanting to make his company look bad for having missed such an important issue, Marcus started by calling his boss from a pay phone outside. Their conversation didn't go well. At least he got the man to grasp the severity of the situation and to agree that something "might" need to be done. On the other hand, Marcus was told to keep his mouth shut and proceed with the ceremony as planned. They would deal with this matter later.

Marcus hadn't been happy about that, but he'd done as instructed. Investors, local officials, the architect, some media, and a handful of local citizens all came to the ceremony.

Once the symbolic shovelful of dirt had been dug and thrown, a brief question-and-answer session ensued. To his dismay, one reporter raised the issue of building an oceanfront structure with such wide eaves, which would surely be no match for the region's high winds. The architect was the one fielding most of the questions, but when that one came up, he suddenly turned and gestured toward Marcus, saying that might best by answered by their resident engineering expert. After a bit of hemming and hawing, Marcus had finally blurted out that they were "still exploring the matter at this time" and that it "may involve slight modifications to the design."

"But we were told the final design had been approved," the reporter persisted.

Marcus tried not to look like a deer in the headlights as he managed a response. "Every structure is, in a sense, a work in progress, and this one is simply undergoing some final tweaks." He'd meant his words to be vague while still addressing the question, but judging by the glaring looks the investors and the architect all gave him, Marcus had made a serious misstep.

The moment they were alone and behind closed doors, a major shouting match erupted. Apparently "final design approval" was a big issue here on the Georgia coast, and any mention of modifications would set off all sorts of red lights with zoning approvals and committee restrictions and more, possibly even kicking the project into some no-man's land of pre-construction purgatory. In the end, one very unhappy investor got on the phone with Marcus's boss, who promised to take the next flight out and handle things here in person himself.

Brother.

With the boss on the way despite the storm that was closing in, Marcus had no choice but to get in his car and head to the airport to pick the man up. Big, fat raindrops began to fall when he was halfway there, and by the time he'd parked and was running inside, the winds had whipped up so furiously that the rain was practically blowing sideways. Though technically it was no longer a tropical storm, it was still quite fierce.

Marcus didn't know how much longer he could tolerate this job. As he dashed through the rain, two questions pounded in his head: *How much longer can I stand it, and is this really what I should be doing with my life anyway?*

Looking back on that moment now, Marcus could see how the hand of God had been working out the details of his future even in the midst of such turmoil. Had his boss not decided to fly out to the coast, Marcus wouldn't have gone to the airport. Had he not gone to the airport, he would never have met Juliette Taylor. Had he not met Juliette, he would never have found the nerve to make so many big changes in his life.

Taking a deep breath, Marcus could feel himself growing sleepy. Before he drifted off, he said a silent prayer, asking God to bless their coming encounter and to open Juliette's heart to the idea of seeing him again after all these years.

He knew now what he'd refused to admit to himself before, that his hoped-for reconnection with Juliette was every bit as much about the enduring strength of his old feelings for her as it was about protecting her from harm.

Chapter Fourteen

Juliette paddled across the pool and used the steps to climb out. She was done. Though her soak in the grotto had been incredibly relaxing, she was starting to feel uncomfortably hot—not to mention sleepy.

The cool night air felt good on her skin as she dried off and slipped back into her robe. It would've been so lovely to stroll all the way back to her room, but she didn't want to be foolhardy—not to mention that she'd made a promise to Didi. Thus, once she was ready to go, she tossed her wet towel in a bin and approached the nearest security guard. Before she could even say what she wanted, he offered a ride to her room.

Five minutes later she was in the shower.

Ten minutes after that she was in the bed.

The sheets were cool, the pillows fluffy, the blankets the perfect weight and softness. After such a long day, she thought she would fall asleep in minutes, but as she lay there in the darkness, she found that her mind was still racing. Closing her eyes, she surrendered to the inevitable as her thoughts returned, once again, to that day twenty-five years ago, when Marcus came into her life.

There in the airport Juliette had dozed for a while in her alcove hidey-hole. She awoke feeling antsy and unsettled, so she decided to take a walk.

There wasn't much to see. After strolling from one end of the airport to the other, she finally returned to the gift shop in the middle and killed time by flipping through a rack of greeting cards on the far side of the cash register.

As she did, she couldn't help but listen to the running commentary of the woman at the checkout counter, a cashier with a nametag of *Kitty*. Practically ancient, with a sun-wrinkled face and a cap of white hair, Kitty's lipstick had gathered in the vertical lines of her mouth and caked into waxy stripes of bright red. She seemed like one of those perpetually upbeat kind of people, always at the ready with silly cracks and one-liners, the cornier the better. Most of the customers reacted favorably, with a laugh or chuckle. Juliette was glad. She could use an encounter with a sunny disposition herself.

At one point a mother and child entered the store, complaining that they'd lost a quarter in the nearby vending machine. The little boy was whiny and petulant, but as Kitty reached a wrinkled hand into the register, fished out a coin, and gave it over to the mother, she asked if either of them had ever heard the joke about the sun.

They both looked back at her, their faces blank.

"You ain't heard the joke about the sun? Oh well, never mind. It's way over your head."

It took a moment to sink in, then the mother laughed and her tight stance relaxed. She thanked the checker and led her child from the store, explaining the joke to him in a voice far less harried than it had sounded when she'd first come in.

Juliette was still smiling to herself when someone else entered. From behind the card rack, she stole a glance at the customer and saw that it was a man in his late twenties— a strikingly handsome man, despite the fact that his expression was surly and dark. Pulling out a card and opening it, Juliette pretended to read as she listened to what might happen next. If Kitty could get a smile out of this one, she deserved a medal or something.

Without a word, the guy slapped a pack of gum and a newspaper on the counter.

"Gum and a newspaper, that's all for you today?" Kitty asked brightly as she began to ring him up.

"Yes," he snapped. Then he reached into a candy bin next to the register, pulled one out, and tossed it onto the pile. "And a Peppermint Pattie."

"Fine, and one peppermint." After a beat, Kitty added, "But don't call me Patty."

A giggle burst from Juliette's lips, she couldn't help herself. Much to her surprise, however, the man didn't laugh at all—nor even crack a smile, for that matter. Instead, without saying another word, he simply paid, accepted his bag of goods, and walked out.

Feeling bad for poor Kitty, Juliette moved to the cash register herself and set down a card. With a smile, she told the woman how much she'd been appreciating her humor. "You're one funny lady."

Kitty rang up the purchase, bagged it, and handed it over. "Yeah, I guess sometimes I can be a real *card*."

Groaning, Juliette handed the woman a five-dollar bill for the two-dollar total, telling her to keep the change. "And keep the humor too. The world could use more cheery people like you."

"Hey, thanks." Kitty sounded genuinely touched as she made the change and slid it into her pocket.

Moving out of the shop, the smile remained on Juliette's face all the way back to the main terminal. She found her crew—the men snoring loudly, the women reading magazines—and still didn't feel like dealing with them.

Modeling was such a lonely profession sometimes, especially when what she wanted most was just another person to hang out with who really understood what her life was like. A lot of people thought models traveled in packs and spent plenty of time together. But for Juliette—and the other models at her level—nothing could be further from the truth. Nine times out of ten she was the only woman on a shoot. Even when the project used other models, the women were usually photographed in sequence, not simultaneously. At the most, supermodels passed each other in transition, like vaguely friendly ships in the night.

Feeling a surge of sadness, Juliette decided to return to her little alcove and read her Bible. Maybe some time in the Word would comfort her aching soul.

She settled down and began to read, though it was hard not to be distracted by the scene outside the massive airport windows. From where she sat, she could see trees whipping around in the wind and debris skipping across the tarmac. The storm was so mesmerizing, in fact, that eventually she gave up for the time being and put the Bible away.

Others must have also realized that this vantage point offered a perfect view of the storm, because frequently people would come and stand at the window to look out for a while. Most didn't even notice her there.

When someone new came to the glass, she glanced up and saw that it was a man, his posture tense, his jaw clenched. With a start, she realized it was the same guy who'd been in the gift shop earlier, the surly one who'd bought the Peppermint Pattie and hadn't even cracked a smile at Kitty's joke.

For some reason she called out to him. "Hey. You. Didn't you see the movie *Airplane*? 'Don't call me Shirley,' and all that?"

The man glanced at her and then looked to one side and then the other, obviously trying to figure out to whom she was speaking.

"That's right, I'm talking to you," she continued. "Remember in there, in the gift shop? When the woman said don't call me Patty? It was just a joke. The least you could've done was be nice to her."

After a pause, he focused in on Juliette. "Why are you saying this to me?"

Gazing back at him, she realized that his eyes were a vivid blue-gray, the color of sea glass. His thick, dark hair was clipped short, and over a muscular build he wore dark slacks and an oxford button-down shirt. Studying him, Juliette thought he was one of the most handsome men she'd ever seen, far better looking than any of the male models she knew.

"Look, the woman was just trying to be friendly, but when you didn't even laugh at her joke, it hurt her feelings." Trying to lighten the mood, she flashed him her famous smile. "Sorry. I'm aware that this is none of my business, but I just felt bad for her is all."

At that point Juliette expected one of two reactions. Either this guy was going to snap at her and tell her to mind her own business, or he was going to spout off some excuse for his earlier behavior and then try to make a pass at her. Instead, he surprised her by doing neither.

"Wow, good for you, calling me out on that." He turned to face her fully, hands on his hips, as she looked back at him, eyes narrowed. "I'm serious. I appreciate you bringing it to my attention. I really didn't even hear her. My mind was elsewhere, totally caught up in my own thoughts." Hesitating, he added, "What did she say to me again?"

"You said to add the Peppermint Pattie and

she said 'fine, one peppermint, but don't call me Patty'."

He frowned. "That was a punch line?"

"Of course. Like in the movie *Airplane*, somebody says 'Surely you can't be serious,' and the guy goes, 'I am serious. But don't call me Shirley.'"

The man's eyes widened then crinkled into a smile. "Ah. I get it now." He chuckled. "Hey, thanks. Thanks a lot."

And with that he turned and walked away. After a moment Juliette leaned forward to peek around the wall and see where he was going. She spotted him making a beeline for the gift shop, where he walked right up to the counter and started talking to Kitty. Though Juliette couldn't hear what they were saying, this was obviously a far friendlier exchange than the one before. Soon Kitty was laughing and the man was talking and gesticulating and the two of them were having a good old time together. Juliette was pleased.

She tried to put him out of her mind, but eventually she peeked around the corner again, looking toward the gift shop. He was no longer there, and Kitty was busily cracking jokes with a new batch of customers. Wondering where he might have gone, Juliette stood and brushed off her slacks, gathered her things, and went for another walk through the airport. Fifteen minutes later she had made the rounds of the entire place, but he was nowhere to be found. Feeling oddly disappointed, she decided to get some coffee.

Soon she was sitting in the airport's lone restaurant, sipping a cup of the nasty brew and trying to pretend it included cream and sugar. Turning to look out of the window, she saw that the sky was a roiling mass of black clouds. Rain pelted the rounded, silver sides of the grounded airplanes and puddled on the dark pavement.

To her right Juliette heard a soft *thunk* against the table, and when she turned she saw a Peppermint Pattie right there in front of her. Glancing upward, she met those blue-gray eyes, sparkling now. It was him, waiting expectantly.

She grinned. "Thanks for the Peppermint Pattie."

To which he replied, of course, "You're welcome. But don't call me Patty."

They both laughed, Juliette's cheeks growing hot when she realized how happy she was to see him again.

"May I join you?" He held up his own cup of coffee as if for proof that he, too, was a paying customer here.

"Please do."

He sat and extended his right hand toward her. "My name is Marcus, by the way."

He seemed so earnest, his movements so formal, that Juliette had to suppress a smile. Though he couldn't have been a day over thirty—and was probably even a few years younger than that—he acted like someone far older. By this point, most guys would've had their hand out for her phone number, not to make a formal introduction. How absolutely . . . quaint. Taking his warm hand in her own and giving it a shake, she replied that her name was Juliette.

"It's nice to meet you, Juliette."

"You too." And she meant it. So much so in fact that she had to hide her silly grin by taking another sip of her coffee.

He gestured toward the window and the storm raging outside. "Your flight grounded?"

"No, I just like the coffee here."

He smiled at her joke.

"Kidding. Yes, of course, I'm here because my flight was grounded. Aren't you?"

He shook his head. "Actually, I'm here to pick someone up. No telling how long I'll have to wait now."

"Wow, you're a lot more patient than I am. Can't you leave and come back later? They could call you when they get in."

He shrugged. "Nah, couldn't do that."

"It could be hours yet, you know."

He met her eyes. "No, it's my boss, and he's not happy with me. I need to be waiting when he arrives. I don't want to aggravate him more than I already have."

"Yikes. What'd you do?"

"Long story." He waved off the question and took another sip of his coffee. From the pained expression that clouded his features, Juliette realized that it had to be something pretty serious.

After a moment she lowered her voice. "Do you . . . feel like talking about it? You did seem pretty upset and preoccupied in the gift shop earlier."

He didn't reply, and after a long moment Juliette felt her cheeks warming. She sat up straight, brushed her hair from her eyes. "You know what? Never mind. It's none of my business."

"It's not that. The truth is, I'd love to tell you all about it, but I don't want to bore you to death. This has been a long time coming. I'm just afraid if I get started, I'll never stop."

Suddenly Juliette wanted nothing more than to be a shoulder for this man to cry on. She gestured around them, palms upward. "Does it look like I've got somewhere else to go? Feel free to spill your guts, and I promise I'll let you know if you go on too long."

"Really? Thanks." Marcus seemed to collect his thoughts as he drained his coffee. Setting the empty cup aside, he crossed his muscular arms, rested them on the table, and launched into his tale. It took him nearly an hour to get through it—yet she remained spellbound the entire time.

He started by explaining his work as an engineer and his constant battle with a world that measured human life in terms of dollars. He seemed disillusioned and angry but also noble and good. The more he expressed his frustrations, the more she could see what a compassionate man he was, and intelligent too. She didn't offer advice, but by the time he was finally done, he seemed to feel much better just for having talked about it.

He bought them each another coffee, and when he came back to the table he told her that it was her turn to unload. "Clearly, something is bothering you too. No offense, Juliette, but you don't seem much happier than I am."

Ouch. He had that right.

She shrugged. "I don't know, it's like you said earlier. I'm afraid if I get started, I'll never stop."

He placed a warm hand on hers. "Try. Like you said, I'll cut you off if you go on too long."

And that was how she found herself sharing with him as well. She told him about her work, about what it was like to live in a world that measured human worth in terms of physical perfection. She said that even as an icon of that world, she was well aware of her every *im*perfection—and if she'd forget, somehow she would be reminded, and quickly. She told him how it had been at first, when designers and photographers would talk to each other right in front of her, complaining about the size of her hips or the freckles on her shoulders. That had changed as she'd become more successful, she said, and yet in a way things hadn't changed at all. She was afforded more respect as a super-model, of course, but all it took was an edi-tor's appraising glare to know that her body still wasn't measuring up.

Juliette told Marcus things she'd never told anyone, for fear of coming across as a diva or of seeming ungrateful. Not even her booker Didi, who was a great friend and sounding board, would've understood what she was getting at. And yet Marcus seemed to hear not just her words but her pain. She began to feel better. Between the two of them, there was enough angst and anger to fill a room, and yet they spent as much time laughing as they did pouring out their deepest anguish.

Somehow just talking things through with

a total stranger ended up being the one element that would turn the corner for them both.

Part of the reason they'd been so honest, of course, was because they knew they'd never see each other again. After hours of sharing their innermost thoughts, however, they both realized they couldn't *not* see each other again. Juliette had never given much credence to the idea of having a "soul mate" out there somewhere, but if that were true, she'd found him in an eastern Georgia airport on a stormy September day.

He seemed to feel the same about her. They eventually left the coffee shop, found some comfortable seats in another part of the airport, and turned the conversation from what they *didn't* want to what they *did*. Somewhere along the way, as he shared his dream of a job where he could focus on safety, and she talked about taking time off and getting back to the person she knew was still inside of her somewhere, they found their fingers entwining. Their gazes lingering. Their shoulders relaxed against each other as they sat there side by side.

"You do know this can't end here," Marcus said finally, turning toward Juliette and reaching out to brush a tendril from her cheek. "Meeting the woman of my dreams wasn't exactly on my agenda today, but now that I have, I'm not about to let this go."

Her heart pounded as she looked into his beautiful blue-gray eyes. How could she, too, have fallen so hard, so fast? She'd never experienced anything like this before.

"On the other hand," he continued, "if we can conclude one thing from the time we've spent together today, it's that we both need to make some big changes in our lives."

Sitting back, she took his hand in hers as she waited to hear what he was getting at.

"I don't want to come to you as this guy"—he gave her a rueful smile—"this angry, confused, soon-to-be-jobless sad sack. This isn't really me, you know. If I'm going to go back to Atlanta and do what I know I need to do, that's got to happen first. That makes sense, right?"

She nodded. Strangely it did, and she thought she knew why. If this was just a fun, casual dating relationship, to delay would be silly. But this felt like nothing of the sort. Marcus Stone wasn't the kind of man she wanted to see casually.

He was the kind of man she wanted to end up with, for good.

She nodded. "I know what I need to do now as well. And I agree. I say we go back to our separate lives and take the big actions we need to take, and when we're finally free and clear of all that drama, we meet back up and start from there."

They decided not to pick a date to reconnect nor a rendezvous point, fearing that either one might hinder them both from accomplishing their plans. If they were going to succeed at a personal relationship, their respective work situations had to be sorted out first.

She gave him her contact information and he tucked it safely in his wallet, promising that when the time was finally right, he would be in touch.

Eventually he took her in his arms and just held onto her for a long, long time. When they finally pulled apart it was only by inches. She wanted him to kiss her. Their lips were so close, she could feel the aching pulse of her own need. He, too, seemed almost there and yet he hesitated, placing a cheek against hers instead.

"I want to kiss you so bad," he whispered. "But I'm afraid if I get started, I'll never stop."

Inhaling deeply she rested her head on his shoulder, fitting like a hand to a glove. Somehow she felt more deeply connected to Marcus Stone than to any man she'd ever known. It was crazy, but it was true.

He was just so very kind and respectful, so

genuinely interested in her, and so utterly different from anyone she'd ever met. The words that came to mind were old-fashioned ones that people didn't use much anymore. Trustworthy. Dependable. *Solid*, both in build and in character. With him, she could see not just the man he wanted to become but the woman she hoped to be someday as well. Best of all, he was a Christian too, just like her, a man of faith who clearly walked the talk.

Guys like him didn't exactly grow on trees.

All too soon their time together came to an end. An odd energy began to radiate through the terminal, and soon the announcement was official: The runways had been cleared. The airport was back in business.

Marcus and Juliette decided to say their good-byes where they were, away from the prying eyes of her crew. His boss would arrive soon. She needed to get to her gate to catch her plane. Standing, they indulged in one more long, fierce hug. Then she simply gazed into his eyes, memorizing his beautiful face until she would see him again.

"This wasn't all just words, was it?" He held her close, one hand resting at the small of her back. "We're really going to do this, I mean. I'm going to give my boss an ultimatum? You're going to end your modeling career and give yourself a chance to heal?"

She nodded. "I will if you will."

"And I will if you will."

"It's a deal," they said in unison, shaking on it, then sharing a deep smile.

"You know," Juliette added, "I wouldn't have had the nerve to do this without our time together, without you. Without today. Now it seems like the simplest choice I never made."

He chuckled. "Me too! Now all that's left for me is to stand firm and let the chips fall where they will."

"Keep your eyes on God, Marcus, and you know you can't go wrong."

"Back at you, Taylor. I'll keep you in my prayers."

He pulled her in for another hug and held her close, speaking into her ear. "Just be patient, okay? It may not happen right away. First I've got to wrap things up with this job and then I've got to figure out where I'm going from here. I need to do both before I can focus on a relationship. Before I can even really *begin* a relationship. You get that, right?"

She pulled back so she could look into his eyes. "I totally get that, Marcus. Trust me, I've got plenty of work to do on my end too." With a laugh, she added, "I do believe this is the smartest, most mature entry into a relationship I've ever had."

"Yeah, well, I do believe this is the fastest, most impulsive leap my heart has ever made. But it feels completely right. You and I feel completely right."

He placed his hands on each side of her face and kissed her on the forehead, the heat of his lips searing her skin like a branding iron. "If you can be patient, it'll be worth the wait, I promise. When I come hobbling up to you in that nursing home and tell you I'm finally ready to get started—"

She slapped him on the arm. "Don't you dare wait that long."

Their expressions grew somber. The dings and whirs of a building coming to life surrounded them.

It was time to go.

Sharing one last long look, Juliette said, "All kidding aside, Marcus, don't come until you're ready. But when you are ready, please, do come. Come and find me."

"I will. I promise."

Those were the last words he said to her.

She never heard from him again.

Chapter Fifteen

Juliette woke early. her muscles were still relaxed from last night's soak in the grotto, but her mind was eager to move forward. The time for nostalgic indulgences was over.

She needed to spend an hour or two preparing for the retreat that would kick off later today, but otherwise she planned to spend her time until then looking into the whole Raven/Brooke situation and getting more solid information.

Juliette's mind swirled with questions as she got ready for the day, so finally she grabbed a pen and notepad from the bedside table and jotted them all down:

What did Raven mean by her threat at the airport?

Why was she here at Palm Grotto?

Who are the men she wanted to be near?

Why are they here under fake names?

What was the cause of Raven's death?

If her death was related to her treatment, were any of the products counterfeit?

If so, how did counterfeits end up here at Palm Grotto?

She returned to the bathroom and brushed her teeth, her mind rolling around that last question. What her company had been finding since this whole counterfeiting issue first came to light a few months ago was that there seemed to be two kinds of nefarious goings-on that had been leading salons and spas to send back counterfeit JT Lady products rather than the real thing. When an entire returned shipment was made up of fakes, more often than not the problem traced to a disreputable distributor. When only a few random products in a shipment were fake, that usually traced to someone at the salon and spa level, such as a dishonest employee who'd been helping herself to the real thing and leaving counterfeits in exchange.

In both cases it wasn't hard for them to get away with it because the packaging for counterfeit products were nearly indistinguishable from the real thing—at least to the untrained eye. Everyone at JT Lady had been shown what to look for, of course, such as printing issues with the labels, or odd odors or colors with the product. But they couldn't train those at the receiving end, and that's where the problems came in.

To verify the validity of the return stock, JT Lady's project manager had chosen a couple of warehouse workers who seemed to have a pretty good eye for spotting fakes and had assigned them to verification duty. Their job was to examine each return shipment as it came in. Shipments found with even one counterfeit in them were flagged and analyzed, placing a real burden on the chemists, not to mention a major expense for the company. In the long run, their trouble would be worth it if they could stamp out the counterfeiting.

But for now, it was a living nightmare.

Finished at the sink, Juliette ran a brush through her hair, feeling a surge of guilt that she hadn't brought this counterfeiting issue to the attention of the police yesterday. If they'd been aware going in that the cause of death might just have been a counterfeit jar of chai soy mud, they might have been able to save quite a few steps and expedite their investigation. The experts had talked about how counterfeits had been known to cause burns and rashes and numerous other physical complications. Whether or not they might cause an actual death as well, Juliette wasn't sure.

At the very least, she knew, they could inflict serious harm.

Thinking about that now, her mind went to Brooke, and she was struck with a terrible thought: What if speaking sooner would've allowed the doctors to determine more quickly the substance that may have poisoned her—maybe even find an antidote? Could Juliette's silence have had an impact on Brooke's outcome?

Pulse surging, she went straight to the phone on the bedside table and called the resort's security department to get the name and numbers of the police detectives who were handling this case. She tried both but got only voice mail, so she hung up without leaving any messages. Juliette thought about calling the hospital next but knew they wouldn't talk to her because of privacy laws.

Trying a different approach, she dialed her home office back East, and soon she was on with Elsa Gresh, the project manager who'd been handling the whole relabeling program and, consequently, the counterfeiting mess.

"Elsa, I hate to ask this, but I need to know if any counterfeit products have been found in the shipment of old-label stock returned by Palm Grotto."

"Just a moment, I will check." Elsa's voice carried a hint of her Scandinavian lilt. Juliette heard the computer clicking in the background as Elsa typed. "Here we go. Palm Grotto's return of old-label stock . . . Hmm, there's nothing here. Hold on." A few more clicks. "Oh, okay, I see. They have not yet sent back their shipment."

"Thanks, Elsa, that's what I needed to know." Juliette hung up, wondering why she hadn't thought to look into this before coming out here. It just never crossed her mind to consider whether or not Palm Grotto might be one of the spas on their watch list. This was such a classy place, one they'd been doing business with almost since the beginning. She couldn't imagine anyone here being involved with counterfeiting. The spa's low employee turnover made that even less likely.

Still, until her company received Palm Grotto's return shipment, she couldn't be sure. Maybe when she had a chance to talk with Ty about the storage, retrieval, and preparation of the products used for mud wraps, she could also get a look at their old-label stock. If she found any counterfeits . . . she'd know to pursue the issue.

Until the spa opened, though, she'd focus on the other questions on her list. Starting with a discreet look at the cluster of rooms where Raven stayed. The three men Raven came to see were probably still in their adjacent rooms. If Juliette could figure out who they really were and what Raven had wanted with them, perhaps she might understand her odd threat at the airport.

Juliette pulled on her running clothes, took a long drink from the water bottle on the bedside table, pocketed her cell phone, and headed out. From all appearances she was simply a guest of the resort on an early morning jog.

That she had plans for a little sleuthing during that jog was nobody's business but hers.

Crystal usually enjoyed her morning stroll from the employee parking lot to the main spa building, but today she found herself reluctant to go inside. She dreaded all the gossip and the drama. She *did* want an update on Brooke, but otherwise she wasn't interested. At last night's meeting Reggie had instructed the spa staff to refrain from discussing the situation anywhere outside of the break room, but she wasn't sure if that was really going to happen or not. A story this juicy—Former supermodel dies on the table during a treatment! Therapist giving fatal treatment found babbling in the corner!—would not be easily contained.

Inside the main spa building Crystal

clocked in, stashed her things in her locker, and grabbed the two papers in her cubby. One was her schedule for the day, the other was a handwritten note from Andre, asking her to come to his office as soon as she got in.

Pulse surging, she did as requested and was relieved to hear what he wanted. He asked if she would be willing to take Brooke's place with the retreat, which meant primarily that she would lead a few morning hikes and give a lecture. She agreed, flattered to have been asked.

She had another twenty minutes before her first massage, so with a much lighter step, she headed to the break room behind Arrowscale to make herself a cup of tea and collect her thoughts. As she went, she wondered if they were planning to use Tamarisk today, where the woman died. Crystal hoped not. The thought seemed . . . disrespectful somehow.

When she reached the break room, she realized too late she was coming in on a scene she would rather have avoided. Over in the kitchen area Xena was yelling at several employees, her hands clenched around an empty coffeepot, her eyes blazing.

"How many times do I have to *tell* you people this?" Xena demanded. "*News flash*, *w*hoever takes the last cup of coffee brews the next batch. Is that not *clear*?"

The three workers nodded and apologized, all of them cowering except Ty, who just stood there with a mug in his hand, body language exuding belligerence.

"I can do it now," one of the younger women timidly offered.

"It's too late. I'll do it myself." Xena turned her attention back to the machine, handling it much too roughly as she went about making a fresh pot.

Though the others seemed frozen in place, unsure whether they'd been dismissed yet or not, Ty simply headed for the door, mug in hand. As he passed Crystal, he gave her a sly wink. Ignoring the gesture, she squared her shoulders, sucked in a breath, and headed into the fray.

Juliette did a few stretches in her private courtyard, then began moving down the walkway in a warm-up pace. As she began to pick up the speed, the pull on her muscles felt so good she wished she really *were* just out for a simple jog. Maybe later. For now there were questions to ask and answers to find—and no time for a loop or two around Palm Grotto's fabulous jogging trail.

Instead she stayed on the sidewalks, choosing the route that would bring her directly past the cluster of rooms where Raven had been staying. When she finally spotted the building up ahead, Juliette slowed her pace and then came to a full stop beside a potted olive tree about twenty feet away. She placed one foot against the slats of the huge wooden planter and stretched her hamstrings as she allowed her eyes to wander over to the area in question.

Though the stone-and-stucco design elements were similar throughout the resort, the architecture for each grouping of rooms was different. This cluster looked to be four separate structures connected by a single roof. Like a square donut, the center of this little domain featured a courtyard open to the sky, with what looked like a hot tub or maybe even a small pool at its center. Nice.

Three cars were parked in the allotted spaces, but Juliette's mouth almost fell open when she realized those cars were a Rolls Royce, a Lamborghini, and what she had a feeling was a Bugatti. Goodness. At a place like Palm Grotto, one expected to find the occasional Porsche or Jaguar or Mercedes, but this was unbelievable. Whatever the identity of these three mystery men, they weren't hurting for money, that was for sure.

If Raven wasn't rich in her own right, Juliette would've wondered if she'd come here hoping to acquire a Sugar Daddy.

She was doing a quad stretch when she spotted movement in the courtyard of the cluster. Heart pounding, she tried to act nonchalant as she watched a man emerge, walk to the Rolls, and open the door to the back seat. He sat down sideways and traded out the flip-flops he was wearing for a pair of sneakers. Stealing several glances at him, Juliette thought she might recognize him, but she didn't. He had a very nondescript look—trim physique, blond hair, too-dark-for-May tan.

The guy's phone rang, and from where Juliette stood, she could easily hear his side of the brief conversation that ensued.

"Ferguson here. No, I was just about to head up to the restaurant. Meet me at the fountain in five."

Putting away his phone, he stood, closed up the car, and began moving toward the sidewalk. He noticed Juliette and gave her a polite nod—one early morning jogger to another—then he turned and started uphill slowly, away from her. She was tempted to follow along but decided to do an end run instead, using a shortcut across the grounds that would get her to the top of the hill much sooner than his more circuitous route. There was a ladies room with an exterior entrance along the side of the restaurant, and she had a feeling it would give her a clear view of the fountain area.

Sure enough, when she finally reached the top of the hill, she stepped into the small bathroom, locked the door, then went to the window and slid it open just wide enough to peek out. Pulse surging, she watched and waited until the jogger finally appeared at the fountain and began doing some stretches. She settled in to watch for the person he was meeting, eager to see what might happen between them. The resort was even quieter than usual, most of its guests asleep, the daytime employees at the very beginning of their shifts.

Juliette's hip pressed against the cold porcelain of the sink as she kept her vigil. A minute or so later she suddenly spotted movement off to the right. She leaned in closer and saw that it was a security guard, walking over from the area of the front gate around the corner.

As he came closer, she was shocked to realize that the guard was none other than Orlando. He came to a stop at the fountain and handed "Mr. Ferguson" a big, fat envelope. The man offered up a folded bill in return, which Orlando pocketed.

This was starting to be a recurring theme.

Juliette was hoping there might be some further exchange between them, but after that the guy's attention was focused fully on the package in his hands. With a quick

"Thanks" on both sides, the two men parted, Ferguson walking toward the restaurant's entrance and Orlando retracing his steps back to his post.

Eager to continue her surveillance, Juliette closed the window, washed her hands, and then exited the bathroom and headed around front to the restaurant. Once inside she saw that the place was completely devoid of customers except for Ferguson himself, envelope under his arm and an empty mug in his hand. He was near the beverage service area, tapping a foot impatiently as a restaurant employee fooled with the coffee dispenser. Across the room a breakfast buffet was being set up, which, according to the placard, would be open in another ten minutes. At least the coffee was available now.

Soon Juliette was sitting two tables behind her subject, sipping from a cup and discreetly observing his actions. So far, all he'd done was empty the contents of the envelope—an inch-thick stack of loose papers that appeared to be covered with text—onto the surface in front of him and then begin reading through them.

As soon as the buffet opened, the man jumped up and went to it, leaving the papers just sitting there on the table, where anyone could see. Heart pounding, Juliette stood, then she watched as he claimed a plate and begin working his way down the fruit bar, his back fully turned to her. Unable to resist, she moved closer to the table and allowed herself one long moment to look down at the page and read what she could. It began at the top, mid sentence, with the words:

hardscrabble existence, it's easy to understand how she turned out this way. Though her face is lined, her hands calloused and stained, there's still a regal sense of nobility in her, that hint of Anglo-Scottish forebears that managed to trickle down through the generations to this one woman in this tiny Appalachian village.

Was this about Raven? Certainly, she had come from Appalachia, though Juliette didn't know if she'd been of "Anglo-Scottish" descent. She definitely had a regal carriage, but it was highly doubtful that Raven's hands had ever been calloused or stained, at least not in the past thirty years.

The words went on from there, but Juliette dared not push things any further. Instead, she tore herself away, walked over to the complimentary buffet, and grabbed a banana and a whole wheat English muffin. Then she left Ferguson and the restaurant behind, not sure whether to be proud of her brief attempt at surveillance or ashamed.

Perhaps she was a bit of both.

Outside she was crossing to the gift shop to buy a newspaper when she spotted two workmen at a nearby flower bed, erecting a big sign that faced the parking lot. Changing her direction, she walked some distance away, then turned around and took it in, unable to keep the smile from her face.

**Welcome to this Juliette Taylor
event, where it's your turn . . .**

. . . to be nurtured

. . . to be pampered

. . . to be restored.

If only her joy in the new look and slogans weren't so bittersweet, thanks to the counterfeiting issues they had ended up bringing to light.

If only her excitement about the impending retreat weren't tempered by yesterday's tragedy and the many questions that had arisen from it.

With a sigh, she took one last look at the sign and then she walked away, reminding herself to turn the situation over to God and trust Him for the outcome, whatever that may be.

Chapter Sixteen

Marcus awoke at 8:30 a.m.—11:30 back home—surprised that his body had let him sleep that long. He must have been more worn out than he'd realized.

With a yawn and a stretch, he swung his legs over the side of the bed and sat for a moment. The flight had landed on schedule, but by the time they'd claimed their luggage, rented a car, and gotten all the way to the spa, it had been well into the early hours of the morning. His mom had been a trooper, never complaining despite her obvious exhaustion. He hoped she would sleep in for an hour or two yet, so she'd have enough energy to enjoy the retreat—not to mention that would give him time to slip out and find Juliette. He wanted to have that critical first encounter alone, no matter what.

Last night on the plane he'd allowed his

mind to wander back to the past, but now he was thinking that was a mistake. Those thoughts stirred up things he'd put to rest ages ago. Why wake all that up now, when he had a far more important task at hand?

Marcus rose and moved to the window. The whole thing was ridiculous, really. Who falls in love with someone during a single encounter? Who admits that that love never really died? What kind of idiot was he, still carrying a torch for a woman he barely knew?

Get a grip, Stone. You're here to keep her safe, not to sweep her off her feet. Deal with it.

Still, he wasn't going to rule out any possibilities.

With a grunt he pushed such thoughts aside along with the heavy drapes, eager to let in some light and get rolling. The sight that greeted him took his breath away. The resort had seemed nice enough last night, in the dark, but now in the daylight it was incredible. From his window there on the first floor, he could see the gentle curve of a lake, its banks dotted with occasional groupings of chairs and benches. The grounds were as lush and green and meticulously tended as a golf course, with enough unique trees and bushes and flowers to keep his mother in gardener heaven, trotting around with a pair of scissors all weekend long.

Beyond the lake loomed a large building that was probably the conference center. Seeing it reminded him that time was of the essence, so he pulled himself away from the window and headed for the shower.

Thirty minutes later he was dressed and ready to go. Time to take a walk and scope this place out, not to mention grab some grub at the free breakfast buffet. On the retreat schedule Juliette was listed as "unavailable" until 1:00 p.m., when she would greet retreat guests. He felt pretty confident that their paths wouldn't cross just yet, though he decided to keep the Peppermint Pattie with him anyway, just in case.

Marcus Stone was nothing if not prepared.

He tucked the silver-wrapped candy into his pocket alongside his room key and headed for the door. But when he swung it open he found himself face to face with Beverly Stone, holding up a tray laden with food and newspapers. They both gasped.

"Mom?"

"Marcus! Goodness! You scared me. What are you doing right here at the door?"

"I was on my way out. What are you doing up and around? I thought you were still asleep." Taking the tray from her hands, Marcus stepped back to let his mom inside. Judging by her colorful resort-wear outfit, freshly made-up face, and neatly coiffed hair, she'd been up for a while.

"I was so excited I couldn't sleep in, so I went exploring. The food's for you." She gestured toward the tray he was still holding. "They have a lovely breakfast buffet in the restaurant. I ate mine there, but I got yours to go, in case you overslept and missed it."

Marcus blinked. *"Recalculating route,"* as Zoe liked to say whenever plans had to be rearranged.

"Thanks. Appreciate it." Moving stiffly, he carried the tray over to the breakfast bar that divided the kitchenette from the sitting area and put it down. This was all well and good, but somehow he needed to get out of there without his mother waiting to come along with him.

Mind racing, he pulled up a barstool, sat, and lifted the stainless steel cover from atop his plate. The food looked delicious, and it was. With the first bite of cheesy eggs, all thoughts of leaving temporarily flew from his mind.

As he ate, his mother flitted around the room, chatting about all she'd seen during her morning jaunt. "This place is gorgeous, even more beautiful than in the photos. It really is 'casually elegant,' as they say, with a contemporary Southwestern architecture and décor throughout."

"What'd you do, Mom, memorize the bro-chure?"

She smiled. "Just about. The Brood kept taking me online to show me stuff. They were more excited about this trip than I was, at first."

"And now?" He bit into a fresh, juicy straw-berry.

Her face broke into a broad grin. "And now, well, I guess you could say I'm ready to get my grotto on."

Marcus laughed. Why was he surprised? His whole life his mother had embraced new experiences with gusto.

"Though I'm not sure about this whole bathrobe policy."

"Bathrobe policy?"

Beverly went into her bedroom and came back out with a white robe draped over her arm and small cardboard triangle sign, which she handed to Marcus to read.

We invite you to don the Palm Grotto robe and wear it throughout your stay, wher-ever you may wander or dine or relax on our sixty-acre property.

"They're not kidding about that, Marcus. Almost every person I saw was in robe and slippers. Can you imagine? Inside, sure, but outside? I'd feel like I was in my pajamas!"

Marcus chuckled, handing back the sign. "I'm with you there, Mom."

"Then again, can't hurt to try it on. 'When in Rome' and all that." With a wink, she headed back to her room and closed the door.

Chuckling to himself, Marcus glanced down at the folded newspaper on the tray and then did a double take. Nearly choking on his food, he dropped his fork, grabbed the paper, and unfolded it so that he could read the headline in full: *Supermodel Dies at Palm Grotto Resort*.

No! Please, no!

Heart pounding, stomach churning, he had to skim the first paragraph several times before he had assured himself that the super-model in question was *not* Juliette Taylor. It was someone named Raven, and apparently she'd passed away yesterday during a beauty treatment here at the spa.

Juliette's okay. It's not her. It was someone else.

Exhaling loudly, he lowered the paper to his lap and closed his eyes.

Thank You, Lord. I'm sorry for this other woman, but thank you just the same.

Marcus sat perfectly still, his heartbeat slowing, but his mind spinning. Once he'd calmed down, he opened his eyes again and read the entire article. What he found was not encouraging.

Though the report said nothing outright about foul play, it wasn't hard to read between the lines. Something was fishy about this woman's death, and the police knew it.

Suspicious death.

Supermodel.

Palm Grotto.

Knowing what Marcus knew, he could only hope this had nothing to do with Juliette or her company and the counterfeiters who were profiting at her expense.

Had this death been some sort of warning sign, intended to scare Juliette into silence?

Taking a deep breath, Marcus had no choice but to call Nate and let him know about this disturbing new development.

EXCEPT FOR A GLIMPSE at the headline, Juliette waited until she was back in her room, showered and dressed, before she read the newspaper article on the front page of the local daily.

Supermodel Dies
at Palm Grotto Resort

Raven, 55, the model who rose to fame in the 1980s and was known worldwide for her signature vivid red hair, died Thursday in Cahuilla Springs of undetermined causes during a spa treatment at Palm Grotto Resort.

Though the California Department of Public Health is conducting lab tests to determine the cause of death, police said they suspect it was caused by some sort of toxin in the products used during treatment.

Injured in the same incident was massage therapist Brooke Hutchinson, 35, of Cahuilla Springs, who was taken from the scene to Seven Springs Community Hospital and admitted for medical care. Hutchinson is in stable condition, said George Lewis, a spokesman for the hospital. The results of lab tests to determine the cause of Raven's death and Hutchinson's injuries are pending, Lewis said.

Some sort of toxin likely entered the bloodstream of both patients through the skin, according to County Coroner Dr. Scott Smith. "The difference between life and death here was due to the amount of exposure to the toxin," Smith said. He stated that while Hutchinson was likely exposed only through her hands, the client was exposed over a much broader area of skin, and for a longer period of time.

The two women were heard making significant noise and "being uncharacteristically loud" during the massage session preceding the incident, according to Palm Grotto Spa manager Andre Leveque. "They didn't seem to be in distress at the time but instead were overheard laughing and talking. As soon as the sounds grew more dire, we looked into it and realized something had happened," said Leveque.

According to resort manager Reggie Roberts, this is a first for the posh resort known to cater to the Hollywood elite. "Nothing like this has ever happened here," Roberts said.

In conjunction with the Department of Public Health, Cahuilla Springs police are looking into the incident. Spokesmen will neither confirm nor deny whether a criminal investigation is underway.

Juliette swallowed hard. Her worst fear had been confirmed: The death was caused by some sort of toxin in the products used during treatment.

Stomach churning, she headed next door to show the article to her business partner, who had also just finished getting ready for the day. Good 'ol level-headed Didi went right into action, dissecting the issue, contacting the home office, and even getting on the phone with the company lawyers. When all was said and done, they'd mapped out a plan: While Didi handled preparations for the retreat solo, Juliette would contact the detective to alert him to the counterfeiting issue, then go to the spa and get the inventory information she'd been wanting since the day before.

Feeling much more at peace and in control, Juliette returned to her own room and made that difficult call to Detective Bryant. It went better than expected, mostly because he said that the spa manager had already told them yesterday about the problems her company had been having with counterfeits. Still, Detective Bryant sounded appreciative that she'd called and he told her that he or Detective Lopez might be in touch for further information as things developed.

After that, Juliette headed up to the spa to pay a visit to Andre and request a full review of their inventory procedures.

On the way she thought again about her and Didi's conversation with their lawyer. According to him, they all better *hope* the toxin was from a counterfeit version of the mud lest they face legal liability regarding one of their own legitimate products. At least a follow-up call afterwards with Natalie, JT Lady's head chemist, reassured them that there was nothing in the real chai soy mud that could spoil or otherwise somehow become tainted along the way. As far as Natalie was concerned, there was nothing to worry about on their end at all, that this couldn't possibly have happened because of some chemical flaw in the real product. Thank goodness.

By the time Juliette got to Andre's office, she felt calm and composed as she made her request to have a look at Palm Grotto's inventory supply system. In response he said that they were shorthanded for the day, but that he would pull Ty from his duties for a brief period.

"Please, though, try to make it quick, would you, Sweetie?" Andre rolled his eyes dramatically. "We're absolutely *swamped* today."

Juliette assured him that she would take up as little of Ty's time as possible. Andre made a quick call, and soon she was standing out back, watching the handsome young aide coming her way from the direction of the mud pits and the Watsu pools.

Though Ty had always seemed polite and efficient, Juliette hadn't had many dealings with him in the past. As he came closer now, she greeted him with a handshake and a big thanks.

He shrugged. "I've been running like crazy all morning, it's nice to get a break."

Juliette smiled. "In that case, I'm sorry we have to rush. I promised Andre we'd do this as quickly as possible."

"Sure. He said you want to know about inventory controls?"

"Yes, I'd like you to walk me through the whole process my products go through from when they first arrive at the spa to when they're finally used on a client."

Ty's eyes narrowed. "This have something to do with all that mess from yesterday?"

She nodded. "Considering that it was supposedly my company's mud that caused the problem, I'd be more comfortable if I understood the policies and procedures here with regards to inventory control."

His chin set, lips tight, the young man thrust his hands into his pockets and took a step back. "Okay, then. I guess we should start at Shipping and Receiving."

With that, he turned and walked away. After a moment's startled hesitation, Juliette caught up and matched him stride for stride.

Crystal was thrilled when Greg sent her a text asking if they could have lunch together. They weren't supposed to be texting during work hours, but she shot back a reply between massages: *Schedule packed, just have half hour today.*

His response came quickly: *Half hour better than nothing. Meet at stone bench by mud pits. Time?*

Grinning, she sent a response and then muted her phone and tucked it into her pocket. A picnic lunch with the best-looking guy in Cahuilla Springs, maybe in all of California? She was so there.

For a moment she thought of her mom, who'd been nagging her for years to date more. Sandy Walsh would like Greg—his looks, his good manners, the way he could rattle off quotes without sounding the least bit pretentious. Of course, she wouldn't be so crazy about his aspirations to become a police officer. Like Moonflower, Sandy hated cops. But unlike Moonflower, her stance wasn't some countercultural thing. It was borne of experience.

Cops evicted you. They tried to institutionalize you. They checked your daughter for bruises to make sure she wasn't being abused.

Crystal felt a surge of sadness rise up from within. Her mother was a mess, mentally speaking, but she'd never physically hurt her, never even spanked her when she was small.

Instead, Sandy had simply taken her daughter along for the ride.

The Crazy Express . . .

Swallowing back her grief, she realized she missed her mom for the first time since leaving home three weeks before. Crystal would never go back to Seattle, but she could stay in touch. She really should. Taking a deep breath, she patted her pocket, feeling the weight of her cell phone there.

One of these days, very soon, she would give her mom a call.

Chapter Seventeen

"I can see why you're concerned, Marcus."
Nate's voice was somber on the other end of
the line. "I mean, when you get down to it,
how many supermodels were there back in
the eighties anyway? Five? Six? Now two of
them are in the same place at the same time,
one is on a terrorist list and the other one
ends up dead? This whole thing has a real
stink to it, if you ask me."

"I know. Let's hope it was all just a big,
sad coincidence." Marcus was standing at the
window in his bedroom, gazing out across the
lush grounds at the conference building in the
distance. Was Juliette there now? Should he
take matters into his own hands, go find her
right away, and get that all-important first
encounter over with right now? If this other
model's death really had been a warning sign,

Juliette needed to understand as soon as possible that she could be in serious danger.

"I need you to do something for me," Marcus said into the phone as he turned away from the glass. "With this new development, I think it's important to take things to the next level out here. She needs to know the truth, and I'd like permission to tell her."

"Permission denied. For now. Let me take this up the chain of command a bit and get back to you."

Marcus grunted, tempted to tell her anyway, permission or not. "Fine, but make it quick. If it turns out this other supermodel's death was intentional rather than an accident, all bets are off."

"Look at it this way," Nate said, "at least you're out there and can keep an eye on her. Keep her safe. You do that and I'll work the situation from this end as fast as I can."

"While you're at it, can you find out who determines the Threat Levels in those reports of yours? The dossier listed her as 'Moderate, not believed to be a direct target of the larger organization at this time.' Who decides that? On what do they base that conclusion?"

Nate was quiet for a moment before he spoke. "That comes from a team of highly qualified sifters."

"Sifters?" Marcus began to pace back and forth at the foot of the bed.

"Sorry, that's what I call the agents who specialize in analyzing evidence and examining data. They sift through all the info and draw certain conclusions based on what they find."

Marcus tried to keep his voice level. "I assume they've been known to make mistakes in the past?"

"Come on, Stone, lose the attitude. You know as well as I do, we're doing the best we can. This isn't some scientifically quantifiable engineering issue, like a steel beam that can be tested and measured to an exact degree of weight-bearing capability. This is *subjective*. We make informed predictions. Educated guesses. Of course mistakes happen. We're talking about people here, not products, not formulas or figures. But I've yet to encounter a single sifter who didn't take their job very, very seriously. They don't just toss out these things at will, regardless of what you think. Am I making myself clear?"

Marcus exhaled slowly. "Yes." He wanted to say "Yes, *sir*!" but held back on the sarcasm. Nate was his superior on this project, after all.

"Good." Nate seemed to calm down. "Now. It seems to me that, yes, this Threat Level should be revisited. We'll look into that. But in the meantime, I have to wonder about another issue with the report, one that we hadn't considered before."

Marcus felt a shift in his gut. "What's that?" He listened to the sound of papers being shuffled until, finally, Nate spoke.

"Here we go. The name Juliette Taylor appeared on a terrorist cell's list, and the sifters came up with two reasons why they think that happened, listed here under 'Probable Reason for Inclusion.' You've seen it before, but I'll read it to you again. One, 'Subject has recently become aware of counterfeited products and has initiated an internal investigation.' Two, 'As a public figure, subject has been invited to join forces with anticounterfeiting organizations to increase awareness.'"

Marcus tried to understand what Nate was getting at. "Yeah, okay. That's from the same report you and I were looking at yesterday."

"Uh-huh. And yesterday these seemed like valid conclusions. But now that there's been a death, we need to reconsider whether she really was on the terrorists' list for these reasons . . ."

Nate's voice trailed off, but Marcus realized where he was going with that thought. He lowered himself to the edge of the bed and finished the sentence. ". . . or if there's some other aspect to the situation that we don't know about."

"Exactly. Bottom line, I think there's more to it than this. I think we need to reconsider why her name ended up on that list in the first place."

Juliette followed Ty's lead as they walked past the spa building, down the slate steps, and along the front of Arrowscale. When they reached the main road, he turned right and headed up the hill for a short ways before angling left across the street toward a wide driveway that cut through a thick stand of olive trees. The two of them followed that driveway around to a long, low utility building all but hidden from view behind the greenery.

There seemed to be two entrances, one at each end of the building, and when she commented on it, Ty explained that Shipping and Receiving shared the structure with House-keeping, but each department had its own separate access.

Ty opened the door marked *Delivery Check-In* and they stepped inside. "Shipments to the resort always come in through here."

He introduced her to the woman in charge and explained that she and the others in her department were responsible for opening all packages and verifying each delivery by comparing the contents against the original order and the packing slip.

"We also make sure there hasn't been any breakage or spillage or whatever," she added, popping her gum for emphasis.

"Once they've done that," Ty continued, "they shoot me an e-mail to let me know an order has arrived and is ready for pickup. I'll come here to get it, then I bring it back to the main spa building, do another count myself, and log everything into the computer. When I'm finished, I'll take the stuff to the supply closet and unload it onto the shelves."

After some questions and answers, Juliette was satisfied with that part of her tour and suggested they continue.

"Sure." Moving just as quickly as before, Ty led her back down the hill and around to the spa. Once inside he brought them through a door marked *Employees Only* and down a hallway lined with a punch clock and a row of lockers. He continued past a janitor's closet and finally came to a stop at what had probably once also been a closet but was now set up as a workstation complete with computer terminal, packing supplies, a handcart, and more. The space was small and packed full of stuff, with just enough room to get the job done.

Standing at the computer, Ty brought up the inventory control system software and gave Juliette a brief overview. That took about fifteen minutes, then they returned to the main hallway and concluded their tour with a visit to the supply closet, the very one where Juliette had cowered from Raven the day before. Swallowing down her guilt, she watched and listened as Ty showed her how the closet's inventory was organized and tracked.

"From here it gets a little more confusing." His muscular arms crossed at the chest, Ty leaned one shoulder against the sturdy shelving and continued. "Once a week I'll take a look at all the upcoming treatments and where they'll be given, then I pull the supplies from here and move them to the temporary storage areas of the various rooms where they will be used. Of course, things can change, and more treatments are always getting added, so every day around four thirty, I'll take a look at the next day's schedule and make sure I've got everything on hand where it's supposed to be."

Juliette nodded, impressed with Ty's command of the whole system. He wasn't the most personable fellow in the world, but at least he seemed to know what he was doing as far as inventory was concerned.

"Tell me about the chai soy mud Brooke used on Raven yesterday. I'm assuming it came from in here?"

"Yeah, on Monday, the schedule showed five wraps in Arrowscale this week, so I moved five jars from here to the back room over there. Two of those already got used, but the jar in question stayed in that cabinet until yesterday morning, when I took it out and put it in the warmer in Tamarisk."

Juliette nodded, thinking about that. "And the other jars that were already used this week, none of those clients had any problems?"

"Not that I'm aware of." His jaw set, he added, "We run a tight ship here, Ms. Taylor. Whatever happened in that room yesterday had nothing to do with any inventory issues, I promise you that."

Juliette met the man's gaze. "I hope you're right, 'Ty. But as I'm sure you're aware, we at JT Lady recently discovered that counterfeit versions of our products are being made and sold under our label."

"Yeah, I saw the memo."

"So you can understand my concern, that the toxin in question came from a counterfeit that somehow ended up in place of the real thing."

His mouth was a tight, straight line. "I've

been keeping my eyes open, but as far as I know, nothing like that has come through here."

Shifting her weight, Juliette tried to appear nonchalant as she asked why he hadn't yet sent in his return shipment of old-label stock to JT Lady.

"The deadline's not for a few weeks. I'll get to it in time. I've just been really busy."

Juliette chewed her bottom lip. "Where are the old-label products now? I've seen only new-label stuff since I got here."

"That's what all those boxes under the table in my workstation are. I did the switch to the new stuff the week it came in, but before I tape up the packages and send the old stuff out, I wanted to do one last sweep of all the various treatment rooms and temporary storage areas to make sure I haven't missed anything."

Juliette took in a breath and held it for a moment. There was something odd in Ty's demeanor, but for now she would give him the benefit of the doubt and assume he was just feeling defensive about having his inventory procedures questioned and challenged.

Eyes narrowing, she asked if she could have access to those boxes of old-label stock waiting to be returned. "No offense, but I need to go through them and see if there are any fakes among the real."

Dropping his arms, Ty glanced at his watch and gave her a shrug. "Sure, as long as you can do it without me—and you don't mind working in such a tight space."

"No problem. I'll let you get back to your job and make do on my own."

"Okay. Have fun with that."

He stepped into the hall and began to walk away but Juliette leaned out and called after him in a soft voice.

"Ty?"

He paused and turned. "Yeah?"

"Keep your eyes open for counterfeits, will you? This problem is far from over, but the more cooperation we can get from the spas, the faster it can be resolved."

Averting his eyes, he gave her a nod. Then he turned and continued down the hall and out the back door.

Lunch with Greg went way too fast. He was in a really good mood, his funniest, flirtiest self yet. Crystal responded in kind, and soon they were laughing and joking like old friends.

This was Crystal's favorite bench for people-watching, situated just ten feet or so from the spa's main thoroughfare, yet nestled among the trees. The spa was super busy today, and the broad sidewalk saw a lot of traffic. After a while Greg and Crystal invented a counting game: He got one point for every man that walked by, she got one for every woman, with extra points given if they were wearing robes or flip-flops. Soon they were neck and neck, so they added extra point opportunities for sunglasses and hair color.

"Oh, and ten points if the person is a celebrity," Greg added in a whisper.

Crystal giggled. "I'm not very good with that stuff. I don't have a TV and I rarely read those kinds of magazines."

"Seriously? Staying up on all the celebrity gossip isn't, like, required for spa employees?"

"Not that I know of. What difference would it make?"

He shrugged. "I don't know, we got a lot of VIPs here. I figure they're supposed to get better treatment or whatever."

She tried not to sound offended as she told him that *all* of her clients got excellent treatment. He apologized, she accepted, and then they shared a smile and returned to their game.

Soon a robed couple came walking past, holding hands as they walked.

"Guess that was a push," she said once they were gone.

"No way, that guy had blond hair *and* knobby knees."

She giggled. "I still say knobby knees are too objective."

"How about hair plugs?" He gestured toward the next man coming down the walk. "Shouldn't I get a point for that?"

Crystal cringed, recognizing her client from yesterday. She shushed Greg and sat absolutely still until he had moved on past, relieved that he hadn't noticed her there.

"You have a problem with that guy?" Greg sounded as if he might leap to her defense at any moment.

"No, not at all. It's just that he's the one I was massaging yesterday when everything happened in the room next door." She took a sip of water.

Greg turned to face her. "Really? The guy who threw on his clothes and ran away the moment he realized what was going on was Quentin VonTassel?"

She shook her head. "His name's Elwood Dowd."

Greg stared at her for a moment. "That guy? He may be registered as Elwood Dowd, but his real name is Quentin VonTassel. He's a big Hollywood director."

Crystal's eyes widened.

"You didn't know that? Boy, you weren't kidding that you're not up on that sort of thing. The guy's a major celebrity. Probably why he took off so fast yesterday, because he didn't want to be connected in any way with such a bizarre situation."

Maybe Greg was right. Dowd had seemed utterly panicked. He'd left without even taking the time to slip on his shoes.

Speaking of time, Crystal pulled out her phone to check the hour then showed it to Greg. They stood to go.

"Anyway," he added as he balled up their trash, "I'm glad he walked by."

"Why?"

He looked at her, his handsome brown eyes twinkling. "Because even without points for the hair plugs, he had on a robe, sunglasses, flip-flops—and he had brown hair *and* knobby knees. And he's a celebrity." He grinned. "I win, by a landslide."

It didn't take long for Juliette to get settled inside the small workstation closet and get down to business. Under the bar-height table were nine cases of JT Lady products that she would need to go through, item by item. If she found even one suspicious-looking bottle or tube or jar in any of them, she would know for sure that counterfeits had infiltrated Palm Grotto's inventory.

She didn't have much time, so she worked

as quickly as possible, going through one box at a time by putting its contents onto the table then examining each item as she loaded it back in. At first she did so while standing at the tall table, her back to the hallway, but eventually moved around to the other side and perched on a small barstool instead.

As she worked, she wasn't necessarily being all that quiet, but no one seemed to notice her anyway, not even when they walked right past. After a while she began to feel like an auditory voyeur. There was a water cooler just outside and to the left of the door, and twice she overheard private conversations that took place right there, the first involving gossipy complaints about a coworker, and the other going into great detail about somebody's hot date the night before.

At least with every box she examined, Juliette found herself growing more certain that there were no counterfeits here. Still she persisted. She was on the fifth box when she overheard a new conversation—only this time it wasn't in the employee hallway in front of her but instead somewhere on the other side of the wall, behind her.

Trying to ignore the low rumble of voices, she continued on with the fifth box. She was moving to the sixth when the voices began to grow so loud and clear that they were impossible to ignore. Juliette decided that the gist of their argument had to do with someone having found out something they weren't supposed to know. The man's voice was too muffled to make out more than the occasional word, but she couldn't help but hear the woman, who kept saying things like, "She *knew*!" and "How did she find out?" and "What do we do?"

Juliette wondered if perhaps the couple had been involved in a secret affair and his wife had learned about it. As the fight continued and she heard phrases like "damage control" and "cost-risk ratio," however, she decided that it sounded less like a matter of the heart and more like something to do with money or business. Eventually the voices grew so loud that Juliette couldn't help but hear almost every word.

"But why *now*?" the woman demanded furiously. "She never did before."

"Keep your voice down," the man hissed, but she went on as if she hadn't heard him, her next words even louder.

"News flash: It's not January and it's not July! It's *May*! So why now? I'll *tell* you why now."

"I'm not going to say this again: *Keep your voice down!*"

After a long silence, they began speaking

again, but back at a lower volume where Juliette couldn't quite make out the words. Soon the sound began to fade away entirely, and by the time she had finished with the eighth box and moved on to the ninth and final one, she could no longer hear the voices at all.

It wasn't until she was sliding the last box back into place, zero counterfeits having surfaced, that she gasped, eyes wide, as a part of this puzzle clicked together in her mind. According to Iliana, Raven had come here to the spa twice a year for twenty years.

Every January. Every July.

The argument had been about Raven.

Chapter Eighteen

Once Juliette realized the argument she'd overheard had something to do with Raven, she wished she'd paid more attention to it when it was happening! With no instant replay, no tape to rewind and listen to again, the most she could do for now was figure out where it had taken place. Hopefully on the other side of that wall was someone's office, which should reveal the identity of at least one of the arguers.

She finished neatening up the workstation then headed out of the employees-only area into the spa's main hallway. Trying to act like she belonged there, Juliette made her way around the maze of side hallways and treatment areas, passing the occasional employee or customer, none of whom paid any attention to what she was doing or where she was going. Finally she came to what she felt sure was the room in question.

The door was open and the light was off inside, so she chanced a peek—and was disappointed to realize that it wasn't an office at all, but just a treatment room.

Hoping she'd judged the spacing wrong, she checked several rooms to each side as well, but the whole row was nothing but treatment rooms. At least she understood why someone would have chosen to have a sensitive conversation in one of them. This particular section of the spa was tucked down a side hall of a side hall and felt very secluded. More importantly, at the moment, every single one of the rooms here was empty.

Now what did she do with the information she had gleaned from what she'd overheard? She decided to get Didi's opinion. After winding her way back out, Juliette finally exited the rear door of the spa and began to move down the walkway toward the conference center.

As she went, she must've hit a cellular hot spot, because suddenly the phone in her pocket began to vibrate and ding. She pulled it out and waited until it seemed that all messages had been received. She'd probably been out of range for nearly an hour, and in that time she'd gotten six texts and two voicemails. A nervous flutter in her stomach, she went through each one—some from Didi and some from Elsa—and realized they all said about the same thing: Call the home office immediately. Juliette did as instructed and soon was on with Elsa.

"Sorry to freak out and send so many messages, but I could not reach you and it was important."

"That's okay. What's up?" Juliette started when a squirrel scampered across the path in front of her.

"We're going to have some visitors here today that I thought you might need to know about."

"Oh?" Juliette continued walking toward the conference center as she waited for Elsa to elaborate.

"Somebody from the FBI called, about half an hour ago. They're coming here in about an hour. They need to ask us some questions."

Juliette blinked, wondering if she was hearing correctly. The *FBI?* "Questions about what?"

"They said it has to do with the counterfeiting issue. I explained that both you and Didi were out of town, but they insisted on coming anyway. I mean, I can handle it, but I thought perhaps you two might want to be on speakerphone at the time."

"Yes, of course." Juliette pinched the bridge of her nose, thinking. Given that the retreat's opening session was to start at two o'clock, the timing couldn't be worse. Depending on how long the FBI stuck around, she and Didi might not be able to participate in the entire conversation.

Nevertheless, they worked out the details of how they would handle the phone call, and by the time Juliette hung up, she was almost to the conference center. Didi must've spotted her through the big front windows, because she came outside before she even got there. She stood waiting on the sidewalk, hands clasped, teeth gritted.

Juliette came to a stop. "I just talked to Elsa. We'll need to shift things around a bit if we want to be a part of that meeting."

Didi nodded, her eyes narrowing. "No problem. There's something else, though. We need to talk, somewhere private. It's important."

Marcus was at the desk in his room and absently glanced toward the window when he spotted the tall blonde striding along in the distance. Jumping up from his chair, he moved to the glass and peered out, his heart skipping a beat.

Juliette Taylor.

There she was, live and in person.

Juliette. His Juliette.

Holding his breath, Marcus watched as she came to a stop just outside the conference center, where she was met by a short, heavy woman with dark hair. The two of them stood talking for a moment and then they turned and began to walk along the sidewalk that ran in front of the building.

Now that he had her in his sights, it was time to act—especially because once the conference began she'd be too busy. Heart pounding, he gave one last quick mirror check. His mom napped in her room, and as Marcus came out, he was relieved to see that her door was still closed. He paused just long enough to make sure the Peppermint Pattie was still in his pocket, and then he headed out.

Heart pounding in his ears, Marcus emerged into the sunshine and walked in the direction the two women had gone. He soon spotted them, up ahead and to the left. They had settled on a bench a short distance down a winding pathway beside the lake.

Not wanting them to notice him, he chose a different bench, one closer to the conference center and somewhat obscured by a tree, where he would wait until they came back this way. As soon as Juliette was close, he decided, he was going to step up, tell her hello, and hand her the Peppermint Pattie.

It was the longest wait of his life. As he sat there, his resolve and confidence began to waver. What if she didn't get it? What if he came across like some sort of stalker? What if she knew exactly who he was but didn't want to see him? He should have planned better, come out a day earlier, approached Juliette in a proper manner, and without an audience.

Mind swirling, he thought about getting up to leave, just go back to his room for now and figure out some other way to have this initial encounter later. He always planned every-thing, leaving as little as possible to chance. But Juliette was a variable he could not con-trol.

He took a deep breath, blew it out, then forced himself to relax and look around. The scenery here really was breathtaking. If this first encounter went well, and despite the primary reason he was here, he could imagine coming back at some point with her and sit-ting on this same bench, side by side, catching up on their lives.

Marcus leaned forward and peeked around the tree. She and her friend were still deep in conversation. Suddenly he realized that these eleventh-hour nerves weren't about planning or preparation. This was about trust.

In God. In himself.

All along he'd felt God's leading in this, so why was he ignoring Him now? He closed his eyes, focusing on that small, still voice, then settled back against the bench. This was right where he needed to be.

And so he would wait. And gaze at the beautiful lake—and watch for the beautiful woman he had come to see, the one he'd come to protect.

Didi wouldn't tell Juliette what was wrong until they were off by themselves on a bench beside the lake. Even once they sat down, she seemed hesitant, so Juliette finished telling about her tour with Ty and the argument she'd overheard from the closet. When she was done, she settled back against the seat and looked out at the sparkling water in front of them.

"All right, Didi, your turn. Spill. You had something to tell me?"

Didi took in a deep breath then turned to face her friend.

"Two things, actually, two new developments I just heard about fifteen minutes ago."

Juliette swallowed hard, waiting for Didi to continue.

"For starters, the toxin that killed Raven

was definitely in the mud. The JT Lady chai soy mud."

Juliette closed her eyes. She wasn't surprised to hear that, but that still didn't make it easy to take.

"The good news is that it wasn't some random chemical from a bad batch. And, hallelujah, it was not from a counterfeit product. So at least we know we won't have any liability here."

Juliette exhaled in relief. No counterfeit involved. *Thank You, Lord.*

"The bad news is on a more personal level. Well . . . I guess the easiest way to do this is to just say it all at once." She paused to reach out and take Juliette's hand. "Raven was murdered, hon. Poisoned. The toxin that killed her was added to the mud intentionally."

Juliette shook her head, trying to understand. "How do they know that?"

Didi shrugged, giving her hand one final squeeze and then letting it go. "Because of the substance that was used. It was a drug of some kind, one that could only have ended up in the jar if someone had intentionally put it there. From what I understand, this drug is pretty common—and safe at a normal dosage. The problem is that by adding so much of it into the mud, she was basically given a fatal drug overdose. Through the skin, no less."

Juliette was finding it hard to breathe. "And Brooke?"

"She got overdosed too. The only reason she's still alive is because it only got on her hands. Poor Raven had it slathered all over her whole body."

Juliette turned away, trying to take this in. Finally she told Didi she'd like a few minutes to herself. "I'll be fine, I promise, I just need to be alone for a bit. Please go."

Didi rose, her voice reluctant. "Okay, but watch the time. Don't forget about our conference call."

Juliette nodded, her eyes focused on the distant mountains, her heart aching from the grief.

Marcus came alert when he saw Juliette's friend walking up the path alone. Juliette was still on the bench by herself.

Could he ask for a more perfect opportunity than this?

As the friend walked past, they gave each other a nod. Then he rose and started toward Juliette. Now or never.

The distance to where she sat was only about a hundred feet, but it felt like miles. He would go and sit next to her on the bench then say hello and give her the candy. What a perfect spot for their reunion, a peaceful spot by a pristine lake in a lush setting.

Just as he was getting close, Juliette stood and began walking up the path toward him, her head down.

Well, this changes things.

His usual strength at being able to alter plans in an instant when dealing with a crisis left him, and he felt like an awkward schoolboy. Before he could come up with a new plan, he and Juliette Taylor were crossing paths. He stepped forward and spoke.

"Hello, stranger." With that he looked into her face and handed her the Peppermint Pattie.

A man spoke to Juliette as she was walking up the path, but her head was pounding so loudly, her mind swirling with such confusion, that she couldn't even make out his words. It didn't matter. She simply nodded and tried to continue on, stopping short only when he thrust out his hand. She glanced down to see a quick flash of a silver wrapper. Candy? This man was offering her candy?

Her temples throbbing, Juliette chose the quickest way out of this unwelcome encounter—she took the candy, shoved it into her pocket, and mumbled a quick, "Thank you, but excuse me," and kept going.

She picked up her pace as she continued onward, veering left on the walkway that would bring her to her room. There wasn't much time to spare, but she needed to be alone for at least a few minutes. She needed to think. Soon she realized that she was barely breathing. Murdered! Raven had been murdered.

Juliette fumbled to unlock the door then walked in, shut it, and leaned back against it, trying to catch her breath. Once she had calmed down a bit, she began to pace back and forth across the cold marble floor. The pacing only made her feel more agitated, so finally, she sat, closed her eyes, and began to pray.

Why murder, God? Why her?

Juliette knew she was overreacting to Didi's news, but she just felt so out of control. She couldn't even wrap her head around the idea that someone had murdered Raven, much less that they'd used one of Juliette's products to do so. Unbelievable. Simply unbelievable.

Marcus stood frozen on the path for several minutes after Juliette was gone. Her reaction to him had been all wrong. In fact, she barely noticed him at all. In the many scenarios he'd played out in his head, he never imagined this one, that she just wouldn't care.

What an absolute fool he had been. Their encounter all those years ago had meant nothing to her. He was carrying a torch that had never been lit.

Even the Peppermint Pattie had been a complete flop! For all he knew, she was laughing at him right now, mocking him as just one more pathetic man throwing himself at a supermodel. He trudged back to his room, hoping his mother was still asleep. By the time he got there and went inside, his face still burned.

Feeling an absolute fool, he went into his room, closed the door, and just sat there for a while. He felt like a tire with a slow leak. Finally he forced himself to look at the situation objectively. The best thing to do at this point would be simply to avoid her as much as possible. But that was not an option. Their own personal issues aside, he had come here to help protect her and that's what he was going to do. What other choice did he have?

What was he going to do now?

He pulled out his cell to see if Nate had called him back yet, but he had not.

Obviously Marcus only had one option. He needed to forget everything about his past personal relationship with Juliette and focus solely on the danger she was in. Surely if he tried again and kept things much more casual this time, she might at least give him five seconds and a proper hello.

Man, this was tough.

Needing to work off this nervous energy, Marcus decided to go for a run. He'd seen a jogging trail on the resort map, so he would go there now, get in a good workout, and try to clear his head.

After a quick change into shorts and a T-shirt, he left a note for his mom, headed outside, and aimed for the nearby path, starting out slow until his muscles warmed up.

The dream he had carried for so many years, the one he had nurtured and finally allowed to blossom, had now been plucked and squashed. That dream was a lie he had told himself—a mirage he'd gazed at for years, deceiving himself into believing it was. How could he have been so foolish?

You'd think life would make you smarter about things like this. You'd think after all the heartbreak he'd endured—not just on the job in the aftermath of great disaster but at home as well—something like this would be a piece of cake. But pain was pain, and just admitting he should've known better still didn't make it go away.

Marcus found the jogging loop and was glad to see that it wasn't paved but was instead a dusty gravel path that began at a break in some trees, wound past a great big boulder a little further out, and then basically formed a long, wide curve that ran along the outer fringes of the resort's property. The rest of the resort was hidden from view by trees, and after the first twenty feet, he felt like he was out in the middle of the desert, it was that dry, that deserted.

If only he could keep running. If only he could run all the way back home and forget he'd ever come here at all.

Chapter Nineteen

Juliette looked at the clock, relieved to see that she still had ten minutes before she needed to head next door to Didi's room. Their phone call with the home office and the FBI would be disturbing enough in and of itself. She didn't need to bring any extra anxiety into the matter, but right now anxiety was all she was feeling.

Standing, she began to pace again, more slowly this time. She wasn't self-unaware, she knew where this gut-wrenching fear was coming from and that it wasn't just about the murder of an old colleague and friend. It had to do with an earlier time, with the death of her parents. She'd been just fourteen when they passed away, leaving her and her younger sister Katherine in the care of distant and aloof grandparents.

The news of Raven's death yesterday hadn't

hit Juliette this hard. But now that she knew it was murder, that changed things. She couldn't quite put her finger on why, but it had something to do with the *intentionality* of it. Raven was dead because someone *wanted* her that way, someone *made* her that way.

Again having a seat on the edge of the bed, Juliette closed her eyes, remembering herself as a young teen in the aftermath of her parents' death. At first she'd felt certain that they, too, had been murdered. Their death had been so unexpected, so random and inexplicable. Several years prior to that, she had become convinced that her father was a secret government agent—a suspicion he and her mother had laughed off, insisting that she read too many spy novels for her own good.

But then they were killed under mysterious circumstances and her imagination had gone wild. For months she had pored over the newspaper reports about the tragic accident, looking for clues and suspects and motives. She'd never come up with any solid theories nor been able to convince anyone else of her suspicions, and eventually she'd had no choice but to let those notions go. As she matured, she'd come to understand that sometimes people died and there was no reason for it, the only villains a dark night and a slippery road and a sharp downhill curve.

Juliette opened her eyes and glanced at the clock again. Seven minutes.

She reached out a hand to the bedside table drawer and slid it open to see if there was a Bible inside. There was, God bless the Gideons. Though she had a great Bible app on her phone, at the moment she needed to hold the Word in her hands, needed its heft and weight and the crinkling of the pages as she turned to the book of Deuteronomy, to the verse that had given her so much strength over the years. She found it now, and though it wasn't in the translation she usually used, there was something lovely and lyrical about good ol' King James.

"Be strong and of a good courage, fear not, nor be afraid . . . for the LORD thy God, he it is that doth go with thee; he will not fail thee, nor forsake thee."

She focused on the last part: *He will not fail thee, nor forsake thee.*

Her mind went to the more familiar translation she had memorized years ago, which put it, *Never will I leave you; never will I forsake you.*

That was God's promise, and she knew it was true.

As a young woman, she had railed against it, though. She could still see herself at eighteen, the night before her graduation from high school—the graduation her parents had not been alive to attend. She had found this verse that night and it had made her furious.

"Everyone leaves!" she had cried in prayer, shaking a fist at the sky. "Everyone forsakes you in the end!"

Yet somehow God had remained steadfast.

Never will I leave you; never will I forsake you.

She remembered herself at twenty-six, the morning after she'd broken her engagement with Mike. That time she'd been the one to do the forsaking. She'd broken a good man's heart just because she hadn't loved him enough for a lifetime.

She'd forsaken him, but God had not forsaken her.

Never will I leave you; never will I forsake you.

She pictured herself at her surprise fortieth birthday party, surrounded by family and friends and employees. The party had been lovely, but the occasion it marked bittersweet. She didn't mind getting older. What she minded was getting older *alone*. Where was the husband she had always expected to find? Where were the children she had always dreamed would fill her life? It's not like she hadn't dated. Over the years she'd gotten at least a dozen proposals but even the two times she'd said yes, she ended up changing her mind and calling things off. She'd never found anyone she loved enough for a lifetime.

Later that night after her party, once she was finally home and by herself, she had wept from the heartbreak of it all.

"Why, God? Why put the desire for husband and kids in my heart if You weren't going to bless me with either?"

He hadn't given her any answers. But somehow He had given her comfort.

Never will I leave you; never will I forsake you.

That promise had proven true at the lowest points in her life and at every moment in between.

Looking around the empty hotel room now, Juliette knew it still held true. God was there with her. He always was. He always would be. No matter what insanity raged around her, He would not leave nor forsake her. He would be steadfast.

With that thought, the anxiety began to fade. Once again closing her eyes, Juliette allowed God's promise to sink in to the bone, to saturate her to the core. She prayed aloud, thanking God for being with her, always. As she spoke, a calm surged deep into her soul.

She stayed there, in prayer, for as long as

she could. Then, with a final "amen," she rose and headed for Didi's room, one minute to spare.

Moonflower sounded scared.

Crystal didn't know what had frightened the aging flower child so, nor why she kept denying it when Crystal pointed it out, but from the tone of Moonflower's voice over the phone and the odd, disjointed things she was saying, there was no question. She was terrified half to death.

Crystal had thought about Moonflower all morning and intended to call during her lunch break, but had spent that time with Greg instead. Now she was in transit between two treatment huts and only had a few minutes to spare.

"Please tell me what's bothering you. I'm sorry to be so pushy, but I don't have much time and I'm really worried about you."

"It's just been a hard day." Moonflower's voice cracked. "It's never easy to lose a client, especially not like this. Now I'm not even sure if I can go back to work at all. Ever again."

"Why on earth not?" Palm Grotto without the peaceful, motherly presence of Moonflower Youngblood? Crystal couldn't even imagine such a thing.

"Because of what was done to Raven."

"I know it'll be hard at first, but in time—"

"It's not that." She lowered her voice. "Okay, you're right. I am scared."

Crystal remained silent, willing her friend to explain.

"Now that Raven's been killed, I'm afraid the killer might come for me too."

Crystal was so startled she could barely form a reply. "What? Why?"

Moonflower sniffled. "Never mind. I shouldn't have said anything."

"No, really. What do you mean? Why would anyone want to hurt you? Tell me. Maybe I can help."

Moonflower paused, and then spoke, her voice low and foreboding. "Raven was being blackmailed."

Crystal stopped in her tracks, trying hard to keep her mouth from hanging open. "Blackmailed? I don't understand."

Again Moonflower tried to backpedal. "Look, I shouldn't even be talking about this. Forget I said anything."

"No way." Crystal forced herself to start walking again. "Moonflower, Raven was *murdered*. If you know she was being blackmailed, you have to tell the police."

"Tell the *pigs*? Absolutely not! Never trust anyone in a uniform, don't you know that?"

Pigs? Oh, right. Just as Greg had mentioned the day before. Best to drop it for the moment lest Moonflower decide to clam up again. "You're not being blackmailed too, are you?"

"Of course not."

"Then why do you sound so frightened?"

Moonflower exhaled slowly. "Because I'm the one who told Raven to turn the blackmailer down, to call his bluff and refuse to pay. She took my advice and now she's dead. If the blackmailer killed her for refusing to pay, then what's to stop him from killing me too?"

Crystal shuddered, trying to wrap her head around what she was hearing. "If you tell the police, they'll protect you."

Moonflower sighed. "No pigs. I told you that already."

Good grief. "Well, at the very least, I'm coming over there after I get off work. I have to hang up now, but I want to talk about this some more later. Okay?"

"I'll text you my address." Moonflower sounded relieved.

As they said their good-byes and hung up, Crystal knew she had to find some way to convince her aging hippie friend to talk to the police. Before the unthinkable happened.

And someone else ended up dead.

Juliette hated having to do this by telephone, where she couldn't look these men in the eye nor observe their body language. She had hoped she and Didi might at least be able to Skype in, but the FBI agents had nixed that idea right off. They weren't exactly keen on bringing them into the conversation via conference call either, but at least they had allowed it.

Now they were fifteen minutes into that call, with Elsa, Natalie, and two male agents on speakerphone on that end and Juliette and Didi each on her own phone on this end. So far, almost the entire conversation had been just one long rapid-fire question-and-answer session. The two agents weren't big on explaining much, but there sure was a lot they wanted to know.

Had any strange calls come into the company lately?

Had any unusual orders been placed?

Had there been any unique customer requests of late?

Had there been any recent repairs done to the facility, or had any workmen shown up claiming to be from the phone or gas or electric company?

"Basically, we're looking for anything out of the ordinary," the agent said, stating the obvious. He went on to say that they needed information about all new accounts opened and all employees hired within the past year.

Juliette bristled at the request. Why hadn't she thought to bring the company lawyers in on the conversation as well? It sounded like Elsa was typing into the computer, already complying, but Juliette called that to a halt.

"We're happy to answer some basic questions, but I'm afraid that's as far as it goes for now. If you want confidential information like this, you'll have to speak with our lawyers."

Didi's eyes widened as she peered over at Juliette and gave her a thumbs-up.

On the other end of the line, the two agents blustered a bit, but Juliette knew her rights. Before she handed over a single piece of the requested information, she wanted to know a whole lot more about why they were asking these things and what this investigation was about. Their earlier explanation that this had to do with the counterfeiting situation wasn't enough.

By the time the two men hung up, they were clearly unhappy with her, but what else could she do? She preferred to err to the side of caution and leave such matters in the hands of her lawyers, who were the experts.

Once they were off the phone, Juliette and Didi rehashed the entire conversation, going back over each of the questions. Though neither one could think of any recent abnormalities or aberrations, they called Elsa back and told her to ask around a bit among some of the other employees to make sure. They also asked if she would take a closer look at the information the agents had wanted, details on new accounts and new employees, just for their own in-house knowledge for now. Elsa promised to get right on it and said she would contact them if she came up with anything unusual.

By the time all was said and done, it was nearly 12:30 p.m., which gave Juliette just an hour and a half before the start of the retreat—time enough to grab a light lunch, see to the final details of the event, and renew her notes for her talk. She had spent the entire day thus far on matters related to Raven's death and to the counterfeiting issue. And though she wasn't even close to finding the answers to her many questions, she would need to put all of that out of her mind for now regardless and focus on the event that lay ahead.

Already attendees were no doubt arriving, checking in, getting settled. They had each come here expecting a great retreat, and it was up to Juliette to meet—and hopefully exceed—their expectations. God willing, this weekend would be all about its stated theme,

Serving While Preserving: Helping Others without Ignoring Ourselves. These women deserved her full attention despite all the turmoil that seemed to rage on every side.

Chapter Twenty

Juliette stood in the shadows to the side of the stage, smiling as she watched the retreat's introductory session get underway. They were starting with a skit, and though she knew the script by heart, it was fun to see it acted out, especially when the women playing the roles were as talented as these two volunteers from a local church's drama team.

Each character represented opposite ends of the spectrum, one a constant do-gooder kept so busy with volunteer duties and other acts of service that she was at her limit and completely frazzled. The other was all about self, lazy and demanding and pampered. The two women played their roles perfectly, and by the volume of the laughter coming from out front, it was clear the audience thought so too.

The scene ended with both women realizing that something needed to be done. They said their final line in unison, "There's something very wrong here," then the lights came down and the two women moved to stand at each side of the stage as Juliette strode out to the center. When the lights came back up, the crowd got their first sight of their well-known hostess for the weekend and burst into enthusiastic applause.

Smiling, Juliette looked out at them and waited for the sound to die down. She had prayed for these people often over the past few weeks, prayed that they would come here with open hearts and open minds—and that God would have her say the words they needed to hear during their time together. And though she would have several opportunities to speak to them over the next few days, this opening address was one of the most important, as it would set the tone for the entire weekend.

Once the applause finally wound down to a close, she began.

"If you saw yourself in either of these two women, there really is something very wrong here."

Audience members smiled, and many nodded.

Juliette gestured to the woman on her left, who gave a red-carpet-like pose, one hand behind her neck, the other on her hip. "For example, if you related a little too closely to our pampered princess here, well, let's just say it's time to start looking beyond the end of your own nose."

"What's wrong with my nose?" the woman cried in faux offense as she whipped out a hand mirror and examined her face. "This nose cost more than my last trip to Vegas!"

The audience chuckled.

"If, on the other hand, you related more to our over-burdened do-gooder, as I suspect many of you did . . ."

She gestured toward the woman on her right, who gripped her hair in both fists and let out a yell of frustration, much to the audience's delight.

"Well, then, let me just say you've come to the right place. Ladies, thank you so much for your help, let's give our actresses a hand."

The audience cheered as the two women bowed and made their exit. Waiting, Juliette looked out at the crowd and noticed a sprinkling of men among the women, no doubt family members and friends accompanying some of the guests. Though much of the retreat would be limited to attendees, a few parts were open to all, including this introductory session.

Juliette continued her speech once the

applause tapered off, explaining that Christians often had trouble finding the right balance in the area of service. "Some of us really do too much. We feed, we give, we tend, we comfort, we work hard to bless others in the name of Christ. And that's wonderful. We're great at caring for others. The problem is how difficult it is to allow others to care for us in return."

She paused, again looking out at the group. Eager eyes gazed back at her from around the room. Scanning the faces, she hesitated on one person in particular—a strikingly handsome man sitting in the next-to-last row. For some reason, his expression was not one of curiosity but rather of . . . what? Animosity? Irritation? Did this guy have something against her?

Forcing herself to ignore him for now, she continued with her talk, gesturing toward the screen behind her, which lit up with the words of a familiar verse.

"The Bible says a lot about the necessity of taking time to rest and rejuvenate, and today we're going to start by focusing on Psalm 46, verse 10, 'Be still and know that I am God.'"

Juliette dropped her arm and faced the audience straight on. "You know that verse well, but hear it again. Look at what it's telling us to do. Be *still*." She was silent for a long moment, her voice echoing in the quiet. "Be still," she said again, whispering this time, and once more followed her words by a long moment of silence.

Finally she took a step forward, making eye contact among the crowd, and spoke in a soft voice. "Do you ever stop and think how utterly un-still our lives have become? Friends, it's time to heed these words, to turn down the noise, to halt the activity, to stop the running, running, running. 'Be *still* and know that I am God.'" She took a deep breath and let it out slowly. "My prayer for this weekend, my prayer for you, is that you reconnect with what it truly means to 'Be still.'"

Marcus's mother gently elbowed him in the ribs then leaned in to whisper. "She's really something, isn't she?"

He nodded, unable to tear his eyes from the stage, where Juliette held the undivided attention of everyone in the room. *Really something* didn't begin to describe it. She was amazing. Luminous. Spellbinding.

"I wonder if she's married?" she added, eyes twinkling.

Not trusting himself to speak, Marcus merely grunted in reply. Prior to the disaster of his encounter with Juliette out by the bench, he would have silently rejoiced at the answer to that question, which was no. But once the woman had summarily rejected him, what difference did it make? Married or not, Juliette didn't want *him*, and that's all that really mattered. Marcus wanted to be bitter at that thought. After all he had gone through to get here, he had the right to a little self-pity. And yet . . .

And yet.

Watching her now, Marcus's heart ached, not from the pain of rejection, but from the thrill of seeing her this way, in her element. He just couldn't believe they were under the same roof again after all these years. They were breathing the same air, inhabiting the same space. Despite the fact that she wanted nothing to do with him, Marcus allowed himself to treasure those facts regardless.

As he'd suspected twenty-five years ago, Juliette Taylor was born to encourage and inspire. Already she had these women in the palm of her hand. Clearly she had been using her God-given gifts exactly the way He intended her to.

If only God had also intended for the two of them to be together. Obviously, that was not going to happen. But as Marcus watched the woman he'd come clear across the country to see, he knew he'd have to proceed regardless. She may not be interested in him romantically or even care that he was here. She may not even remember him, for that matter. But he'd known going in there would be no guarantees, emotionally speaking. And as difficult as it may be, he would persist with his original goal of connecting, friend to friend, for the purpose of keeping her safe.

He just wished it didn't hurt so bad.

Fifteen minutes later Juliette wrapped up her introductory talk to enthusiastic applause and took her seat at the side of the stage as Didi came out to the podium to review key information about the more logistical elements of their weekend—sessions, lectures, small groups, treatments, meals, and more.

As Didi spoke, Juliette peered out at the audience, her eyes again wandering to the man who was sitting in the next-to-last row, the one who'd been looking at her oddly earlier. His features seemed to have softened somewhat since then, thank goodness. Suddenly, as if he sensed her attentions, he shifted his eyes to meet her gaze. They locked in on each other for a long moment, and then Juliette looked away.

She just had the oddest feeling . . .

Did she know this man? She stole another glance and realized where she'd seen him. He was the one who came up to her on the path earlier, just moments after she learned that Raven had been murdered.

Her mind racing, Juliette tried to remember exactly what he'd said to her, and if she'd said anything in return. She couldn't recall. He did speak, she remembered that. A simple greeting? At the time his words had been drowned out by the pounding of her heart and the spinning of her mind. Now she tried her hardest to bring it back, but it was no use.

Thinking through their brief encounter, Juliette caught her breath, remembering something else. Not only had he spoken to her, he had also given her something. He'd handed it to her, something shiny, and all she'd been able to do was mumble and push past, shoving whatever he'd given her into . . . where? Her pocket?

As discreetly as possible, Juliette pressed her hands to her pants pockets, but both lay smooth and flat against her hips. No, she realized, not her pants pocket, her *jacket* pocket. Currently, that jacket was hanging across a chair in the back of the room. Looking toward it, Juliette's gaze once again met that of the handsome man. What had he given to her? Suddenly she very much wanted to know. For some reason she couldn't help but feel like whatever it was, it had been important. She needed to check that pocket!

The problem was that if she waited until Didi was finished, it would take forever to get back there. The crowd would spring from their seats and fill the aisles. People would try to talk to her, some of them at length. She didn't want to wait that long.

Better she go back there right now, while Didi was still talking and the audience members were still in their seats. Moving quietly Juliette stood and stepped down from the stage, avoiding all eye contact as she walked up a side aisle toward the back of the room. She'd almost reached the jacket when Didi launched into the closing prayer. Juliette stopped to join in, then she kept going after Didi's "amen." As expected, the room sprung to life, women laughing and talking as they stood and began to mingle. Seizing the moment, Juliette thrust her hand into one pocket and then the other until her fingers closed around something. Something small. She pulled it out and opened her hand. There in her palm was a silver foil packet with blue lettering.

A Peppermint Pattie.

In a flash the knowledge conveyed by that single piece of candy struck Juliette with such force that she had to sit for fear she might fall down.

It was him.

Marcus.

The one who got away.

Heart pounding, mind racing, Juliette looked up, hoping against hope that he would still be there, that he'd been watching and now understood by the shock in her eyes that she just didn't "get it" before.

But he was gone. The woman he'd been with was still there, chatting with several other guests, but Marcus Stone was nowhere to be seen.

Trying to keep her breath even and slow, Juliette stood and worked her way closer to that woman, who must be his mother. She had the same blue-gray eyes. Juliette had never forgotten his eyes.

Barely trusting herself to speak, Juliette introduced herself to the woman, who greeted her with a broad smile in return. "How nice to meet you. I'm Beverly. Beverly Stone."

Stone. So it really was true. Hearing his last name spoken out loud hit her like a sucker punch.

Somehow she managed to chat for a full minute before asking the question that was burning inside her. "The man sitting next to you—I assume that was your son?"

Beverley nodded, beaming. "That's my boy, Marcus. He insisted on bringing me, and I'm so glad he did."

Marcus Stone. After all these years.

Juliette knew it was probably time for Beverly to get to her first spa treatment, but she couldn't bring herself to end their conversation just yet. As the room emptied around them, she pressed onward. "Marcus Stone? Why does that name sound familiar? Did he say anything to you about whether or not he and I had ever met?"

Juliette knew she was being sneaky, and though she felt a little guilty about that, her brain was too addled at the moment to broach this topic any other way. Had the man not shown up here and given her a Peppermint Pattie at the get-go, she would have played things differently. But the candy changed everything. Clearly he wanted to remind her of what the two of them had once shared.

"No, but I hear that a lot with him. You've probably seen his picture in the papers or on the news, maybe read about him in *Newsweek*."

"*Newsweek* magazine?"

Beverly nodded. "He's an expert in disaster prevention and recovery. He's shown up in there a few times, once with a photo and everything."

"I see." Juliette's heart soared. An expert in

disaster prevention and recovery? So he'd done it! He really had changed the course of his life!

"Maybe I could introduce you to him tonight at dinner," Beverly added with a smile. "Right now I need to go, it's time for my first-ever scalp massage."

Juliette thanked her and watched as the woman turned and walked away. She stood in the quiet of the empty conference room for a long moment after that, pinballs pinging around inside her head and heart.

She had so many questions! Was he married? Did he have children?

Had their single encounter in that airport twenty-five years ago really changed his life as much as it had changed hers?

Taking a deep breath, Juliette headed out the door, pausing in the sunny lobby when she passed a resort employee. "Excuse me, may I ask you a strange question?"

"Yes. Of course." The woman gave her a polite smile.

Juliette took a deep breath and slowly blew it out. "Can you tell me if there's somewhere around here where I could buy a bag of Peppermint Patties?"

Marcus sat on the couch in his suite, remote in hand, flipping back and forth between a

Braves pregame special and an NFL Playoff analysis, unable to focus on either. He'd been sitting there for the past hour, ever since the opening session of the retreat came to a close, and he made a beeline out of the conference center auditorium to head straight back to the room. He'd have given anything not to go in the first place, but his mother had practically begged him, so he'd relented. The moment it was done, however, he had murmured an excuse and left. He just wasn't ready to come face-to-face with Juliette Taylor and get rejected again, even though he knew he couldn't put it off forever. He'd come here to see her and talk with her, and that's what he would do. Eventually.

He just needed some time to reframe things in his mind first. Time to recalculate the route.

Marcus groaned. He wasn't used to feeling like this. He was the one who alleviated other people's suffering, who stayed calm and cool-headed when disaster uprooted other people's lives. He showed them how to survive, how to cope, how to start over. Now he would have to take his own advice—only instead of navigating floodwaters or earthquake-damaged buildings, he would have to make his way through matters of the heart.

Not exactly his specialty.

Before he could even decide where to begin, the door opened and his mother walked in, raving about her first-ever spa treatment.

"That was simply amazing! I never knew that you could pay someone to massage your scalp, let alone that it would feel so grand!" Her eyes were sparkling, but her hair was a filthy, scrambled mess, like a greasy version of the tumbleweeds he'd seen on his earlier jog.

"Glad to hear you're enjoying yourself, Mom. Not sure what I think of the new 'do, though."

She laughed, reaching up to pat the top of her head gingerly. "It's all the conditioning oils. They said I'm supposed to leave them in for as long as I can stand it, but I think I'm about at that point already."

He chuckled. "You look like one of those ducks after the Macondo blowout, like we need to dip you in a tub of cleaning agent and tag you for release back into the wild."

She laughed again, and Marcus couldn't help but think how adorable she was. She'd always been an upbeat person, but he hadn't seen her this light and carefree in a long time.

"All teasing aside, Marcus, you've been looking pretty tense since we got here. You should think about getting one of those scalp massages yourself." She gestured toward the door. "That is, if they don't kick you out first for littering."

"Me? Littering?" Had the scalp massage scrambled her brain?

"Yes, dear, didn't you notice the mess you made out front when you spilled your candies?"

"What are you talking about, Mom?"

"I saw you with a Peppermint Pattie earlier today. I didn't know you had a whole bag, but it must have ripped open between here and the car, because they're spread all over the walk. A real mess."

Marcus stared at her but she simply clucked her tongue and told him he was far too old to expect his mother to clean up after him. "Besides, I have to get in the shower. I've had it with the oil, I know it's softening and conditioning, but it just feels too icky." She headed for her room, adding, "Don't forget, dinner's at six."

It couldn't be . . .

Could it?

Once she'd disappeared into her bedroom, Marcus jumped up and flung the front door open. One look confirmed what he hadn't dared to hope: There on the path outside was a long line of wrapped Peppermint Patties, practically forming a trail.

It *was* a trail. Had to be.

He paused only long enough to grab his room key and put on his shoes, then he set off to follow where it led.

That pursuit brought him down the walkway toward his car but then veered off to the right, in the direction of the jogging path. The foil-wrapped candies were spaced farther apart as he went, but it was still a definite and distinctive trail. He followed it across the parking lot, around the edge of the wooded area, and onto the jogging path. He made it through the stand of trees, and as he neared the bend around the big rock, he held his breath. When he got to the other side of that rock, he stopped in his tracks.

Standing before him, a smile on her face and a Peppermint Pattie in her open palm, was Juliette Taylor.

Chapter Twenty-One

Juliette stared into Marcus's vivid blue-gray eyes, her heart pounding. It had worked. Her cornball, chancy ploy had brought him to her just as she'd hoped.

"Hello." His greeting was tentative, cautious.

Juliette's throat went dry. She held out her hand. "Care for a Peppermint Pattie?"

He smiled then, the slightly crooked, incredulous smile that had melted her heart all those years ago. She'd remembered it, and yet she'd forgotten how powerfully it affected her.

"Yes, I would." He reached out to take the candy. "But don't call me Patty."

They grinned, eyes locked, neither one to look away.

"Marcus," she whispered.

"Juliette," he replied.

They continued to hold each other's gaze.

"I'm so sorry about earlier," she said. "I don't know what to say except that you showed up at the exact wrong time. I had just gotten some really bad news and I could barely think—or even see, for that matter. I had no idea why some guy was talking to me and trying to give me something. My mind was a trillion miles away."

His eyes filled with concern. "Is everything okay?"

She shrugged. "Long story, I can explain later. I just wanted you to understand it had nothing to do with you."

He nodded. "Well, I'm sorry for whatever happened that was so upsetting, but I'm glad to hear this just the same. The whole encounter was rather, uh, humiliating."

Juliette couldn't help but smile. How endearing he was! How honest. She'd forgotten that. "I can imagine. I saw you during the opening session, and though I had no idea who you were, I could tell by your expression that you were put out with me, like I'd hurt your feelings or something. The more I thought about it, I realized you must have been the guy who approached me earlier. Then I remembered being handed something. By the time I could check my pocket and found the candy, you had already left the auditorium."

The corners of his mouth twitched ruefully. "Yeah, I went to the session for my mom's sake, but I didn't feel like hanging around afterward and risk getting snubbed again."

"Aw. Forgive me?"

"Absolutely. And I'm sorry too, about the timing, I mean."

She waved away the thought. "Not your fault."

"Is there anything I can do to help?"

"No, but thanks for asking. It's complicated.

He looked like he wanted to say something but then changed his mind, glancing away as he slipped his hands into his pockets.

"Right now, I just need to ask the obvious question," she said.

He waited, eyebrows raised.

"Marcus, what are you doing here? Obviously, you knew I would . . ." Her voice trailed off as she gestured toward the silver-wrapped candy he still held in his hand. "Well, they don't exactly have those things in the resort's vending machines. You came prepared."

"The truth is . . ." He faltered, cleared his throat, tried again. "I came here specifically to see you. I mean, my mom definitely deserved the trip, but I'm feeling kind of guilty because she doesn't know I was just using her to get myself here."

"She doesn't know about—" Juliette caught herself in time, but then he finished the sentence for her anyway.

"About us? Nope. I probably should've told her, but that would've made me too self-conscious. After all, what if I walked up to you to say hello and you just snubbed me, like took the candy and kept going?" Glancing at her, eyes twinkling, he added, "Oh right, that *is* what happened."

She chuckled.

"Anyway, at that point I was really glad I hadn't told her. I mean, it was bad enough by myself, but it would've been far worse if she'd known our history and had witnessed such a complete and utter rejection."

Again Juliette chuckled. Again, he was being so honest. It made her dare to be honest in response. She looked at him, her head tilted.

"But why now, Marcus? Why now, after so many years?"

He looked away, a cloud passing across his eyes for a long moment. "It's hard to explain. For one thing, the timing seemed right, I guess."

"The timing," she echoed. "Are you saying you've come to find me at last?"

His cheeks colored at her words, but to his credit he didn't try to bluff his way out. "That's part of it. Too extreme?"

She chewed her bottom lip, unsure whether she wanted to punch him or kiss him. Maybe both. "About as extreme as the fact that I've been waiting for you to show up for the past twenty-five years."

And there it was, she had laid her heart out on the table too. Suddenly emboldened, she took it a step further. "I ought to deck you right here, you know."

"Deck me?" His confusion was tinged with startled delight.

She raised two fists. "Yeah, like punch your lights out? Knock your block off?"

Marcus laughed. "Knock my block off? I don't think anyone's used that expression since we were kids and boxing robots were all the rage."

He was charming, but she maintained her stance, unwilling to back down.

"Seriously," he added, smile fading. "Why do you say that?"

She couldn't keep the sarcasm from her response. "Um, do you own a calendar, Marcus? Do you even grasp the concept of time? It's been twenty-five years! What took you so long?" She lowered her fists and placed her hands on her hips.

"Juliette, I—"

"I'm serious! Sorry, but as thrilled as I am to see you, I won't let you off that easily. You said you would come and find me and you didn't."

He cleared his throat, a pained expression on his face. "Actually, I did."

"Oh? When?" Her eyes narrowed.

"Exactly two years after the day we met. I knew you were making an appearance at a big charity benefit, and I was going to surprise you by showing up there."

Juliette took a step back, her mind racing. Two years after they met, she'd been living in Philadelphia with her sister, significantly healed from the trauma of her modeling years and trying to decide what she wanted the next phase of her life to look like. She'd been doing a lot of volunteer work back then and also lending her celebrity to various causes, which was how she'd met Mike.

Her fiancé, Mike.

Juliette's eyes widened as she looked at Marcus, afraid to hear what he was going to say next.

He nodded somberly. "That very afternoon I was all checked in to my hotel and had about an hour before it was time to get ready for the event. I was just reading the sports section of the Philly paper when I saw your picture with Mike Parshall and read the little headline, 'Eagles Wide Receiver to Marry Supermodel.'"

Juliette's hand came up to cover her mouth. "Oh, Marcus."

"Yeah, not the best moment of my life. Needless to say, I packed up and headed out."

"Without even contacting me?"

He shrugged. "You were newly engaged, I had no right to come in and mess that up."

"But to not even let me know?"

He studied her face for a long moment. "In retrospect, I guess I could have dropped you a note or something after the fact. But I was hurt. Idiot that I am, I thought you would've waited for me."

Much to her surprise and embarrassment, Juliette's eyes suddenly filled with tears.

In response Marcus stepped closer and took her hands in his. "Hey, hey. Look, it was all my fault, not yours. It took me too long. I should've come sooner. I should've stayed in touch with you instead of waiting until I was established and ready. That was really dumb on my part. I mean, come on. What was I thinking?"

Blinking away her tears, Juliette looked down at their clasped hands, unable to meet his eyes as he continued.

"At least I learned some valuable lessons from all of that." He gave her hands a firm squeeze and released them.

Juliette dropped her arms to her sides.

"Oh? What, snooze you lose? Strike while the iron's hot? Don't count your chickens before they hatch?"

His face flushed. "All of the above. But the whole experience also taught me to live a more balanced life. To not surrender one area for another. Like, don't sacrifice love for the sake of work. That kind of thing."

"That kind of thing," she echoed.

"I mean, from the day you and I met, I spent the next two years living with complete tunnel vision, totally focused on breaking away from the firm and establishing myself in the field in a new way."

"That's exactly what you were supposed to be doing."

He nodded. "Yeah, but not at the expense of everything else. Once I got home from my failed trip to Philly, I took a long, hard look at my life. Started dating again. Tried to forget about us and move on."

So Marcus had moved on—even as she and Mike eventually called off their engagement and she spent more than the next two decades *not* moving on, romantically speaking, at least not in any significant way. Unbelievable. Fearing her knees might buckle, she looked back for the bench they had passed, spotting it not far from the big rock, tucked amidst flowering shrubs.

"I need to sit down," she murmured as she began walking toward it, her head pounding with one thought, *If only I had known.*

If only I had known.

As soon as Crystal was done for the day, she changed out of her work uniform into shorts and a T-shirt and beelined to her car. She pulled out the county map and studied it until she located Canyon Drive, where Moonflower lived. It looked like quite a trip—maybe fifteen or twenty miles—but she needed to talk to the woman in person regardless.

Half an hour later, she was there. As she turned in, she saw that the driveway was in worse shape than the road. She had to dodge potholes right and left as she inched her way toward the house.

If it could be called a house.

The structure was a geodesic dome, constructed of wood with a natural finish and blending in with the background foliage. Wildflowers grew along the walkway and beside the steps that led to a small deck at the front door. Beyond the dome, more wildflowers peppered a small meadow between house and woods. A stone birdbath and some feeders dotted the yard, and numerous wind chimes tinkled from where they hung among the trees. As Crystal began to climb the steps, the door swung open.

"You made it." Moonflower was wearing a shapeless, flowing muumuu, tie-dyed in varying shades of blue and green. "Any trouble finding the place?"

"Nah," Crystal said, not wanting to complain. When she reached the doorway, Moonflower welcomed her with a tight hug, smelling of jasmine and rose petals.

The older woman brought her inside and offered her tea, and soon Crystal was sitting at a small, rough-hewn table in the kitchen, watching her friend set water to boil on the stove as she launched right into the topic of Raven.

Grief darkened Moonflower's lovely face as she told how they'd met twenty years ago, when the supermodel first came to the spa. "Almost right away, I could see how empty her soul was. I poured all the compassion I had into that girl."

"I'm sure she appreciated it."

"Maybe. She didn't show her gratitude like most people."

"No?"

She sighed, placing loose tea in a ball and hanging it in a brown pottery teapot. "Raven was angry on the outside, but on the inside she was just a scared and helpless child. She had a hard life before she made it big. The wounds went very, very deep."

Crystal wanted to know more but it wasn't her right to ask.

Once the water was hot enough, Moonflower took it from the stove and poured it into the teapot. After replacing the lid, she took a step back from the counter. "Now we give it time to steep. A lot of people don't do that, but we all need it—time to steep. That's what I've been trying to do today."

"To steep?"

Moonflower nodded soberly. "While I was steeping, I realized something. I know you want me to talk to the cops, but you need to understand, it's not always up to us to change things. Sometimes we need to sit back and contemplate what life has done to us, not rush out with the blind idea that we have to do something *to* life."

Crystal struggled mightily to keep her voice calm. "And Raven's killer? If you don't tell the police what you know, don't you think he'll seek and find his next victim in due time?"

Moonflower's head jerked, as if the peaceful aura she'd spent the afternoon building had shattered in one quick blow. When she spoke, her lips were tight. "Other forces are in play here, and changes will happen whether we interfere or not."

Crystal's lips went tight as well. "But somebody *already* interfered, big time—with Raven's life, with Brooke's, with yours. With a lot of people's, including everyone at Palm Grotto."

Moonflower seemed sadder and more distressed than Crystal had ever seen her, and yet on some level she retained that calmness, every movement one of purpose.

"Come on, let's sit. Bring the mugs, will you?" Moonflower grabbed the pot with both hands and carried it into the living area, where she set it on a low table and then took her seat in a nearby rocking chair.

Crystal chose a recliner and sat, looking around at the simple furnishings of Moonflower's home. A loft extended partway across the room, and hanging from its rafters were bunches of herbs. Underneath was a work area filled with large jars and pottery crocks, a stone mortar and pestle sitting idle on the table.

"Is that where you create your rubs and oils?" Crystal asked.

"Yes, that's my workshop. Currently I'm perfecting a new lemon foot scrub made with Sea Salt."

"Nice."

Finally Moonflower poured their tea. Crystal accepted hers and took a sip, the fragrant blend unusual but soothing.

Glancing over at Moonflower, Crystal decided to drop the whole police matter for now and come at things from a different angle. Wrapping both hands around her warm mug, she lowered it to her lap and fixed her gaze on her friend. "On the phone earlier you said that Raven was being blackmailed."

Moonflower nodded ever so slightly, avoiding her eyes.

"Why don't you tell me a little more about that?"

The woman shrugged, her face growing a deep red.

"It's okay, really." Crystal spoke in the soft, cajoling tones one might use with a skittish horse or a nervous child. "Think of it this way, Moonflower. Your friendship with Raven got you into this mess, whatever it is. Maybe your friendship with me can help get you out."

There was so much that needed to be said, and yet neither one spoke at all. Instead Juliette and Marcus simply sat side by side on the bench by the big rock, sharing a contemplative silence. This she remembered about him, that he didn't rush to fill the quiet spaces.

And she wanted quiet at the moment, to

think things through and regain at least some control over her emotions. She hated that he had seen her teary eyes and wobbly knees. Breathing deeply she prayed for peace and composure.

Finally, aware of the passing time, Juliette pulled out her phone to see how much longer until her one free hour of the afternoon was done. Nine minutes.

Not nearly enough for all she needed to say, for all she wanted to know.

Juliette opened her scheduling app to take a look at the rest of the day, and Marcus must've realized what she was doing, because he quickly apologized for holding her up if she needed to be somewhere. She explained that she hated to cut things short, but that she had to lead a small group starting at 4:00 p.m. After that, she would be busy with retreat matters straight through until 9:00 p.m.

"I knew you'd probably be kept pretty busy, but please tell me we can get back together afterward. We've got a lot of catching up to do."

He sounded so earnest, so eager, that once again she found herself utterly disarmed. Guys usually went one of two ways with her, either they fawned all over her, smothering her with attention and adoration, or they worked hard to play it cool around her, like they thought she'd be impressed with their indifference.

Not so this guy, which was one of the things she had liked most about him way back when. Even now, all these years later, his genuineness remained. Marcus Stone was a good guy, definitely not the kind who put on a fake persona in an attempt to manipulate.

Leaning slightly closer to him now, Juliette showed Marcus the screen of her phone, pointing out that guests were welcome to the last three parts of the evening, which were dinner at the restaurant, a sunset hike, and an hour of fun and games.

"Great." His grin warmed her to her toes. "Sounds like I'll be having dinner at the restaurant, taking a sunset hike, and enjoying an hour of fun and games."

She returned his smile, feeling far less shaky now. "Of course, I'll have to circulate during all three, but once game time is over, maybe we can be alone again to talk some more."

He nodded, locking his blue-gray eyes on hers. "I'd really like that, to talk some more."

She held his gaze for a long moment but finally forced herself to look away. "Right now, though, I really need to run."

"I understand. How 'bout I clean up the candy trail while you get to where you need to be."

"Thanks. I appreciate that."

They both stood and began walking up the path toward the tree line. As they got closer, Juliette hesitated, unable to save her most burning question for later.

"You know I broke off that engagement, right? To Mike?"

Marcus paused there on the path as well, his expression unreadable. "I know."

Her eyes widened. "So why . . ." She couldn't even bring herself to finish the sentence.

He seemed to understand regardless. "That didn't happen until, what, like nine or ten months later? And then I didn't hear about it for a few months after that. By the time I found out, it was too late." He cleared his throat. "By the time I found out, I was married."

Married?

Juliette froze, crestfallen.

Married.

Seeing her expression, Marcus quickly added, "Oh, sorry, not anymore. I'm not married now."

She waited, needing more than that.

"It's a long story," he added. "Bottom line, she left ten years ago. These days, she's remarried and living in France."

She wanted to ask about kids but knew they didn't have time right now. So instead she just nodded and thanked him for telling her. Then she was off, walking across the grounds of the resort, feeling sad and happy and confused and ecstatic and heartbroken and hopeful—all at the same time.

Chapter Twenty-Two

Crystal sat back, intent on Moonflower's explanation of what the blackmailer had on Raven. The aging therapist took the long way around to get to the point, but the story she told was fascinating.

And heartbreaking.

According to Moonflower, Raven's real name was Rayleen, and she'd been born in some backwater town in the Appalachian mountains. She'd been a gangly child, but by her early teens had begun to blossom, eventually growing tall and stunning. Rayleen's mother was a horrible woman, a part-time barmaid and full-time drunk with six kids, all from different fathers. Rayleen was the oldest, and she didn't even know who her father was.

She did, however, know who her mother's boyfriends were. That's because most of them made a point of visiting her late at night, once her mother had passed out drunk. By the time Rayleen was sixteen, she'd learned to defend herself, and she was doing whatever she could to get out of there for good. Her dream was to be an actress, and she waitressed at a truck stop out on the highway, trying to make enough money to go to California and pursue a film career.

Then one day a customer strode into the truck stop, a man wearing nice clothes and with an expensive haircut. As he chatted with the tall, beautiful waitress, he explained that he was a filmmaker from New York, in the area to scout out filming locations.

Rayleen had learned long ago to trust no man, but this guy seemed different. He never made a pass at her, for one thing. Instead, he encouraged her dream of becoming an actress but said he thought she should start on the stage, in New York, rather than out west in L.A.

"If you live in New York, I can use you for some film work, too, if you're interested," he'd said. "But I think Broadway's where you really belong." Before he left, he gave her his card and said if she ever made it up to the Big Apple to give him a call.

Three months later she did just that. In that very first conversation, he offered her an "extended audition." She'd been thrilled, thinking this would be her big break.

"You're okay with nudity, right?" he'd asked just before hanging up the phone, his voice insinuating that if she wasn't, then she couldn't possibly be a serious actress.

She had mumbled out some sort of reply, saying she might if it were "justified." But she hoped the issue wouldn't come up at all.

"Back then Raven was savvy in some ways but not in others." Moonflower sounded like she wanted to weep. "In the end, that extended audition was recorded on film—and it involved nudity and more. The man seemed legitimate, so she'd let her guard down—acting out a scene with him exactly as directed. Afterwards, when she realized how he'd tricked her, it was too late."

"Oh, no." Crystal's mug of tea grew cold in her hands. "What'd she do?"

Moonflower pressed her lips into a tight line. "Well, she started by begging the guy to destroy the film, but he refused. It absolutely killed her that she had trusted him. She'd even signed a release. There was nothing she *could do*."

"What happened?"

Moonflower shrugged. "I'll tell you one thing that happened, the day she walked away from that, she built a shell around her heart—a hard, thick shell that no one could ever crack. Dyed her hair vivid red, changed her name to Raven, and never looked back."

"Poor thing."

Moonflower glanced down at her mug, then set it on the small table beside her as she continued. "At least she landed on her feet. Stuck it out. Kept trying to pursue her dream. Sadly, all she wanted to be was an actress, but she had far more success as a model. She tried to do both for a while, but once her modeling career took off, the acting kind of fell by the wayside."

Crystal leaned forward, elbows on her knees. "What about the film?"

"It never surfaced, at least not that she knew of. We discussed it in some of our earliest sessions, and eventually she seemed to work things through. At least she found a peace about it—or she had until a few months ago, when a letter came out of the blue. A blackmail letter."

Crystal's eyes widened. "After all these years?"

Moonflower nodded. "The person who wrote it said he had an explicit film of her as a young woman, and unless she forked over twenty thousand dollars, he was going to post it on the Internet. Her first thought, of course, was that the photographer himself was doing this for some reason, but she looked into it and learned that the man died years ago."

"Wow."

Moonflower nodded. "Her manager advised her to call the guy's bluff, said it wouldn't hurt her career, that in this day and age an explicit film could actually give her a career *boost*."

"Wait—career? I thought she retired from modeling a long time ago."

"She did. For the past ten years or so, she's been living in L.A., trying again as an actress."

"So is that what she decided to do? Turn the blackmailer down?"

Moonflower pulled a loose thread from her muumuu, her face unreadable. "Not immediately. The letter came in January, just a couple of days before her semiannual visit here, so she brought it with her and showed it to me, to get my advice. I told her I needed a day to think about it, then I spent most of that afternoon and evening reading through her entire file, trying to refresh my memory by going over all of my old treatment notes. The next day—"

"Wait, what did your treatment notes have to do with anything?"

Moonflower blinked, surprised by the question. "They provided a good record of all the things she'd shared with me over the years."

"The things she shared? Verbally?"

"Of course. Don't you keep treatment notes?"

"Yeah, sure, about *physical* issues. In a million years I wouldn't write anything down about *emotional* things. Especially if it was something I'd been told in confidence."

"I only saw the woman twice a year." Moonflower shrugged. "How else was I going to remember all the stuff she told me if I didn't write it down?"

Crystal frowned. While Moonflower may have been a fully trained and licensed massage therapist, she was definitely not a fully trained or licensed *mental health* therapist. And yet it sounded as if she'd practically been conducting private counseling sessions along with Raven's massages!

"Anyway, once I'd done some reading and brought myself up to speed, I told Raven that I agreed with her manager, that she should refuse to pay and let the chips fall where they may."

Crystal's eyes widened.

"Oh, not for the same reason he said. I just felt it was important that she not be ruled by another's threats. Also, I thought if the film actually did get out, she might find it liberating, in a way."

"*Liberating?*"

"Secrets can be like battery acid, eating

away at the soul. The threat of that stupid movie had hung over her for so long, I thought that having it out there might put an end to the matter. No more waiting for that other shoe to drop, you know?"

Crystal sat back. While she understood what Moonflower was saying, she certainly didn't agree. It sounded like poor Raven had been a victim her whole life. The last thing she needed was for the world to witness a filmed version of that victimization.

"So anyway, she said she was going to take my advice. As far as I know, she went back home and turned the blackmailer down."

"And the movie came out?"

"Not that I ever heard, actually. When I learned Raven was coming here outside her regular biannual schedule, I thought maybe she needed to talk about whatever happened with all of that." Her expression grim, Moonflower met Crystal's eyes. "Now that she's been murdered, I have to believe it all ties in together somehow."

"But how?"

Moonflower's fingers returned to the loose thread, only now her hands were trembling. "I'm not sure, but I've been thinking about it all day. My guess is that the blackmailer was bluffing, that maybe he *knew* about the film but didn't actually *have* it. Then when she called his bluff, he got so mad that he killed her."

Crystal's eyes widened. "And because you were the one who advised her to turn him down, you think that means you're next?"

Moonflower shrugged, dropping the thread and clasping her hands together in her lap. "I didn't think that at first. But then I tried calling her manager to get more information, and it's like the man has ceased to exist."

"What do you mean?"

She sighed. I think he's gone into hiding—and that maybe I should too. Because if Raven's killer isn't caught soon, I just might end up becoming the next victim."

Much to Juliette's relief, for the next hour she somehow found a way to put Marcus from her mind and focus on the task at hand. She loved doing these retreats so much, it wasn't difficult to immerse herself in it. The women in her small-group session were delightful, and their discussion about priorities and time management ended up being as helpful to her as it was to them. Juliette taught a seeker's Sunday school class back at home, and though she appreciated the opportunity to tackle the doubts and confusions of those new to or considering the faith, sometimes it just felt good to be surrounded by mature Christians instead, women who knew exactly what they believed and why they believed it.

After small group came the dinner hour, which ended up being a bit more difficult to get through. At every retreat Juliette tried to use the mealtimes as a way to connect with her attendees on a more casual level. She would sit with a different group each meal, and once she was finished eating, she always tried to circulate a bit, pausing at the different tables to chat. Usually she enjoyed it, but having Marcus Stone there in the very same room made it nearly impossible to focus. As her partner in this secret bond known only to them, he tormented her ruthlessly with flirty winks and sly glances clearly designed to tease.

She shot him one or two pointed looks in return, but Didi was far too omnipresent— not to mention perceptive—for Juliette to get away with more than that. At least Marcus's mother seemed oblivious to their interactions. Clearly a natural in social settings, she was too busy chatting with newfound friends to notice anything beyond her own table.

As for that table, Juliette avoided it for as long as she could, but eventually she had no choice but to make the obligatory stop there as well. As she did, she positioned herself with one hand on the back of Marcus's chair, ready to give him a discreet poke if he tried any monkey business. He stayed on his best behavior, however, even when his own mother "introduced" them.

Somehow Juliette managed to muddle through, but as dinner ended and the group set off on their sunset hike, she discreetly pulled him aside to let him know that his antics weren't funny.

"These people paid good money to be here," she whispered as they started down the walkway. "It's hard enough to give them the attention they deserve without you constantly making faces at me from across the room."

He apologized, but from the slant of his grin she could tell he wasn't really sorry.

They continued trudging along, taking an uphill trail past the mud baths and the Watsu pools. Eventually they came to a broad clearing where they could spread out and watch as the sun set behind the mountains in the distance.

Tonight's sky was cloudless and clear, and as the glowing orb slipped down behind the far peaks, the horizon took on a beautiful pinkish–purple hue. The hike was being led by a resort employee, and as one by one the brightest of stars and planets began to appear in the sky, he pointed them out by name.

A few of the hikers had brought along their cameras, and many of those who hadn't were using their camera phones. Juliette was standing a short way behind the crowd, taking in the happy sight of everyone snapping away, when she sensed a presence beside her. Marcus.

She had trouble tearing her eyes away—she could gaze at him forever. She'd never been able to imagine him as older than thirty, but here he was, a gorgeous specimen of a mature man. Turning away, Juliette told herself to calm down, that she was being ridiculous. She barely knew this man. She'd spent time with him only once, and that had been many, many years ago. For all she knew, he was a psychopath or a serial killer.

Then again, she admitted to herself with a small smile, the very thought of that was ludicrous. Stranger or not, Marcus Stone exuded goodness from his very pores. To spend five minutes with the man was to know he was about as solid and dependable and kind as they come. To think that she'd blown it all those years ago by accepting the proposal of a man she didn't love enough simply broke her heart. Earlier Marcus had said it was his fault, that he shouldn't have waited so long to come and find her. But she knew the truth, that she shared the blame. She should have waited.

She should have trusted that he really would show up once he was ready.

"A penny for your thoughts," he said now, his voice a warm whisper in her ear.

Feeling her cheeks flush with heat, Juliette gave him a shy smile and replied, "I was just playing a little 'what if.'"

"Ah, yes, the ol' 'what if.' When it comes to you and me, babe, that's a game I know well."

They shared a rueful smile, and for just a moment she felt the warmth of his hand brush across hers. Then he simply moved away, going over to stand beside his mother to ooh and ahh at the pictures she'd taken.

Fun and game time back at the conference center followed, and though team assignments were random, the two of them somehow ended up in the same group. Marcus proved to be every bit the competitor she was, and together they were nearly undefeatable. After a while, however, Juliette sensed Didi watching her, and she realized she needed to tone down her behavior lest she give away her biggest secret—that her TOTGA, as Didi liked to call him, was alive and well and sitting right next to her on the sofa! Juliette made a point of separating herself from him during the refreshment break, but once that break was over and it was time for the final round of competition, Didi pulled her aside.

"The guy is a major hunk, I'll give you that." Didi spoke softly as she tossed a paper cup into the trash can. "But you might want to tone things down just a tad. As my mama used to say, when you meet a fellow you really like, it never hurts to play it a little close to the vest."

Juliette rolled her eyes. "Point taken, Ms. Finkelton."

When fun and games drew to a close half an hour later, Juliette found herself nearly breathless with the anticipation of spending time alone with Marcus. She wasn't sure where they might find some relative privacy where they could talk, but if need be they could always head into town and look for a coffee shop or something.

Extricating herself from Didi, however, was going to be an issue. Every time they did these retreats, the two of them made a point of ending each day back in one of their rooms, sitting in their pajamas, debriefing and discussing the day. Juliette supposed she could make up some fib about having a headache or something, but that wouldn't be right. Besides, she already felt guilty enough about not telling her very best friend in the world the truth about who this man was.

She would tell her eventually, of course, but not yet. Definitely not yet.

Juliette was still trying to decide how she was going to get out of her debriefing with Didi when the evening drew to a close. The group gathered for a prayer, and though it lasted perhaps a minute at most, she felt the telltale vibration in her pocket of at least three text messages coming in while she prayed. After a hearty group "amen," she pulled out her phone and noticed Didi doing the same as well.

Looking down at the screen, Juliette saw that there were, indeed, three messages, and that they had all come from Elsa, back at home. Elsa? At this hour? At 9 p.m. here, it was midnight there. Looking more closely, she saw that even though the messages had come through all at once, they'd each been sent about an hour apart, starting about two hours ago. Pulse surging, she read them in order.

> Sorry to interrupt, but I've been going through some records as per our earlier conversation. We need to talk. Call when you get a minute.

The next one sounded a bit more urgent.

> Did you get my text? Really need to talk! Am heading home now but will keep cell handy. Please call ASAP.

Juliette swallowed hard as she moved on to the third message.

> Still up, still waiting to hear back from you.
> Will try calling your rooms.

Raising her head, Juliette's eyes met Didi's. Whatever Elsa had turned up, it couldn't be good.

By the time Crystal left Moonflower's house, it was late. Though she felt bad leaving her friend in such a state, there wasn't much else she could do for her at the moment. Moonflower remained adamant on not calling the police, which now left Crystal in the difficult position of having to choose between going to them herself or respecting her friend's trust and privacy.

As she barreled down the quiet, empty highway, she once again reviewed the blackmail situation in her mind, trying to make sense of it all. One thing Moonflower had said kept coming back to her: *My guess is that the blackmailer was bluffing, that maybe he knew about the film but didn't actually have it.*

If the film never surfaced after Raven called the blackmailer's bluff, then that theory made sense. According to Moonflower, only four people even knew it existed: the now-deceased photographer, Raven, Raven's manager, and Moonflower. Given that, how could the blackmailer have found out? No sooner had Crystal asked herself that question than the answer popped into her head.

The notes!

Moonflower's treatment notes!

If someone had gotten hold of those and read through them, they would've learned all about Raven's youthful indiscretion. Then, once they had that information, they could've put together a blackmailing scheme even without having the film itself. If that's what happened, then it really was true. The blackmailer was only bluffing, so when Raven turned him down, he must have decided to kill her instead.

Crystal's mind raced as pieces of this puzzle began to click into place. Everyone at the spa knew that Raven confided in Moonflower. If someone also knew that Moonflower kept a written record of those confidentialities—and where she stored that record—all he'd have to do was break into that locker and read Raven's file.

Certainly the late redhead had had enough enemies around that place. Was it really that big of a stretch to imagine that one of them chose blackmail as a means to get even?

Crystal's heart pounded with a sudden

realization: Raven's killer was someone they knew, someone with whom they worked at the spa, side-by-side, day after day.

Chapter Twenty-Three

Didi stayed in the game room and tried to get Elsa on the phone while Juliette herded the last of the group from the building. As she led the handful of stragglers toward the lobby exit, Marcus fell in beside her to ask if something was wrong.

"Just an issue at the home office. I'm sorry I can't slip away yet."

Though his face showed deep concern, Marcus didn't push. Instead, he assured her he didn't mind waiting, that he could use the time to help get his mother settled in their suite for the night. They exchanged cell phone numbers so she could text him when she was done, then Juliette called out a friendly, "See you in the morning!" to everyone and closed the door behind them all.

She returned to the now otherwise empty

game room to find Didi sitting on the couch, Elsa on speakerphone.

"So what's up?" Juliette plopped down next to Didi.

"We were waiting for you to get into the details, but it has to do with the FBI."

Juliette nodded, listening as Elsa launched into an explanation for them both.

"I was doing some in-house follow-up on the questions the FBI agents were asking us earlier, you know, like talking with employees and going through records and stuff. The reason I wanted to talk to you guys is because I may have found something, a new account that seems kind of odd."

Juliette and Didi exchanged alarmed glances as Elsa went on from there.

"The thing about this company that first caught my eye was the fact that it showed no affiliation with any salon or spa."

"That's unusual, but not unheard of," Didi interjected.

"Worth taking a closer look, though," Juliette added.

Elsa continued. "I thought so too. Anyway, the contact's name is David Walden, the company is JSM Enterprises, and they're located in Phoenix, Arizona. According to our records, they placed a small order just once, back in September, for less than $100."

Juliette's eyes widened. "A hundred dollars? Anyone with an order of that size should be buying retail, not wholesale."

"Ordinarily yes," Elsa replied. "But this was a sample request. Ruth handled the sale, and she has it marked as a 'new vendor.'"

"Did she follow up after the fact to see how the company liked the products and if they wanted to place a full order?"

"Yes, her file notes indicate that she tried to contact the man two weeks after the order was sent but that the phone number had been disconnected. I tried it myself and it still is."

Elsa went on to explain how she decided to do a quick Internet check on the address—only to learn that it was bogus. Rather than being a legitimate location in some Phoenix office building, it was actually that of a shipping store, the kind that could be used by people who wanted to receive packages anonymously.

"I spoke to the manager there, and she was able to confirm that the shipment was received by them and picked up by the customer on the same day. Not surprisingly, no one on staff there at the shipping store remembers that particular transaction at all. Ruth doesn't remember much about it either, other than her surprise that the phone number didn't work when she tried to follow up."

Juliette wasn't sure what to think. This could be nothing—or it could be really important. There was just no way to know for sure without more information. She said as much, and Didi and Elsa both concurred.

"I think I've done everything I can to track this down on our end," Elsa told them. "Though I imagine if anyone could take it from here, it would be the FBI."

Juliette suggested they wait until they heard back from the lawyers before doing anything else with the information. Elsa and Didi agreed. Once they thanked Elsa and concluded their call, Juliette and Didi just sat there together for a while in silence, one thought going around and around in Juliette's mind. Her life had been on an even keel for so long . . .

Why was everything falling apart *now*, just when she'd finally found Marcus again?

Marcus waited until his mother went to bed, then headed back out into the night. Juliette hadn't texted him yet to say she was finished, but in the meantime he could scope out some place at the resort where they could chat with relative privacy.

According to the literature in his information packet, the only public areas open at this

hour were the grotto and the patios that surrounded it. That was near the resort entrance,
so he decided to drive up rather than walk,
thinking that if it didn't pan out, his car
would be handy to take a quick run into town
and look for something there. No telling how
long Juliette would be, but if he could find
a place before she did, that would give them
more time to focus on each other.

From the main parking lot he headed
toward the grotto, pausing at the top of the
stone steps, surprised to see that the grotto
area wasn't illuminated at all. There were
no underwater lights to create the glowing
blue of a nighttime pool, no overhead beams
shining down on the patios. Instead, the
grotto pools looked inky black in the moonlight, the bodies in them mere shadows. He
would've thought such a setting unsafe if
not for the visible presence of roving security guards.

Candles flickered on a few of the patio
tables, which lent a small amount of light to
the scene. But otherwise the only bright spot
in view was about fifteen feet past the far
pool, the vivid orange flames of an outdoor
fireplace. Several empty chairs were clustered
in front of that fireplace, and Marcus realized
that might be the perfect spot for them to sit
and talk—innocent yet intimate.

He grunted, amending that last thought. As much as he wanted to reconnect with Juliette on a personal level, he had a more important task to accomplish first, that of figuring out how to keep her safe.

Marcus was about to head down the steps for a closer look at the fireplace area when he felt the gentle vibration of a text. It was from Juliette:

All done, where should we meet?

Marcus realized he was smiling like an idiot as the two of them went back and forth with several rapid texts. No, she didn't need him to pick her up; yes, she was catching a ride with a security guard. Yes, he'd be waiting for her at the fountain.

It was all he could do not to pump his fist as he moved to the fountain and stood there waiting. When the cart finally pulled up and Juliette climbed from it, his heart was pounding like crazy.

Once the cart drove off the two of them just stood there for a long moment, alone, the cool night breeze gently caressing the hair around her face. Unable to stop himself, Marcus reached out and brushed a tendril from her cheek.

He was about to speak when he heard what sounded like breaking glass. They both turned to look at a nearby building, the one that housed the resort's check-in desk and gift shop. Marcus could tell that the gift shop area in front was dark, but some lights were on in the back. His first thought was that someone was creeping around in there and had accidentally knocked something over. But then loud voices followed another crash of glass, and he nixed that theory. Thieves didn't yell, they whispered.

When a third crash of glass could be heard, Juliette suggested they call security.

Marcus gestured toward the steps. "There's a guard right down by the grotto. You go get him, I'll take a closer look."

"Be careful."

"You too." Marcus strode to the building and peered in through the glass. He could see a man and a woman standing in the back, behind the desk, deeply embroiled in an argument. Though the guy seemed relatively calm, the woman was livid. As Marcus watched, she grabbed something from a nearby shelf and threw it toward the man. Again came the sound of breaking glass.

Marcus's first thought was of a spurned female on the attack, but then he realized that this could just as well be a situation of self-defense. For all he knew she was throwing things to keep the man from advancing on her. Unwilling to risk it, Marcus tried the door, found it unlocked, and stepped inside.

"Why are you doing this?" The woman sounded near hysteria.

The man, however, replied with an exaggerated calm. "You violated company policy. I'm sorry, but it's as simple as that."

Marcus hesitated, as yet unnoticed. This didn't sound like an attack.

The man continued. "Look, you broke the rules, so now you're fired. It's that simple. Please finish clearing out your desk. I'm calling security to escort you from the property."

Ah, so it was a firing. Marcus turned to go, eager to slip out before either of them realized someone had been eavesdropping on this very private exchange.

"Rules can be bent sometimes!" The woman's voice was voice thick with tears. "Don't you know that? Didn't you learn your lesson last summer? Wasn't one death enough for you?"

Marcus froze, hand on the knob. What did she say?

Wasn't one death enough for you?

Juliette followed behind the security guard, holding her breath as he swung open the door to the main office. They both gasped, startled to see Marcus right there, as if he'd been about to come out. He stepped aside to let the guard pass, then moved out of the building, took Juliette by the elbow, and led her a safe distance away.

He relayed what he'd overheard in there, ending with an odd comment the woman had made to the man about a death. Eyes wide, Juliette moved toward the glass of the front window to peer inside. As she suspected, the people in question were Reggie and Iliana. From the conversation Marcus just described, it sounded like Reggie had found out that Iliana gave more info than she should have to Raven—and now Iliana had been fired for it.

But what did Iliana mean, *"wasn't one death enough for you?"* . . . ?

Together Juliette and Marcus went to sit on the edge of the fountain and wait for someone to emerge. It didn't take long. Soon the door swung open and out came a sobbing Iliana, an overloaded cardboard box under her arm, followed by the security guard.

Juliette jumped up. "Iliana, are you okay?"

The woman turned, but when she saw Juliette, her grief gave way to pure rage and her lips curled back in a snarl. "Get away from me! I lost my job, thanks to you!"

Juliette took a step back as Iliana went on, her voice growing even louder.

"You just *had* to tell him how I violated company policy!"

Juliette shook her head. "No. I didn't breathe a word of that to anyone. Neither did Didi."

"Oh yeah? Well, you two are the only ones who knew!"

Marcus stepped forward, but Juliette put a hand on his arm to keep him from overreacting. "We didn't tell a soul, I promise."

"*Liar!*" Iliana turned and marched off toward the parking lot, the security guard falling in step behind her.

Juliette watched them. Regardless of what Iliana believed, there was still an important matter to be settled. "What did you mean in there when you said wasn't one death enough? Whose death? Raven's?"

Iliana picked up the pace as she spat out her reply. "Sorry, I don't speak to traitors."

Once they reached the car, Juliette and Marcus watched Iliana shove the box into the trunk and then get in and head out. They stood there, silent for a long moment as the car disappeared around the stand of palm trees. A few seconds later they heard the squeal of tires as it pulled out onto the road and sped away.

"Well, that was a shame."

"You can say that again." Marcus clicked

341

his tongue. "She was definitely *not* speaking just above a whisper."

The tension broken, Juliette flashed Marcus a small smile. "Funny man."

Even the guard chuckled as he excused himself and returned to his post.

Now that the drama was over, Marcus suggested they head down to the grotto, but Juliette wanted to talk to Reggie first. She wanted to know what Iliana had meant by her comment.

When they got to the office, they found Reggie standing at the check-in desk in back, talking on the phone. As they moved forward, he glanced up and saw them. His eyebrows arched.

"Never mind. She's right here. Yes, at the front office. Okay." He hung up the phone and looked again at Juliette. "That was the guard at the front gate."

"Is this about Iliana?"

Reggie shook his head, somber. "No. There's someone here to see you."

Juliette glanced at Marcus. "To see *me*? At this hour?"

Reggie nodded, coming around the desk and gesturing toward the door. "It's the police. You're wanted down at the station, for questioning."

Chapter Twenty-Four

Marcus was going nuts. Juliette had been in the interrogation room for over an hour, with no signs she'd be emerging any time soon.

What could possibly be taking so long?

He had called Nate the moment the police car took her away from Palm Grotto, waking the man up and demanding to know what was going on. The groggy FBI agent said he had no idea but that he would try to find out. He called back fifteen minutes later, just as Marcus was turning into the parking lot of the Cahuilla Springs police station.

"The best anyone on this end can figure, this is a local action, not one that has anything to do with the agency."

Marcus hadn't known whether to be relieved or not.

At the moment he just wanted to be in there with Juliette. He needed to be there, at her side. Not surprisingly the officer manning the front desk looked at him like he was crazy for even asking such a thing. Clenching his jaw, Marcus marched outside and called Nate yet again, asking the man to pull a few strings and get him in there.

"Tell them this woman needs to be protected at all costs."

Nate agreed to try, but so far it didn't seem to be working. A half hour later, Marcus stood outside, waiting to hear back from his friend. Then the station door opened and out stepped a tall, muscular young man in a green polo shirt, one that bore the now-familiar logo of Palm Grotto Resort and Spa. He moved past Marcus and down the front steps, then stopped and pulled out a cell phone.

"Hey, excuse me!" Marcus took the steps two at a time.

"Yeah?" The young man barely glanced back as he pressed some buttons on the phone and raised it to his ear.

"Are you from Palm Grotto?" Marcus came to a stop beside him. "I saw the shirt."

"Yeah, so?" He turned his face away and spoke into the phone. "I'm done. Come get me."

Marcus waited. If this kid was calling for a ride, maybe they would have a few minutes to talk before it came.

"So wake her back up. Whatever. I don't care. Just come get me." He disconnected the call without saying good-bye.

A real charmer, this one.

He shot Marcus a glance. "What do you want?"

"I'm not sure. An update, I guess. Information. Are you here because of that supermodel who got murdered?"

The man squinted, reaching into another pocket for a pack of cigarettes. "What are you, a reporter?"

"No. I'm a guest at the resort." Marcus flashed his room key at the guy as proof, then held out his hand for a shake. "Marcus Stone, nice to meet you."

Ignoring the outstretched hand, the kid began slapping the cigarette pack against the heel of his hand. "So? Why should I tell you anything?"

"Do you know Juliette Taylor?"

"Of course. What about her?"

Marcus fixed his gaze on the guy. "She's a friend of mine. A good friend. I'm just trying to help her get a handle on the situation."

"Oh yeah, they knew each other, back in the day, right? Her and the one who died?"

Marcus nodded, watching as the kid shook out a cigarette, held it between his lips, flicked a lighter, and sucked in its flame until the tip glowed orange. With two fingers the guy pulled it from his mouth, then blew a long, straight stream of smoke into the chilly night air. When he returned it to his lips for another drag, he surprised Marcus by extending his hand this time. "Ty Kirkland. So what do you want to know?"

They shook. Marcus relaxed then, leaning one hip against the railing behind him. "I'm not even sure. Just facts. Information. Do you know who their main suspects are at this point?" *Do you know if Juliette is one of those suspects?* He never would've expected such a thing, but the cop who'd picked her up from the resort had treated her oddly, with suspicion. Like a common criminal.

Ty studied him through another deep drag. "They think *I* did it."

"Seriously?"

"Yeah, cop shows up at my house tonight, says I have to come with him. I'm like, you're kidding, right? My wife and kid are both sick. She's been waiting all day for me to get home from work so I could take over, and they want to drag me down here and start firing questions at me?" He flicked his ashes toward the parking lot. "I was no fan of that cougar who died, but I sure didn't have any reason to kill her! I'm thinking that's why they finally released me, 'cause they got no proof and I got no motive. No means either. Opportunity, sure, okay, I probably had more opportunity than anyone else, but I didn't have any motive. And I sure haven't got any poisonous drug. Like I would waste two seconds on some dried-up old has-been anyway."

Marcus worked to keep his expression blank as Ty continued.

"See, the killer put some drug in the mud, and I'm the one who put the mud in the warmer. Since I was the last person to handle the jar before Brooke, they think I'm the one who put the drug in there. Yeah, right."

"Let me ask you something, when you say 'mud,' do you mean actual mud? Or is that just what it's called?"

Ty shrugged. "Well it's not like they just go outside and scoop it up from a mud puddle. I mean, it looks kind of like mud, you know, except it's green. Comes in a jar, like cold cream."

Marcus nodded. Beauty products weren't exactly his area of expertise. "So what do they do with it, actually? How is it used?"

"Basically, they exfoliate the person's body, then slather on the mud, then wrap the person up in cloth so it can soak up real good into their skin."

Marcus grunted. "Sounds like a pretty clever way to drug someone, if you ask me."

Ty thought about that for a moment. "Guess so, now that you mention it."

"So any idea who put the drug in the mud?"

Ty took a final drag on his cigarette, then tossed it to the ground and stubbed it out with his toe. "No clue."

"When would someone have had access to it? You think somebody snuck into the treatment room after you put the mud in the warmer and added something into it then?"

Ty pulled out his pack of cigarettes, started to light another, then thought better of it and slid the pack back into his pocket. "Highly doubt it. Between therapists, clients, and aides, those rooms are almost continually occupied all day long. It'd be hard to pull off something like that in the daytime without being seen."

"So when do you think it was added?"

Ty turned his face to look off toward the parking lot. "I'm thinking early that morning, or maybe even the night before. I kept telling the cops that, but they're not hearing what I'm saying."

"Which is . . ."

Ty returned his gaze to Marcus. "Which is, I'm in charge of inventory. I'm the one who stocks the mud jars in the cabinet. There should've been *three* jars in there yesterday morning, but there was only one. I didn't have time to worry about it right then, but it did bother me. Where did the other two jars go? All three had been in there the day before— and I knew they hadn't been used with other clients. Anyway, I only needed one jar right then, so I pulled it, brought it into the room, and put it down in the warmer. Figured I'd worry about the inventory issue later."

Marcus didn't quite follow.

"Don't you get it, man? I think the killer snuck in the night before or early that morning and put the poison in the jar then."

"What does that have to do with two missing jars?"

Ty exhaled loudly. "Think about it. The killer needed to make sure I would use the jar that had the poison in it. So my guess is he took away the other two jars, just to be safe. Can't grab the wrong jar if there's only one in there."

The men were interrupted by the sharp honk of a car's horn as it pulled in at the curb. Ty's ride.

Marcus thanked the young man for his help.

"No problem, Ms. Taylor's a real nice lady. I only talked to you for her sake." Ty began moving toward the car, then he turned back with a smile. "Of course, you're welcome to leave me a big tip at checkout, if you want."

Once the kid was gone, Marcus turned and made his way back up the steps, his mind swirling with all he'd just learned.

What a nightmare.

Nate still hadn't called, so he decided to go back inside where he could sit down. To his surprise, however, as soon as the cop behind the desk saw him come in, she waved him over.

"There you are. Your name Stone?"

Marcus nodded.

She reached for the phone. "Good. Somebody was just out here looking for you."

"Oh?"

She spoke into the receiver for a moment and then hung up. Before she could explain any further, a uniformed officer appeared in the doorway and invited Marcus to follow him down the hall.

Marcus exhaled slowly. Good ol' Nate had come through for him after all.

He thought the guy was bringing him to join Juliette, but instead they ended up in a small, dark observation booth that looked in on the room where she was being questioned. Through one-way glass Marcus saw Juliette sitting at a table in the next room, across from a grizzled old guy in a suit.

"That's Detective Lopez." The cop jerked his chin toward the man sitting opposite Juliette. "He's the lead detective on the case."

Marcus resisted the urge to roll his eyes. The lead detective? In a sleepy little desert town like this one? "Get a lot of murders out here, do you?"

"More than you'd think." Clearly the cop didn't pick up on Marcus's sarcasm. "Usually, though, it's just some homeless person who got rolled for his dough, or maybe a bar fight that went too far. This is our first real high-profile murder in a long time."

Did the guy have to sound so excited about it? A woman was dead, after all. Marcus thought about pointing that out but held his tongue. This was a time to listen and think, not to act. No need to make an enemy here just because he was ready to hit something.

Or someone.

Marcus focused on the conversation on the other side of the glass, and it didn't take long to understand that the detective wasn't just asking Juliette some basic questions. He was interrogating her about Raven's death.

Just as Marcus had feared.

Ty wasn't their only murder suspect.

"You've got to admit, Ms. Taylor, your behavior here looks very suspicious."

Juliette watched herself on the computer screen for the fifth time in a row. Why did he insist on showing her this same film clip over and over? What was the point of the repetition? She'd already explained her actions— the first four times.

"I told you why I did that." Juliette brushed back her hair. How long was this going to go on? It felt like she'd been in here an hour at least. "Raven was just so difficult, sometimes it was easier to disappear than to risk a confrontation. Trust me, I'm not the first person to hide from her, not by a long shot. I just happened to get caught doing it on film."

The video had come from a Palm Grotto security camera that was mounted over the back door of the main spa building. In the grainy black-and-white image, Juliette could be seen running in from the waiting room and dashing into the supply closet then peeking back out a minute or two later. Next, Ty appeared, walking up the hall, his muscular back to the camera.

"If you could see the expression on his face, you'd know he was feeling the same way I was, like he wanted to turn around and run. Can't you tell by his body language?" Juliette was trying not to sound as exasperated as she felt, but it was getting harder each time they made her go through this.

On the screen the door to the treatment room swung open and Ty slowed to a halt.

"What's he saying to you there?" Detective Lopez spoke as if he might catch her in an impulsive confession.

"I already told you, I don't think he said anything to me. There wasn't time. The door opened, he stopped walking, and out came Brooke."

Sure enough the film showed the therapist coming into the hallway from a side room and giving a small wave to Juliette, who responded by putting a finger to her lips and gesturing toward reception.

Stifling a groan, Juliette put her hands to her temples, massaging her scalp. The throbbing had mounted to a serious headache.

The detective's voice sounded almost matter-of-fact. "We have two witnesses from the airport. They both heard Raven threatening to kill you yesterday—and then here you are, not an hour later, hiding from the woman."

She looked at the screen, then asked him to rewind it a little. In response, he took it back to the part where she interacted with Ty and Brooke.

"There. Now, play it in slow motion."

The images became a jerky sequence of single frames. Leaning forward, Juliette pointed to her own face. "Look at me. Look at my expression. Do I seem traumatized here to you? Do I look like someone who's hiding for her very life, or plotting some sort of preemptive murder myself? No. Of course not. I'm not proud of it, but I look like someone who's hiding from a woman she doesn't feeling like running into. If you look closely, you'll even catch me smiling once or twice. See?" On the screen during her interaction with Brooke and Ty, Juliette did indeed smile several times. And even as she ducked back into the closet, her expression wasn't one of fear or rage, but rather something more like chagrin.

Juliette folded her arms across her chest and fixed her gaze on Detective Lopez. He put the film on pause and met her eyes. The man was in his late fifties or early sixties, and he had a world-weary air about him, the puffy bags under his red eyes and the elongated wrinkles around his mouth reminding her of a basset hound.

"So where does atropine come into this?"

Juliette's head jerked up. "Atropine?" This was new territory. "I'm not even sure what that is. It sounds like a drug."

"Is atropine ever used in your company's products?"

She blinked. What was he really asking her here? Was atropine the poison, the substance used to kill Raven? "I . . . not that I'm aware of, but I'm not a chemist. You'd need to talk to my home office to get a definitive answer to that."

"We already have. I just want to hear what *you* know about it."

Adrenaline surged through Juliette's veins, and in that moment she understood the "flight or fight" reflex. "What I know"—she choked out—"is nothing. I know absolutely nothing about atropine, and I have no idea who killed Raven or why."

Chapter Twenty-Five

Marcus peered at Juliette through the glass. She was tough and feisty, for sure, and holding her own. On the other hand, she looked so scared and small and vulnerable. Eventually the detective excused himself and left the room, and Marcus watched, his heart aching, as Juliette simply hunched over the table, her head in her hands, the picture of dejection.

If only he could get in there with her, he'd tell her not to worry, that these hayseeds didn't have a clue what they were doing. If what Ty said about the missing jars and the mud having been poisoned prior to the start of the business day was true, then she was in the clear. He wasn't exactly sure on her timing, but he knew she'd been in transit until the workday was well underway.

Marcus glanced at the man next him. "So

what time did the atropine get put into the mud in the first place?"

The cop shrugged. "Not sure. We're still working with a couple different theories at this point."

Well, at least that confirmed atropine was the drug the killer used. "So what do you make of Ty Kirkland's claims that it had to have been done when the spa was closed?"

The man grunted, shifting his weight. "Kirkland? I don't believe a word that comes out of that man's mouth. Shame we don't have enough to hold him yet. *He's* the killer, if you ask me."

"Oh? How's that?"

He raised a hand and counted off on his fingers. "Ample opportunity, of course, him being the one with access to the mud. Motive, it was a known fact he couldn't stand the woman—"

"From what I can tell, everyone who met her felt that way."

"Yeah, but not everyone who met her also has a list of priors."

That gave Marcus pause. He'd actually kind of liked Ty, once he got past the rough exterior. "Priors. Really? Violent crimes?"

"A mix. Assault. Simple assault. Some check kiting. Possession."

Marcus was disappointed to hear that,

but he wasn't exactly surprised. The kid had looked like he'd been around the block a few times. "Okay, I get what you're saying, but still. What he says makes sense to me, that someone poisoned the mud the night before, while the spa was closed. Any chance the building was wired for security? Maybe a camera or two? I'm sure you guys have looked into that."

"Yeah, we looked into it. No alarm system. Single deadbolts on all the doors. No signs of forced entry."

"Oh well."

"There is a camera, an exterior one out in back of the building, but it's broken."

Marcus's eyebrows raised. "A broken security camera? For how long?"

"I dunno."

That sounded fishy. If it had been broken for a while, that was one thing. But if it had happened recently, that was something else entirely. These guys should look into that some more, try to find out how long ago the camera broke, and how. Marcus thought about saying as much, but he knew it wouldn't go over well. He had yet to meet the cop who appreciated being told how to do his job.

The door to the interrogation room opened, and the detective strode back in and told Juliette she was free to go.

For now.

As they left the room, the uniformed cop turned to Marcus. "Guess that's our cue. I'm not sure what your interest is in this case, but let us know if we can do anything else for you."

They stepped into the hallway, only to see Lopez and Juliette headed in the opposite direction. "Where are they going?"

"To get her belongings, I imagine. We don't allow purses or cell phones or anything like that in interrogation."

"Oh, right. Of course not."

They turned and headed the other way.

"It was nice to meet you," the cop said as they reached the lobby. "We don't get a lot of Feds out here."

Marcus nodded. What in the world did Nate tell them to open this particular door? Probably that he was "with" the FBI. Technically that was true, he supposed, though only as a consultant.

"Well, keep up the good work." It was the most noncommittal thing he could think of to say. Then he stood and waited for Juliette.

If only he could make all of this go away.

They found an all-night pancake house one town over and were soon settled into a booth,

Juliette ordering Greek yogurt with fresh fruit and Marcus the Big Bronco Breakfast. Still rattled from her interrogation, she was glad they could sit and talk for a while rather than head straight back to the resort. It was late, but she needed some time to collect her thoughts and recover from the trauma.

In the car Marcus had been so sweet, so concerned. Now as she sat across from him in the restaurant, she still couldn't quite believe he was there. Marcus Stone. Her TOTGA. If only Didi knew!

Once the waitress finished taking their orders and walked away, Marcus focused on Juliette, his voice soft even though the room was nearly empty. "So you really think those are the only two things they have against you? The threat at the airport and the surveillance video?"

She nodded. "He threw me with that question about atropine. I mean, I've heard of it, but I'm not even sure what it is. Was that the drug that killed her?"

Marcus nodded. "I'm not all that familiar with it myself, but I've seen it used in emergency situations. Actually, now that I think about it, it's a WHO Essential."

"A who what?"

He smiled. "The World Health Organization, or WHO. Atropine is on their 'essential drugs' list. It's kept on-hand primarily in case of exposure to nerve gas, but I've also seen it used to stop a heart attack. From what I understand, in certain situations, it can make the difference between life and death."

The waitress returned with coffee for both and a large orange juice for Marcus, who continued as she walked away.

"Anyway, I can look into it some more. Shouldn't be hard to find info about atropine online."

Juliette studied him as he stirred cream and sugar into his coffee, captivated by the handsome angles and planes of his face. "You don't have to do this, you know. It's my fight, not yours."

Eyebrows raised, he stopped mid-stir. "What?"

"This whole Raven mess. If these cops are as inept as you say, they're never going to find the real killer. That's why . . ." Her voice trailed off as she looked away.

"What?"

She shrugged and met his eyes. "Maybe I shouldn't tell you this, but that's why I've decided I'm going to try and solve this myself. Figure out who killed Raven, and why. I *have* to."

"To protect yourself?"

"Well, partly."

"Why else?

Juliette sucked in a deep breath. How to explain? "I *owe* her. It's too late to save her life, but at least maybe I can give her justice."

She braced herself, certain he was going to try to talk her out of it. Instead, much to her surprise, when he finally spoke, his words were simple and direct.

"Let me help."

She looked at him, eyes wide.

He leaned toward her across the table. "We can do this together, Juliette. I can help you. Just since we left the police station, I've already thought of half a dozen different things they should be checking out. The broken surveillance camera, the security of the resort's perimeter, the—"

"I appreciate that, Marcus, but you didn't even know Raven."

He shrugged. "I'm not doing it for Raven. My concern is you. Clearing your name. Keeping you safe. Helping you with this thing that's so important to you."

His ready support flowed over her, warming her to the core. She nodded, resisting the urge to reach out and take his hand as she met his beautiful blue-gray eyes. "Thank you, Marcus. I think I can use all the help I can get—especially since I have a retreat to conduct at the same time. It's going to be a busy weekend."

"Well, consider me at your service."

A comfortable silence fell between them.

"Why do we do things so backwards, you and I?" she asked finally. "We haven't even had the chance to catch up on each other's lives yet and we're already joining forces to investigate a murder."

He smiled. "I guess there are a few things we should cover, especially now that we're alone and can really talk."

She eyed him, nodding. "You're right. Why don't we start where we left off this afternoon? With your marriage."

Marcus's face colored, but their food arrived at that moment. Once the plates and bowls were down in front of them and the waitress walked away, Marcus said grace for them both, then picked up his fork and began eating. Juliette scooped a few sliced strawberries onto her yogurt as she waited, unwilling to fill the silence for him.

"Actually, why don't we start with you so I can eat my food while it's still hot? Yours is supposed to be cold."

"Um hmm. Nice sidestep, Mr. Stone."

He grinned as he reached for the syrup. "Go ahead, tell me about your life. We'll get back to my marriage, I promise."

With a sigh, Juliette settled back into her seat. "What would you like to know?"

"Everything. But I guess question number one is if you're currently seeing anyone. I Googled you the other day and saw some recent pictures of you with a senator."

She smiled. Marcus's lack of guile was so refreshing. He wanted to know if she was available, and that was that. "I go out occasionally, sure, but there's no one special right now." *Except you. It has always been you.*

"You never married, never had kids?"

She shook her head. "Came close to marriage a couple of times. But I just never found the right guy, you know? I really wanted the whole deal—husband, house full of children, all that—but it wasn't in God's plan for me, I suppose. I've had a very happy life just the same. And my sister has four children now, so at least I have them."

"Bet you're the fun aunt. I can just picture it."

She grinned. "I guess you could put it that way. And they're good kids."

Juliette went on to tell him about her business, how she and her best friend Didi founded a skin-care company ten years before and developed a product line that was sold primarily through salons and spas.

"And your business, it's done well?"

She hesitated. Yes, very well—until a few months ago, when they learned about the counterfeiting and their world had been turned upside down. "We've, uh, hit a few bumps in the road lately, but overall it's done great."

Juliette could see that Marcus was about to probe further, so she headed him off. "And now it's your turn. You were going to tell me about that marriage of yours."

Marcus wiped his mouth with his napkin, settled back against the seat, and gave her an appraising look. "Okay. It's kind of complicated, though."

"I'm listening." She scooped some blueberries in with the strawberries, swirled them together with the yogurt, and took another bite.

"If you remember back when you and I first met, my plan was to quit my job at the firm and find something more in line with my main focus, which was safety. Specifically, disaster-related safety."

"Yes, I've wondered about that for years, if you ever found what you were looking for."

"Not at first—at least not within the confines of an engineering firm. So I decided to get a job with Uncle Sam. Ending up spending the next fifteen years working in the field of disaster response."

"Wow."

He nodded, looking away as he continued. "Eva was with an international humanitarian aid group. We became friends in the aftermath of Hurricane Gilbert. A year later I went to see you in Philly, learned about your engagement, and realized you and I were a nonissue. So when I saw Eva again after Hugo, I decided to pursue a more romantic relationship with her. She was a lovely woman, with a big heart for those in crisis. And, like I said, I was trying to get on with my life at that point."

"Stop apologizing, Marcus. It's not necessary."

His smile was sheepish. "We were married in Hawaii the following spring."

"How romantic." Juliette tried not to picture it.

Marcus waved away the thought. "Don't be too impressed. We were there for the recovery effort after the Kilauea Volcano."

With a smile Juliette sat against the vinyl backrest of the booth and crossed her arms over her chest. "So is that how you measure your life, Marcus? By disasters?"

He shrugged, and an odd expression came over his face. Looking down, he focused on his food again, finishing off the last of the pancakes.

"Did I say something wrong?" Juliette's voice was soft.

He hesitated, shoulders sagging, and then he met her eyes.

"No, you wouldn't know. It's just that . . . you're right. I guess I do measure my life in disasters. The thing is, some disasters have taken a higher toll than others."

Juliette's eyes widened.

"Eva was headed for Oklahoma City after the bombing when she had her first miscarriage."

"I'm so sorry."

He nodded. "She was only three months along, but the loss really . . . well, it was devastating, especially to Eva. She quit her job, found one that wouldn't involve travel, tried again. Took another few years, but we finally had a daughter. Zoe. Unfortunately the little stinker decided to show up early, born while I was away in the wake of Hurricane Floyd."

Juliette gasped with delight. "You have a daughter?"

He nodded, smiling as he pulled out his phone, opened the photo app, and handed it to Juliette over the table. She took it from him and scrolled through the pictures. The girl was gorgeous, tall and slender, a carbon copy of her father except for her eyes, which were a rich amber brown. In each of the photos, she was either alone or with kids her own age or with Marcus. The mother was nowhere to be seen.

"Thirteen, you said?" Juliette smiled at an image of father and daughter in a stadium at a ball game, arms around each other as they grinned for the camera.

"Yeah. Thirteen going on thirty, I guess."

She chuckled. "She could be a model."

"Don't tell her that."

Handing the phone back, Juliette asked if they'd gone on to have any more children. Immediately Marcus's face clouded over.

Wrong question.

"Like I said, some disasters took a higher toll than others. We, uh . . . We lost another baby, a boy. Only this time it wasn't a miscarriage. He was stillborn. At eight months. Again, I was away, that time at the World Trade Center. Eva never forgave me—and she never got over it. Eventually she decided to leave. I thought it was just a temporary separation, especially because she left Zoe behind as well. Eva went back to live with her family in France, saying she had to sort things out. Next thing I knew, I was being served with divorce papers. I tried as hard as I could to reconcile, but she wouldn't even consider it. She remarried a few years later, and that was that."

"Oh, Marcus. I'm so sorry."

He nodded, avoiding her eyes as he caught the waitress's eye and gestured for the check. Juliette was stunned. Marcus had lost a child. A son. She couldn't fathom a deeper, more agonizing pain! And she couldn't even think about the wife part of the equation. The whole thing was just such a tragedy.

Finally he met her eyes. "The good news is, I got full custody of Zoe. She was only three when Eva first left, so I had to make some big changes. No more government job for me, and no more disaster recovery. A buddy and I started a company of our own, one that focused primarily on disaster prevention—like, training, consulting, evaluating. That allowed me to stay local for the most part—or at least to plan my trips in advance rather than having to run off at the drop of a hat every time disaster struck. And we've done pretty well. Just celebrated our ninth anniversary."

"That's great, Marcus. Sounds like you and your friend were starting your business right about the same time Didi and I were launching ours."

"Brilliant minds think alike, I guess."

They shared a smile, then silence descended. Juliette looked down at the table. Had it been too long since their first meeting? They were different people now. Older. More battle-scarred. And twenty-five years was an awfully long time to carry a torch for anyone, even someone as special as Marcus.

"Anyway"—his voice drew her gaze back to his face—"I didn't mean to focus on just the bad stuff. There's been some pain, sure, but overall I've had a very happy life. Great job, great kid. I'm doing well. I really am."

She gazed at him for a long moment, an odd sort of joy filling her heart at the thought. "You can't imagine how thrilled I am to hear that, Marcus. Over the years I've thought of you so often, prayed for you sometimes. Wondered about you. To know that you're happy . . ." She couldn't finish the sentence for fear she might tear up again.

"I feel the same about you." His expression intense, Marcus reached out and laid the back of his hand on the table, opening his palm to her. After a moment's hesitation, she slipped her hand into his.

"Juliette, this may sound crazy, but I need you to understand what a tremendous impact that one afternoon you and I spent together had on my life. More than you could ever imagine."

She shook her head. She didn't have to imagine it. "It was the same for me too. You gave me the courage to change my whole world."

His fingers tightened on hers. "The weird thing is, that one day we spent together feels more real to me than any of the thousands of days I've lived since."

She nodded, so close to tears. Thankfully the waitress showed up then with their check, giving her time to regain her composure.

In the car, as they drove toward the resort, Juliette reached out and gave Marcus's arm a squeeze. Her hand lingered there for a moment, comforted by the warmth of his skin, the hardness of his muscles underneath. When she pulled it away, Marcus reached out and took it again, placing it back on his arm. Smiling in the darkness, she kept it there, feeling utterly connected to him as they drove on in silence through the night.

When they finally reached the resort, he drove to her building and pulled to stop, putting the car in park and turning off the lights but leaving the engine running. Looking over at the small strip of guestrooms, Juliette was reminded of Didi . . . Oh, was she ever going to be shocked when she learned the truth about Marcus.

"Something wrong?"

She glanced at the man next to her, pulse quickening at the sight of his handsome face in the moonlight. "I was just thinking about Didi. I have to tell her who you really are."

He cleared his throat. "Good luck with that. I don't think she likes me very much."

Juliette gave him a reassuring pat. "She's just watching out for me. I don't usually get so friendly with a man so fast."

"Yeah, right. Twenty-five years fast."

Juliette smiled. "She tends to be a tad over-protective. She'll get over it."

Didi did need to know the truth, and soon. It wasn't fair to keep her in the dark any longer. Juliette had enjoyed having this special secret, but now she had to tell Didi that not only was Marcus not a stranger, he was, in fact, her TOTGA.

"How about your mom? Does she know about us?"

"No, not yet." He grinned. "I couldn't tell her ahead of time because I was afraid you'd reject me, and I didn't want anyone to witness that."

"Which I did, actually. I totally rejected you." Juliette pressed her lips together.

"That was a matter of bad timing on my part."

"But you couldn't have known."

"At least we got another chance." Marcus's voice was thick with emotion. "Not everyone does, you know."

She gazed into his eyes. There was just enough moonlight to see his tender expression. He was *too* good-looking, her real-life white knight.

Marcus leaned toward her, a flash of shyness in his eyes. Her pulse raced.

He's going to kiss me.

She caught her breath. "Maybe Didi's right. Maybe we are moving too fast."

Marcus tilted his head to one side. After a beat, they whispered in unison. "Yeah, right. Twenty-five years too fast."

They shared a smile, and then Marcus brought his lips to hers. The kiss was gentle at first, then strong, almost fierce. As she slid her hand up to his cheek, felt his arms wrapping around her and pulling her in closer, a small moan escaped from her throat. This was what she'd wanted, longed for, *craved*, half her life. When the kiss was over, she could scarcely breathe.

"Well," Marcus whispered, also trying to catch his breath. "I'd say that was definitely worth the wait." A slow smile eased across his features. "And then some."

Chapter Twenty-Six

Crystal couldn't believe she was getting to work so early. When Andre asked her to handle Brooke's duties this weekend, he mentioned a "morning hike" but hadn't specified until later that it was a *sunrise* hike. Thanks a lot, boss.

Night still blanketed the scene as she turned into the resort, though the promise of morning hovered on the horizon, offering just enough light so she could see the buildings ahead. The quiet of the dawn felt like a lull before a storm. She didn't know why she had such an odd sense of foreboding, but she hoped she could shake if off before they embarked on the hike.

Crystal pulled up to the employee gate as usual, but then the guard came out and told her there was no one available to escort her up from employee parking right now so she should use the main parking lot instead. She was happy to comply, though as she steered around the cluster of palm trees and the main lot came into view, she was surprised to see a police car near the entrance of the resort. Several of her fellow employees clustered around.

When she spotted Ms. Taylor's business partner among the group, her heart sank. The hikers were supposed to meet at the nearby fountain. Surely nothing bad had happened to one of those sweet ladies from the retreat!

Crystal parked and joined the others. Drawing closer, she saw that a Palm Grotto golf cart was parked on the grass, its headlights illuminating the big sign on the lawn, the one that had been put up yesterday to welcome people to the Juliette Taylor Event. Didi was near the sign, bending over and snapping pictures of the ground with her camera phone.

Crystal took a closer look at the sign. It read, as it had before:

It's your turn . . .
. . . to be nurtured
. . . to be pampered
. . . to be restored.

Then she gasped. Underneath the last line someone had added a few more words, spray-painted a vivid, dripping red:

Marcus drew in a deep breath of the clean morning air. He felt energized and rarin' to go despite getting less than five hours of sleep. It was 8:00 a.m. and already a beautiful day. The sun shone, the birds sang, and all was in place for an impromptu breakfast picnic. He'd gotten the food and found a relatively private rendezvous point.

Now all he needed was Juliette.

What was taking her so long? She only had an hour to spare, and Marcus could feel himself growing more impatient with each passing minute. Finally she appeared, coming around the corner on the path, all done up for the day and looking like a million bucks. The very sight set Marcus's heart to pounding. Adrenaline coursed through his body.

Brother. What a woman.

"There you are." Juliette came to a stop, a shy grin on her face. "Why do I feel like a sixteen-year-old girl meeting up with her big crush?"

Grateful for the cover of the thick foliage surrounding them on three sides, he stepped closer and took her into his arms. "I was just wondering the same thing."

Marcus leaned in for a kiss but Juliette

held back, a teasing glint in her eye. "Really? I make you feel like a sixteen-year-old girl?"

He growled. "Such a comedian." Then his mouth was on hers and he didn't want to come up for air.

Why did she feel so right in his arms?

Why had he waited so long to find her again?

Finally they pulled apart, then he took her hand and led her to the bench where their breakfast was waiting.

"The flowers are beautiful." She sat and looked around. "You were right, Marcus. This is a great spot."

He nodded. "Not to mention secluded enough to steal a kiss or two."

"Steal a kiss? If you say so."

Juliette playfully reached for him and pulled his face to hers. Once more he was lost in the feel of her lips on his—like they'd been custom-made to fit right there, soft and warm and willing.

He was falling too far, too fast. How could this possibly feel so right even though they barely even knew each other?

When the kiss ended, he lingered there for a long moment, lightly kissing her cheeks, her forehead. He knew he could stay like that forever—but time was short and they had a lot to talk about. Finally he wrenched himself away.

"Hungry?" He sat back and reached for the two take-out boxes on his other side. "I wasn't sure what you'd like, so I just went down the buffet and tried to get a little of everything that was even remotely healthy."

He handed her one of the boxes then opened his own, inhaling the delicious scent steaming up from the food within. As he unwrapped his plastic utensils and dug into a fresh-made waffle, Juliette poked through her box and opted for the melon balls, spearing one with a fork and nibbling it delicately.

"Oh, I got coffee too." Marcus handed her one of the insulated cups then sipped at his own. "I know you don't have much time, so I guess we should jump right in with 'Operation Raven.'"

"Operation Raven?"

He smiled. "Whatever you want to call it. If we want to figure things out here, I think we should start by brainstorming, just like I used to do with my team before going into a disaster situation. It never hurts to toss out ideas. Information. Concerns. Suggestions. With the right combination of people, things can really get done."

"Sounds good." She speared another melon ball.

"We can start with just the two of us now, but maybe later we could widen the circle a bit, bring in a few others who might be useful as well."

She nodded. "Didi, certainly. She should be a part of this." Juliette thought for a moment. "We probably need an insider, too—a spa staff member—though I don't know who we could ask. I trust Brooke, but she's in the hospital. Other than that . . ."

Marcus set aside his take-out box and grabbed the pen and small notepad he'd brought from the room. "Well, we can decide as we go. For now, why don't we start with the sequence of events? I've read the news reports and you've given me some of your own details, but it would help if I was a hundred percent clear on how everything played out, beginning to end."

"Okay."

"You said you flew in on Thursday, right? What time did you get here?"

Sitting back against the bench and taking an occasional bite of her breakfast, Juliette recounted everything from the moment she got off the plane Thursday afternoon until she was released from the police station last night. He took notes as she talked, and he wasn't surprised that in the process he learned a number of details he hadn't known before, like how Raven had wrangled her way into a room right next to the three men who were here under fake names. Once Marcus constructed a time line of events, they went back through and added in other details. Finally he asked Juliette if there was anything else she could think of that they might have missed.

She was quiet for a moment, sipping her coffee. "Yes. There is one other thing. Did I happen to mention that Raven was extremely adept at self-defense?"

"No, you didn't." He made note of that.

"She knew street fighting, and, trust me, she could really hold her own. I told this to the detective, but he didn't seem very interested. Didn't even write it down."

Marcus rolled his eyes. "Like I said, hayseeds." He took a bite of turkey sausage.

"I know, right?" Juliette shook her head sadly. "I just keep thinking about how she was killed. It makes so much sense, the place and the timing, I mean. No way could someone have overpowered Raven, like to strangle her or stab her or something. They must've known that they'd have to wait until she was all wrapped up, arms bound at her sides. And even then they did it with some drug overdose, rubbed in through her skin, rather than confronting her directly. She probably never even realized what was going on—and then it was too late."

Marcus studied Juliette's face as she talked, wishing more than anything that he could protect this woman, prevent this pain, preserve the sweetness of her very soul. She wasn't naïve or foolish, but there was an odd sort of innocence to her all the same, a kind of trusting vulnerability that shone from her eyes and spoke through her words. By this age, most folks had had that childlike innocence crushed out of them, but not Juliette. At heart she was still the same, sweet girl he met on that fateful stormy day so long ago. Only now she was older, wiser, and even more beautiful.

"I'm sorry you're having to go through all of this."

She looked at him, her eyes filling with tears. "At least I don't have to go through it alone."

His heart surged with protective tenderness. There were no words, so instead he simply set aside pen and paper and took her into his arms.

He was still holding her tight, gently rocking back and forth, when her cell phone began to ring.

The last thing on earth Juliette wanted was to tear herself away from the warm embrace of this dear, sweet man, but she couldn't ignore the call given all that was going on. With a sigh, she sat up straight, pulled out her phone, and glanced at the screen. Didi.

"Where *are* you?"

"Didi? Why? Is something wrong?"

Didi grunted. "You can't imagine."

Juliette felt a catch in her breath. "What is it?"

"In person. Where are you right now?"

Juliette glanced at Marcus, who was watching her, a frown on his brow. "I'm on a bench out past the grapefruit orchard. Should I come to you?"

"No, there are too many people around. Is it quiet there?"

"Very."

"Then I'll come to you. How do I get there?"

Juliette explained which path to take, again glancing at Marcus, who began to gather the trash from their breakfast.

"Perfect. I'm not far from there at all. Stay put, I'm on my way." Didi hung up without a good-bye.

In less than a minute, the short, heavyset woman came huffing and puffing up the trail. She and Juliette spotted each other at the same moment, but then Didi's eyes shifted to Marcus and she hesitated, a shadow crossing her features. Obviously she'd expected her friend to be alone.

"Sorry, I didn't realize you were with someone. Can we speak privately, please?"

Juliette glanced at Marcus, who nodded and excused himself. Carrying the trash, he moved away toward a large can a short ways up the path.

An odd lurch in her gut, Juliette gestured for Didi to have a seat on the bench. "What's up?"

"You're not going to believe this." Didi heaved an exhausted sigh. "Elsa just called. The FBI showed up at JT Lady headquarters with a warrant and now they're walking out the door with our computers, our files, and who knows what else, even as we speak."

Crystal walked into the break room and headed straight for the vending machine. The combination of dry desert air and the various aromas and scents of the products she worked with sometimes made her feel so parched. She put in her quarters and pressed the button for mineral water, which dropped into the tray with a liquid *thunk*. Pulling out the bottle, she twisted off the lid and began to drink, glad she had this fifteen-minute window between treatments.

Finally she took a moment to catch her breath, have a seat, and look around. The room was empty except for a pair of spa staffers, Lisa and Beth, and a nice, older man from the maintenance department named Vin. They were also on break, drinking coffee together two tables away. She glanced their way and saw they were all peering at her oddly in return.

She paused, the bottle at her lips. "What?"

"Sorry," Lisa said, "we were just talking about you."

Crystal bristled. "Oh?"

Lisa wrapped both hands around her coffee mug, a sympathetic expression on her face. "Yeah, Vin was telling us about this morning, with the sign. You poor thing. Seems like you keep coming onto the scene right after some terrible event has happened."

Crystal hesitated. Just what were they insinuating? She looked for guile but saw only concern—especially with Vin. He'd been the one to take down the sign that morning, as soon as the policeman gave the go-ahead.

"Are you doing okay?" he asked.

Crystal shrugged. "Sure, I guess." She wasn't used to people expressing concern for her welfare and didn't quite know how to respond.

"What were you doing here so early?" asked Beth.

"I was supposed to lead the retreat guests on a sunrise hike."

Lisa gasped. "With all that's been going on here? A hike in the dark?"

"Well, that was the plan. But we ended up making it a sunrise stretching session instead. Security didn't want a bunch of women trooping around alone in the woods, and there weren't enough guards on duty to go with us. I knew we could get a pretty good view of the eastern sky from the tennis courts, so we walked over and did our stretches there as the sun came up. It was nice, actually. And it helped calm me down. The sight of that sign *was* pretty disturbing."

"You can say that again." Vin shook his head. "I can't imagine what kind of a sicko would do that."

"I heard it was written in blood," Beth said, her eyes wide.

Vin grunted. "Not blood, just red paint. See, that's how rumors get started." He got up from the table and left after that, though Crystal wasn't sure if that was because his break time was over or if he was just irritated at the turn in the conversation.

"Well, it's no rumor that Raven's death was a murder," Beth said once he was gone. "They confirmed it on the news this morning, that it was intentional and not an accident."

"I know, I was so shocked when I heard." Lisa took a sip of her coffee. "I felt sure it was an allergic reaction, especially given what happened that other time."

Crystal again looked their way. "What other time?"

"Last summer. That big mess when Raven filed a complaint and Reggie forwarded it to corporate?"

"I've only been working at Palm Grotto for a few weeks."

"Oh, right. Of course. So you wouldn't know." Turning in her chair, Lisa leaned forward and lowered her voice, eager to share some tidbit with the newbie. "Last summer, when Raven was here for her regular visit, she had an allergic reaction to one of the products used during a treatment."

"A reaction? Like a rash or something?"

"More like a burn, if you could call it that. I mean, it wasn't all that bad. She didn't need to see a doctor or anything. Her skin was just a little pink. But of course this is *Raven* we're talking about. She made it into a huge deal. Filed complaints all the way up the line."

Beth jumped in to finish the story. "Reggie was new at the time, and he didn't realize that Raven filed at least one complaint with every visit. The old manager had always just played along—and then tossed her report in the circular file once she was gone. But stupid Reggie took her seriously. Sent the report about the 'burn' along to corporate."

"Oh no."

"Yeah. A couple of people here ended up getting in big trouble for the way the incident was handled. One was even fired. Spa management was furious at Raven—and at Reggie."

Crystal's mind began to swirl. This must be what the cook had been talking about yesterday when he said folks like Xena and Andre didn't want anything to do with Raven any more. No wonder. The woman got them all in trouble with the head office!

"Anyway," Lisa continued, "that's why I felt sure Raven's death was caused by an allergy, because of that reaction she had the last time. When I learned it was murder this time, I was shocked."

Beth shook her head. "I didn't buy your allergy theory because the same thing has happened too many times, with too many other clients. We've had other burns before, but nobody else has ever *died*."

Crystal nearly choked on her last gulp of water. "Wait a minute. Other clients besides Raven have gotten burned here?"

Both women nodded.

."It's gotten worse in the last year or so." Lisa shook her head. "I think it's a quality control issue at JT Lady. Their products are usually fine, but then once in a while you open up a jar or a tube and it smells odd or it looks funny—or, worst of all, it's uncomfortable to the client. I've been bugging Andre to switch to a different brand for a while now, but so far he hasn't. I figure after all this, he just might."

Crystal was stunned. She wasn't sure what was going on here, but she'd been working with and selling JT Lady products from her previous spa back in Seattle for years and they'd never, *ever* had a single incident of spoilage or toxicity. Something had to be wrong on this end, like maybe Palm Grotto was storing the products at too high a temperature.

She was about to say as much but then held her tongue when she saw a pair of spa aides, both known for gossip, coming up the walk. The last thing she wanted was to discuss JT Lady quality control issues in front of these two. Ironically named Harmony and Karma, they seemed to stir up trouble wherever they went.

Sure enough, as soon as they stepped inside and spotted Lisa and Beth, Harmony headed toward them, speaking in a loud whisper.

"Guess what we just found out? You'll never believe who's one of the prime suspects in Raven's murder case."

Crystal rose from her chair and tossed her bottle into the recycling bin as Harmony went on to answer her own question.

"Juliette Taylor!"

Crystal's head jerked around. Juliette Taylor? A murder suspect? Oh please. Not in a million years. Not in a trillion. She hesitated, trying to think of a way to nip such a ridiculous rumor in the bud.

"How do you know?" Lisa looked like a puppy begging for a treat.

"My sister's boyfriend is a cop. He said that a patrolman came here late last night and picked Ms. Taylor up then brought her down to the station for questioning. She was there for a long time."

"No way!" Lisa gushed.

"Unbelievable!" cried the esthetician.

"Wait till you hear what happened next." Harmony's face was alive with the drama of it all. "While she was in there being interrogated, the chief got a call from none other than the *FBI*, saying that they were working a different but related case that involved Ms. Taylor and wanted to send someone in to observe the interrogation."

"No way!"

"What did they mean? Why?"

"Nobody knows for sure." Glancing at Karma, Harmony nodded. "You want to tell them the last part?"

Karma grinned as she turned to the others. "Okay, have you guys seen the guest here, he's a super-hunky older man—real muscular, silver hair, killer blue eyes?"

"The one who brought his mother for the retreat?" Lisa sighed. "He's yummy."

"That's the one. Well, guess what?"

Crystal listened with rapt attention, no better than the others.

"The agent that the FBI was talking about was *him*. That guy works for the FBI—and I think he came here to spy on Ms. Taylor!"

Chapter Twenty-Seven

Juliette gaped at Didi, her breakfast turning to a cold, solid lump in her gut as she tried to take in the news. The FBI was conducting a raid of the JT Lady offices? At that very moment? Incredible!

How had they managed to get a warrant for the files they'd been denied just the day before? And what was with this timing? On Saturday mornings the main office at JT Lady was closed, with just a handful of people on duty in the warehouse and in Shipping and Receiving. Had the FBI been aware of that, and shown up just when they wouldn't have to deal with management or a building full of irate employees?

Outrageous.

Didi went on. "The good news is that the moment the FBI showed up, the warehouse guys contacted Elsa. She rushed right down, but by the time she got there, things were well underway. The FBI agents had already run backups of the computers and the server, disconnected everything, and were loading up a van with their equipment and boxes of files. She couldn't do a thing but watch."

"Poor Elsa."

"I know." Didi's face grew even more somber. "There's something else. Unrelated to that."

Juliette's eyes widened. What *now?*

Didi took a deep breath. "This morning around five, I got a call from Palm Grotto security. They needed me to come up to the main parking lot because, well, here." Didi pulled out her cell and tapped the screen. "It's probably easier to show you the pictures than try to explain."

Juliette took the phone and braced herself as she took a look. The photo was of their new sign, the big one near Palm Grotto's main parking lot that welcomed their guests to the event. Someone had added graffiti to the bottom, but it wasn't until she enlarged the image that she could make out what had been written there: . . . *to be murdered.*

Unbelievable.

Pulse surging, Juliette turned and gestured to Marcus, who'd been hovering in the distance but now came rushing to her side. She handed him Didi's phone and watched as he absorbed what he was seeing.

His eyes were riveted to the screen. "Who did this?"

Didi's mouth grew tight. "We don't know. At least it's being taken seriously. Police came and dusted for fingerprints and everything, and even one of the detectives came to take a look."

"I can't believe this." Juliette shook her head. "Who would do such a thing?"

Without reply, Didi reached out and flipped to the next photo. "That's a partial shoeprint I spotted near the base of the left pole. I was hoping the police would do a plaster cast of it or something, but they seemed more interested in fingerprints than footprints."

Juliette studied the picture, which showed a distinct impression in the soft brown earth of the front half of someone's shoe.

Didi took back her phone and pocketed it. "At least we were able to get the whole thing down and out of sight before the sunrise hikers started showing up. But a whole handful of Palm Grotto staffers saw it. Who knows what kinds of rumors are flying around here now?"

"This is just awful." Juliette closed her eyes.

"Didi's right, though, it's good that the detective is taking it seriously."

Juliette knew Marcus was trying to console her, but she opened her eyes and gave him a sharp glance, unable to contain her anger. "You mean the detective who thinks I'm a murderer?"

Didi gasped.

Marcus kept his voice even and calm. "You know as well as I do that they're grasping at straws."

"Thorough? Right. Those cops can't even catch some vandal with a can of spray paint, and we're expecting them to nab a killer? Please."

Didi was staring at the two of them, her mouth slack. "What are you talking about? Who thinks you're a murderer?"

Juliette felt heat rush to her cheeks. Oh boy. She'd known she would have to tell Didi about last night at some point, but she hadn't meant for it to come out like this. Quickly she launched into an explanation, but as she spoke she could see Didi's jaw clenching ever tighter, her eyes narrowing into slits.

"And why didn't anyone think to notify me of this development?" Didi's voice was tight.

"It was so late, there was no reason to wake you up last night. Marcus came down to the station and was waiting for me when they released me, so I didn't even need a ride. I was going to tell you about it this morning, as soon as we could get a few minutes alone."

Didi glared at Juliette and then at Marcus. "Clearly you chose to spend your alone minutes with someone else. Excuse me for breaking in on your private little party."

With that, she stood and walked away. Juliette sighed, watching her go.

"Will she be okay?"

Juliette turned back to Marcus. "Yeah. This is just how Didi fights. I'd rather settle things up front, but she likes to cool off first and talk later."

"I see."

Juliette checked her watch, just seven more minutes before she'd have to head to the conference center. She sighed again, wondering how this beautiful morning could've fallen apart so quickly. On the other hand, why was she surprised? Things had begun to fall apart the moment she stepped off that plane and spotted Raven in the crowd at the airport.

"How about you? Are you okay?"

"I don't know." She hadn't even told him yet about the whole FBI mess back home. Now there was the matter of the sign to contend with as well? Weariness filled her soul.

"Why would someone write that, Marcus? Do you think it was done by whoever killed

Raven? Or was it someone else, just trying to make some sort of statement?"

She looked at him, wishing he had all the answers. In response he simply shrugged, but then he reached out and took her hand, clasping it tightly in his. The gesture reminded her that though he may not be able to stop this avalanche of disaster from falling on her head, at least she wasn't facing it alone.

There was nothing Marcus could say in the moment that would make the situation any better, so rather than spout some empty reassurance or platitude, he simply held onto Juliette's hand. After a beat, he could feel her leaning into him, her head fitting perfectly against his shoulder. They sat there for a long while, the only sound was the birds chirping from the trees. Soon Marcus could feel a prayer rising up within him, and he closed his eyes, intending to offer a silent supplication. But somehow the words found their way to his mouth and out into the morning air.

"Father, I just ask Your protection on this woman and her ministry and her business. Thank You for bringing her back into my life again, and please help us both to seek Your will in this relationship. Keep us safe, and help us today and in the days to come as we seek the truth about all that has happened. Guide her through this difficult time, and make Your presence so real that she'll find strength and encouragement and reassurance in Your loving grace with every moment of every day. Amen."

A part of him almost felt embarrassed, like he'd had no right to do something so intimate as pray for her, with her. Even though they had discussed their mutual faith at length twenty-five years ago, he wasn't sure how she felt about it now. Perhaps she would view his act as inappropriate. He was trying to decide what to say when she sat up and turned toward him, her eyes brimming with tears.

"No man has ever done that, just prayed for me, out of the blue, in a moment when I so desperately needed it." With a brave smile, she wrapped her arms around Marcus and gave him a hug, whispering a soft "thank you" in his ear before pulling away again.

"You're welcome." The scent of her hair filled his lungs and made his head spin.

"I'm out of time, but there's one more quick thing before I go. The main reason Didi came out here."

Marcus waited, hoping she had some good news for a change.

"I can't explain in full right now, but I'll

give it to you in a nutshell. Do you know what counterfeit goods are?"

Marcus froze. Surely she could hear the sudden pounding of his heart. "Yes. I'm very familiar with the term—and the problem."

She sighed her relief. "Good. Well, long story short, my company, JT Lady, has become a target for counterfeiters. There are fake products bearing our label for sale all over the world."

He nodded, not trusting himself to speak. Glancing again at the time, she explained that yesterday afternoon her home office had a visit from the FBI, who wanted information that might help with their counterfeiting investigation. They were nice and all, she said, but when they requested more info than she was willing to give, she put them off, telling them she needed to speak with her lawyer first.

"The main reason Didi came over here just now was to let me know that the FBI showed up at our office again this morning—but this time with a warrant. They're probably still there now, seizing our records and our computers. And apparently there's nothing we can do to stop them."

Marcus stared at her. A *warrant*? A search-and-seizure? What on earth were they thinking? He couldn't even begin to come up with a response, but he was saved from having to try when Juliette once more checked her watch and told him she had to go.

"I'll be tied up all morning, but I have a little free time after lunch. Meet up with you then? We can connect at the restaurant."

"Absolutely." It was all he could manage to say.

She gave him one last quick kiss and was on her way.

Marcus dragged in a deep breath, his hands clenched into fists as he realized what the FBI had done. When he called Nate last night and told him that the police had picked up Juliette for questioning in Raven's murder, he'd handed over "probable cause" on a platter. No doubt the matter of getting a warrant was a breeze after that. What judge wouldn't green-light the search-and-scizure of a company whose products were being counterfeited—and whose owner was on a terrorist list *and* the subject of a murder investigation?

Incredible.

Heart pounding, Marcus wanted to call Nate right there but couldn't chance being overheard. Glad that his mother would be tied up with retreat functions all morning, he set off down the path for his suite. Once he was behind closed doors, he was going to give his FBI buddy a piece of his mind and then some.

Brother.

Crystal was in torment. She *had* to tell Ms. Taylor what she'd learned in the break room, she just had to. Even though they'd only really spoken that one time when they met in the supply closet, she'd always had great respect for the woman and thought she deserved to know what was going on. Crystal's boss at the spa in Seattle had thought so highly of Juliette Taylor and of JT Lady. To hear her and her products being maligned here among Palm Grotto staff was heartbreaking.

Worse, she'd seen Ms. Taylor hanging out with that handsome man yesterday. Somehow Crystal had to tell her he wasn't at all who he said he was. Ms. Taylor needed to know the truth, that he was an FBI agent, one they'd planted on the inside, right here at the resort, to spy on her.

Marcus had been pacing for the past hour. Why hadn't Nate called him back yet? He checked his phone again, just to be sure.

Nothing.

The longer he was forced to wait, the

angrier he grew. Nate had passed along the information about Juliette to his superiors knowing they would use it in some unscrupulous way to their advantage!

When Nate finally called back, that was the first thing Marcus said to him.

"What can I tell you, man?" Nate's reply was calm. "The agents from that branch tried to get the records they needed with her cooperation yesterday, but she turned them down. What other choice did they have but to get a warrant? Sure, I guess it was kind of a cheap shot to manipulate the murder situation for their own gain, but they're only trying to do their job. It's not that easy to convince a judge to give the go-ahead on an S-and-S. A good agent will do whatever it takes."

Marcus took a deep breath, trying to calm down. At least Nate wasn't trying to deny the truth or talk his way out of it. He was just telling it like it was.

"Are your people after Juliette personally?"

"Not that I know of. They're just trying to preserve any relevant records before the counterfeiters have time to cover their tracks."

Weary, Marcus lowered himself to the side of the bed and listened as Nate continued.

"Here's what I can tell you. It might make you feel better."

"I'm listening."

Nate lowered his voice. "The L.A. office has an informant. A counterfeiting informant. Thanks in part to his tips, we now know that the whole area you're in is heavily linked with the buying and selling of fake beauty products. Palm Springs. Desert Hot Springs. Cahuilla Springs. And not just her brand, but other brands as well."

Marcus tried to digest that information as Nate continued.

"If you think about it, it makes sense. These buyers and sellers of fake goods can be pretty aggressive. They recruit spa insiders who are in a position to manipulate inventory—underpaid, disgruntled spa employees who see an opportunity to make a little extra cash on the side and go for it."

"What are they being paid to do?"

"Different things. Siphon off legit products and sell them to the vendors. Replace what they took with fake products so that no one's the wiser. Every shill needs legitimate goods to use as a front. The fakes come into the picture on the back end. There are a lot of variations, but even just the old bait and switch at the cash register comes into play. The customer selects a jar of the real thing and hands it to the vendor, who bends down to put it in a bag and trades it out for a fake version he's gotten hidden under the counter.

Voila, a twenty-dollar sale on a two-dollar product."

Marcus nodded. "I guess it makes sense. But why is it happening so much in this area?"

"Because the region is dominated by the salon and spa industry—I mean, there's practically one on every corner. Most of those places are legit, of course, but we have managed to root out more than a few where employees are buying and selling inventory on the side."

"Including Palm Grotto?" Marcus stood and paced again.

"Possibly. There were a few indications, but Juliette Taylor's hosting of an event there and the death of her old cohort once she arrived has raised more red flags. We need to gather as much information as we can—and if some of that gathering requires a warrant, then, sure, our people will do what it takes to get one. That's just the facts of life. I understand why you're upset, but it's nothing personal against her."

Marcus was quiet for a long moment.

"At least we're making progress, Marcus. We know of three different online vendors who operate out of Cahuilla Springs. They advertise real products on their websites at super deep discounts but ship out fakes when the orders come in. We're also aware of several flea markets in the region that are rampant with counterfeit sales."

Marcus shook his head. "So why aren't you cracking down?"

"We are. Just this morning the local FBI branch raided the biggest flea market in the Coachella Valley. They're still processing things as we speak."

"And?" Marcus returned to his perch on the bed.

"And the raid itself might not seem to do much in the end. All the sellers will claim that they were duped into buying what they thought were real items. Not a single one of them will know anyone higher up in the counterfeiting chain than the man or woman who sells them the stuff. The Bureau will confiscate all the fakes, but there might not be any real leads. Worse, all those people will be back up and running in a month or two."

"So why bother?"

"Because every lead on a supplier puts us one rung higher up the crime ladder. See, counterfeiters are cockroaches. Turn on the light and they scatter. A raid like the one today might not seem to net much, but send a few counterfeiters running scared and things can begin to happen."

Marcus exhaled slowly. "I understand that, Nate. But why scatter those cockroaches while Juliette is still in town? Couldn't this have waited until she was on the plane out of here?"

Nate sighed. "Look, buddy, I know she's important to you, but she's not our only consideration. We don't have the luxury of waiting for one person to get out of the way. We're constantly moving ahead, step by step, and we take each break in the case where we can get it. This isn't a small problem, and it won't have a quick fix."

Marcus grunted.

"Hey, at least we're making a dent. Every new development helps."

"Fine. I understand that. I just don't see what the records in JT Lady's home office have to do with it."

"Neither do we—yet. But remember, Marcus, your friend showed up on that terror cell's list for a reason. We thought we knew the connection between her and the terrorists. But in light of the supermodel's death and the local police's suspicions, we need to take a closer look."

Marcus held his tongue. After all, the man was right.

Nate's voice softened. "I do have some good news for you. Or, at least news you'll be glad to hear."

"Oh?"

He cleared his throat. "I think you're safe to go ahead and tell Juliette about her name being on a terrorist list."

Marcus sat up straight. "Really?"

"Yeah. Bear in mind, the FBI can't offer her any protection, nor can we give her any further information about our investigation. But now that there are lawyers involved, the news about the list is going to come out anyway. She might as well hear it from you first."

Chapter Twenty-Eight

Juliette stood off to one side at the front of the auditorium and watched as the women trickled in from the doors at the back and chose their seats. What a pleasure it was to see the camaraderie they already shared, the smiles on their faces as they chatted among themselves. This was one reason she did these events, as a springboard for women to form new relationships.

Of course, just that word, *relationship*, brought only one person to mind. Who would have believed she and Marcus would reunite after all these years, much less that their old attraction would rise up so quickly, or that it would be so intense and all encompassing? She felt more comfortable and alive and whole with him than with any other man she'd ever met. It was that way when she was twenty-four and it was still that way now, at forty-nine.

No question, she was smitten.

All thoughts of romance aside, however, Juliette knew she needed to focus on the talk she was about to give, her second keynote of the weekend. Today's verse was from Luke: *"But Jesus often withdrew to lonely places and prayed."* Her goal for the session was to show these women how important it was to follow His example and take time out from all of their hard work and good deeds to refresh and regroup. Everyone needed to withdraw to the lonely places once in a while and spend time with their Creator, just as Jesus had done throughout His ministry on earth.

Juliette was lost in thought, doing a quick run-through of her notes, when she heard an odd sound behind her. Turning, she realized someone had cracked opened the exit door beside the stage.

"Pssst."

It opened a few inches more, and in popped the head of a spa employee, the cute little blonde named Crystal, who'd been so sweet and effusive when they met on Thursday. "Ms. Taylor? Can I speak with you for a minute?"

Tucking her notes into her pocket, Juliette glanced around at the auditorium, which was half full. Then she nodded, moving toward the door and joining Crystal on the cement walkway outside.

Crystal's face was a myriad of emotions. "I am so sorry to interrupt you. I was going to approach you inside, but then I thought it might be better to come around and speak to you out here. It's more private."

"No problem, though I only have a few minutes."

"Me too. I'll be quick."

Hands on hips, Juliette waited for Crystal to explain. The young woman had been such a help so far this weekend, filling in for Brooke and tirelessly pampering these women during their treatments. She was such an upbeat little thing, but at the moment the young woman's face and body radiated anguish.

"Are you okay?"

Crystal nodded. "I'm fine. I'm so sorry to bother you right before you have to give a talk, but there's something I need to tell you, and I won't be free again for hours."

"What is it?"

Crystal swallowed hard. "It's the staff. Spa staff mostly, I guess." The girl hesitated.

"Yes? What about them?"

She blushed furiously. "Well, as you can imagine, there have been a lot of rumors floating around since the, uh, the death on Thursday."

Juliette rolled her eyes. "No surprise there. Listen, the best way to handle gossip is just to ignore it."

"This is different. People are saying bad things about JT Lady, about your company's quality control. The thing is, I know it isn't true, because I worked with your whole line at my last job and we never had a single problem with any of it."

Wow. This wasn't what Juliette had expected to hear.

Crystal continued. "Apparently people have been getting skin burns from some of your products. Even Raven was burned here before."

Juliette's eyes narrowed. "Seriously?"

Crystal hesitated. "That's what I heard through the grapevine. I don't know if it's true or not, but I bet Andre could tell you. Just . . . well, keep my name out of it if you can, please. I'm no tattletale, but I couldn't keep quiet about this."

"Of course." Juliette nodded, unsure how else to respond. On the one hand, this was terrible news. On the other hand, at least it answered one question: This place really was dealing in counterfeits.

Juliette thanked the girl for sharing this with her and turned to go.

"There's something else."

Oh, great. Juliette turned back again and braced herself for Round Two. "Yes?"

Crystal's cheeks grew an even brighter shade of red. "There's a guest here at the spa, a really handsome man? About your age? I've seen you talking with him."

Juliette felt a lurch in her gut. Oh boy. Someone must've spied them kissing and spread that little tidbit around until it had grown into something lurid and altogether untrue. "I assume you mean Marcus Stone? Gray-blue eyes? Great smile?"

"Yeah, that's the one. Listen, I don't know how well you know this guy . . ." Crystal's voice trailed off as she met Juliette's eyes.

"It's complicated."

Crystal nodded. "Okay, well, for what it's worth, rumor has it he's an FBI agent. Worse, they're saying he was sent here to spy on you."

Crystal wasn't sure if going to Ms. Taylor had been the right thing to do or not. The woman hadn't seemed as upset as she'd expected about the news of the burns and the quality-control issues. But then when she learned about that guy and his connection with the FBI, she looked like she was going to faint.

Poor thing!

At least she managed to recover enough to

go inside and start in on her speech. But now that Crystal had thought things over en route to her next treatment hut, she was regretting the timing of their discussion. Why had she thought it would be okay to give Ms. Taylor news like that just before she had to go on a stage and address an auditorium full of people?

Dumb, dumb, dumb. Next time she'd hold her tongue till a more appropriate moment.

Crystal got to the hut two minutes late. She could hear movement inside, and as she swung the door open, she braced herself for a scolding from Ty. Though she outranked him in the Palm Grotto hierarchy, so to speak, he was a tyrant when it came to punctuality. She had a feeling upper management let him get away with such behavior because, after all, staying on schedule was in everyone's best interests.

Blinking as her eyes adjusted to the dimmer light inside, Crystal was surprised to see a client sitting there waiting for her. What on earth? That wasn't procedure. Late or not, it was the aide's job to wait until the therapist was present and ready before delivering the client. Yet here on the table sat a plump, middle-aged man in a Palm Grotto robe, smiling in her direction.

"Are you Crystal? That fellow said you'd be along any minute."

Flustered, she moved to the sink to wash her hands in preparation for the massage. "Yes, hi. Nice to meet you." She lathered her hands. "'That fellow' being the aide who brought you here?"

"Yep. Shaggy hair, big 'ol muscles? He gave me a message for you."

"Oh?" Crystal rinsing her hands, then turned off the water and reached for a towel.

"He said to tell you he was sorry, but he had a family emergency and needed to leave early."

Immediately Crystal's attitude changed. A family emergency? Oh. That was different. Of course Ty could change up procedure if he needed to.

"Did he happen to say what kind of an emergency it was?"

"Nope. But he sure was in a hurry to get out of here."

"Okay. Well, sorry about that. But thanks for letting me know."

"No problem."

Taking the completed intake form from the client, Crystal sucked in a deep breath and let it out slowly as she looked it over. Regardless of Ty's absence, regardless of the bad timing for her conversation with Ms. Taylor, at the moment she had a man in front of her who was here for a treatment. He deserved her undivided attention.

The drama swirling around this place would simply have to wait.

Juliette managed to get through her entire talk, but once it was over, she couldn't bear the thought of having to make it through lunch as well. During retreats she always tried to use the mealtimes for socializing with her guests. But even light banter took a certain amount of effort, and she simply didn't have it in her right now to be witty, friendly, or engaging.

This day just kept getting worse and worse. Not only did she need to find Didi to make up, she needed to find Marcus to break up. Throw in a dog and a truck and her life would have all the makings of a good country song!

At the thought of either encounter, she could feel a weariness settle deep in her bones. She wasn't ready to speak with either of them just yet. All she really wanted to do was to go back to her room, crawl under the covers, and take a long nap, so she headed that direction.

Maybe, if she were lucky, somewhere along the way there'd be an earthquake and the ground would simply swallow her whole.

By the time she got to the room, she was so tired she could barely stand. Within moments she had kicked off her shoes, emptied the contents of her pockets onto the bedside table, and draped her jacket over a chair. Then she slipped under the covers and quickly went to sleep.

Though she dozed for just half an hour, when she awoke, she felt much better. Power naps always did wonders for her energy and her mood—especially after a night like last night, when she'd hardly gotten any sleep at all.

Lying there under the cozy blankets, she tried to gather the energy she needed to get up, freshen up, and then get out there and have those difficult conversations. Marcus first, and then Didi. Hopefully, what Crystal had told her about him being an FBI agent was pure rumor, nothing more.

Juliette raised herself onto her elbows and was about to sit all the way up when she spotted something on the pillow next to her.

Odd.

It was a paper, folded into a square. Like a note.

Apprehension filling her gut, she stood up and simply stared at it for a long moment. She was certain that had *not* been there when she'd climbed into the bed and fallen asleep half an hour before.

Heart pounding, she stared at it for a long

moment. Something told her this thing might have fingerprints on it—and that that would be important. She dashed into the bathroom and came out with the tweezers from her makeup bag.

Then, hands trembling, she carefully used the tweezers to unfold the page. Sure enough, it was a note, printed in a messy, masculine hand:

Tell your boyfriend I'll be in touch. I'm ready to confess, but I want a deal—immunity in exchange for information.

Chapter Twenty-Nine

Marcus looked around. Why wasn't Juliette at lunch? The longer he waited for her to appear, the more concerned he grew. Something was wrong. She said she'd be there, circulating among her guests, but there was no sign of her. Even more worrisome, she hadn't answered a single text he'd sent her in the past half hour.

Where *was* she?

He was about to go looking for her when she finally texted:

COME TO MY ROOM. NOW!

What man wouldn't want to get that message, especially from a supermodel? But even as he read it, he knew something was wrong.

On my way.

Then, trying to act nonchalant, he excused himself, saying there was a matter he needed to attend to.

His mother looked dismayed. "What about your dessert? Didn't you order the Chocolate Tuxedo Pie?"

"Someone else can have it. Ladies? You do know that a dessert given to you by someone else has no calories, right?"

The women giggled as he gave a quick bow and turned to go. He made his way across the dining room, surprised to see Didi also headed that way. They reached the door at the same moment, and she looked at him, alarm in her eyes.

Marcus pushed the door open for them. "You got a text from Juliette?"

She nodded as she stepped through. "You too?"

"Yes. Hope she's okay."

Once outside, they chose the shortest route, which brought them around the building, down the slate steps, and toward the path marked "Tennis Courts." They were moving so fast that as they rounded the first bend, they nearly crashed into someone. Marcus stopped short then took a step back, realizing it was Reggie Roberts—the man who'd fired Iliana last night and then escorted Juliette into the arms of the police.

"Sorry about that," Didi muttered as she tried to regain her balance.

"No problem at all," Reggie said to Didi, and then he turned to Marcus and grinned. "What a coincidence. I was hoping to run into you today—though not literally, of course."

"Oh?" Marcus glanced at Didi, who looked about as happy with this encounter as he was.

Reggie continued. "Yes. Do you have a minute?"

"Not really, I need to get somewhere."

"No problem, I can walk with you as far as the yoga hut."

Didi harrumphed as the three of them continued on together.

Reggie didn't seem to notice. "I'll make it quick. I just wanted to offer you an apology."

Marcus tried not to groan. Couldn't this wait?

"You see, when you told me your name last night, it sounded familiar but it didn't register who you were. Then this morning it came to me, and I felt so stupid. Of *course* I know who you are. Let me just say, it's a real honor to meet you in person. I try to stay abreast of all incoming VIPs, but I never thought to check the names on the retreat roster. I do apologize for the oversight." Reggie extended a hand.

Marcus gave it a shake, the heat rising in his cheeks. "Don't give it another thought. I just brought my mother out for a little R and R. No recognition necessary."

"Your mother? How nice. Does she like citrus? Because we'd be happy to send over a complimentary fruit basket to your suite."

Marcus upped the pace as the path veered left and continued alongside the small lake. "She does, but to be honest she'd prefer a cutting from a couple of your grapefruit trees. She's big on gardening."

Reggie laughed. "I'm sure that can be arranged. For now, I just wanted to welcome you to Palm Grotto. And to let you know how integral you are to our Facilities division. It's corporate policy, all new construction must be based on the very guidelines *you* established. Our designers use the SSSD as their starting point. I thought you'd like to know that."

"Yes, that's gratifying to hear. Thanks."

"I've always been a fan, but I'm especially grateful for your contributions to the field now that I've been transferred here, to a vortex. Can't be too careful, as far as I'm concerned."

As they reached the other side of the lake, Reggie again shook Marcus's hand, then he bid them both good-bye, broke off, and disappeared into the dome-shaped yoga building.

They continued onward, Marcus again increasing the pace.

"What was *that* about?" Didi huffed and puffed to keep up. "He was gushing over you like you were a rock star."

"Yeah, that happens sometimes."

"Why? Are you really some kind of VIP, like he said?"

Marcus shrugged. He hated having attention called to himself in this way. "I'm just an engineer."

Didi grunted. "What's the SSSD?"

"The Stone System of Structural Dynamics. It's a construction concept I worked up in conjunction with the Earthquake Engineering Research Institute."

She pursed her lips, waiting for him to elaborate.

"I'm an expert in disaster prevention. Over the years I've worked to establish engineering guidelines for various disaster-prone areas—earthquake zones, tornado alleys, hurricane regions, things like that. For the people who are into that sort of thing, like Reggie there, I am kind of like a rock star, I guess. I put up with it if, at the end of the day, it means that lives are being saved. That's all."

Didi nodded, her expression softening somewhat. *Recalculating route*, as Zoe would say.

Marcus turned his attention back to the path in front of them. As they got closer, he began to run. Before they even reached the walk, Juliette's door flung open and she stood there waiting for them.

Please, Lord, let her be okay, he prayed. But from the look on her face, Marcus could see that she was not okay.

She was not okay at all.

Crystal prepared for her next massage, rubbing the warm oil onto her hands as she studied the woman in front of her. Though Mrs. Stone's posture was vaguely stooped, her face was smooth and calm, even beautiful. Soft wrinkles nestled around her eyes and mouth, hinting at a life filled with laughter. To Crystal's surprise, the woman was studying her, too, a curious and kind expression on her face.

"What did you say your name was, sweetheart?"

"Crystal."

"Well, Crystal, why don't you call me Beverly?"

Crystal smiled. Something about this woman was so appealing. "Okay, Beverly, I'm going to start your massage off with a heated mint extract oil to warm your hands and refresh the skin. Mint also relieves anxiety and is good for mental fatigue. Not to mention it smells great." Crystal took Beverly's hands in her own, working her thumbs against the palms. Almost immediately, Beverly closed her eyes and leaned her head back against the chair rest.

Crystal worked in peaceful silence for a while, but eventually Beverly let out a long sigh. "This is wonderful." She opened her eyes. "You're so young, but I can tell you really know what you're doing. Have you worked here long?"

"Thanks. Just a few weeks, actually. But I have a two-year degree in massage therapy. And before this I was at a day spa back in Seattle."

"Seattle? How did you end up here?"

"One of my clients had some connections. She knew I was looking to move so she put in a good word for me. It was a big step up, for sure."

"Well, Seattle's loss was Palm Grotto's gain. You're very good at what you do."

"Thank you. It's almost like my hands have ears. I use them to listen to what your body has to say."

"Really?" Beverly's expression was kind, but skeptical. "What does my body tell you about me?"

Smiling, Crystal used her thumbs to probe

both sides of Beverly's right hand. "See this slight swelling around your knuckle of your little finger? That's the palmar metacarpal area. It feels tight and looks swollen, which tells me without even looking at the rest of your body that you have tension in your shoulders. That's probably where you hold stress. Maybe you even get stress headaches?"

"That's amazing," Beverly said. "You're right."

Crystal moved up to Beverly's wrist, wondering what a woman her age had to be stressed about. She didn't want to pry, but she was perfectly willing to listen if Beverly wanted to talk. Unlike Moonflower, Crystal knew exactly what her job did and did not entail. She was a masseuse, not a counselor.

"It's all this commuting," Beverly blurted. "Having to get in and out of downtown Atlanta is a nightmare. I'm too old to hop from subway to train to bus, but there's no way I can drive, not in city traffic, anyway. I'm not sure how much longer I can keep it up—but I want so desperately to be there."

"What do you do in the city?" Crystal pumped some more oil into her hands and switched to Beverly's left side.

"I work in a soup kitchen on East Point Street."

"*No.*" Crystal just blurted it out, unable to

stop herself. She knew soup kitchens. She'd *lived* soup kitchens. The very idea of this little, defenseless woman working in an area like that horrified Crystal. "Sorry. It's just . . . Soup kitchens aren't usually in the safest places. You could be hurt or something."

Beverly smiled. "It's worth the risk, don't you think?"

Crystal focused on her work as the memories crashed back. The gnawing ache of hunger. The humiliating walk down the food line. The well-meaning volunteers who gazed at her, sympathy mixed with condescension.

"We have the sweetest regulars. Some of them are quite picky over their soup, but not a one of them can resist my homegrown, homemade tomato and basil."

Still drowning in the flood of memories, Crystal wrapped Beverly's hands in the heated towel and moved her stool so she could work on her feet.

"Is something wrong?" The woman's hands were covered, but the gentle tone of her words indicated that, if she could, she would have reached out and touched Crystal on the cheek.

"No, it's just that I've, uh, I've spent a little time in soup kitchens myself."

"Really?" Beverly's tone was friendly, casual. One volunteer to another.

Crystal hesitated. For some reason she wanted to tell this sweet woman the truth. "From the other side of the table."

Beverly was silent for a long moment and then she seemed to get it. "Ah."

They fell quiet for a while after that, but Crystal could tell her client was deep in thought, probably trying to decide what to say to this stupid girl who just admitted a humiliating fact about herself. Then, all of a sudden, Beverly gazed off in the distance and started to speak, her words sounding like a poem or some kind of quote:

> *"He who sits on the throne*
> *will shelter them with his presence.*
> *'Never again will they hunger; never*
> *again will they thirst.*
> *The sun will not beat down on them,'*
> *nor any scorching heat.*
> *For the Lamb at the center of the throne*
> *will be their shepherd;*
> *'he will lead them to springs of living*
> *water.*
> *And God will wipe away every tear*
> *from their eyes.'"*

Beverly gave Crystal a big grin. "I may be ancient, but I knew I could dig that one up from my memory in there somewhere. *'Never again will they hunger.'* I thought you might like that line best."

"The whole poem is lovely. What is it?"

"God's promise to you."

She said the words casually, but for some reason they hit Crystal like a punch to the stomach. Inexplicably her eyes filled with tears.

God's promise to her? If only that were true! But she'd had enough promises in her lifetime, thank you. And not a single one of them had ever been kept.

An hour later Juliette's room was getting crowded. Marcus and Didi were there, of course, as was Detective Bryant, a fingerprinting technician from the local police department, Reggie Roberts, and the head of housekeeping—a tough, heavyset woman named Lucita.

Juliette felt her throat tightening with claustrophobia, so she moved to the small patio just outside, Didi and Marcus following behind.

"Sorry, I couldn't breathe in there." Juliette moved to the nearest chair and sat, placing her elbows on her knees and her head in her hands. Soon she felt a warm body settle in next to her, and a whiff of Casmir told her it was Didi.

Juliette kept her eyes closed, trying to stop her mind from spinning. If only she could make sense of all that was going on! It didn't help matters that things were still strained between her and Didi and that she could hardly bring herself to look Marcus in the eye at all.

She'd been so relieved when they'd shown up after her call for help, both of them loaded for bear. But between her explanation of what had happened and their quick and decisive response, there'd been no chance for settling rifts or validating rumors.

And though that letter had now been discussed at length, not one of them had a clue who had left it. If it could be believed, then Raven's murderer had come into Juliette's room while she was sleeping and put it on her pillow.

The very thought chilled her to the bone.

At least things finally seemed to be winding down. Juliette heard a noise and looked up to see the fingerprinting lady breeze past them on the patio without so much as a goodbye. Lucita left next, pausing to assure all three of them that nothing like this would ever happen again.

Next, Reggie and the detective emerged

together then stood there on the patio giving their final wrap-up. Detective Bryant promised to keep them posted. Reggie spouted the party line about how terrible he felt that this had happened and would she like to be upgraded to a different room or maybe even a suite.

Juliette declined, knowing it wouldn't make any difference. Whoever had gotten into her room here would be able to do the same wherever she was in the resort. She would just have to remember to use the security bolt at all times.

Finally, both men said their good-byes and walked away, leaving a heavy silence between those that remained.

Didi was the first to speak. "Are you okay?"

Juliette sighed heavily. "I guess. At least I don't have to be anywhere for a while." They both knew that treatment appointments and free skin-care evaluations took up the next few hours of the retreat. And though Juliette usually helped out with the latter, her presence wasn't really required. Didi, on the other hand, needed this time to handle a variety of behind-the-scenes retreat matters.

"You can get going if you need to, Didi. I know you have lots to do." She glanced up and was surprised to see hurt in her friend's eyes. Then she realized how she must have interpreted that statement, i.e., *Get lost because I'd rather be alone with Marcus*. "Or stay. Either is fine."

Didi stood, her expression blank. "I'll be up at the conference center. Let me know if you need anything."

"Um, okay. I will. Thanks."

With that, Didi left. As Juliette listened to the sound of her footsteps moving down the walk, she wanted to go after her, to settle their argument from earlier. To apologize for keeping her out of the loop. To tell her that Marcus wasn't just some random guy, he was her TOTGA.

But before she could do any of that, she needed to know the truth about Marcus Stone.

The whole truth.

It wasn't just rumor any more. Thanks to the note left on her pillow, he'd been forced to explain to the police why it had been directed at him, of all people. In front of everyone, he'd admitted that whoever wrote that must've known he had "connections" with the FBI. But then the details of those connections had been relayed to the detective outside, in private.

Marcus hadn't offered a word of explanation to Juliette since.

With a heavy sigh, she looked at the man

across from her now and spoke in a low voice. "There's no way to get around this, Marcus, so I'm just going to ask you straight out." She met his eyes, her heart heavy as a rock. "What does the FBI has to do with this? And what do *you* have to do with the FBI?"

He ran a hand over his face with a loud sigh. "It's complicated. I'm not sure how to answer you."

"Are you an agent?"

"No." He sucked in a breath, blew it out. "But I do consult with them from time to time."

"Is that why you're here?"

"Again, it's complicated. But to an extent, yes, that's one reason I came."

She swallowed hard. "To spy on me?"

Marcus jerked his head back. "What? No! Where did you get that idea?"

"Don't play games. Don't try to mess with my head. I just want the truth. You owe me that. Are you here to keep an eye on me?"

He hesitated for a long moment, then he leaned forward and fixed his gaze on her. "Not in the way you mean. I'm here to keep you safe. To protect you. Believe me when I say that spying on you had nothing to do with it. The FBI didn't send me. In fact, I came here against their wishes, but I knew you were in danger and so I came anyway."

Juliette shook her head. Though his expression was earnest, she didn't know what to believe. If what he was saying was true, then why hadn't he told her any of this before?

"Why don't I go back to the beginning?" He sighed. "To the day, six months ago, when an old acquaintance of mine called me up and asked me to join a newly-formed FBI task force as a consultant."

"An FBI task force?"

He nodded. "An antiterrorism task force. Their office had located an active terrorist cell in Atlanta and needed me to run disaster scenarios as they worked toward an eventual raid. I accepted and got to work."

Juliette waited, clueless as to what this could possibly have to do with her, especially when Marcus went on to explain the cell structure and how it worked.

"The one we were focused on is what's known as a 'support cell.' Their job was to raise money for the cause, which they did primarily through the buying and selling of counterfeit goods."

And there it was.

At the word *counterfeit*, Juliette's stomach dropped, like on a fast-moving elevator suddenly shooting toward the sky. Heart pounding, she leaned forward and hung on Marcus's every word, desperate to know where he was going with this.

"The raid was a success, though of course there was a lot of processing that had to be done after the fact. I can't go into detail, but just a few hours ago I was finally given permission to tell you this: One of the documents recovered from the cell showed a list of ten names. The best we could figure, these were ten people the cell considered detrimental to their objectives. I can't give you any specific names, of course, but think politicians, legislators, those who speak out against counterfeiting. That sort of thing."

Juliette nodded, waiting for what she feared was coming next.

Then Marcus's beautiful blue-gray eyes met hers. "I'm sorry to tell you this, Juliette, but number six on that list was you."

Chapter Thirty

A half hour of questions and answers later, Juliette was still quite shaken, but at least she felt like she had a basic understanding of the situation with the terrorist list and the task force and the counterfeiting industry. There was much that Marcus wasn't allowed to say, and she respected that. Her bigger issue was with why her name had shown up in this way at all. Why would a terrorist organization target her? What had she ever done to make anyone think she was a threat?

It couldn't just be the corporate changes they'd made at JT Lady to deal with the problem. It couldn't just be what the FBI had suspected at first, that the terrorists feared she would use her celebrity to draw attention to the issue. Plenty of celebrities, some far more well known than she, had spoken out publically against counterfeiting. Sure, the people at *Harper's Bazaar* may have invited her to speak at their next anticounterfeiting summit, but she hadn't even accepted yet. And, again, there were already some big names on the roster. Why her and not them? What made her different? That was the most disturbing part of the whole puzzle.

Aside from all of that, then, just one question remained. Marcus had to know she would get to this—and that his answer could very well impact the course of their lives. As she looked at him now, the pain was like a fist wrapped around her heart, holding on tight and ready to squeeze even tighter.

She took a deep breath, but as she began to speak, she had to look away, afraid to see the truth in his eyes. "There's just one more thing I want to know, but I need you to promise you'll be a hundred-percent honest with me, no matter what. Okay? Promise?"

"As long as it's not privileged information."

"It's not."

"Okay, then. I promise."

She took a deep breath. "Now that I know you came here not to rekindle a romance but to keep an 'old acquaintance' from harm, I have to guess this whole thing has been a lie. Has it?"

"What whole thing?"

Juliette forced herself to look him in the

eye. "Us. The attraction. The reconnecting. All of it. Were you just pretending so you could stay close? Were you just doing your duty as a friend?"

She braced herself for the answer, but Marcus didn't speak. Instead, he simply sat there, silent, for a long moment. That silence told her all she needed to know.

Closing her eyes, Juliette whispered, "Fine, then. Thanks for your friendship, but I can take it from here. Please just go."

The creak of the chair as he stood sounded the breaking of her heart. How could she have fallen for this man not once, but *twice* in a lifetime? What a fool she had been!

Juliette was startled when she felt hands on hers. Her eyes flew open to see Marcus Stone kneeling on the ground in front of her. He gazed at her with such intensity that all she could do was sit there and look back at him as he spoke, his voice low and melodic.

"Twenty-five years ago I met the woman of my dreams. I spent a single afternoon with her, then we parted. But I was certain she and I were going to share a future somehow. I knew it was ridiculous, but that's how I felt, that quite possibly I had met 'the one.'"

Juliette nodded. She'd felt the same.

"Twenty-three years ago I went to find that woman, to tell her I was set with my career and finally ready for a relationship. But I was too late. She'd moved on."

Her eyes filled with tears as he spoke.

"My heart was broken—which is crazy, since I barely knew her, but there you go. Afterward, I guess you could say I kind of sealed off that part of myself and tried to get on with my life. I thought of that woman fondly and often, but in a very removed sort of way, almost like the entire encounter had been a figment of my imagination. Eventually I found someone else, started a family, was blessed with much joy. Endured a lot of heartache."

Tears spilled onto Juliette's cheeks. She looked down, waiting for him to get to the point, to put her out of her misery.

"Five years ago, when my ex-wife remarried, I sat down and Googled that person I'd met so long ago, the woman of my dreams. Thanks to the Internet, I found enough information to know that she was doing really well—but that she'd never married. I thought about looking her up. I *wanted* to look her up. But I had a little girl and a new business and a lot of baggage. So I left well enough alone. I'd blown my opportunity the first time around. I figured that chance had passed, for good."

Juliette shook her head, unable to stop herself.

"Then, three weeks ago, I read a list of names, and when I got to number six, my heart practically stopped. Juliette Taylor. *My* Juliette Taylor. I was dumbfounded."

His warm hand touched her cheek, tilting her face upward until she met his eyes.

"You ask if the reconnecting has been a lie? A means to an end?" His voice was soft and low. "Though I'm not proud to admit it, the truth is the exact opposite. Yes, I was concerned about an old friend. Yes, I wanted to protect you from this danger you knew nothing about. But to be completely honest, I also used that as an excuse to reconnect, to come here and find you and see if at least some small spark remained between us."

Juliette's pulse surged as fresh tears filled her eyes.

"Two days ago I followed a trail of Peppermint Patties that led me straight to you. And in one instant all twenty-five years evaporated. Just like that. You are still the most beautiful woman I have ever met. You are still that same sweet, fascinating, spunky girl you were way back then, when you fussed at me for hurting a cashier's feelings by not laughing at her joke."

Marcus raised his hands and cupped them on each side of her face. "Juliette, that's the one-hundred-percent honest truth. I have never forgotten you, and I have never gotten over you. I came here to protect you, yes, but mostly I came here to find you. To see if there could be an us. Surely you can understand what I'm saying. Surely you believe me."

Juliette swallowed hard, swiping at her tears. "I do believe you"—her voice came out a hoarse whisper—"But don't call me Shirley."

It took a moment, then he burst out laughing. With a guttural sound, he wrapped his arms around Juliette and pulled her close. They remained that way for a long moment, holding onto each other, rocking side to side, clinging to the hope of their past and the promise of a future.

In spite of everything going on, she had never known such joy.

After a sweet parting with Marcus, Juliette went in search of Didi and finally tracked her down in a back room at the conference center. She was shoulder-to-shoulder with several volunteers, assembling the farewell goodie bags that each retreat attendee would receive at the conclusion of the event the next day. When she saw Juliette come into the room, she turned her eyes downward without even acknowledging her presence.

Didi wasn't going to make this easy.

"May we speak privately?" Juliette's intention was to go outside, where the two of them could be alone to talk. Instead, Didi gave the workers a ten-minute break, apologizing to them that she hadn't thought to do so sooner.

The three women were chatting and laughing as they left, making the silence that much more noticeable once they were gone. Juliette closed the door behind them even as Didi continued moving down the line, filling a goody bag and placing it into a large cardboard box at the end of the row. Then she went back to the beginning, pulled out a new bag, and repeated the process.

"I know you're upset with me." Juliette stepped up to the other side of the table, grabbed an empty bag, and began to work her way down the line as well. "But I was hoping we could clear the air. Marcus and I want to have a brainstorming session at three-thirty, and I don't think we can do that if you're all mad and everything."

Didi paused, looking at Juliette. "A brainstorming session? About JT Lady?"

"Not just that. About the whole mess here. Raven's death. The vandalized sign. The note. Other things. I just have so many questions, but I think if a few of us put our heads together, we might be able to come up with some answers."

"I see." Lips pursed, Didi started up again, stuffing the bags with extra intensity. "Sorry, but three's a crowd."

Juliette thought for a moment, trying to figure out what was really going on here. She worked her way down the line, but after she put the filled bag into the box, she gave up and instead pulled out a stool from under the table and sat, facing her friend.

"What is it that bothers you about him? With the exception of a few bad apples, I've never known you to have a problem with any of the men I've liked. Why Marcus?"

Didi continued to the end with one more bag before answering. "Because you're carrying on with a complete stranger, acting like you've known him all your life. Sneaking off with him whenever you can. Even riding alone with him in his car last night." She paused to look straight at Juliette. "Do I need to remind you that a woman was *murdered* here, just days ago? How do you expect me to feel when I see you acting so careless in the wake of that?"

"I know that's how it seems, but—"

"But nothing. Don't you understand? This isn't about him. He's probably fine, a perfectly nice guy. Then again he might not be at all who he seems. Who knows? We're talking about a complete stranger. The reason I usually don't have a problem with the guys you date is because you choose carefully. You move slow. You check things out first. The way you've been the past few days is absurd."

"But there's something you need to—"

"Even if Marcus is drop-dead gorgeous, your behavior is completely over the top. I mean, some dashing stranger shows an interest in you, and suddenly it's like he's the center of your world? Honestly, Juliette, you're acting like a naïve child. You don't even know this man!"

Tired of being interrupted, Juliette raised her voice. "Actually, Didi, I *do* know this man."

Didi crossed her arms over her chest. "What do you mean?"

Taking a deep breath and letting it out slowly, Juliette met her friend's angry, confused glare. "He's TOTGA. Marcus Stone is The One That Got Away. After twenty-five years he's finally come back into my life."

There. She'd said it. Out loud. She felt a deep thrill, as if telling someone else had finally made it so.

In response Didi's eyes grew wide. Her face paled. She fumbled for another stool, pulled it out from under the table, and sat. When she spoke, her voice was hushed and strained.

"Are you sure? Twenty-five years is a long time."

Juliette nodded, unable to keep a smile from easing onto her lips. "I'm sure. He's here for me, Didi. The One That Got Away finally came to find me after all. And he's even more wonderful than I remembered. He's amazing, actually."

Again her friend grew silent. Slowly Didi's expression went from shock to hurt. "So why didn't you tell me sooner? Why did you let me worry like that?"

Juliette let out a long, slow breath, not sure how to answer that question. "You're right, I should've said something before now. But it was all such a shock. I needed to grasp the situation myself first before I could share it with anyone else."

Closing her mouth, Didi nodded, though the look on her face remained troubled. "Well. Good for you." Her voice was flat. She stood, walked to the door, and swung it open. "I'll, uh, I'll let you know about the brainstorming." She hesitated there in the doorway for a long moment.

Then she simply turned and walked away.

Crystal clocked out at 3:05 p.m., glad to be done for the day—or for the next four hours, anyway. Despite having risen before dawn for the sunrise hike, she had to be back on duty tonight at 7:30, to help with the final session of the conference.

She was just leaving when she checked her cubby and discovered a pink phone slip inside, from Juliette Taylor no less. Crystal's stomach clenched. All the note said was to call ASAP, with a phone number written in underneath.

Oh boy. This couldn't be good. Was she in trouble? Did it have to do with their earlier encounter, when Crystal told Juliette about the rumors she'd heard?

Hands shaking, Crystal dialed the number from her cell and soon was talking to Ms. Taylor, who didn't sound mad at all. She just asked if they could meet up, away from the resort if possible, the sooner the better. Crystal agreed, but her mind churned with possible explanations for what this could be about.

She had already ditched her white lab coat, but now she returned to the ladies' locker room and went ahead and changed her clothes as well, switching back into the more casual Palm Grotto sweat suit—dark green with a white logo—that she'd worn for the sunrise hike. Soon she was in her car and on the way to Desayuno, a little 24-hour pancake house about fifteen miles from the resort.

Crystal was a nervous wreck by the time she got there. Knees trembling, she made her way inside and found Ms. Taylor waiting for her in a booth by the window. To her surprise, that super hunky FBI guy sat next to her. Introductions were made, and he insisted that Crystal call him Marcus.

"And I'm Juliette. Please. No more 'Ms. Taylor,' okay?"

"Okay."

In a soft voice Juliette added, "Just so you know, that rumor you told me about Marcus was partly right, he has worked with the FBI in the past. But he's not an agent and he wasn't sent here to spy on me. That's all I'm allowed to tell you, except that I do trust him implicitly and I assure you that you can too."

Crystal nodded, feeling both mortified and flattered. Why did they care what she thought anyway?

A waitress came and took their orders. Once she was gone, Juliette finally launched into an explanation of what was going on, saying that this was a brainstorming session and they wanted Crystal to be a part of it.

Her eyes narrowed. "A brainstorming session? What's that?"

Juliette glanced toward the handsome man beside her. "Marcus and I have been trying to get answers about some of the things that have been happening around the resort this week. So we've decided to brainstorm a bit. We thought it would be good to include an insider in the discussion, someone we can trust who works for the spa. We're hoping that person is you."

They trusted her? They barely knew her! Still, a warmth began to spread inside Crystal's chest.

"Um, of course. Sure. I'll do what I can. But I've only been here a few weeks, so I might not be all that helpful. I don't know much."

"I don't think any of us knows much, individually." Juliette gave Crystal an encouraging smile. "But maybe if we put our heads together, we'll find we know more than we think we do."

Chapter Thirty-One

The brainstorming session went along better than Marcus had expected. Didi showed up just as they were getting started, and despite the tension between her and Juliette, the mood around the table was upbeat and productive. Just as Juliette had predicted, Crystal was a welcome addition, especially as she was able to elaborate on the many behind-the-scenes spa procedures that were relevant to the murder.

Marcus started out with the theory he'd been working on, that Raven's killer was an employee at the resort. He asked Crystal how an employee might sneak onto the grounds unnoticed after hours, and she said they couldn't, that the only way to get back in was by scanning an employee keycard at the front gate.

"How about coming onto the grounds

somewhere else?" he asked. "Do you know if the perimeter is secure?"

"No clue. But I'd be happy to ask my friend Greg. He's a Palm Grotto security guard."

"Or I could just give Orlando a call." Didi reached for her phone.

Juliette nixed that idea. "No offense, Didi, but I'm not sure anymore if we can trust him." She went on to explain how she'd seen Orlando give one of Raven's three "mystery men" a package—and received a payoff in return.

Didi's expression soured. "That doesn't sound like a payoff to me. It sounds like a tip. A courier must've dropped the package off at the front gate, and Orlando simply took responsibility for delivering it."

Marcus nodded. "I'm with Didi on this one. I don't think his behavior sounds suspicious."

"Do you know what was in the package?" Crystal asked.

Juliette hesitated. "Papers. About an inch-high stack of papers, all of them covered with printed text. I got a look at one page, and it was almost like a story. It described a woman, and parts of it could've been about Raven, but other parts not. I wasn't sure what it was."

"Maybe she was writing a book," Crystal mused.

Didi barked out a laugh. "Gotta be able to read one before you can write one."

Ignoring her attempt at humor, Marcus pulled out a paper and handed it over to Crystal. "I brought along the resort map. Any thoughts on where someone might be able to sneak onto the grounds after hours, in the dark, unnoticed?"

The young woman studied the page then pointed out several issues, including a ten-foot fence that ran parallel to the highway along the north, a cliff-like drop on the east, and thick brambles and underbrush blocking the south. That left the west as the most vulnerable.

Crystal looked at Marcus. "They'd have to hike half a mile or so first to get there, but that's about it."

Nodding, he pointed out the six circles that he'd drawn in on the map earlier and explained that he'd taken a walk around the resort, scoped out the security cameras, and drawn those circles to indicate his estimation of their viewing radius. "See if you can trace a route from that western entrance point all the way to the building where Raven was killed, without crossing into any of those circles."

Crystal did as she was told, her finger zig-zagging across the page. "Yes." She looked up at him, eyes wide. "Except for one, the camera behind Arrowscale."

"The camera that just happens to be broken."

They shared a knowing look. If Marcus's theory was correct, then the murderer knew the resort well.

The waitress showed up with their food, so Marcus took back the map and put it away for now. Once they'd been served, he said a blessing and they all turned their attentions to the various plates and platters in front of them.

Eager to keep things moving along as they ate, Marcus led them to the next point of discussion, which was Iliana's comment from the night before. Turning to Crystal, he asked if she knew what the woman might have meant by her exclamation of "wasn't one death enough for you?"

Crystal shook her head. "I can ask a few people, but honestly, no one's ever mentioned any other deaths at Palm Grotto."

From there they moved on to the argument Juliette overheard when she was examining the products in Ty's workstation closet. Marcus had her repeat that argument word for word, as much as she could remember anyway, in the hopes that something the man and woman had said might click with the others. Sure enough, as she neared the end of her tale, Crystal gasped.

"'News flash'? She really said it that way? 'News flash'?"

Juliette nodded.

"Wow. Well, I don't know for sure if it was her, but I can tell you who uses that expression all the time. In fact, I heard her say it yesterday, when she yelled at Ty in the break room. 'News flash! Whoever empties the coffeepot has to refill it!'"

Marcus glanced at Juliette then back at Crystal. "Who?"

She met his eyes. "Xena. Xena says 'news flash' all the time."

"There's more." Crystal's heart pounded as she looked around the table at the others. "I might know what they were talking about. But I need to make a call before I can say anything."

As the others looked on, their expressions perplexed, Crystal excused herself, grabbed her cell phone, and headed outside. In moments she was on the phone with Moonflower, once again attempting to get permission to share what she'd been told in confidence.

This time she tried a different approach.

Rather than arguing about the detectives' right to know, she played on Moonflower's distrust of the cops by telling her how poor, sweet Juliette Taylor had been hauled down to the police station as a suspect in Raven's murder.

Moonflower took the bait, ranting about "abuses of power" and "keeping women down" and other such things. From there it wasn't hard to convince her that Juliette deserved to know about the blackmail to protect herself.

Back at the table Crystal shared all of it, the entire sad tale of Raven's early days in New York City, the film she'd made, and the way it had come back to haunt her so many years later via blackmail. When she was done, Juliette chimed right in.

"Okay, I totally agree that the conversation I overheard could've been about blackmail. That would make a lot of sense, actually. When Raven showed up at the wrong time of year, Xena and whatever man she was talking to must've concluded that she'd found them out and was coming here to do something about it." Juliette wrapped her hands around her coffee mug. "But what I don't get is how on earth someone like Xena could get her hands on a film that old. We're talking thirty years ago, give or take."

Crystal nodded. "To blackmail Raven, she

didn't need to have the movie itself, she just needed to know it existed. The *threat* of that film is what was important here, not the actual film itself."

Juliette frowned. "But how would Xena have known about it? I highly doubt Raven would've shared such a thing with anybody, much less someone like Xena."

Crystal smiled. "Raven didn't tell Xena. She told Moonflower. And though the information was kept in confidence, Moonflower made the mistake of writing it in her treatment notes."

Didi gave a slow nod. "So all Xena had to do was look through Moonflower's notes to get the goods on Raven?"

"Exactly."

"Why, though?" Juliette frowned. "Why would Xena have done something so extreme?"

Crystal thought for a moment, sucking in a breath as her earlier conversation with Vin and Lisa sprang into her mind. Quickly she explained to the others what she'd learned, how Raven had been burned by a beauty product during a treatment and filed a complaint that ended up wreaking havoc on several lives—including Xena's and Andre's. "They did it out of revenge. They were so furious at Raven, they probably wracked their brains to come up with some sort of payback.

They probably dug through Moonflower's treatment notes hoping to uncover some perfect little secret. Then they threatened Raven with revealing that secret unless she paid up."

Juliette nodded. "The man I heard arguing could have been Andre."

"And did she?" Didi asked Crystal. "Pay up, I mean?"

She shook her head. "Moonflower urged her to call the blackmailer's bluff, which Raven did. She refused to pay—and now she's dead and poor Moonflower is terrified for her life."

Didi's eyes narrowed. "I don't know. Xena and Andre as blackmailers, maybe. But as killers? I don't see it."

Everyone grew silent for a long moment until finally Juliette spoke. "At least I just figured something out." She looked from one to the other. "I think I know what Raven meant by her threat to me at the airport."

It was all coming together—and it was breaking Juliette's heart. "I don't know why I didn't realize it before. It's so obvious. And so sad."

"What?" Didi leaned toward her.

"Raven never made any secret of the fact that modeling was just a stepping-stone to her real dream. Even as a supermodel, all she talked about was her future movie career. It never happened, not in a big way, but maybe she was still pursuing it all these years later."

Didi stared at her, face blank.

Tears filled Juliette's eyes. "Don't you get it? When Raven told me, 'That part is mine,' she was talking about a part in a movie. That *part* is mine."

Didi frowned. "Why here, though? This is a spa, not an audition studio."

Juliette looked from her to Marcus. "Maybe so, but Palm Grotto is a haven for the Hollywood elite. What do you want to bet those three men she wanted to stay near are producers or directors or whatever."

"That would explain their expensive cars," Marcus replied. "And the fact that they chose film characters for their fake names."

Juliette nodded. "Raven must've come here hoping to convince them to cast her in their next movie. When she learned I'd be here too, she must've thought I was after the same thing, the same part. So she read me the riot act."

Didi exhaled slowly. "'That part is mine.'"

Juliette sat up straight, another thought coming to her. "This would also explain the package Orlando delivered yesterday. It wasn't a book I saw, it was a *script*. I was probably reading a character description—more than likely for the character Raven was hoping to play." The more Juliette thought about it, the more she knew she was right. "Somehow Raven must have known those men were coming here under Jimmy Stewart character names, but not which ones. So she gave Iliana a list of every single possibility and just hoped there'd be a match in there somewhere."

"Lucky for her, there were three matches," Didi said. "George Bailey, Elwood Dowd, and Scott Ferguson."

Crystal sat up straight. "Did you say Elwood Dowd?"

They looked her way. "Why? Do you know him? Who is he?"

The young woman hesitated. "I'm not at liberty to say. But you must have seen him around. Him . . . and his hair plugs?"

Juliette gasped. "Quentin VonTassel! We saw him in the spa's restaurant Thursday night."

Didi met her eyes with a wry smile. "Just think. All this time we've been wanting to learn more about Raven's mystery men, when there we were that first night, having dinner not ten feet away from them."

Marcus skimmed through his list, eager to wrap things up. "Okay gang, there's just one issue left to discuss, that of who vandalized the JT Lady sign, and why."

They debated the various possibilities—that the murderer did it, perhaps as a warning or threat that there were more deaths to come. That it was a malicious stunt engineered to malign either JT Lady or Palm Grotto Spa. That it was just some stupid prank pulled by a mischievous employee or guest.

Though Marcus didn't voice his own opinion to the group, his fear was that it somehow tied in with the counterfeiters—perhaps as a warning of some sort to Juliette. He hoped he was wrong, but until he knew for sure, he planned to keep his eyes peeled and assume the worst.

At least there was one promising clue: the unusual footprint that Didi had photographed. She said the print looked familiar to her for some reason, though she couldn't think why. Juliette suggested that she upload the pictures onto the computer and see if an enlarged version might help jog her memory.

Didi agreed to try. "I need to get back to my retreat duties, but if I leave now, I can probably take a few minutes for that first."

She left, and then the three who remained divvied out the other tasks. Crystal agreed to look into Iliana's odd comment to Reggie. Juliette said she'd try to confirm her theory about Raven's threat meaning a part in a movie. Marcus said he would tell the detectives about the blackmail then take a closer look around the resort's western perimeter to search for signs of entry.

Before they left, Crystal told them she had one more issue to discuss. "Sorry, but I'm still confused by everything that happened on Thursday. The weird noises Raven and Brooke were making. The whole, 'I need another drink' thing. The way Brooke was so out of it when I finally went in there. Do you guys . . . have an explanation for any of that? I assume it has to do with the drug that was used to poison them? It's called atropine, I think?"

Marcus flipped through his notes. "Yes. I knew some about the drug already, but I checked it out online to get more info." He skimmed what he'd written. "Okay, let's see . . . Atropine is used for everything from optical surgery to stomach-related issues—like colitis and ulcers—to Parkinson's, and even brain tumors. It can be a real lifesaver. Literally."

"If it's so great, why did Raven die from it?"

"In a large dose, atropine can paralyze the motor nerves. It causes dry mouth, racing heartbeat, dilated pupils, high fever . . ." He skimmed further. "Flushed face, disorientation, hallucinations."

"Wow." Horror resonated in Crystal's whisper. "I saw and heard all of that. At first I thought they were drunk, but that must've been the disorientation and hallucinations. One of them kept saying she wanted another drink. I thought she meant alcohol, but I guess she was just asking for water because of the dry mouth."

Marcus glanced at Juliette, who seemed pale and withdrawn.

Crystal continued. "When I got in there, Brooke was sitting on the floor, staring straight ahead and making this high-pitched noise. Her skin was super hot and flushed, and her eyes were so dilated I couldn't even see the color in them." She looked up at Marcus. "Sounds like almost everything you just described."

Marcus nodded. "At least Brooke's symptoms stopped there. Poor Raven would've gone through the next steps too: respiratory depression, coma, circulatory collapse, and then death."

Crystal shook her head. "All while I was right next door."

"You couldn't have known," said Juliette.

Crystal looked at Marcus. "It probably took a lot of atropine to poison them that bad. Can't the police just check pharmacy records or something? Find out which one of their suspects had a prescription?"

"It wouldn't necessarily had to have come from a pharmacy," he replied. "From what I saw online, atropine is in plants that grow all around this area. The killer could have gone out and picked a big batch of belladonna or deadly nightshade and taken it from there, no prescription required. There's also jimson-weed, moonflower—"

Crystal's eyes widened. "Moonflower?"

The four of them looked at each other.

"Coincidence?" Marcus asked.

"Must be," Juliette replied.

"Yeah. Must be." But by the look on Crystal's face, Marcus had a feeling that a new suspect had just been added to their list.

Chapter Thirty-Two

When their brainstorming session was over and the check paid, they said their good-byes and headed out. Crystal was just sliding her keys into the ignition when her cell phone rang.

She took a look. Moonflower. Pulse surging, Crystal sucked in a deep breath and then answered, hoping her voice didn't give away her apprehension.

The older woman jumped right in. "Well? Did you tell Juliette about the blackmail?"

"Yes, I did. She appreciated your help."

Moonflower sighed. "I don't relish the thought of her sharing that information with the police. But if that's what it takes to secure her freedom, then so be it."

Afraid that her older friend might launch into yet another rant, Crystal cut her off by blurting out the question that was foremost on her mind. "Hey, where did you get the name 'Moonflower'?"

"I . . . huh?"

"Your name. Moonflower. Is that a nickname or is it real?"

"My real name is Doris. People started calling me Moonflower back in the sixties. I went through a bit of a wild phase, I'm afraid. Did so much moonflower they started calling me that. Eventually it just kind of stuck. I can't say I minded too much. I do seem more like a 'Moonflower' than a 'Doris,' don't you think?"

"Yeah, I guess." Crystal's narrowed her eyes. "But I'm confused. You said you 'did' moonflower. How does one 'do' moonflower, exactly?"

"Oh, hon, I really don't recommend it. That stuff makes for a nice high, sure, but it's actually quite dangerous. I can't believe how we used to play around with it back then. It's a miracle one of us didn't end up dead."

If Moonflower drugged Raven, would she be speaking so matter-of-factly like this now? Crystal decided to take it a step further. "You do realize that's what killed Raven, right?"

"What do you mean?"

"The drug that comes from moonflower— or jimsonweed or belladonna or a couple of other plants that grow wild around here. That's what was put into the chai soy mud that did Raven in."

"No, it wasn't," Moonflower sputtered. "The newspaper said she died from an overdose of atropine."

"Right. And where do you think atropine comes from?"

"No way!" Moonflower cried. "From *moonflower?*"

Crystal was glad her friend was so dumbfounded. She really couldn't fathom that this sweet older woman, who was filled with such life, could be capable of inflicting death.

Settling back into her seat, Crystal interrupted her friend yet again, this time to ask the other pressing question on her mind. "Do you know if there have been any other deaths at Palm Grotto? Like, prior to Raven?"

"Um . . . Yeah. Sure. Three or four that I can recall." Moonflower's voice sounded so casual, but as she continued, Crystal realized why: She was talking about deaths that had occurred over the several decades she'd been working there, each from natural causes.

"Sorry, I meant, have there been any other deaths in the recent past, like, say, since Reggie came on board last year?"

"Oh. In that case, no." After a beat, Moon-flower amended that thought. "Well, we did have someone die last year. But it didn't happen *at* Palm Grotto."

Crystal sat up straight. "Did that death involve Reggie in any way?"

"Yes, actually, it did. Raven too, for that matter."

Crystal's breath caught. "Tell me about it."

"Well, let's see. It was last summer. Raven came for her usual July visit, but her regular manicurist was out of town. Xena assigned a different manicurist instead, and that's where the trouble started. It wasn't the poor girl's fault, but something was wrong with the exfoliating cream and it ended up burning the skin on Raven's hands and forearms. Of course, Raven being Raven, she put up a huge stink. Filed a complaint with Andre—and when that didn't seem to do anything, she went over his head and filed another with Reggie."

Crystal closed her eyes and pinched the bridge of her nose. Why did that incident from last summer keep coming up? More important, why hadn't anyone bothered to mention the part where someone *died*?

"I've already heard some of this, how Reggie was new and didn't realize that Raven was just up to her usual shenanigans and all of that."

"Exactly. Like a real rube, he conducted an official inquiry. Treated it like a big deal. In the end he wrote up the aide, the manicurist, the scheduler, and the spa manager—and sent the full report on to corporate."

Crystal watched a wasp hover at the front windshield as Moonflower continued.

"The poor manicurist got fired. The aide nearly did as well. At least Xena and Andre got to keep their jobs, but there were all kinds of consequences for the both of them—no bonuses or promotions for at least a year, stuff like that. They were *not* happy about it."

"Yeah, but come on. A burn isn't exactly a small matter."

"No, you're right. It's not. Raven had every right to report it. But she didn't have to make such a big fuss over it. Screaming, crying, finger-pointing. It was way over the top. If everyone disliked Raven before, they positively despised her after that. When she came back for her January visit, nobody would even talk to her. I tried to warn her that would happen if she persisted with all the drama, but she wouldn't listen to me. Now she was paying the price. The poor woman was completely ostracized."

Crystal sighed. "And the death? Where did that come in? Who died?"

"Oh, it was such a tragedy. The manicurist. A few days after she got fired, she killed herself. It was so heartbreaking. She was the sweetest, saddest girl."

Crystal sucked in a sharp breath. "What was her name?" she asked, realizing she knew the answer even as Moonflower said it.

"Valentine. Valentine Overstreet. I think you know her brother, Greg, the security guard? He was devastated, of course. Kept insisting it was murder, not suicide. But we all figured that was just his way of coping. I mean, the signs were pretty clear."

Anger flared within Crystal's heart. Maybe so, but how dare they all dismiss Greg's suspicions entirely? Even if suicide had been the more obvious conclusion, they could've at least considered the alternative.

Moonflower continued. "Val was clinically depressed, I do believe, plus she'd been having an affair with a married man, and it ended badly. Losing her job was the last straw. She just went off the deep end. Almost everyone blamed Raven, but I say it was Reggie's fault too. If only he weren't such a stickler."

Again, Crystal gasped. What was it that Marcus had overheard Iliana say to Reggie?

Wasn't one death enough for you?

It made sense now.

The death Iliana had been talking about was Valentine's!

"Her ex was the one who broke off the relationship. Told Valentine he had to call it quits because he just couldn't live with the guilt anymore. Guilt, schmilt, the guy cheats on his wife all the time. That was just an excuse."

The wasp landed and began inching its way along a windshield wiper. Crystal watched, her mind spinning as Moonflower continued.

"I mean, their affair wasn't exactly common knowledge, but Val confided in me sometimes. I know she loved him desperately. Losing him devastated her."

Crystal's mind raced. What was the quote the police had taken for a suicide note? *"If you lose control of your heart, you lose control of your head, too?"*

No wonder everyone had jumped to that conclusion.

"Who was he?" Crystal hated to ask, but she simply had to know.

On the other end of the line, the older woman was quiet for a moment. "I'm no gossip, Crystal. Ordinarily, I wouldn't violate a confidence like this, but I guess it doesn't matter now anyway. I think I'll make an exception, purely as a cautionary tale."

"A cautionary tale?"

Moonflower sighed. "The man was someone she worked with. You work with him now too. I'd hate to see you fall into the same trap she did. He is awfully handsome."

Crystal's mind raced. "Who, Moonflower? What's his name?"

"It was Ty Kirkland. The spa aide. Before she died, Valentine had been having an affair with Ty."

Juliette had no idea who Raven's agent was, but it shouldn't be hard to find out. She waited until Marcus finished his call with the detective, then as he drove them back to the resort, she started checking around. Sure enough, after just a few calls, she had the agent's name and office number.

Crystal had said the man might be in hiding, but Juliette had a feeling he'd just been avoiding Moonflower's calls. And though Juliette hated to throw her own "celebrity" around, she invoked it now. It must've worked, because after less than a minute on hold, the man's secretary put her through.

In her most charming voice, Juliette apologized for the intrusion but said that she needed to talk to him about her "old friend and colleague" Raven. Then she launched right in, telling the man her theory about Raven's threat at the airport and the three men who were staying at the resort incognito. Much to her relief, the agent confirmed all of it.

"Let's just say that Raven was *desperate* to get that part." He spoke in a thick Brooklyn accent—despite the fact that he worked in Beverly Hills. "She managed to get a glimpse of the script, and she was convinced that was the character she was born to play. The role called for a 'woman of a certain age,' a hardworking Appalachian type who also happened to be tall and stunning."

Just like the paragraph Juliette had seen in the restaurant. "Any chance she was actually going to get the part?"

"No ma'am. No way. Between you and me, Ms. Taylor, I couldn't even get her an audition. They said they needed a more, uh, *natural* look."

"Ah." In other words, one not so obviously altered by cosmetic surgery. Poor Raven. Why had she clung so desperately to her youth when she could have grown into such a beautiful older woman?

The agent continued. "Somehow she got it in her head that if the director would just spend a little time with her, he'd look beyond the obvious and see how perfect she was for the part anyway."

"So she arranged to meet up with him here?"

"Uh . . . not exactly. You might say she kind of *stalked* him there."

He went on to explain how Raven had been hovering around VonTassel for a few weeks, waiting for the perfect opportunity to corner him. Apparently she had busboys on the payroll at all of his favorite restaurants, to keep their ears open on her behalf. Last week she finally hit pay dirt when one of her paid informants told her that not only was VonTassel going to a spa this weekend— which was, to her mind, the perfect place to connect in a relaxed setting—but he was going to *her* spa, the one she'd been using for years.

"She must've been thrilled."

"Yep. Took it as kismet. Wanted to book a room near his but there was just one problem—she had no idea what name he'd be registering under. All her informant knew was that he was staying incognito, as a character from an old Jimmy Stewart movie."

Juliette nodded. "So why all the secrecy? From what I understand, people in the entertainment industry come to Palm Grotto all the time."

"It's the *combination* of the three people involved." The man's voice grew intimate. Conspiratorial. "This is all very hush-hush, you understand, but rumor has it that those three are in talks about forming their own studio. If they do, it'll be very big news."

"I see."

"From what I understand, this is supposedly going to be their flagship film."

A flagship film from a new studio—and Raven dreamed of being the star.

Taking a deep breath, Juliette thanked the agent for his help and said there was just one more thing, the matter of the blackmailer.

He sounded surprised that she knew about that but told her what he could. His version of events was similar to Crystal's, though when he mentioned having discussed it with the police, Juliette interrupted him. "Wait. You reported the blackmail to the police?"

"No, Raven didn't want that. I'm talking about yesterday, when the lead detective on the murder case called to question me. I went ahead and told him everything—about the blackmail scheme, about Raven's threat to you at the airport, about the three men and why she was there at the spa."

Juliette thought about that for a moment. "Did you happen to mention how Raven gave the list of Jimmy Stewart character names to the reservationist?"

"Yeah, of course."

Well. At least that explained who had tattled. Just knowing made Juliette feel oddly vindicated. Take that, Iliana.

Marcus made a right turn, and Juliette realized they weren't far from the resort. Eager to wrap things up, she asked the agent her final question, if he thought the blackmailer might've been the one to kill Raven.

"Huh. Never crossed my mind. That's been all over and done with for a while. The letter came back in January, Raven responded to it a week or two later, and nothing's happened since. I've been monitoring the Internet—just to keep an eye out, you understand—but as far as I can tell, no movie has ever surfaced. I think the blackmailer was bluffing. Once she called that bluff, there was no other response but to let it drop."

Marcus slowed as they neared the entrance up ahead.

The agent continued. "If you want to know the truth, Ms. Taylor, there are plenty of viable suspects much closer at hand. Raven had no shortage of enemies, as I'm sure you know. I hate to say it, but given the number of people who wished she were dead, I'll be surprised if they *ever* figure out who actually did it."

As Juliette hung up, a wave of sadness swept over her. It was almost as if Raven had intentionally alienated people, to keep them away. She probably figured if she never let anyone get close, she'd never get hurt.

How wrong she had been!

Juliette tried to put those thoughts from her mind as Marcus slowed and turned in to the resort. They pulled to a stop at the security booth, surprised to see Didi there, chatting with Orlando, laptop tucked under her arm.

As soon as Marcus rolled down the window, Didi instructed them to park the car around the corner and come right back. Juliette didn't have much time to spare before she would need to return her attentions to the retreat—dinner with the attendees was in half an hour, followed by an hour of preparation and her final keynote address at eight— but they did as requested and were soon back at the gate on foot.

"You'll never believe what I found." Didi's eyes glowed as she opened her laptop and thrust it toward Juliette. "This is the clearest shot I got of the footprint near the sign."

Juliette looked at the photo on the screen, which was quite clear. It showed the rich brown soil of a flowerbed, into which had been pressed the front curve of a shoe with a very unique tread.

"Now, if you zoom in here . . ." Didi pressed a few buttons and enlarged the image. "You can see a tiny irregularity on one of the treads."

Juliette squinted at the screen, conscious of the heat of Marcus's body as he stood close and looked on as well. Didi was right, the tread pattern consisted of rows and rows of round dots, but one of those dots looked different from the others—intentionally so.

"Now"—Didi pressed a few more buttons— "I had an idea, so I did a little Googling. And *voilà*."

With one more click, the photo of the dirt was replaced with a slick advertising image of an actual shoe, tilted on its side to reveal the unique tread along the bottom. The rows and rows of dots were an exact match for the shoeprint in the dirt.

Without a word, Didi zoomed in closer on this image as well—until Juliette could see exactly what had caused the irregularity in the dirt. One of the dots of the tread held an imprint, the familiar logo of the overlapping letters *L* and *V.*

Louis Vuitton.

No question, the shoe that had made that footprint was a designer ballet flat, straight from the Louis Vuitton spring collection.

Chapter Thirty-Three

Juliette couldn't believe Iliana had been the one to vandalize their sign. Then again, she *had* left the resort last night in a fury, blaming the owners of JT Lady for her misfortune. Was it really all that surprising that she'd come back here later to strike out in revenge? At least her only weapon had been a can of spray paint. Considering the events of the past few days, Juliette shuddered to think what could have happened instead.

Marcus frowned. "Guess we should call and share this with the police."

"We can tell them in person," Didi said. "They're on their way now to get Xena. They called Orlando and told him not to let her leave the property."

Juliette glanced at Marcus. Thank heaven the police were already acting on the info they'd called in just after leaving the restaurant.

Juliette glanced at her watch and rethought her schedule. She had intended to freshen up and prepare for her talk before dinner, but that would mean heading on to her room now. Instead, she decided to wait and do that between the meal and the closing session, which would buy her another half hour before she'd have to go. Maybe she'd get to see how events unfolded.

A handsome young security guard came to deliver a status report to Orlando, and Juliette strained to listen as they spoke. From what she could hear, Xena was still at the spa for now but was almost done for the day and should be heading out soon. When they finished talking, the young man slipped into the booth as Orlando rejoined them at the gate.

"I wish the police would hurry up and get here." He looked toward the road, his expression tense.

Juliette cleared her throat. "While we're waiting, I have a question about Iliana. She was escorted out of here last night in a rage, so why on earth was she allowed back onto the property later?"

Orlando shook his head, looking surprised at the very question. "She *wasn't*. She snuck in somehow, probably during rounds."

"Rounds?"

He returned his gaze to the road. "Yeah,

we try to keep the booth manned continuously during the day, but that's not as easy at night because there's fewer guards on duty. Once an hour, starting around midnight, whoever's manning the gate usually has to lock it up, hang out the *'Back in 10 minutes'* sign, and drive the loop, just to make sure things are okay."

Juliette pursed her lips. "But hasn't security been sort of amped up the past few days?"

Orlando nodded. "We've had extra personnel since the death, but there were a few hours last night—around three to six this morning, I think—where there was no overlap. My guess is that Iliana parked her car on the road around the corner and out of sight, watched until the guard took off on his rounds, then came in on foot, painted the sign, and slipped back out again before he returned. She probably could've done that in ten minutes—and if not, she knew this place well enough to hide for a while and slip out during the next rounds an hour later. That's my theory anyway."

Crystal had to talk to Greg. She had to tell him that she believed his theory about his sister's death, even if no one else did. She wanted to describe the afternoon's brainstorming session, to let him know that the people who were trying to solve Raven's murder might be willing to try and solve Valentine's as well.

He was probably still on duty, so she drove straight to the resort. When she got there, she was surprised to see Juliette, Didi, and Marcus all standing at the guest entrance gate, talking with Orlando. Something strange was going on.

Swallowing hard, Crystal scanned her card to clear the employee gate, then she pulled ahead and parked on the shoulder. She climbed out and ran over to join them, hoping they wouldn't mind her butting in.

They didn't seem to. With a welcoming smile, Juliette explained that they were waiting for the police, who were coming to get Xena. "Also, Didi identified the shoe print. It was *Iliana*."

Crystal gasped. "Iliana wrote those horrible words on the sign? No way!"

Suddenly a voice called out from the booth—Greg's voice—telling them that Xena was on the move, headed to employee parking.

Crystal hadn't even noticed Greg there before, but now their eyes met and he gave her a quick wink before returning his focus to the screen and the walkie talkie inside. Watching him, she felt a surge of electricity that shot clear down to her toes.

There was a noise behind her, and she turned to see a sedan pulling into the resort entrance, Detective Bryant at the wheel, followed by a police car.

"It's about time," Orlando mumbled as both vehicles came to a stop.

Leaning down, he updated the detective on the situation, then got into the backseat of the second car, the cruiser, so he could lead them to the parking lot to apprehend Xena.

Greg raised the gate as Orlando had them back up and pull through the employee entrance instead. Then they were off, racing down the narrow road. Crystal thought Detective Bryant would follow, but instead he stayed where he was and spoke to Juliette. "I'm glad you're here. I was just about to contact you. Do you have a moment?"

She nodded. "We'll meet you in the main parking lot, around the corner."

"Sounds good."

Crystal stayed there beside the booth and watched everyone go, wondering why, after such commotion, all of a sudden things seemed so quiet.

Maybe it was the calm before the storm.

Even if it wasn't mutual, Marcus was starting to have a lot of respect for Didi. She was protective of Juliette, of course, and not exactly warm and fuzzy toward him. But as he watched her with the detective, he couldn't help but think how competent she seemed, how clearly she laid out the facts and presented her case about Iliana and the shoeprint and the vandalized sign.

The four of them were at the far end of the half-empty parking lot, standing beside the detective's car in the shade of a big tree. A radio crackled inside the vehicle, at one point interrupting them with the report that Xena had been apprehended at her car without incident. They all cheered. After that, Didi jumped back into her tale and soon had Bryant so convinced about the shoeprint that he radioed in for another cruiser to round up Iliana Hernandez, wherever she may be.

After that, Didi put away her laptop and they all listened as Bryant launched in with the news he'd come there to deliver. According to him, the fingerprint report had returned with a hit. The man who snuck into Juliette's room while she was sleeping and left a note on her pillow was none other than the spa aide Ty Kirkland.

By his own admission in that note, Ty was the one who'd killed Raven.

Juliette paled at the news. Marcus took her by the elbow even as Didi moved into place on her other side and grabbed her forearm. Their reactions as dueling protectors would've been almost comical had the situation not been so serious.

The detective's expression was grim. "Worse, Kirkland has disappeared. Around noon he told people here that he had a family emergency and had to leave early. But according to his wife, there *is* no family emergency and she hasn't seen or heard from him since he left for work this morning."

Marcus and Didi grunted in unison.

The man continued, his eyes on Juliette. "We've checked out the timing and think he must have gone to your room right after he left the spa. No one knows where he went after that."

Juliette pursed her lips. "Any idea why he killed Raven? Or why he decided to confess, for that matter?"

Detective Bryant shook his head.

Didi's eyes burned with rage. "Why did he go into Juliette's room? Why confess that way?"

"You think he was trying to threaten her? Scare her? What?" Marcus could feel his blood boil.

Bryant shrugged. "He was probably making a point, trying to show that he *could* do harm if he *wanted* to. It's not uncommon, a type of 'posturing.'"

Marcus scowled. "Yeah, it was just posturing this time. Next time, we may not be so lucky."

The detective nodded, his expression grave. "I'm concerned about the placement of the fingerprints. We found them on the doorknob and the note, both of which make sense. But there was another match." He looked at Juliette. "On your cell phone."

Juliette's eyes widened. "Wait. You're saying while Ty was in my room, he fooled with my cell phone?" She glanced from Marcus to Didi. "I put it on the bedside table while I slept. When I saw the technician fingerprinting it, I thought she was wasting her time."

Bryant leaned in closer. "Ms. Taylor, can you think of anything he might've been doing with your phone? We could send it over to the digital forensics lab in L.A. and get them to figure it out, but I hate to do that if we don't have to."

Her expression blank, Juliette reached into her pocket and pulled out her cell, holding it like a dirty diaper. Sensing her reluctance, Marcus offered to help and took it from her, unlocked the screen, and then double-tapped the main button to bring up the icons that would indicate which apps had been used most recently. There were only three: phone, text messaging, and contacts.

Taking a deep breath, he touched the phone icon first and pulled up a list of activity. One quick look at the time stamps showed there had been no calls, in or out, during the period in question.

Ditto for text messages.

That left the contacts, which carried no time stamp. Marcus looked at Bryant. "Either he was smart enough to erase his tracks, or he rooted through her address book," he said, then he met Juliette's eyes. "His note did say he would be in touch. My best guess? I think he went in here to get *my* number."

It felt so strange to be with Greg, alone, afraid she was intruding on his work. Crystal could tell this was the wrong time to bring up Valentine. She stayed anyway, moving to the doorway of the booth and filling the sudden silence between them by asking about the equipment inside. He seemed pleased by her interest and proud to show off some of his favorite toys—high-powered spotlight, elaborate snakebite kit, night vision binoculars.

She gestured toward the little black-and-white monitor mounted on the shelf, which showed a view of the grotto, nearly empty here at the dinner hour. Soon the screen flickered and jumped to a new image, that of the spa interior, also empty.

"Is this where you guys monitor the security cameras?"

"Partly. This one hops from camera to camera, with each image holding for about twenty seconds before changing. I much prefer the control panel over at the security office, which has six screens, each one dedicated to a single camera. You can watch them all at the same time, no hopping required."

"I heard one of the cameras is broken," she said, trying to sound nonchalant.

"Yeah, behind Arrowscale. I'm the one who reported it, actually."

"Oh?"

He nodded. "Doesn't happen often, but once in a while one of the cameras goes out. A chipmunk chews through a cable or whatever. Anyway, I was manning the panel on Wednesday morning when I realized screen four had gone blank. First I thought it was a loose wire, but I fiddled for a while there at the monitor and never could get it to work. So finally I went and checked out the camera itself. It's mounted up kind of high, but it wasn't hard to see even from down on the ground that the lens had been busted. I figured maybe a rock got thrown up there by a lawnmower or something."

"What did you do?" Crystal asked, thinking how cute Greg looked when he was being so official and all.

He shrugged. "Followed procedure. Wrote up a priority maintenance request, turned it in. They checked it out right away, and, sure enough, for some reason the glass lens was shattered. They ordered a replacement, said it would be two or three days before it came in. I didn't think much more about it—until everything happened the next day. Then . . ." His face colored. "Well, never mind."

"No. What? What were you going to say?"

He shrugged. "I just keep thinking how convenient, you know? Of all the cameras on the property, the one that breaks is the one pointed at the building where there's a murder? That sounds more than a little suspicious to me."

"You're not the only one. Did you tell this to the police?"

"Yeah, but they hardly seemed to care. I don't know if they even followed up on it. Can you imagine? It seems so obvious but they were like, yeah, okay, whatever. They remember me from when Val died, I'm sure. Probably think I'm some kind of nut job. Paranoid. Delusional."

Taking a deep breath, Crystal moved closer and put her hands on each side of Greg's face.

"I believe you, Greg, about the camera—and about Val's murder."

Tears filled his eyes. There was such gratitude in his expression, she wondered if she was the very first person to say that to him since his sister's death.

She continued, her tone softening. "Once this whole Raven mess is over, I'm going to help you. I have an idea about solving your sister's death."

He blinked, sending twin tracks of tears down his cheeks.

Tempted to wipe away those tears, Crystal withdrew her hands instead, not wanting to cross a line. "But let's get through all of this stuff with Raven's death first. You need to talk to the police again about the camera issue. *Make* them look into it. Tell them exactly what you told me. Surely you can convince them how significant it is."

He took a deep breath, let it out. Wiped his cheeks with the back of his hands. "I tried, Crystal. Seriously, they don't care."

"Then maybe you and Marcus should talk to them together."

"Marcus?"

"The guy who was just here. With Juliette and Didi? He says the same thing, that the killer must have broken the camera on purpose, ahead of time. He thinks it was probably an employee, one who familiarized himself with the security coverage throughout the resort and figured out the best way to come and go without being seen."

Greg gestured toward the road. "You mean like Iliana did? Sneaking in while the front gate was unattended?"

Shaking her head, she tried to explain the circles Marcus had drawn on the map and how he'd concluded that the safest and most logical entry point for not being seen would have been to come in somewhere along the jogging trail, hiking in from the west. "If someone knew what they were doing, they could've made it all the way into Arrowscale unseen, if not for that one camera."

"Exactly. You really think Marcus might be willing to bring me into the loop? Join forces?"

"Yes. I do. He's a good guy."

Greg's eyes shone. "You know what this means, don't you? If I could help solve Raven's murder, then people just might take me more seriously about Val's death too."

Crystal studied the handsome man in front of her. She wanted to tell him it was even better than he thought, that Marcus was affiliated with the *FBI*—which meant he had access to resources that were even more vast and effective than the police. But that wasn't her secret to share. Instead, she just touched his arm and whispered, "Let's hope so. At least you're not alone in this anymore, you know?"

Greg's beautiful brown eyes focused in on her, and for a moment she thought he might kiss her. Instead, he leaned close and whispered in her ear.

"It's so true, 'He that can have patience can have what he will.'" Pulling back, he gave her a nod and a grin. "That's what Benjamin Franklin says anyway."

Half confused, half intrigued, she angled a look at him. Did he mean his dream of solving his sister's murder?

Or Crystal's dream of a relationship between the two of them?

Standing there beside him now, she could only hope he was talking about both.

Chapter Thirty-Four

Marcus couldn't bear to let Juliette out of his sight. At the moment she was in her room, freshening up for her final keynote address while he waited on her patio. Once she was ready, he would walk her to the conference center, after which he could finally go check out the western perimeter for signs of entry. Even with a pending confession, Marcus knew that any additional proof of the crime would be useful. They just needed to hurry, because the sun would set in about twenty minutes and then it would be too dark to see.

Taking a deep breath and blowing it out, Marcus told himself to chill. Waiting for a possible phone call from Ty Kirkland had Marcus's nerves on edge—as did the various developments that were unfolding down at the station.

First had come news about Xena, that the moment she was brought into interrogation, she started to squeal, admitting she black-mailed Raven—with Andre as her partner in crime. In response, police apprehended Andre too, and now both were in custody and pointing fingers at each other with vigor.

The detectives were also holding Iliana Hernandez. Thanks to Didi's discovery about the shoeprint, police had gone to her home to round her up for questioning. While there, an eagle-eyed lieutenant spotted an empty spray-paint can on the floor of her car, at which point Iliana broke down and confessed to vandalizing the sign.

Thus far, then, they had three suspects in custody, owning up to two different crimes: Xena and Andre and their blackmail scheme, and Iliana and her vandalism. But all three denied having anything to do with Raven's murder. Still, if the note left on Juliette's pillow could be believed, there was a good chance they were lying about that. In his note Ty had offered "immunity in exchange for information." He probably meant to implicate others with his confession—most likely these three—though at this point that was mere conjecture. Whatever information he had, or why he thought it so valuable, wouldn't be known until he made contact.

Marcus glanced at his phone, willing Ty to call.

What is taking so long?

Why leave a note saying you'll be in touch and then not follow through?

At least everything was set on this end, the various people poised to spring into action at a moment's notice. The DA was standing by to hear Ty's offer, and police were ready to head out and pick the man up as soon as they had a location.

Obviously Ty had heard the rumor about Marcus being with the FBI, which must be why he'd chosen Marcus as his go-between. That Raven's murder was a matter for the police and not the Bureau probably hadn't even dawned on him.

Just in case there was more to it than that, however, the FBI was on alert as well. Depending on what Ty had to say, they may need to be a part of things after all.

Marcus knew his biggest challenge would be controlling his own temper once he and Ty were on the phone. The thought of that man breaking into Juliette's room and hovering over her as she slept enraged him. But if he wanted to bring things to a close, he would hold his tongue and deal with the matter at hand.

He was trying to build up his resolve on that thought when the door opened and

Juliette emerged, the sight of her banishing everything else from his mind. He stood, eyes wide. She was a vision in white and smelled like azalea blossoms in springtime. How had he ever been so foolish as to let this woman slip through his fingers?

Thank You, Lord, for giving me another chance with her.

"No call yet?" Her brow furrowed as she closed her door and made sure it locked.

He shook his head. "I can't believe I have to miss your final talk for this."

"It's worth it. You need to be ready if and when that phone rings." She gave him a sweet smile. "And I can always recap things for you later if you'd like."

"Yes, I would like that, my own personal recap, from *the* Juliette Taylor herself." Marcus stepped closer. "May I kiss you? Or would that mess up your lipstick?"

She shrugged then gave him a wink. "Eh, lipstick can be repaired."

He breathed her in as he slid his arms around her waist. "How can one woman be so beautiful?"

She didn't answer but instead touched her lips to his—tender, sweet, lingering. He gently kissed her in return, his embrace tenuous, as though squeezing too hard might mar the perfection.

Finally he stepped back and gave her one last perusal. "You sure do clean up nice, lady."

She flashed him her million-dollar smile as she pulled from her bag a hand mirror and a pink tube to fix the damage. "Yeah? Keep saying things like that, and I might let you mess up my lipstick again later."

Greg was relieved from his post in time to escort Crystal to the conference center, where she would begin part two of her long work day. She moved her car to the employee lot as he followed along behind in a cart, then she climbed in beside him and they were off, Crystal relishing the heat of Greg's body, the coolness of the evening air, and the streaks of orange and gold that filled the sky as they drove across the lush grounds of the resort.

When they reached their destination, she was thrilled to see Marcus up ahead, just walking into the conference center with Juliette.

Pulse surging, Crystal turned to Greg with a broad smile. "What time do you get off?"

"In a few minutes, as soon as I punch out. Why? Don't you have to work?"

"Yeah, but this isn't about me. Park the cart. It's time for that introduction."

Once Marcus delivered Juliette to the safety of the conference center—and Didi's watchful eye—he moved back outside and picked up the pace, gaze on the sky. The sun was at the horizon, but hopefully the light would linger long enough for him to accomplish his goal.

Just as he reached the parking lot, however, he was intercepted by Crystal and the young security guard from the booth. The girl seemed intent on introducing them, though Marcus wasn't sure why until she explained that Greg was the one who first discovered the broken security camera behind the Arrowscale building. "His theory about what happened pretty much lines up with yours."

Now *this* was worth the interruption. Marcus had been planning to ask Orlando about the camera issue later, but a firsthand account would be even better.

Crystal had to get to work, so she excused herself and left the two of them there. As she walked away, Marcus turned to Greg, who seemed rather shy, and asked if he had a few minutes to take a walk.

"Of course, sir."

"Great, let's go. But drop the 'sir' stuff, okay? It's just Marcus."

"Sure, Marcus."

They headed off together and made it out

to the empty trail with just a few minutes of daylight to spare. On the way Marcus explained what they were looking for; once there he divided the perimeter between them and they both got to work, searching for signs of trespass.

Marcus walked along his section, eyes open for footprints, broken branches, any sort of disturbance to nature. He couldn't find any definite signs of entry, but at least he confirmed that it was doable. The brush was thick, yes, but there were thinner patches of growth here and there where someone could've gotten through if they'd really wanted to.

After that, he peered down the hill from various vantage points and finally spotted some large construction equipment about half a mile away, sitting idle amid a smattering of foundations and half-framed structures. A new housing development.

Bingo.

More than likely a place like that would hum with activity during the day but be silent and deserted after hours, as it was now. That would make it the perfect place for a killer to park his car and hike up here to the resort under cover of darkness.

Marcus called over his young helper—who hadn't been able to find any signs of entry either—and pointed out the sight. Greg agreed with his theory, and as they headed back toward the conference center in the gathering darkness, they discussed and debated it, trying to refine their scenario. When they reached the parking lot, they were about to part ways when Marcus's cell phone rang.

With a start, he asked Greg to stay put as he pulled it out and looked at the screen. *Blocked*. This had to be Ty. Police were already patched in to listen, but just in case that didn't work, he reached into his shirt pocket, took out Detective Bryant's card, and thrust it toward Greg. "Phone this number right now and make sure they're aware of this call and are listening in, would you?"

Greg asked no questions, but instead got right to it. As he began to dial, Marcus took a deep breath and answered his own phone with a quiet, brusque, "Hello?"

"Marcus Stone?"

"Yeah. Who's this?"

"Ty. Ty Kirkland. We met last night at the police station?"

Marcus's jaw clenched. He glanced at Greg, who handed back the card and put the phone to his ear.

"I know who you are." Unable to stop himself, Marcus blurted, "And if you ever go near Juliette Taylor again, I will personally see to it that—"

"Yeah, yeah, sorry about that. I know I kind of crossed the line."

"*Kind* of?" A cluster of nearby guests glared their way, and Marcus realized he was shouting. Taking another deep breath, he gestured for Greg to follow him and then began walking as fast as possible toward his suite. "Kirkland, you went well over that line the minute you even *thought* about breaking into her room."

"Look, I'm sorry, Stone, but I had to find some way to reach you. When I was leaving the spa, I saw Ms. Taylor walking by so I, uh, borrowed a master key and followed her there. I figured she'd have your number, and she did."

Greg dropped back to talk on his phone, but Marcus continued on to his room, trying to stay focused on Ty. "You've got some nerve, Kirkland."

"Yeah, well, I was desperate, okay? And this is important."

Marcus blew out a breath. *Calm down.* He reached the door, unlocked it, and stepped inside, leaving it open for Greg to follow once he'd ended his own call.

"Okay. Fine. Talk to me. Your note said you want to turn yourself in?" Marcus grabbed a blank pad and pen from the end table and carried them to the kitchen counter, where he stood and listened, pen poised at the ready.

"Yeah. I do. I've been . . . involved with this stuff for a while now, but I've reached the point where I just want out. I'm ready to cut a deal. It's just not worth it, man. I don't want to do this anymore. I want out, and I need you to arrange it for me."

Marcus glanced toward the door, where Greg was just stepping inside. Their eyes met, and the young man gave him a solid nod.

Good. At least that much was under control. Police were tuned in and listening.

Just in case further assistance was needed, he gestured for Greg to close the door and have a seat.

Marcus turned his attention back to the person on the other end of the line. "I'll do what I can, but you have to understand, I have zero authority when it comes to making deals. We'll need to bring someone else in on this, most likely the District Attorney."

Ty grunted. "The DA? This has nothing to do with him. I need FBI. That's why I'm calling you. You *are* FBI, right?"

Marcus let out a breath. "Not exactly, but I do have some . . . uh . . . connections."

"Fine. Then let's get on with it."

"No problem. But why don't we start there,

with why you see this as a matter for the FBI rather than the police."

Ty didn't reply, staying silent for so long that Marcus feared the connection had been broken. Had he pushed too hard? "Hello?"

"I'm here," Ty growled. "And this is how it's going to go. We will hang up. You will contact the FBI and get them to send over someone who *does* have the authority to make deals. In one hour the two of you will meet me at the pavilion at Laskey Park. Any police nonsense, any backup teams or whatever, and I won't be there. I'll just disappear—for good. That's a promise."

With that, he disconnected the call, leaving Marcus with nothing but dead silence on the phone and a knot the size of a fist in his gut.

"You okay?"

He turned to see Greg still there on the couch, watching him. Marcus exhaled and ran a hand over his face. "I'm fine. I just have a funny feeling about this guy. There's something going on here, some element to this case that I don't understand."

"What makes you think that?"

He shrugged and met Greg's eyes. "He won't deal with the DA. Wants the FBI or nothing at all."

"So what are you going to do?"

Feeling weary to the bone, Marcus began

to dial the number that was already loaded and waiting. "What else *can* I do? I'm calling in the FBI."

Juliette stood behind the curtain one last time, listening to the closing lines of the skit and trying to put the afternoon's drama aside for the next hour or two. Unable to clear her head, she finally put it to prayer, asking God to keep Marcus safe while they were apart, especially if Ty made contact.

She felt better after that, and soon her thoughts were focused on her impending talk and on the women who'd be hearing it. With all that was going on, Juliette hadn't been able to give this retreat her all, yet somehow God filled in the missing places and worked in the lives of these women anyway. She'd seen it during the dinner hour especially, the hearty camaraderie, the happy expressions, the relaxed postures. They'd gotten her point, loud and clear—that even the most dedicated servants really were supposed to take time out from the Lord's work once in a while to rest, recover, and rejuvenate.

Tonight she would speak from 1 Kings, the part where Elijah was told to stand on the mountain "for the LORD is about to pass by."

Elijah did as he was told, and soon he

endured what amounted to a tornado, an earthquake, and a fire. Yet after each event, the Lord was not in them. The passage concluded, "And after the fire came a gentle whisper. When Elijah heard it, he pulled his cloak over his face and went out and stood at the mouth of the cave."

As it turned out, God was in the whisper.

"Help me hear Your whisper, Lord, every time it comes," Juliette prayed.

Then she took a deep breath, smoothed the front of her white Chanel suit, and waited for her cue to go on.

Forty-five minutes later Marcus was speeding toward Laskey Park in a Chevy Tahoe, Agent Tim Wilson of the FBI's Palm Spring branch at the wheel. As they drove along, Marcus chafed at the stiff, bulky Kevlar vest the man had given him to wear, but he was glad he had it on. Something about this situation still didn't feel right, and a little extra protection couldn't hurt.

He would've felt even safer had Agent Wilson allowed the police to follow at a discreet distance, but instead the man had arranged for them to wait at a location in town, ready to roll if need be but stationary until then.

Wilson slowed and put on his blinker,

and as he turned into the park where their rendezvous would take place, Marcus peered out at the scene, searching for some sign of activity. It seemed deserted, though it was too dark to know for sure.

The car eased to a stop near a small wooden pavilion and they sat there for a long moment, lights on and engine running. Marcus expected Ty to step out from behind a post or a tree or something, but he did not. In fact, nothing happened at all.

Marcus looked down at the phone in his hand, willing it to ring, wishing Ty hadn't blocked his number in his earlier calls. Surely the cops had tracked it back and knew what number he'd been calling from. Maybe Marcus should get it from them then use it to call Ty and demand to know where he was and what was going on.

Marcus glanced at Wilson, who was studying their surroundings through a pair of small night vision goggles.

"How long before we give up and drive out of here?"

"Not much longer." Wilson turned his head to scan the horizon. "In fact, hold on a sec." He put down the binoculars, picked up his phone, and made a quick call. "It's Tim. We're at the park, but subject is E and E. Can you give me a location update? Good. Thanks."

As Tim waited, he put the car in reverse, backed up, then began to edge forward, retracing their route to the main road. "All right. Stay on it live from here on out, would you? We're in pursuit. And give me a viz too, please."

He put the phone on speaker and set it in a holder on the dash. As he pulled onto the blacktop and accelerated, he explained to Marcus that they had a lock on Ty's phone, and though he'd been at the park before, he was now on the move, headed west on Dillon Road.

Suddenly the screen of the phone sprung to life. Apparently *viz* meant *visual*, seeing as a small green dot moved slowly along a horizontal line. Marcus grunted. Why hadn't they kept a closer eye on Ty?

"Looks like he's turning onto sixty-two, heading north," a woman's voice said from the phone.

His eyes still glued to the tiny screen, Marcus watched as the dot changed direction and moved upward along a vertical line. Over the next ten minutes, as they sped along trying to catch up, the dot made two more turns, onto Mission Creek Road, and then onto South Springs Road. Finally it came to a stop, and a moment after that Marcus got a text from Ty. New location, 291 South Springs Road. Go now. Am waiting.

Marcus relayed the message to Wilson, eyes back on the dot. If they were lucky, it would remain stationary and this would be their final stop. He didn't care where they had to go to get this done. He just didn't feel like spending half the night on a wild goose chase.

Once they finally turned onto South Springs Road and he got a look around, however, Marcus changed his mind about wanting this to be their final location. They were in the middle of nowhere, nothing but dust and scruffy bushes to either side. His eyes darted back and forth between the numbers on the occasional mailboxes and the purple dot—indicative of their own vehicle—that had appeared on the screen and was now moving toward the green.

When they finally got there, Wilson turned into a driveway of sorts, the sweep of his headlights illuminating two dilapidated old farm buildings in front of them, a half-rotted barn off to one side, and a smaller, more intact structure to the other. There were no vehicles to be seen. As they rolled to a stop, another text came through. Am in shed, to your right.

Marcus read the words aloud, then looked at the agent next to him.

Frowning, Wilson grabbed the binoculars and surveyed the structures and the surrounding area for a long moment. "I don't like the looks of this." Nevertheless, he put down the binoculars, told the woman on the phone what they were doing, and then climbed from the car. Marcus followed suit. Though both men were armed with heavy flashlights, Wilson was the only one with a gun. Pulling it from a shoulder holster, he held it at the ready and instructed Marcus to stay back.

Way back.

The shed was about twenty feet away, and though it looked pretty ramshackle, at least they could see that there was a light on inside. They approached the structure, Wilson waving Marcus back even further when he got close and moved into place, his shoulder against the wall beside the door.

"Ty Kirkland? It's Agent Tim Wilson, FBI. I'm here with Marcus Stone."

Marcus realized he was holding his breath as they waited for a reply.

None came.

Instead, all they could hear were the sounds of the night: rodents scuffling, birds calling, insects buzzing. The desert was a busy place after dark.

Wilson looked like a coil about to spring as he reached out and flung open the door to the shed.

The next thing Marcus knew—the only

thing he knew—was that he'd never seen a brighter light, never heard a louder boom, never had his body propelled through the air so far or so fast.

Never landed so hard.

Never knew that the world could simply go black.

Chapter Thirty-Five

Juliette looked around the broad lobby once again but saw nothing to settle her sense of unease. Marcus was nowhere to be found.

She'd looked for him during her talk, to no avail, which wasn't all that surprising. What had surprised her was that when she looked again later, at the beginning of the reception, there'd still been no sight of him. Now that the reception was almost over, he remained a no show. She wanted to call his cell but Detective Bryant had told her not to use that number until after the whole Ty mess had been settled. Unable to wait any longer, she excused herself and found a wall phone out in the hallway instead. She called his room but got no answer.

As she hung up, her concern deepened.

Where *was* he? Had Ty made contact?

Was he off meeting with him at that very moment?

Busy with final photos and questions, Juliette told herself Marcus was okay and tried to focus on the women for now. They all seemed thrilled about their retreat experience, and several even said that tonight's talk had been a highlight. Their praise brought tears to Juliette's eyes. She, too, had felt the Spirit move, and she was oh so grateful that God had given her all the right words even when she had failed to give Him all of the right prayer and preparation.

Eventually the last of the guests filed out, the other employees went home, and she and Didi and Crystal were wrapping things up. Juliette's feet were killing her, so she decided to switch over to her flats. She was just pulling them on when she heard from Marcus, via text: Big news! Ty is in custody and has confessed to the murder!

With a deep sigh of relief, Juliette texted back her reply: Super! Where r u now?

His response came quickly. With FBI and police. U shld come too. They want statements from you and Didi.

She didn't hesitate. Can leave now. Where do we go?

She waited for him to supply an address,

her heart surging with relief. At least this part of the nightmare was over. Looking from Didi to Crystal, she let out a long sigh and told them police had Ty in custody at last.

Raven's murderer had been apprehended.

"Is that it up there?" Crystal peered out from the backseat. Far ahead in the distance, she could see bright lights that seemed to indicate police activity.

Juliette glanced where she indicated but then returned her attention to her phone's GPS app. "No, this is South Springs Road. We're supposed to take the next right, go about half a mile, and then make a left on Bismark Lane."

Crystal wasn't so sure, but she didn't say anything. She was just glad they'd let her tag along. Marcus's text had asked for Juliette and Didi, but Crystal wasn't about to miss out on the final big wrap-up if she could help it. She only hoped Marcus had let Greg tag along as well, because that might mean he'd be out here now too.

Didi slowed to make the right turn just as an ambulance came from up ahead and went speeding past. Following Juliette's directions, Didi continued down the side road until they came to Bismark, where she turned left, putting them parallel with the road they'd been on before. Maybe they were coming up to the same scene, but from the opposite side. Something big had been going on out there, that much was clear from all the lights she'd spotted before they made their turn.

Finally the GPS said they were getting close to their destination, though it was so dark and deserted, it was hard to tell exactly where they were in relation to the flashing emergency lights.

Juliette peered out the window. "What do you think, ladies?"

Crystal craned her neck for some indication of the address as Didi slowed the vehicle to a crawl.

Gazing out into the darkness, Crystal saw a parked car with a Palm Grotto window sticker that looked familiar, though she couldn't remember whose it was. There was another vehicle parked up ahead on the left, so they kept going. As they got closer, Crystal exhaled her relief. "There! That's Greg's black pickup!"

Didi slowed. "I don't see any people, though. I'm not getting out until I see people."

"I'll text Marcus." Juliette's fingers flew, and a moment later read them his response: Greg's here. Will send him out to wave you down.

Didi turned in next to the truck but let the

car idle until they saw the beam of a flashlight waving to get their attention. It came closer, and behind that beam Crystal could just make Greg's face.

She exhaled. "That's him, we're good."

Didi turned off the car and they climbed out.

"Where are we?" Juliette asked as she came around the front. "Why aren't there any police cars here?"

Greg politely shone the light down on the ground rather than in their faces. "You probably saw them as you drove in. They're all parked out on South Springs Road, but things were getting pretty congested over there so they're relocating as many people as they can to this side. Come on, I'll bring you over."

As he raised the light, its beam illuminated Crystal, and his head jerked back. "Oh! Hey! I didn't even see you there, Crystal."

She understood why he was surprised, but for a moment she feared he wasn't *happily* surprised. Instead, he seemed . . . disconcerted, somehow, as if he didn't want her around.

"Is there a problem?" she asked, cheeks hot.

"No, not at all." He ran a hand through his thick brown hair. "But do me a favor and wait here at the car, would you? I'll walk these two over and then come back so we can talk. I have something important to tell you."

Something important to tell her? Pulse surging, she wondered if that meant he'd gotten some sort of lead on his sister's murder. Maybe he and Marcus had really hit it off, and the FBI had been willing to help out in some way.

Eager to know what info awaited, she agreed to stay behind but asked Didi to unlock the car door so she could wait in there.

With a squeeze of the remote, the locks popped up; Crystal slipped into the driver's seat and closed the door. As she watched the three of them trudge off into the darkness, she hit the lock button. Then she settled back against the cool leather, hoping Greg wouldn't be gone too long.

"Right this way, ladies."

Greg pointed the beam of his flashlight at a rough path on the ground that had been strewn with fresh straw. "Stay on the trail, though, because you never know what kind of creatures might be out here at night. We don't need any snakebites."

Juliette shivered and did as he instructed, falling in behind Didi and moving with cautious steps. They trudged onward, Greg and his flashlight leading them off into utter darkness. The further they went, the more confused she grew.

The police weren't out here. They couldn't be. There were no lights, no activity, just a stupid straw path and a single flashlight and three vulnerable people. In the desert. At night.

A wave of apprehension rippled through Juliette. She pulled out her phone, but rather than texting Marcus this time, she touched the buttons to call him.

They kept walking, Greg leading the way, but then he paused as they neared a big boulder and stepped to the side of the path, gesturing for them to continue onward.

"It's not much further now. We should see some lights once we get around the other side of this giant rock." He shone the beam ahead of them and held it steady as they made their way past.

Juliette followed Didi but her focus was on the phone, waiting for the call to go through. She checked the screen. One bar. That should be enough, yet it made no sound. Finally she pressed it back to her ear and was relieved to hear it ring once. A connection. But then it rang the second time—

And she also heard it ring out loud. Like Marcus—and his phone—were near. Physically near.

Like . . . right behind her.

She spun around to see where the sound

was coming from, but as she did, she began to feel herself fall. With a loud *whoosh*, all three of them were falling—falling and screaming— as if the very earth itself had opened up and was trying to swallow them whole.

Crystal heaved another bored sigh. What was taking so long? More important, why hadn't she asked Didi for the keys instead of just having her hit the unlock button? If she'd done that, then at least she could be listening to the radio now. Instead, all she had to entertain her were the sounds of the night.

Which she didn't like to think about.

Coyote howls, owl screeches, lonely kill-deer—they all sounded like screaming women to her. She put her hands over her ears to muffle the distant cries of some creature or another that she'd rather not listen to.

Was she safe here?

If so, then why did she feel like a sitting duck?

Pressing the lock button again just to be sure, she swallowed hard and stared out at the darkness. She thought of the familiar car they had just passed, the one with the Palm Grotto window sticker. It was a Range Rover. A metallic red Range Rover.

Then she remembered. *Reggie*. That's

whose it was. Reggie Roberts drove a red Range Rover.

And she sells seashells by the seashore.

Crystal chuckled at her own joke, trying to settle her unease.

It didn't help matters that as her eyes adjusted to the lack of light, she began to make out the shape of a creepy-looking structure in the distance. Was that a house? If so, she felt sure that no one lived there—and hadn't for a long time.

Marcus opened his eyes and found himself looking into the face of a woman he didn't recognize. She had dark skin and long eyelashes, and she was moving her mouth as if she were talking.

Except no sound was coming out.

He tried to sit up but was knocked flat by a searing pain at his ribs.

What was going on?

The woman sat back as a man leaned in from the other side, but he, too, was flapping his jaws and making no sound. Blinking, Marcus looked around—and frowned. From the looks of things, he was inside an ambulance. These two were talking, machines were flashing, probably a siren was going. Yet everything was eerily quiet.

No, not quiet exactly. There was a hum, or a buzz, some low kind of white noise. But nothing else at all. No voices. Nothing.

At least he could see. And he could smell. Man, could he smell—an acrid, burning stench that turned his stomach.

Marcus closed his eyes, remembering a light. A loud noise.

What happened?

Telling himself to stay calm, he kept his eyes closed and tried to focus on the gentle jostling of the vehicle as it rumbled toward its destination. After a few minutes spent just lying there, the noise in his head began to shift to a lower pitch, and he thought he could detect the sound of voices underneath. He was starting to hear.

He was also starting to feel, unfortunately. The pain was mostly at his ribs, but he grew aware of a sharp throbbing in his left thigh too. Though his throat felt raw and parched, he once again opened his eyes and tried to speak.

"What . . . happened?"

The woman eyed him cautiously, her lips moving once more.

"Louder, please," he rasped. "My ears . . ."

She leaned closer and tried again. "There was an *explosion*. You were *blown back onto the ground and struck by debris.*"

He thought about that for a moment. "Was I alone?"

The woman and the man exchanged glances. *"No, you were with someone else."*

Marcus closed his eyes and thought about that. Agent Wilson. Of the FBI. The two of them had gone somewhere together . . .

To meet with Ty Kirkland.

It had been a trick. A setup.

Marcus's eyes flew open. Juliette. Where was Juliette? Could Ty have somehow tricked her too?

Heart pounding, he patted at his pockets. "My phone. Please. Do you see it?"

The two attendants checked, but to no avail.

"Nope, sorry." The woman shrugged. "You must have dropped it in the explosion."

She turned away, studying something on one of the machines, but he managed to raise a shaky hand and place it on her arm.

"Please," he urged. "I have to reach Juliette Taylor. I have to warn her before it's too late."

Juliette didn't know how far they had fallen. She didn't understand what they had fallen into. All she knew was that every inch of her body hurt.

At least she was alive.

She looked around, realizing with a start that Didi was lying next to her, face down, her eyes closed.

"Didi!" Without thought of her own pain, Juliette sat up and began shaking her friend by the shoulders. "Wake up! Didi, wake up!"

With a groan, the woman finally opened one eye.

Juliette bent closer, frantic. "Are you okay? Where does it hurt?"

It took a long moment and then Didi murmured, "The pinkie toe on my left foot."

"What do you mean?" Juliette jerked around to take a look. "What about it?"

"That's the only thing that *doesn't* hurt."

A joke. Didi was making a joke. That meant she might be okay.

Juliette sat back and forced herself to breathe. In. Out. In. Out. She checked Didi over with care then worked her hands along her own body, feeling for seeping blood or broken bones. She felt neither. She remembered hitting feet first, then falling backward. And though her tailbone ached and her lower legs still throbbed from the impact, she knew something must have broken her fall. Looking down, she saw that they were on a pile of brush and sticks and palm fronds. Looking up, all she could see was a circle of blue starry sky, framed by white stone walls.

Where *were* they? What happened?

She called out for help, but there was no answer. She realized there was no sign of Greg at all—at least not that she could see.

"Greg? Where are you?"

Nothing—yet he'd been right behind her. She assumed he'd fallen in too.

If he had, though, where was he?

For that matter, if he *hadn't*, where was he?

She took in a breath and yelled again, as loud as she could this time. "*Greg!*" Nothing. "*Help! Help!*" Nothing.

If only it weren't so dark!

Willing her eyes to adjust, Juliette rose to her knees with a groan and tried to study their surroundings, but it was hard to see very far. She did spot her cell phone on the ground nearby and eagerly grabbed it—only to realize that the screen was shattered. She tried turning it on anyway, but it was no use.

She instructed Didi to check hers and felt a surge of hope when her friend pulled it out and announced that the screen was still intact. Those hopes were dashed, however, when she reported that hers had also broken in the fall.

"Let me try." Juliette took the phone from her and fooled with it, but no matter what she did, she couldn't get it to come to life.

As she handed the dead phone back to Didi, she saw that her friend had rolled up one pants leg and was examining her ankle— which was unmistakably bruised and swollen.

"Guess Wimbledon's out now," Didi quipped.

"Ha ha." Juliette met her friend's eyes, wincing to see a streak of blood along the side of her face. "Your cheek is cut too. Or maybe just scratched. Hard to tell."

"Oh, great. Now I'll never get another *Vogue* cover either."

Juliette managed half a smile. Needing to do *something*, she tried again to look around, hoping her eyes had adjusted more to the darkness. Sure enough, from where she was sitting, she could tell that they were in some sort of pit. It was about fifteen feet across and perhaps eighteen feet or so deep. Judging by the rubble around them, she realized what must have happened. They had walked out onto a "false ground" of sticks and leaves and then fallen through.

Into a trap.

She thought of that old movie, *Swiss Family Robinson*. Just like the boy caught a tiger in the movie, someone had caught them here by luring them onto what looked like a floor but was actually a ceiling. A fragile ceiling, at that.

At least they both seemed okay except for Didi's ankle and Juliette's aching lower back.

She decided to try and stand, but as she did, she was startled to feel the ground underneath her begin to shift.

She screamed and jumped away, her mind going to snakes or rodents—or even, absurdly, a tiger. But when she turned back to look, she realized what had broken their fall.

A person. A man. There was a man underneath the debris.

Was it Greg? Because he was heavier, had he landed first and then they'd crashed down on top of him?

Frantic, she and Didi pushed away the wide leaves that were covering his face and body, praying he would be okay.

More bored than ever, Crystal was elaborating on her new tongue twister—Reggie and Rhonda Roberts ride regularly in a ruby red Range Rover—when she was startled by sudden movement up ahead. With a gasp, she sat up straight and tried to find the switch for the headlights.

Was that Greg? Reggie? Someone else?

She couldn't tell, but whoever it was, he seemed to be weaving, like he was tired, or maybe even injured. Squinting, she watched as he paused and bent over, hands on his knees, catching his breath. Finally, she found the button and twisted it, flooding the scene with light. It was Greg.

Thank goodness.

Crystal jumped from the car and ran to him, surprised to see that somehow he'd gotten all sweaty and dirty since leaving just minutes before. "Are you okay? What happened?"

"I slipped and almost fell in a hole."

"A hole?"

"Yeah, like a pit. At least I was able to hang on and then climb out. I'll be okay." Standing up straight, Greg began to brush straw and other detritus from his clothes. "It's an old Cahuilla Indian well, one that should've been filled in and covered up years ago."

"That's dangerous! We need to warn the others."

"Good idea." Greg finished brushing himself off then met Crystal's eyes, an odd expression on his face.

"Are you sure you're okay?" She reached up to flick a piece of straw from his hair.

He shrugged, thrusting his hands in his pockets. "I guess. There's just been a lot going on tonight. It's a little overwhelming."

She nodded, eager to hear all about it. "Why don't we talk as we walk? Just let me close up the car."

She ran back over to it, twisted off the

lights, locked and closed the door. As she did, she heard a rhythmic *thunk* coming from somewhere nearby. Startled, she twisted around, wondering what it was, hoping it was something benign, like a woodpecker or a beaver. Well, she amended as she started toward Greg, not likely a beaver here in the desert, but some kind of mammal with a tail that could make a *thunking* sound.

Thunk. Thunk. Thunk.

"What is that?" She dashed the rest of the way to Greg's side, hoping he'd put his arms around her. The noise was so near—and so unsettling. Somewhere in the distance, from the other direction, she heard a bird call that gave her the shivers, its sound mimicking a woman's cry for *"Help! Help!"*

"I don't like this," Crystal said, taking Greg's arm and holding on tight. "And that thing doesn't help." She pointed toward the building she had spotted from the car.

"Why? It's just an old, abandoned house."

"I guess. But the desert is so creepy at night. Aren't you scared?"

He looked at her, but his eyes were distant. "Nah. I grew up here, remember?"

She nodded, wishing they would hurry and join the others. Ordinarily she would've loved being alone under the moonlight with Greg Overstreet. But something about this situation had her feeling edgy, every hair standing on end.

"Yeah, well, let's go," she said, giving his arm a tug. "You said you had something important to tell me. What is it? I'm dying to know."

He neither responded nor moved, so finally she looked up at him, surprised to see the myriad of emotions flooding his face. Sadness. Regret. Pain. *Anguish*, even.

"Greg?"

He was acting so weird. So not himself.

Her eyes narrowed. "Hey, no offense, but you didn't by any chance hit your head when you fell, did you?"

As if returning from some faraway place, he finally met her gaze. "No, I didn't hit my head."

"Are you sure? Because you seem—"

"Can I ask you something, Crystal?"

She blinked. "Of course."

His eyes radiated sadness. "Why did you come here tonight? The text asked for Juliette and Didi only, not you. Never you."

Crystal took a step back, offended. "It's a free country." Hearing the sharpness in her tone, she sucked in a breath, blew it out, tried again. "I've been so involved with this case, when I heard it had been solved, I wanted to come along and see what was going on first-hand. Why is that a problem?"

In the distance another bird called for *"Help! Help!"* Behind them, the animal's odd *"Thunk, thunk, thunk."* It sounded like it was coming from the other vehicle. *Greg's* vehicle.

Crystal swallowed hard, forced herself to meet Greg's eyes. Something was really wrong here.

Something was wrong with Greg.

"Listen, why don't we join the others?" she suggested, her voice ringing hollow in her ears.

"You want to join them?" He trained his gaze directly on her. "You really want to join them?"

As he gazed at her, the sadness on his face slowly contorted into rage.

She took another step back. "Maybe not?" she whispered.

"Too late. Let's go." Springing into action, Greg grabbed Crystal by the wrist and began dragging her away from the road, along the same path he'd led Juliette and Didi a short while before.

He moved fast, too fast.

Crystal asked him to slow down, but it was like he didn't hear. She stumbled on a loose rock, but his grip on her wrist was so strong that he kept her upright, kept her moving.

She looked down at Greg's hand, at the

way his fingers dug into her skin. She looked at his face, the way his jaw was set so firm.

Unable to stop herself, a whimper gurgled from her throat.

At the sound, he turned to look, mouth curling into a snarl even as his eyes filled with tears. *"You left me no choice!"*

He tightened his grip, kept going, his expression wild.

She tumbled along next to him, understanding at last. She'd been so nervous, so afraid of the animals she heard rustling around in the dark. But now she knew. The biggest threat wasn't out there in the dark.

It was right here. On two legs.

Chapter Thirty-Six

Much to Juliette's surprise, once they had the man uncovered, they saw it wasn't Greg at all.

It was Reggie Roberts.

And though he was mumbling and semi-conscious, at least he was still alive.

Didi checked his pulse while Juliette looked for injuries. No blood, no oddly-twisted limbs. Nothing.

"His heart's really racing." Didi placed a hand on his glistening forehead. "He's burning up, too."

They shook him and called out his name until, finally, he opened his eyes—and even as dark as it was, Juliette could see that his pupils were fully dilated.

Atropine.

He'd been drugged.

Swallowing hard, she met Didi's gaze and said the words that filled her brain with such clarity now she couldn't believe she hadn't acknowledged it before. "Greg did this."

Didi blinked. "What?"

Juliette got up, walked the span of the pit as she scanned the debris on the floor. No question, they were alone, just the three of them. Greg was nowhere to be found.

Worse, she realized now, the reason she'd heard Marcus's phone ringing behind her earlier, just before they'd fallen, was because *Greg* had it. Somehow Greg had gotten hold of Marcus's cell phone and used it to lure them there.

She shook her head, trying not to think about the implications of that—especially where Marcus was now, and what Greg had done to get his phone.

Please, Lord, keep Marcus safe!

She looked at Didi. "Greg did this to Reggie, to us. He led us right to this pit and made sure we fell in. He probably intends to kill us."

Greg dragged Crystal all the way to a giant boulder, finally coming to a stop beside it. The huge stone had to be at least eight feet high, maybe ten feet wide. She shuddered. What was he going to do to her?

"Greg, please." The words came out on a

whimper as she tried to pull her arm from his grasp. "I don't understand. What happened? Why are you so upset?"

He didn't answer. Instead he just stood there for a long moment, lost in thought. Then, as if he had come to some sort of a decision, he focused in on Crystal.

"You know that old house back there?" he asked in a soft voice.

"Yeah?"

"That used to be my house. The one I grew up in."

She blinked, gaping at him.

Nodding, he gestured around with a sweep of his arm. "This was all ours, from Bismark Lane to South Springs Road, eighty-two acres of torture. It was worthless, nothing but desert, but it was home."

Crystal studied Greg's face, trying to understand what was going on. This was where he grew up? Here?

Why was he telling her this, and what did it have to do with anything else that was going on tonight?

He continued, his eyes distant and sad. "The place has been abandoned for years. Not just the house, we had other buildings too, at the back side of the property. An old barn. A shed. Well, at least there used to be a shed." He paused, shook his head. Met her gaze. "But this is where she died. Right about there." He shone the beam onto the ground not too far away.

Crystal looked where he indicated, as if she expected to find a dead body still there. "Who, Valentine?"

Greg frowned. "No. Of course not. Our mother."

Crystal's head jerked back. His mother was *dead*? Why hadn't he told her that before? "What happened to her?"

"It was all a terrible accident. She was home alone one morning, out back here, when she slipped and fell into that same old Indian well I almost went into tonight."

Crystal gasped. "She died from a fall?"

He shook his head. "The fall broke her leg. But then she was down in that well for hours. In pain. Overheated. Dehydrated."

"And that's what killed her?"

Again he shook his head. "Eventually, despite all of that, she managed to drag herself back up to the top. She tried to crawl to the house. But on the way there, she ran into a rattlesnake. They're common out here, you know. With her injury, she couldn't back off fast enough, so it struck."

Crystal's hand flew to her mouth.

He nodded. "The tragedy is, she didn't have to die. Rattlesnake bites aren't fun, but they aren't usually fatal. She just needed help. Water, medical attention, whatever. But no one answered her desperate pleas. She ended up dying right there in the dust."

Crystal couldn't even comprehend such a thing. Her eyes filled with tears in spite of herself. "When did this happen?"

"The spring I was seventeen. Val was sixteen."

"Oh, Greg. I'm so sorry. Were you the ones who found her?"

He nodded and looked away. "Val and I. The school bus had just dropped us off. After it drove away, we heard yelling."

"You can't blame yourself, Greg. It's not your fault you didn't make it in time."

"Oh, we made it in time. Soon as we heard her, we came straight over to see what was wrong. Found her there on the ground." Again, he shone the light on an empty spot of dust. Then he turned and tapped the butt of his flashlight against the broad stone surface of the boulder behind him. "See this rock? Once we figured out what was going on, we climbed up on top of it, Val and I. Sat there together and listened to her screams and watched her die."

"You . . . watched your mother *die?*"

Greg looked at Crystal, his eyes empty and flat. "Yeah. We did."

She swallowed hard.

"Then, once we were sure it was over, we called the police. Told them we found her that way. Told them she was already dead by the time we got home from school. Not one person ever questioned it."

Juliette and Didi looked at each other, eyes wide. Though they hadn't caught every word, they had been able to pick up the *gist* of the conversation taking place up above. Bottom line, by letting his mother die out here years ago, Greg had essentially killed her. Now he was unraveling—and he seemed intent on killing again. No doubt, the further he went from reality, the more danger all of them were in.

They had to do something, before it was too late.

Though Juliette's head was spinning and her body ached, she had an idea she wanted to attempt. Greg had called this an Indian well, said that his mother had "managed to drag herself all the way back up to the top." That meant this was probably a *Cahuilla* Indian well, and that somewhere inside would be crude steps, just as Juliette had read about the other day in a magazine.

Looking to Didi, she put a finger to her lips

and crept toward the side wall. Squinting in the darkness, she scanned the surface, searching. She moved counterclockwise around the pit until she came to a series of holes and staggered stones jutting out from the wall. Were these the steps?

Her eyes traced a path diagonally upward. Had to be, though over the years the protrusions had worn down to mere nubs, many of the holes clogged with dirt and debris. She wasn't sure she could make it out this way . . . but she had to try.

Juliette returned to Didi's side and whispered her intentions, explaining that she was going to climb up and go for help. Didi looked horrified at the thought, but she had to know it was their only option. Reluctantly she handed over the car keys, and the two women embraced. Juliette shoved those keys into her pocket and returned to the steps.

She took a deep breath, ears still tuned to the conversation taking place between Greg and Crystal above, and found a foothold. Then, grasping the irregular ridge of stone with her hands, she lifted herself up.

So far so good.

Now if she could do that about twenty more times, she just might make it to the top.

Crystal stared at Greg, astonished. He watched his mother die.

He *let* his mother die.

She had never heard anything so horrifying, yet his voice remained matter-of-fact.

"It was quite the story, those poor teens coming home and finding their mother dead like that. We were in all the papers. Afterwards we went to live with our dad. Up in Utah."

Crystal's mind reeled. "I can't imagine what an experience like that must have done to you. To you and your sister."

"Yeah, kind of messed us up for life, you might say. Then again, our mother had already messed us up pretty good before then."

Comprehension dawned. Of course. After all the abuse, all the craziness, all those years of being a madwoman's victim, Greg and Val had finally fought back. They'd fought by clinging to each other and doing nothing as their mother died. Incredible!

Sucking in a ragged breath, Crystal looked toward the rock and wondered if she could use it to escape. If he would loosen his grip just a little, she could break away and run around to the other side, putting the boulder between them. From there she could either dash back to the road or strike out across the property in the other direction and try to get to those flashing lights she'd seen earlier.

Oh, who was she kidding? Greg was far stronger and bigger than she was. Probably faster, too. Her only hope was to talk her way out.

She had to get him to listen to reason.

"Greg, just because your mother hurt you and Val doesn't mean you have to hurt anyone else."

He looked as if he hadn't even heard her. "You know, I always feared my sister might kill again. I just didn't know she'd end up killing *herself*."

Crystal swallowed hard. "I thought you said she was murdered."

His eyes narrowed into angry slits. "She *was* murdered. By all of them!"

"All of them?"

"Raven. Andre. Reggie. Xena. The counterfeiters. Ty."

"I don't understand."

His grip on her wrist grew even tighter in his rage. "*Raven*, who complained about the treatment Val gave her. *Andre*, who didn't take that complaint seriously enough. *Reggie*, who took it too seriously. *Xena*, who tried to pass all the blame onto Val rather than where it really belonged, on the counterfeit products she'd been given to use. *The counterfeit-*

ers themselves, who don't care who they hurt, or how. *Ty*, for putting the bad product into the treatment room in the first place. Again, *Ty*, for taking advantage of my sweet sister then breaking her heart. She lost her job, her reputation in the business, and the man she loved—a slimeball who never deserved her. She's dead, thanks to all of them. They *killed* her, don't you see that? I can't bring her back, but at least I can even the score. I owe her that much."

Juliette prayed with every agonizing step. She was making progress, but the higher she went, the scarier it got. What if she slipped and crashed back down to the hard stone floor? If she landed wrong, she could break her neck. She could die.

Or what if Greg stopped his babbling and took some sort of action?

What if she made it all the way to the top, only to be spotted and kicked back down? Or run into a rattlesnake, just like Greg's mother?

Never will I leave you, never will I forsake you.

She swallowed hard, claiming that promise more than ever before as she kept going, step by slippery step. Her heart pounded, her legs trembled, her hands could barely hold, and yet she pressed onward. Finally, as she neared the top, she paused and listened, trying to gauge exactly where Greg and Crystal were standing. They had to be close, but from the way their voices carried, it sounded like they were on the far side of the boulder, off to the right. If that were true, then Juliette should be able to climb out without being seen and move to the left side of the boulder.

The last few steps were the toughest. She was dripping with sweat now, her hands and knees slippery and slick. Her terror—at falling, at getting caught—was so real, tremors coursed through her body. But she had to keep going.

It was time for the final push.

As silently as possible Juliette summoned a burst of energy from deep inside and used her legs to thrust herself upward and out, onto the ground. Hands flailing, she scrambled for something to grasp but came up with only dust. Finally her fingers brushed something solid, and she caught hold. It felt like a rock—or at least one pointed end of a rock—jutting out from the earth. Gripping it with both hands, she used every ounce of strength to pull herself forward until her hips were over the edge and she was safely on the ground.

She made it.

Only then did she dare look around. Relief flooded her veins. Her calculations had been correct. Greg and Crystal were just out of sight, on the far side of the boulder.

Wasting no time, she peered over the edge of the pit and gave a thumbs-up, though it was too dark to know if Didi was looking or not. Then Juliette quietly stood, moved to the boulder, and pressed herself against it. Straining to listen, legs wobbling like Jell-O, she inched herself around until she felt like she was exactly opposite Greg and Crystal's location.

What now?

If only she had a working phone!

She would have to use the car to go get help instead. Of course, as soon as she unlocked the vehicle, Greg would hear and see what she was doing and probably come running. But if she moved fast, she should be able get away before he could stop her—unless he had a gun or something, in which case she'd just have to risk it.

First, though, she had to get to the car, which meant making her way from the rock into the darkness, to put some distance between them. Refusing to think of snakes or holes or more booby-trapped wells, she took a deep breath and set off toward the road.

When she finally reached the blacktop, she turned and began to run, despite the pain that jolted her with every step. When she saw the metallic glint of their car ahead, she sprinted the rest of the way then crouched behind the bumper and tried to calm her pounding heart. Knowing her next actions would alert Greg to her presence, she thought through each step she would take—unlock, jump in, lock, keys in ignition, start, *go*—until she felt ready. She was about to spring into action when she heard an odd noise nearby.

Thunk.

She twisted her head around, eyes wide, listening.

Thunk. Thunk.

Greg's truck. The sound was coming from the back of Greg's pickup truck, just a few feet away!

Holding her breath, she rose to get a better look and realized that the bed was sealed over, capped with a solid-looking black cover.

Thunk. Thunk. Thunk.

Someone—or something—was in there, trapped under the lid.

Heart pounding, she crept to the back of the vehicle, pressed her ear to the hatch, and listened. More *thunks*, followed by shuffling noises.

She didn't know what to do. Her instinct

was to open the tailgate and look inside—but what if it was something awful, like a wild animal? What if opening that door was like opening Pandora's box?

On the other hand, what if that was a *person* in there, one who was injured or running out of air, in desperate need of help?

Thunk. Thunk.

She had to do something. Leaning forward, she waited for a break in the thunking and then spoke into the narrow slit just above the latch, praying her voice wouldn't carry all the way over to Greg. "Is someone in there?"

The shuffling stopped, and then came an odd sound in reply—muffled but masculine, like a man with a gag in his mouth, trying to talk.

Juliette gasped. Marcus?

It didn't necessarily sound like his voice, but she wasn't taking any chances.

Heart pounding, she gripped the latch of the tailgate and carefully lifted it upward to disengage it. With a soft, metallic *thong*, it popped free.

She lowered the door then bent forward to peer inside the dark space. It *was* a person, a man, just as she'd thought. He was bound at the wrist and ankles, a blood-stained pillowcase over his head. With a gasp, she ripped that pillowcase off, and he twisted around to look at her, nostrils flaring as he sucked in great breaths of air, eyes filled with terror. It wasn't Marcus after all.

It was Ty Kirkland.

Chapter Thirty-Seven

Crystal could hear the desperation in her voice as she tried to reason with Greg. "It's not too late, you know. Why don't we go somewhere else and think this through? It can still be fixed."

Greg shook his head, features contorted. "No, it can't. Things are already in motion. Raven's dead. Reggie's dead—or he will be soon. Ty comes next, then your friends." He exhaled slowly. "At least I figured it all out. It'll be Ty's fault. Police will think he killed everyone else then ended things by killing himself."

Crystal began to tremble, great spasms of terror coursing through her body. "*Why*, Greg? Why are you doing this?"

He shrugged. "Val had her Nietzsche quote, I have mine. 'It is impossible to suffer without making someone pay for it; every complaint already contains revenge.'" He looked at Crystal, tilted his head. "Don't you see? They have to pay, all of them. Ty most of all."

Crystal shook her head, her heart aching. How had she not seen this side of him before? How had she not known he was capable of this? "You don't have it in you, Greg. I would've seen it if you did. I would've known."

He pursed his lips, clicked his tongue. "Poor Crystal. So naïve. So innocent. So sweet."

She closed her eyes, despising herself even more than she feared him. Not naïve or innocent. *Blind* was more like it. She had blinded herself to his true nature, just as she'd blinded herself to her mother's mental instability for so many years.

Greg touched a hand to Crystal's cheek, making her flinch. "For what it's worth, I am sorry about having to kill the others."

She opened her eyes. "The others?"

"Marcus and Juliette and Didi. They never did anything to me—or to Val. But they're too close to figuring out the truth, so they have to go. I'm just glad my plans were well underway before they came into the picture. The shed. The house. The well. Even with the additional three bodies, I had enough traps already set to handle it. I've had to do some quick thinking and a few alterations, of course, and Xena and Andre still have their turn coming later. But I feel confident it'll all work out in the end."

Work out? He spoke as if he were talking about schedule changes or party plans—not murders!

He continued, his voice growing soft. "It's dominoes, you know? One by one, each person down the chain did something to lead to Valentine's death. She may have tied the rope. But they were the ones who kicked away the stool. Every last one of them who brought her to that place in her mind. They stole her hope. Made her think life wasn't worth living. They *murdered* her, as surely as if they'd pulled a trigger. That's why they deserve to die."

With trembling hands, Juliette put a finger to her lips in warning. Then she reached out and tore away the wide strip of duct tape that covered Ty's mouth.

"What happened?" she whispered. "Did Greg do this to you?"

"Yeah, I was—"

"Shhh! Not so loud! Greg is still close."

"Sorry." He lowered his voice and asked her to untie him.

She shook her head. "Nothing doing. Just tell me what's going on. Where is Marcus? Is he okay?"

He sighed. "No idea. He was supposed to come meet me at Laskey Park. I was out there waiting for him when somebody knocked me out. I'm not sure how long I was unconscious, but when I came to, Greg Overstreet had tied up my hands and was working on my feet."

She took note of the matted, bloody clump of hair on the side of his head. "Did Marcus show up? Did Greg do something to him too?"

"Not that I saw. I think we got out of there before Marcus ever came. Greg was moving pretty fast."

Juliette sucked in a ragged breath, praying Marcus was okay, fearing he couldn't be—otherwise, how could Greg have ended up with his cell phone?

"Anyway, once my feet were tied, he taped over my mouth, put the pillowcase on my head, and crammed me in the back of this truck. That's all I know."

Juliette studied the man in front of her. He'd broken into her hotel room earlier. Admitted to killing Raven in the note he left behind. If that's the kind of person he was, could he be believed now? Her eyes narrowed. "You're bigger than Greg is. You're telling me you couldn't get away from him, even with your hands tied?"

"Oh, I got in one good kick. But then he pulled out a handgun, and that was that."

She gasped. "Greg is armed?"

"Yeah, a large caliber S and W. Between that and the wild look in his eyes, I decided to cooperate."

Juliette swallowed hard. "So then what happened?"

Ty shrugged. "Not much. Once he stashed me in here, he took off and drove for a while. I figured we were heading out into the desert where he could shoot me and dump my body. Instead, he just parked and got out and then nothing. I've been trying to get loose ever since."

Juliette's mind raced. Maybe Ty was telling the truth.

"I'm just glad you showed up. Can you untie me now?"

She pursed her lips. "You're kidding, right? Like I need to deal with *two* murderers on the loose?"

Ty's eyes widened. "What do you mean?"

"Don't play dumb, Ty. You already admitted to killing Raven. How do I know you won't kill me too, the minute your hands are free?"

He eyed her. "I'm confused."

Juliette forced herself to remain calm, but his behavior angered her. How dare he play dumb like this? Did he think she was stupid? "You said it yourself, in that note you left on my pillow."

"That note had nothing to do with Raven."

She grunted. "It said you wanted to confess."

"Yeah, I did. But not to *murder.*"

Juliette hesitated, eyes narrowing. "To what, then?"

Ty let out a soft groan. "My involvement with the counterfeiting. I've been wanting out for a while, but after this morning's raid at the flea market, I realized it was now or never. That's why I needed to talk to somebody from the FBI. I was going to trade names and info on the counterfeiters, in exchange for immunity."

Crystal had to get through to Greg somehow. Summoning her nerve, she reached up with her free hand and held it to his cheek.

"Valentine wouldn't want you to do this."

Enraged, he knocked her hand away, tightening his grip on her other arm. "You don't know that! You didn't know her at all!"

Crystal forced herself to hold his gaze. "Maybe not, but I know the kind of person she must have been. Gentle. Kind. I know because I've seen those same qualities in you."

Finally her words seemed to register. In a

flash his rage seemed to evaporate and leave in its wake only sorrow.

"Please, Greg. For Val. Let it stop here. Don't hurt anyone else."

"I have no choice," he whimpered, eyes again filling with tears. "I already explained that to you."

She took in a breath and held it for a long moment. "And me? Will you kill me too?"

His grip tightened as he began to sob. "Don't you understand? I don't *want* to. You're the only one who. . . . You actually cared."

"I did care, Greg. I do. Please. Don't do this. It's not too late."

"Yes, it is. You're already too close."

"To the truth?"

"No. To me. You're too close to me." He tilted his head back and wailed sobs of pure agony.

Despite everything Crystal's heart ached for this man. Somewhere deep inside he seemed to know what he was doing was wrong, and to regret it.

And yet that wasn't enough to stop him. He was so far gone now, nothing she could say or do was going to bring him back.

Juliette heard someone crying out. She listened, startled. There was such . . . *agony* in those cries. It took a few moments, but she finally identified the voice. Greg. If he sounded like that, then he was near the breaking point. Which meant there wasn't time to take the car and go for help, especially if he had a gun. She would have to stay here, act *now*, before Greg hurt anyone else.

Maybe she should free Ty. He could probably be trusted—in this matter, at least. Then again, why risk the leap from frying pan to fire? Instead, she gave him a quick, "Sit tight, I'll be back," and then set off into the darkness.

She made her way to the boulder in a lesser arc this time, praying Greg wouldn't spot her. Once there she pressed her back against the cold stone and listened. Poor Crystal was doing her best to calm him, but it wasn't working. He seemed to be growing more hysterical by the minute.

It was time.

Holding her breath, Juliette hoisted herself onto the boulder. It was an easy climb, thanks to the stone's craggy face and numerous footholds. She hoped desperately she wouldn't dislodge any loose stones to alert Greg. When she got to the top, she made her way to the other side then lowered to her stomach and dared a quick peek over the edge. Greg's back was to the rock. Crystal faced him, her wrist clutched in his hand. In his other hand, he held a big flashlight. So where was the gun?

If only they weren't standing so close together!

Juliette pulled away from the rim and considered her options. She had just one chance to get this right, and the last thing she wanted to do was to hurt Crystal in the process.

At least she had a good distraction at her disposal. Heart pounding, she stood, reached into her pocket, and carefully pulled out the car keys. Then she got in position at the edge of the boulder, held the remote toward the car, and pushed the alarm button.

The rented SUV sprang to life, honking repeatedly as its warning lights flashed on and off. She looked down to see Greg's reaction. As she'd hoped, he turned toward the sound—then he dropped the flashlight, pulled a gun from his waistband, and pointed it in that direction.

Oh boy.

Gun or not, it was now or never. He would probably move any second, and then her advantage would be lost. Though she dreaded the thought of another hard landing for her sore body, Juliette bent her knees, summoned her nerve, and jumped.

She hit her mark, the full force of her weight knocking Greg forward onto the ground. The gun flew from his hand and skittered off into the darkness. He must have lost his grip on Crystal as well, because she took off running for the car.

At least he was disarmed for the moment, and Juliette prayed the fall had also rendered him unconscious, or at least incapacitated. No such luck. With surprising power and speed, he twisted around and threw her off of him with a guttural growl. She slammed back against the boulder, the impact knocking the breath from her lungs.

She slid to the ground, gasping for air, certain this was the end for all of them. Greg began a frantic search for the gun, and as soon as he found it he would pick them off one by one.

But then came the sound of a scream in the distance. Crystal.

Greg jerked upright, and then he took off in the direction of that scream, the gun still nowhere to be found.

If Juliette could just get some air in her lungs, she realized, she could find that gun herself before it was too late.

She closed her eyes, told herself to calm down, and focused on breathing. Once it no longer felt like she was about to die, she opened her eyes, forced herself to her feet, and began to search. Almost immediately she spotted the flashlight.

Then, with the help of its beam, she found the gun, lying in brush.

Heart pounding, she lifted the cold, hard steel with one hand, flashlight in the other, and trained its beam until it landed on Greg, who had managed to catch up with Crystal and was dragging her back to the scene.

"I've got the gun! Let her go!"

"I've got Crystal!" Greg yelled back in reply. "Drop the gun!"

"No way." Juliette tightened her grip and widened her stance. She had no clue how to shoot, but she'd seen enough TV shows and movies to fake it.

She waited, squinting. As they came closer, she realized Greg was holding Crystal in front of him this time, a muscular arm around her neck, like a shield. Crystal clawed fiercely at his forearm, but he barely seemed to notice.

Juliette feared this would be a standoff, one where she'd have no choice but to drop the gun in the end. She couldn't shoot at Greg, because she couldn't risk hitting Crystal by mistake.

Soon, however, Juliette realized he had something else in mind. Rather than moving in her direction, he dragged his prisoner toward his old house. When they were a few feet from the back steps, he stopped.

"Here's the deal," he called out to Juliette. "Drop the gun and I'll let her go. Nobody else gets hurt."

She took a deep breath as she considered his words. It sounded reasonable, but for all she knew, he had another gun and was planning to shoot them both as soon as hers hit the ground.

She needed to buy time while she tried to think of a plan. "How 'bout this? I'll *lower* the gun, you let her go, and nobody else gets hurt."

"Fine. On one condition. When I do, I want both of you to head around behind that boulder and stay there for five minutes."

"While you escape? No way."

"That's my offer, take it or leave it."

Juliette hesitated. What did he have in mind? Was this a trick, or was he just that crazy? She didn't know, but she had the gun, she had all the power. She would agree to whatever got Crystal out of his grip—then decide from there what her next action would be.

"Okay, here goes." Slowly Juliette lowered her arm until the gun was pointed toward the ground. In response Greg leaned down and whispered something in Crystal's ear.

Then he let her go. As soon as he took away his arm, she ran straight toward Juliette.

"Just do what he says!" she cried, running for the boulder. "Go! "

Juliette didn't understand exactly what was going on, but something told her to do as Crystal said. Together they ducked around behind the giant rock, but then she back leaned out from behind it to see what was going on.

Again she trained the beam toward the house, expecting Greg to be gone, but there he was, still just standing there. As she watched, he turned and mounted the steps, put one hand on the doorknob, and pulled.

Then, with a massive *kaboom*, the structure exploded, lighting the sky as bright as the desert sun.

Chapter Thirty-Eight

Every time there was a knock at the door of Marcus's hospital room, his pulse surged. Then someone other than Juliette would appear around the corner, and it was all he could do to keep the disappointment from showing on his face. He just didn't understand what was taking so long! She'd been down in the ER for more than an hour—for injuries that he'd been told weren't too serious. At least he had his own personal news source to keep him posted: his mother, who'd been monitoring the status of almost everyone involved and reporting back to him with each new development.

Now his mom was back again, and she plopped into the chair next to his bed, still looking peppy despite the fact that it was after midnight. She'd been here at the hospital for almost two hours—the first hour worrying about Marcus and the second worrying *with* him about Juliette and the others.

He was eager to hear what she'd learned this time around, but first she wanted to know if he'd been able to reach Zoe.

Marcus nodded. "I tried to play things down as much as possible, but she got upset, of course, especially once I told her I was an inpatient at the hospital. She started crying, wanted to hop on the first plane out."

"Poor dear."

"I got her to calm down, told her no, that we'll be heading back soon as I'm cleared to fly." Marcus sucked in a deep breath, despite the pain to his ribs. He hated it whenever Zoe cried, it broke his heart. "She's all set to stay with Alison in the meantime, once the class trip is over, but I hope that's not for more than a few days. She needs to see for herself that her dad is fine."

"Maybe we could text her a video later. That might reassure her."

Marcus's eyes widened, and then he grinned. "You never cease to amaze me, Mom, you know that?"

"Why, 'cause this old lady knows the 411? What can I say, I learned it from some of my new BFFs."

Marcus laughed out loud, again wincing from the pain at his ribcage. "Okay, no more comedy till I'm healed. Got any updates for me?"

She nodded. "Yep. Here's the scoop." She placed her eyeglasses onto her nose and referred to her notes. "Juliette was still in with the doctor, so nothing new to report on her yet."

"Okay." Marcus tried to sound like his heart wasn't in his throat.

"Didi definitely needs surgery on her ankle, but they won't know until the specialist gets here whether it's going to be done tonight or if it can wait till tomorrow."

"Got it. Keep me posted."

"Will do." She scanned her notes. "Let's see . . . Crystal has been admitted, I think they're getting her into a room even as we speak."

Marcus's eyes widened. "I thought you said all she needed was a few stitches."

His mother peered at him over the rim of her glasses. "That's what Juliette told me earlier. But apparently the doctors have other concerns. And the girl hasn't spoken a word since the explosion."

Marcus grunted. What could he say? After what that kid had been through, she had the right to keep her mouth shut for a while if she wanted. "So they're doing a psych eval?"

Beverly shrugged. "Probably that too, but I think primarily they're running tests to rule out physical issues—like a brain injury, tissue damage to the throat, that sort of thing."

Marcus nodded. In his field, though he'd mostly dealt with natural disasters, he had been involved in the aftermath of the occasional man-made tragedy as well, including bombings. To his experience, the injuries sustained from explosions were unique, much like those found in combat.

In his work with Nate in the past six months, Marcus's job had been to create disaster-response plans for various Atlanta-based scenarios such as "terrorist cell flies a plane into the Bank of America Plaza" or "cell bombs Underground Atlanta." The work hadn't been fun, but it had been eye-opening, and his reports dealt with everything from where to channel the various injuries—depending on severity of impact, quantity of people needing care, and location of the incident—to how to mobilize and assist MARTA's Emergency Preparedness Unit.

Marcus had learned that explosives were categorized as either "HE" or "LE"—High-Order, such as C-4, or Low-Order, such as a pipe bomb—and tonight he'd been waiting to learn which of the two types they had been subjected to. His own injuries—two broken ribs, a brief hearing loss known as a "temporary threshold shift," and a nasty gouge from a plank that tried to fly through his leg—was more typical of LE explosives.

But considering that Agent Wilson was down in the ICU with pulmonary contusions and an abdominal hemorrhage, Marcus had to wonder if HE explosives had been used instead. Hopefully he'd get a report soon from either the FBI or the local detectives and find out.

In the meantime, at least he had Beverly Stone, ace reporter, who'd done her information gathering not through medical personnel, who were bound by strict confidentiality laws, but by hanging out in the ER's waiting room and quizzing the various patients as they went in or out.

"How's Reggie?" Marcus asked.

She checked her notes. "'Critical but stable.' Most folks seem optimistic about his recovery, though, because of how well that other young woman has done, the therapist who was poisoned when giving the mud wrap to Raven?"

"Brooke?"

"Yes, Brooke. She's still an in-patient here, but rumor has it she'll be going home tomorrow. God willing, Reggie will rally in a few days too, once the atropine is out of his system. Of course, he's also dehydrated and has a broken leg, so that does complicate things a bit."

Marcus nodded. "Do they know how the poison was administered to Reggie?"

Beverly shook her head. "Nothing definite, but I was chatting with that nice young detective in the waiting room, and he had a theory. He said they found a container down in the well holding a few datura seeds. He thinks Greg threw Reggie into the pit and when that didn't kill him, he tossed down that container and forced him to ingest them at gunpoint."

"Why not just skip the seeds and shoot him instead?"

"Too noisy. They believe Greg lured Reggie out there during an afternoon break, so he probably didn't want to draw any attention with a gunshot, especially because that's when he would've been putting the finishing touches on the false floor on top of the pit. He had to go back to work after that, so he must've assumed that Reggie would be dead by the time he returned to carry out the rest of his plan."

Marcus closed his eyes, inhaling deeply. Who could believe that shy, polite young man had had it in him to cause such devastation and destruction? Worse, the kid had managed to pick up important information from Marcus himself, simply by staying near and being helpful when Ty called in and arranged for the time and location of their meeting.

At least Greg wouldn't be able to hurt any-one else.

"Are you okay, hon?"

Marcus opened his eyes and was warmed by the concern reflected on his mother's face.

"Yeah, I was just thinking about the trag-edy of it all."

She nodded, and he marveled at her calm. And that she hadn't asked yet for an expla-nation about Marcus's feelings for Juliette, though he knew it had to be on her mind. She'd witnessed too much tonight: his frenzy when Juliette was missing and no one could find her, his desperation when he got word of another explosion, his utter joy when he learned that Juliette had survived. Through it all Marcus's mom had kept her mouth shut and her "calm face" on, but she had to be full of questions.

Questions that deserved some answers.

Marcus shifted on the narrow hospital bed—daggers of pain shooting through his midsection despite ample medication and a rib belt—and reached for his mother's hand.

"I'm sorry, Mom," he whispered.

Her eyes filled with tears. "Sorry for what, son? For being a hero? For trying to protect Juliette from harm? For caring so much about all of these people?

He studied her for a long moment. "No. For not being completely honest with you."

She looked at him, eyebrows raised. Waiting.

"It's kind of a long story."

She sat back. "Well, it's about time, son. I'm all ears."

Crystal wished everyone would just leave her alone, starting with the guy who couldn't seem to find a vein to draw blood. At least the other bed in her semi-private room was empty, so maybe once all this stuff was over, he would go away and she would get a little peace and quiet.

Well, quiet at least. She'd probably never feel peace again.

For the past hour she'd been poked and prodded and questioned at length, and though she'd willingly submitted to all of their physical demands, she hadn't had it within her to respond to their words. She couldn't speak at all, as if that blast had sucked away every sound from her being, forever.

"Bingo," the phlebotomist said, hitting his mark.

Crystal watched the dark red liquid pull up through the needle and fill first one tube and then another, surprised that blood still pumped through her veins at all.

How could she be so alive when she felt nothing but dead inside?

How would she ever recover from the trauma of this day?

Those questions echoed so loudly in her mind that she couldn't believe this guy didn't hear them. But no, he simply finished his task and went on his way, leaving her there.

Alone.

She would always be alone—had always been alone. Whether back in Seattle or here in Cahuilla Springs, she woke up alone, went to bed alone, and spent every moment in between trying to carve out relationships, like they were accomplishments she could name, or possessions she could hold.

But what good had they done her, really? What consequences had they held for others around her? She still didn't understand all of the details, but she knew this much, that good people had gotten hurt—physically hurt—because of her relationship with Greg Overstreet, because they trusted her and she trusted him, so they had trusted him too.

Could she ever get over the guilt of that? Ever stop wishing she'd never come to this place, never met these people, never even tried to change the sad trajectory of her life?

Who had she thought she was, moving so far from home and thinking she could start fresh here? When life put a target on your back, it stayed there, no matter where you ran.

"Knock-knock."

Crystal looked up. A head poked around the corner and she realized it was Mrs. Peterson, of all people. Her landlady. At this hour? It had to be after midnight!

"May I come in, dear?"

Crystal nodded, though a part of her wanted to push the sweet older woman away, to say, *Steer clear! Danger ahead! Avoid the misguided fool with the target on her back!* But words still wouldn't come, so she watched, helpless, as the woman shuffled into the room and over to the bed, then leaned forward to kiss her on the cheek. She smelled of lavender sachets and bayberry soap, and for a long moment Crystal allowed herself to disappear into that scent, to take comfort in the feeling of her gentle embrace. But then Mrs. Peterson pulled up a chair and sat, and Crystal felt herself slipping back down in the void, back down into the pain.

"I told a little white lie." The woman clasped her hands and tucked them in her lap. "They wouldn't let me in to see you, so I said I was your grandmother. I hope you don't mind. I just couldn't bear to think of you in here by yourself, and I knew the rules were different for family members."

She gazed at Crystal, waiting for a reply. Crystal tried, but the best she could give in return was a nod.

"Oh that's right, they told me you were having trouble with your voice. Well, not to worry. I won't stay long. I just needed to see for myself that you were okay—and to let you know that if there's anything you need, I'm your girl. Don't hesitate to give me a call, okay?"

Crystal nodded, her eyes filling with tears.

"Oh, my, and now I've made you cry." Mrs. Peterson teared up herself. With a sympathetic cluck of the tongue, she scooted forward in her chair and opened her arms.

Crystal couldn't help it, she flung herself forward and buried her face against the woman's soft shoulder, allowing the tears to flow in earnest. Her body was wracked with sobs as sorrow washed over her. In her. Through her.

Scared to let go, she clung to the older woman like a drowning man to a life preserver, holding on tight long after she ran out of tears.

Juliette wanted nothing more than to see Marcus. Only then would she know for sure that he really was okay. The moment the nurse handed over her discharge papers from the ER, Juliette touched base with Didi, then took off for Room 311, where rumor had it that Marcus was "waiting and eager" to see her.

It was all she could do not to run down the quiet, shiny hallways as she made her way there. She didn't even stop to look in a mirror or clean herself up. She just kept going until she was at his door.

Taking a deep breath, she gave a light knock and pushed it open. But as soon as she stepped inside and heard what Marcus was saying, she realized this was the exact wrong moment to interrupt. Deep in conversation, he was finally telling his mother the truth about the past and the real reason for this trip.

Juliette tiptoed back out without either one even realizing she was there. Then she stood in the hallway for a long moment, telling herself she would just have to be patient. This was important, and it couldn't be easy for either of them.

Crystal. Until Marcus was free, Juliette would pay a visit to Crystal. She'd gotten the room number from Didi, so she headed there now, this time taking the elevator in deference to what the ER doc said was a sorely bruised tailbone.

Sore was right.

She stepped out onto the second floor just as a cute little old woman stepped in. Sporting a flowered print dress and brown orthopedic shoes, she looked straight out of central casting, like somebody's tiny, sweet grandma.

Juliette made her way to 216, knocked, and stepped inside. There she found Crystal lying in the bed by the window, eyes closed, skin pale against the white sheets. The poor thing. She'd been through so much.

There was an empty chair beside the bed, so Juliette gingerly lowered her aching frame into it, reached out, and touched Crystal's arm. The girl's eyes opened, and from their red and swollen rims, Juliette could tell that she'd been crying.

"Hey," Juliette whispered. "How are you doing?"

Crystal shrugged.

So, still not talking.

Juliette waved her papers. "I'm all checked out, thank goodness. Nothing serious, except for the next few weeks I'm not supposed to jog or do any heavy exercise, and I've been told to avoid loud noises. Also, they said my tailbone may get worse before it gets better—and that it could take a long time to heal."

Crystal gestured toward Juliette's forearm, which was covered with a bandage.

"Three stitches, no biggie. Doctor said it might not even leave a scar."

Juliette took a deep breath, leaned forward, let it out slowly. Then she met the young woman's gaze. "Crystal, I have to ask you something. Something important."

The girl nodded, eyes wide.

"Just before the explosion, just before Greg let you go . . ." She sat up straight again, adjusted for the pain at her lower back, tried to decide how to phrase what she wanted to know. "He whispered something to you."

Crystal's red eyes filled with tears even as she nodded.

"What was it? What did he say?"

The girl closed her eyes, rivers of tears coursing down her cheeks. As she reached for a tissue and tried to pull herself together, Juliette found pen and paper in the bedside table drawer and handed them over. Crystal grimaced, as if she would rather not.

Still, she held the pad, pen poised over it, looked like she was about to write. Then she lowered both to her lap, met Juliette's eyes, and spoke in a soft whisper.

"He said, 'I know how it has to end now.'"

Juliette sat back, taking that in.

I know how it has to end now?

Of course. This man who killed and kidnapped and lied and injured and tormented all of these people had found a way to turn his own death into something noble, a sacrifice for the sake of this fragile young woman in front of her. Shame on him.

Shame on him.

"What do you think he meant by that?" Juliette tried to keep her voice neutral, glad at least that the girl was able to talk after all.

Crystal dabbed at her tears, looked away and continued in a soft, almost ashamed voice. "That he decided to kill himself rather than have to kill me."

Juliette nodded, letting that sit there for a while, not sure how to respond. Surely Crystal understood there was nothing here to admire.

"Do you respect him for that?" she asked finally.

Crystal's head jerked up and spoke louder this time, her voice filled with emotion. "No! I *hate* him for that! How *dare* he put that on me, like he was giving his life for mine. Yeah, so he died for me, so does that make his death *my* fault? I don't think so. I don't deserve that. No way! His death was his fault. All of us, all of our pain, *his* fault. Period."

Though Crystal was upset, Juliette couldn't help but feel relieved. Despite all of the trauma, this girl still had a solid head on her shoulders.

The two women talked for a while, Crystal sharing about her brief relationship with Greg, what she'd learned of his past, why she'd been so misguided about who he really was. Juliette listened, commented and commiserated. Mostly she just let Crystal work things through.

At some point in the next few days, once the girl had had a chance to recover somewhat, Juliette would make a point of speaking with her again. She wanted to tell her about another man, a very special man.

One who also died for her—but for all the right reasons.

Beverly Stone was nothing if not forgiving. As expected, she was more hurt than mad, not to mention embarrassed. Marcus apologized profusely, and he assured her that he really had been enjoying her as a travel partner—so much so, in fact, that he'd like them to plan another vacation together, one with no extra guests and no ulterior motives. She seemed skeptical, but the mention of a long weekend at Callaway Gardens brought the sparkle back to her eyes.

After that, he insisted she call it a night. Soon she was headed back to Palm Grotto the way she'd come, via police escort. No doubt she'd be back first thing in the morning, but for tonight, at least, he felt better knowing she would soon be sound asleep in bed rather than roaming the halls of the hospital on his behalf.

Much to Marcus's relief, the one person he'd been waiting for all evening finally showed up just as he was about to get out of that bed and go find her himself. First came a soft knock, then her face appeared around the corner.

Juliette.

She stood for a long moment and they just looked at each other. Then the next thing Marcus knew, she was in his arms and they were holding on tight, so tight, despite their injuries. Then she was crying, which made him cry, and then they both had to laugh. What a mess they were!

What a bond they had forged.

Their time together was so short that parting for the remainder of the night would've been nearly impossible had a nurse not found Juliette there and insisted she go.

"The patient needs his rest!" she scolded, and so finally, with one long and lingering kiss, they said their good-byes.

The next morning Juliette and Marcus's mom came back to the hospital together, and he was pleased to see that at least his own deceitful behavior hadn't driven a wedge between the two women. Instead, they seemed like fast friends, laughing and talking and getting to know each other on this new and different level.

His mom made her exit when two FBI agents showed up to talk, but Juliette insisted on staying, and to Marcus's surprise, they let her. Mostly they wanted to discuss the details of yesterday's events, and together they went through the final version of the probable scenario.

The best anyone could figure, Greg's original plan had been to kill Raven first, at the spa, and then use the various booby traps at his old family home—the covered well, the buildings rigged with homemade LE explosives—to kill Xena, Andre, Reggie, and Ty. He'd been successful at murdering Raven undetected, at least initially, but then he'd been thrown several significant curve balls.

First, Marcus, Juliette, and Didi began unraveling the case and getting a little too close to the truth. Second, Xena and Andre were arrested for blackmail. And third, Ty disappeared out of the blue and decided to turn himself in to the FBI. Greg must've known at that point that the rest of his plan was on the verge of crumbling—but then Crystal introduced him to Marcus, which meant he just happened to be present when Ty's call came through. Suddenly he was back in the game.

When Greg left Marcus's hotel room after that call, the FBI surmised he went straight to the rendezvous point at Laskey Park himself, a good half hour ahead of Marcus and Agent Wilson. Once he apprehended Ty—and Ty's cell phone—it had been easy to get Marcus and Agent Wilson to come to the new location. There the two men had walked into his trap and set off the explosion.

Greg probably even hid nearby and watched it happen. And though he would've had to take off right away after that lest he get caught by the emergency responders, he had taken the time first to find Marcus's cell phone in the rubble. His ruse of texting Marcus from Ty's phone had worked so well, in fact, that he used the same trick a second time, by texting Juliette from Marcus's phone. Soon he had lured the women into his final trap on the other side of the property—where he'd been shocked to come face to face with Crystal, the biggest curveball of all.

How events would've played out had she not been there was anybody's guess.

The agents went on to provide more thorough information about Raven's murder as well. They said that on Wednesday afternoon Greg made a great show of trying to deal with a malfunctioning camera at Palm Grotto—first by fooling with the wires at the security building, then checking out that camera in person. What he'd actually done, however, was pull some wires to disable the screen then gone out and busted the lens himself, probably with a well-placed throw of a rock. Turning in a maintenance report had been a clever way to deflect suspicion without risk, because he knew the repair would take several days.

"So my camera theory was right," Marcus said, trying not to sound too smug.

The agent nodded as he went on to tell them the rest. He said FBI satellite images confirmed that around 3:00 a.m. Thursday morning, a black Chevy short-bed truck had been parked at a new housing development not far from Palm Grotto Resort. Clearly Greg hiked up to the jogging trail and entered the resort property via the western perimeter, then he used his knowledge of the security camera placement to make his way to Arrowscale unseen. Once there he slipped inside, put atropine into one of the jars of chai soy mud, removed the extra jars just to be safe, and slipped back out the way he'd come in.

Marcus still couldn't get over how Greg had managed to fool them all, and he said as much now.

"I can't believe he actually intended to kill so many people," Juliette added. "We heard him spout out the full list to Crystal, and it was shocking."

Marcus turned to Juliette, eyes narrowing. "Didn't you tell me that as part of that list, he mentioned 'the counterfeiters'?"

She nodded. "I guess he blamed them because a counterfeit product started the whole thing. Val unknowingly used it on Raven, Raven got burned, and everything fell apart from there."

Marcus grunted. "Even so, what was the guy thinking? How does one take revenge against counterfeiters anyway? If the FBI can't stop these people, what made Greg Overstreet think he could?"

One of the agents held up a hand. "We believe his intention was to go after a specific middle man, the one who procured the fake JT Lady products for Palm Grotto resort."

"You mean Ty?" Juliette asked.

He shook his head. "No, one of Ty's suppliers. It seems that Greg got to the guy by posing as a disgruntled spa employee with access to inventory. But when the supplier took him up on it and requested product, Greg found himself unable to deliver."

He paused in his explanation to pull out a piece of paper from his valise, which he handed over to Juliette. "This is a copy of something we found among Greg's personal papers. It should make sense to you—at least somewhat."

Juliette took it from him and held it toward Marcus so they could study the page together. "That looks like a JT Lady account number," she said, pointing to a combination of numerals and letters separated by dashes.

The agent nodded but did not elaborate.

Marcus continued to study the page, which looked to him like nothing more than some quickly-jotted-down notes. An address, a phone number. Some math calculations. Dollar signs. The only strange thing was what had been written in along the bottom, in prominent lettering: *Justice is Sweet and Musical—T.*

"Reportedly the kid was big on quotes," the agent explained. "We checked it out, that's from Thoreau."

Marcus glanced at Juliette, who was tracing a line from the oversized J of the word "Justice" to three initials in the middle of the page, JSM. With a gasp, she looked up at the agent.

"Justice is Sweet and Musical—JSM Enterprises!" she cried. "Henry David Thoreau. Walden Pond." Turning to Marcus, she explained, "Greg opened an account at JT Lady, under the name David Walden at JSM Enterprises. Unbelievable!"

The agent nodded, and he seemed impressed

that she'd figured it out. "Placed a single order and had it sent to a shipping store in Phoenix, Arizona, about a four-hour drive from here."

She handed the paper back to him. "So in other words, he tried to use my company to get to this guy, to get his revenge."

Both agents nodded somberly.

"Apparently it worked. Now that we have this information, it seems Raven was not the first person killed in this matter by Greg Overstreet. Last September that supplier was found dead, by a single shot to the head, an unsolved homicide. We're still waiting on ballistics, but we believe the report will confirm a match with the gun recovered from the scene last night. Greg took out the supplier, then he bided his time and took out Raven. I daresay, without the hard work of you people, his killing spree might've continued all the way through to the end of his list."

They were all quiet for a long moment as Juliette and Marcus processed that thought.

"And Ty?" Juliette asked finally. "He really had no part in Raven's murder?"

"He thought he did—at first. Thought she died from exposure to counterfeit mud. He knew the counterfeits he put in there had been responsible for her burns the time before, so when he heard she was dead, he says he feared it was the same sort of thing, only fatal this time."

Marcus could only imagine his relief when he learned her death had been intentional! "So did you guys end up cutting Ty a deal after all?"

The agents said yes, and that thus far it was looking like a pretty good trade on both sides. Thanks to Ty, they now had lots of helpful info and several good new leads, though of course the counterfeiting issue—and its impact on JT Lady—was far from over.

"I just hope it doesn't get worse before it gets better," one of them said, his expression grave as his eyes went from Marcus to Juliette and back again.

Juliette waited until Didi was safely out of surgery and resting comfortably, and then she finally agreed to return to the resort with Marcus. Whatever he had up his sleeve, he was practically giddy about it.

Once there she thought he should get to his room and rest, but he insisted on walking out by the lake. Soon she realized why. There by the water, in the shade of a tamarisk tree, was a brand new bench.

Suddenly shy, Marcus actually blushed as he turned to her. "I wanted to give you some closure. I hope you don't mind, but I thought a memorial of some kind . . ."

He gestured toward the new bench and the engraved brass plate that had been affixed to the back. It said:

In Memory of Rayleen Eugenia Humphries,
Known to the world as Raven.
She was a free spirit and a true original.
She also had a pretty mean right hook.

As Juliette read the plaque, her eyes filled with tears, though when she reached the last line, she burst out laughing.

"The engraver's all set to make a new one if you don't like it," Marcus told her quickly. "I wasn't sure if—"

"No"—Juliette hugged him tight—"no, it's perfect just like this. It's absolutely, positively perfect."

Little did she know, it was about to get even better.

At Marcus's request, they sat on the bench together, and then he pulled an envelope from his pocket, which he handed over. She pulled out the contents, looked the papers over for a moment, and frowned. She looked up at him. "Marcus, what does this mean?"

His grin broadened. "Well, as you know, my company is all about disaster preparedness. We teach a lot of classes to the community, including a six-week program every fall on self-defense. Those classes are for paying customers, of course, but I wanted you to know that I talked to my partner and we've decided to earmark an amount that will fund scholarships specifically geared to young women who are on their own for the first time and just starting out. We're calling it The Raven Fund."

Of course she totally lost it then, tears of gratitude welling up in her eyes. It wasn't just the money that touched her so. It was the gesture itself.

It was this man, Marcus Stone.

The one that got away.

Turning to him, Juliette took his hands in hers and looked into his eyes and thanked him from the bottom of her heart. "You know, if this counterfeiting thing isn't over, there is one silver lining. I just might need some more protecting."

He smiled. "I think it's pretty clear you can protect yourself, ma'am, but I agree that an extra pair of eyes wouldn't be a bad idea."

She nodded, sliding closer. "And an extra pair of arms?"

He pulled her in tight, resting his chin on her head. "Um hmm, not to mention an extra pair of lips."

She looked up and he tilted his head down for a kiss.

The one that got away?

Not this time.

Not a chance.